LOVE, LIES & PROMISES

Part two of the Behind Blue Eyes Trilogy

By

Joanna Lambert

Visit us online at www.authorsonline.co.uk

An Authors OnLine Book

ISBN 978-07552-0495-3

Authors OnLine Ltd
19 The Cinques
Gamlingay, Sandy
Bedfordshire SG19 3NU
England

This book is also available in e-book format, details of which are available at www.authorsonline.co.uk

For my husband Steve
with love

ACKNOWLEGEMENTS

MANY THANKS ONCE AGAIN TO GAYNOR AND JAMES AT AUTHORS ON LINE FOR THEIR HELP IN BRINGING THIS BOOK TO LIFE AND TO MY GOOD FRIENDS BARBARA AND JUDY FOR THEIR CONTINUED ENCOURAGEMENT AND SUPPORT

ABOUT THE AUTHOR

Joanna Lambert lives in a village on the outskirts of Bath with her husband, Ruby the Mini and Ziggy her much-loved ginger cat.

BY THE SAME AUTHOR

When Tomorrow Comes

MERIDAN CROSS - MAIN CHARACTERS

Willowbrook Farm
Richard Evas
Peggy Evas (1st wife) d. 1966
Mary Evas (formerly O'Farrell) m. 1967
Niall O'Farrell, her son - now living abroad

Little Court Manor
Laura Kendrick
Ted Williams – her gardener
Ettie Williams – her housekeeper

Saddlers End
Nelson Miller
Rowan, his eldest son
Ash, his youngest son

Village Shop
Margaret Sylvester
Rachel, her daughter

The Somerset Arms
Tom Bennett, Publican
Lily, his wife

Joe 'Doggy' Barker/*Odd Job Man & Poacher*

ABBOTSBRIDGE - MAIN CHARACTERS

Liam Carpenter, Architect
Melissa (Mel), his wife *(Richard Evas's Daughter)*
Nick Kendrick, her son/ *engaged to Jenny Taylor*
Ella Kendrick, her daughter

Bob Macayne/Co-owner of Taylor Macayne Construction
Andy, his son

Jack Taylor/Co-owner of Taylor Macayne Construction
Betty, his wife
Mick, their son/*engaged to Nina Harrison*
Jenny, their daughter/ *engaged to Nick Kendrick*

Tad Benedict/Night Club and Hotel Owner
Faye, his wife
Matt, their son

Ron Harrison/Carpenter with Taylor Macayne
Elsie, his wife
Elaine Lester, their eldest daughter married to Barry Lester
Ryan, their baby son
Nina, their youngest daughter/*engaged to Mick Taylor*

Gerald Langley/Retail and Commercial Property
Caroline, his wife
Justin, their son
Annabel, their daughter/ *engaged to Rich Tate*

Bryan Tate/Garage Owner
Sonia, his wife
Bryony, their daughter *married to Gareth Knight*
Rich, their son *engaged to Annabel Langley*

Oliver Knight/Owner of Stewarts Engineering
Lydia, his wife
Gareth, their son/ *married to Bryony Tate*

Miles Anderson/Abbotsbridge Council Planning Chair
& Local Businessman

Alex Nicholson/Wealthy Local Businessman & Estate Agent

Martin Templeman & Gavin Briggs-Howe/Owners of Mirage Holdings (Development Company)
Gracie Templeman & Selina Briggs-Howe, their wives

Abbotsbridge Rotary Members and their wives –
Charles and Sheila Fitzallen
Maurice and Marjorie Webster
Edgar and Grace Henderson
Tom and Mary Neville
George and Barbara Morris

MATT'S BAND - THE ATTITUDE
Baz Young, Jeff Turner, Paul Fussell, Todd Graham, Steve 'Paddy' Patrick

KINGSFORD - MAIN CHARACTERS

The Bridge Hotel
David Llewellyn
Cheryl, his wife
Isobel (Issy), their daughter

NEW YORK - MAIN CHARACTERS

Doug Henderson - Owner of Maverick Records
Kendal Conway - one of Maverick's recording artists
Marcie Maguire - Doug's Personal Assistant

1968

ONE

Tuesday 24th December

'I'm so sorry Ella. He rang this morning. It was a last minute decision by the record company.' Tad Benedict looked into the face of the pretty dark haired girl at the bar and really felt for her. All around them, in his club, the Mill, people were in celebratory mood. It was Christmas Eve; laughter and music filled the place. Currently the dance floor was packed with revellers dancing to Creedence Clearwater Revival's *Bad Moon Rising.* Not the night at all to be delivering news like this - he could almost reach out and touch her disappointment.

'Switzerland?' Ella's grey eyes clouded and she shook her head as if she could not quite grasp what he was saying.

'Yes, one of their record company's other groups, the Spectators, were due to take part in a Christmas Eve live special out there. Aaron King, the lead singer, decided to get in some skiing when he arrived and is currently in hospital with concussion and a compound fracture to his left leg. So the Attitude were flown out last minute to take their place. Matt phoned from Zurich this afternoon, that was the first I knew of it.'

Ella felt Tad's hand on her shoulder as the news sank in and bitter disappointment washed over her. Switzerland. It might as well be the other side of the moon. And who wouldn't be disappointed on a night like this? She had been waiting since May to be reunited with him; had thought of nothing else. May - that had been a whirlwind time she remembered; Matt's band, the Attitude had been discovered, had a number one hit and been whisked away to London where their record company had completely taken over their lives - first an album, then a UK tour. He kept in touch with post cards from each of their tour stops and had promised to return home for the festive season; to meet her here in the club on Christmas Eve. The record company had no plans for them until spring he said. Ironically, she decided, that was probably why he was now in Switzerland and not here.

This was to have been her moment - an opportunity to reveal her true feelings. To cut through all his diffidence and face him with the fact that what they had had gone beyond friendship. That she loved him.

'When will he be back?' She asked, hoping that at least they would have New Year together and her opportunity had not been lost.

'He didn't say, but as soon as I hear anything I will let you know, I promise.' Tad squeezed her shoulder, 'Sorry I can't be more helpful, but that's as much as I know at the moment.'

Across the room, he saw Ella's two friends Issy Llewellyn and Jenny Taylor coming off the dance floor. Time to leave, to let the sisterhood take over to provide the help and support needed to repair the damage he had just inflicted.

Tad was a philosophical individual with an upbeat outlook on life. Although there had been this setback over Christmas - something that had also left his wife Faye frustrated and upset - he was sure it was just a temporary glitch. In a couple of days he guessed his son would more than likely be returning to the UK and before they all knew it he would be back home to see the New Year in with friends and family in style. In no time at all everyone would have forgotten tonight's disappointment. He wished he could given Ella these crumbs of comfort to buoy her up but was aware that only if he had been dealing in definites would his words have held any comfort for her this evening after receiving such disappointing news.

As he skirted the bar, he stopped and ordered a bottle of his best champagne. 'For the three young ladies in the corner.' he nodded to where the girls sat, Jenny with her arm around Ella's shoulder, all of them deep in conversation. As the person responsible for ruining not only her evening but possibly Christmas as well, it was the least he could do.

Friday 27th December, 1968

'Who was at the door?' Faye called from the kitchen where she was making final preparations for their lunch.

Tad walked in from the hall, he was smiling. 'Telegram from Matt,' He waved the envelope at her, tore it open and began to read, 'Well! We're invited to tea at the Ritz to make up for him not getting home for Christmas.'

'Or New Year!' Faye reminded him, 'It seems to me, that management at Centaur treat the Attitude like a piece of merchandise.'

'Sadly that is exactly what they are Faye, a money-making machine.'

'But Christmas and New Year, Tad!' She raised her hands in exasperation, 'People should be home with their families!'

'I know; it was unfortunate that Swiss millionaire caught the show and thought it would be a good idea for them to stay on and play at his daughter's party. Still, Matt says Centaur cut a good deal for the band.'

'For themselves more likely!' Faye was cynical.

'Faye!' Tad crossed to where she stood. 'Calm down; we have it in here in black and white now,' he waved the telegram at her. 'A table for four is booked for two thirty on the 10th of January at the Ritz.'

She frowned. 'Who else is coming?'

'Ella.'

Faye made a face.

'She's his friend, Faye.'

'Her mother won't let her go you know,' she said, turning back to the cooker and stirring the gravy vigorously, 'not in a million years.'

'Probably not, although maybe it's worth a trip round to Cambridge Crescent to try to melt that hard heart of hers.'

'It's your head on the block.'

'Ah, but if I catch mother and daughter together, it may just swing things in my favour.'

Later that afternoon Tad pulled up outside the Carpenter house. As he reached the front gate, he noticed Mel's red Sunbeam Alpine sitting alone on the driveway. 'Damn,' he muttered under his breath. Ella was out, no point staying; he hesitated then turned quickly away, deciding to return later.

'Did you want something?'

He turned at the sound of the clipped English accent; the front door was open and Mel was standing there, the very essence of domesticity in flowery apron and yellow rubber gloves.

'Ah, Mrs Carpenter. Good afternoon!' He turned and gave her a cheerful smile.

'If you were hoping to catch Liam,' She said, peeling off her gloves as she reached him, 'you're out of luck I'm afraid. He's on the golf course.'

'Liam? No actually it was you I came to see.'

'Me?' She gazed at him stony-faced, 'Whatever for?'

'I need to ask your permission for something.'

'Well, fire away!'

'Matt's has been out of the country; he will be returning to London on the 10th of January and he's invited us up to the Ritz for tea. Ella is included in that invitation.'

The expression on Mel's perfectly made up face told him what was coming even before she had opened her mouth to reply.

'I don't think so,' she said with a regal shake of her blonde head, 'You obviously don't realise that Ella left your son and all that pop nonsense behind her some time ago.'

Tad looked puzzled, 'Well, she was very disappointed he didn't get home for Christmas; they'd made arrangements to meet at the club on Christmas Eve, you know.'

'They'd what!' The annoyance that crossed Mel's face said this was not at all what she wanted to hear. Tad realised he had accidentally scored an own goal; if he had thought he was going to persuade Mel to change her mind, he now knew that was definitely not going to happen.

'Please,' She said graciously, 'do thank your son for his kind invitation, but I'm afraid my daughter wouldn't have been able to make it anyway. She is in Meridan Cross with my father's family and not expected back until the fifth. Then she is returning to college. It would be totally impossible for her to take a day off, her studies are extremely important. Now, if you'll excuse me!'

Audience over then, Tad thought, half amused, half irritated as he watched her walk back to the house. As she reached the door, she turned with an arrogant smirk, 'The Ritz indeed! Don't you realise you have to book weeks in advance to get a table there Mr Benedict? I think your son has rather grandiose ideas!'

'Told you didn't I?' Faye said when Tad reached home, 'The woman's a complete bitch!'

'She certainly is. Poor old Liam.' Tad paused for a moment, and then looked at Faye thoughtfully, 'I could try contacting Ella at her grandparents', I suppose.'

'Tad,' Faye shook her head, 'No. Let's leave well enough alone shall we? If you go against Mel's wishes, she will cause nothing but trouble and that is the last thing we both need. We'll just have to explain the situation when we see Matt and hope he's not too disappointed.'

1969

TWO

Friday 10th January

'This is lovely, just lovely,' Faye Benedict gazed admiringly at the plush surroundings of the Ritz Hotel where she sat with Tad and Matt in the Palm Court about to take afternoon tea.

'I wanted to do something really special for you both,' Dark haired Matt smiled, looking at his mother sitting there, slim and fashionable in her deep turquoise knitted suit. 'The thing is,' he said, 'Centaur has not only managed to wreck Christmas and New Year, they have now decided to send us to Ireland as a post script to our UK tour. So as there's no way I can get home right now,' he gazed around the room, 'I thought maybe this would go some way to soften the blow.'

'Isn't there a waiting list though?' Tad was curious, remembering Mel's caustic comment, 'How did you manage to book so quickly?'

Matt grinned, 'Didn't you know Dad? Fame opens doors - or gets you a table.'

'Well I'm glad it has.' Faye helped herself to a sliver of smoked salmon sandwich. 'This is simply wonderful!'

'Yes it is,' Tad's handsome face broke into a smile, 'and it's good to see you looking so well; your new career obviously agrees with you.'

'It does - I love every minute of it. I am really happy, although…' He gave a sigh, 'I wish Ella could have made it here today with both of you.'

'I am afraid her mother wouldn't entertain the thought of her coming up here.' Tad said as the waiter poured their tea.

'I think Mel Carpenter has very specific ideas about who her daughter spends time with,' Faye added. Ella Kendrick was bad news; secretly she was glad that Mel had sabotaged Matt's invitation. She wanted her completely out of her son's life.

'I'm sorry, I know how disappointed you must be, but I've got an idea that might help.' Tad reached into his jacket, pulled out his wallet and took out one of his business cards, handing it to his son. 'Why don't you write a contact address on the back of this, so she can write to you? I know it's not perfect but at least she will be able to keep in touch with you regularly. And I promise I'll deliver it to her in person.'

'Thanks, that's a great idea.' Matt took it from him and finding a pen began to write.

'Don't worry; I'm sure you'll eventually get to see each other.' Tad said, as Matt handed back the card and he slipped it back into his wallet. 'Now, I suggest you have one of these sandwiches, before your mother eats them all.' He retrieved the china plate from the table and presented it to his son. 'She seems to have developed a thing about smoked salmon.'

'I don't know why you did that thing with the address.' Faye said later in the car on their way home. 'He really doesn't need that sort of distraction. It could affect his career.'

'It's only natural he wants to keep in touch.' Tad argued. 'They were friends for a long time - remember, Ella was with him from the beginning of the band.'

'I was hoping that phase of his life was over.' Faye said dismissively, 'You heard him, Ireland, then a European tour lined up for later this year. He should be moving on, developing his talent, not mooning over a girl who is destined to become a brood mare for the Macayne dynasty.'

'Faye, that's an awful way of putting it and it's her mother's plan, not hers,' Tad replied. 'Ella's nobody's fool; she may be spending time with Andy but she's smart enough to know that he'll never settle down with one woman. He'll always be looking to bed women when the opportunity arises, it's the way he is.'

'The Abbotsbridge Stud!' Faye's words brought a smile to her face.

'Now that is a term I do agree with!' He laughed, 'Come on, cheer up, as I said, I'm sure everything will work out for the best, it usually does.'

'The only problem is,' Faye gave her husband a straight look, 'I don't think my idea of working out for the best is the same as yours.'

'Oh, why not?'

'Because you like her Tad, and I don't. Believe me, I know what I see, and she is trouble!'

Saturday 11th January

As the light dwindled on a grey winter's afternoon, Issy sat in the middle of the huge newly plastered room that would soon become the Brendon Banqueting Suite. The Bridge Hotel, run by her parents David and Cheryl Llewellyn was in the throes of expanding its business and Issy, as newly-appointed Function Manager, was going to run it. She smiled to herself as she looked around the empty room. Another six weeks and they could open for business. Even in its present state, she could clearly see how it would all look. Green carpeted floors, polished oak for the dance area, cream walls and the inclusion of fresh seasonal flowers to accompany each booking. She had spent hours looking at cutlery and crockery samples, the match had to be just right. Her father had given her a free hand; this was her baby and she was going to do everything possible to make sure it was a success.

Perched on an upturned crate surrounded by tins of paint and electrical contractor's cabling she was deep in thought when she caught the sound of noisy footsteps approaching. Looking up she saw Mick Taylor, hands thrust into the pockets of a sheepskin coat glistening with snow, coming towards her.

'Mick!' She got to her feet, feeling an immediate prickle of annoyance. She watched him approach, looking like a younger version of his father - solid and square shouldered, sandy hair falling in his eyes. As he drew closer, she could see the dusting of childhood freckles that trailed across his cheeks and witnessed the emergence of a big grin, something else that always managed to irritate her. He didn't even have to open his mouth, just being there was enough. She knew exactly why she felt the way she did - the accident which had happened when she was fourteen.

Totally smitten with trainee teacher Greg Davies, she was over the moon when he came into the Hotel for lunch one Saturday. She made a point of being the one who took his order, stopping to have a short chat with him. She remembered carrying his lunch across the restaurant so carefully, wanting everything to be perfect. As she reached his table, the door next to it, leading into the hotel lobby burst open, crashing into her and knocking her off balance. Mr Davies' lunch shot out of her hands and straight onto the floor, leaving Issy sprawled uncomfortably face down in his lap. Her mother was there in an instant, rescuing her from her predicament and calling for someone to clear up the mess on the floor. Mr Davies sat there looking at her, red faced with embarrassment, while the other diners stared at her with a mixture of shock and amusement. The culprit turned out to be Mick, standing there with a tin of paint in each hand and that stupid, stupid grin on his face. His excuse was that he thought he was entering the storeroom and having his hands full had simply elbowed the door open. His grin resurrected those embarrassing events every time it surfaced and she hated him for it. Not only was he a clumsy oaf, but his actions had ensured she ended up being the laughing stock of the school.

'Everything is just perfect,' She eyed him coolly as he reached her, 'Dad's extremely pleased.'

'Sorry I'm not with you Iz.' His grey-blue eyes gazed at her blankly.

'The work,' She slowed her words, feeling impatience begin to well up inside her, 'Your boys have done a marvellous job so far. Isn't that why you are here? For a progress check?'

'Actually, my little Welsh wizard,' He rubbed his hands together, 'I am about to be your first customer. My wedding reception.' He said to her empty stare, 'I want to book this place for Saturday 14th June.'

She gazed silently out of the window for a moment. She had completely forgotten he was still engaged to the hateful red-headed girl-from-the-wrong-side-of-the-tracks, Nina Harrison. How strange, she realised that until this moment she had never given him or his situation even a passing thought. Now she was reminded of it, for some reason it annoyed her intensely. Added to that he was grinning again, making her feel even more confrontational.

'You're still determined to go ahead with this madness then, are you?'

'You sound just like my mother,' His smile disappeared and he became defensive, 'I'm not mad, I happen to love her.'

'How come you're booking the reception anyway?' She frowned, 'Isn't that something the bride's parents usually take care of?'

'Issy, be sensible,' He answered in a tone she found annoyingly patronising, 'The Harrisons haven't got the kind of money it takes to book a place like this. Nina wants the best and I'm going to see she has it. So I told her father I'd cover the cost of the reception.' He said with a satisfied smile.

Issy gave a derisory snort. Nina wanted the best did she? 'You're daft Mick Taylor, do you know that? Just plain daft! She's got you dangling on a string. Wedding? Wake up! She's got no intention of marrying you! You're a means to an end.'

'What's that supposed to mean?'

'She wants Andy Macayne back and you're the bait dangling on the hook.'

'No way! Not after what she went through with him. She loves me now and she's going to be *my* wife. Now,' he said irritably, 'Do you want to book this reception for me? Because if not, there are plenty of other places who will.'

'Wait there!' She pushed past him impatiently, 'Never let it be said I turn business away. Oh, and by the way,' she threw over her shoulder as she left the room, 'there's a ten percent non-returnable deposit!'

As Mick watched her leave, he could almost reach out and touch her hostility. From the day he had first seen her outside Kingsford High with his sister Jenny eight years ago, he knew his heart belonged to no one else. In her fair hair and blue eyes he glimpsed the woman she would eventually become. And seeing that, he knew he had no choice but to wait for her. However, the unfortunate incident, which had left Issy sprawled in the lap of one of her favourite teachers, appeared to have wrecked his dreams. She was unforgiving, hostile. Viewed him with scorn and picked on his weaknesses. Rode out to do battle with him on every occasion she could. He had tried everything possible to make his peace with her, but nothing had worked. Now reluctantly, he had given up on the possibility of them ever getting together and turned his affections in another direction Oh yes, he and Nina had a lot in common; they had both been rejected by those they really loved. He was under no illusions; they were both taking second best, but somehow he felt there was a just a chance they could find real happiness together.

'Hello Ella, I've been looking for you. You've been very elusive.'

Buying a round of drinks at the bar, Ella turned and found herself looking at a smiling Tad Benedict.

She smiled back. 'I've been in Meridan Cross for New Year. Well, I didn't really feel like coming to the Mill for the celebrations as Matt wasn't going to be here.'

'Yes, bit of a disappointing time all round wasn't it? We all missed him.'

'Yes, 'she nodded. 'But I gather you've come with good news now.'

'Sort of. Although, I'm afraid he still isn't going to be around for a while.'

'Really?' She gave a disappointed sigh.

'The Attitude are off to Ireland for a few weeks, final leg of their tour.'

'But I thought they had finished?'

'So did we, but the record company felt it would be a good idea to send them on what Matt called a post script to their UK tour.'

'You've spoken to him?'

'Yes.' Tad was relieved at the way she had phrased the question. It avoided the need to lie. He still felt angry with Mel for being so pointlessly mean-minded and spiteful over the invitation. 'After that,' he continued, 'they are off to Europe. However,' he paused, pulling the business card from his top pocket. 'I have managed to obtain an address for Matt which will mean anything you write will automatically get sent on. There may be a bit of a time lapse but you'll be able to keep in regular touch until he's back.'

'Thank you,' She took it from him. 'Do you know when that will be?'

'Early spring I'm told.'

'Unless, of course, the record company decides to send them to Kathmandu?'

Tad laughed. 'I wouldn't put it past them - but no, Matt has a new album to write and he's told them he wants to take time out to do it. Reading between the lines I think Centaur is beginning to realise how hard they've driven the boys. He'll be home when he says he will, don't worry!'

She watched him walk away into the dimness of the club. Turning the card over in her hand she felt a small rush of happiness. Everything was still on hold, but there was light at the end of the tunnel. He would be coming home, and when he did she knew just what she was going to do. Making her way back to the table with the drinks she saw Issy and Jenny's curious expressions.

'Good news?' Jenny asked as Ella set the three glasses down on the table.

'As a matter of fact, yes!' Ella smiled.

'When's he coming home then?' Issy said picking up her glass.

'Not until the spring. But -' She waved the card at them both, 'I have an address, I'm going to write to him!'

Monday 10th February, 1969

Ella was locking her Mini when she caught sight of Jenny crossing the road towards the college.

'Guess what I've got?' She said excitedly, pulling an envelope from her pocket as she caught up with Jenny. 'I managed to intercept the postman on my way here.'

'Well open it then! What does he have to say?'

Ella tore open the envelope and pulled out its contents. She stood there, the wind teasing her hair, her face tight with concentration as she read. 'He got my letter! They're in Rome and it's warm,' she looked up smiling, 'Another full house, screaming fans. Oh and typical! Todd jumped fully clothed into the Trevi fountain and had to be pulled out by the Carabinieri.'

'No mention of when he'll be home then?'

'No, there's nothing here,' Ella shook her head. 'The last letter said late spring. I guess I'll just have to be patient,' she went back to reading the letter. 'This is strange,' she made a face. 'He says he hopes I've got over my disappointment at not being able to make tea at the Ritz with his parents in January. He says maybe just the two of us can do something similar later on in the year.....'

'But you didn't get an invite, did you?'

'No,' Ella folded the letter and slipped it into her bag. 'And no prizes for guessing why not.'

'Your mother?'

'Not my mother,' Ella shook her head, 'His! Faye's done it again hasn't she? I've been deliberately left out, just like when the band had their big celebration at the Mill last May.'

'What are you going to do?'

'Just ignore it. I'm not going to give her the satisfaction of knowing I'm aware of what she's done. I will get to see him, though - I don't know when, but it will happen! And she's not going to stop me, I won't let her!'

Thursday 6th March

Marjorie Webster sat, a large and majestic centrepiece among her assembled guests. She gazed around her lounge, a large airy room with wall to wall Axminster and matching Sanderson wallpaper and curtains. The china cups and saucers on the centrally placed coffee table echoed the pattern in the curtains; pink flowers with dainty green leaves, each cup edge etched with gold. And the crowning glory, the silver service, sitting amongst all of it, polished and bright. Marjorie felt, triumphant. This was her day. Not even Mel Carpenter's spitefulness could dampen the excitement she felt being the hostess for this first gathering of the Rotary Ladies Circle since she had been elected Chairwoman.

The assembled Entertainment's Committee, Marjorie, Sheila Fitzallyn, Barbara Morris, Grace Henderson and Mary Neville, wives of some of the town's most prominent businessmen, sat awaiting the arrival of Mel. The purpose of their meeting was to discuss the forthcoming Easter Ball to be held at the Forum. Marjorie checked her watch; Mel was now ten minutes late. She gave a sigh; why did it always have to be like this? It was childishly pathetic, but so like her. Well Marjorie had had enough of this nonsense. She was Chairwoman now and on this occasion Mel Carpenter was going to be very disappointed.

'Right ladies,' she got to her feet, smiling pleasantly. 'I think we'll make a start.'

Five minutes later Marjorie answered the door to a smiling Mel who breezed past her, expecting to find the whole room waiting for her. Instead, everyone was sitting, the whole room buzzing with conversation. Her expression as she registered this had been one of surprise. Seeing Marjorie smiling serenely behind her it changed immediately to anger.

'Well, we didn't think you were coming,' Marjorie, in her normal well mannered way, ushered her to a chair before pouring her a cup of tea and indicating what was left of the cakes.

'I think I'll pass on the cakes thank you Marjorie. Unlike some I have my figure to think of.' Mel's gaze settled on Marjorie's thick waist and spreading hips, the look on her face guaranteed to do more damage than any words.

Marjorie smiled back undeterred and called the ladies to order. A lively discussion then took place on tactics for the ball - whether it should be a black tie do or perhaps fancy dress; which charity should benefit; the type of music they should have and, of course, their advertising strategy.

Mel sat, looking extremely bored with the whole proceedings, her gaze straying intermittently out of the window. With a sigh she opened her handbag and pulled out her cigarette case and lighter, tapping the cigarette noisily against the case before lighting up. She inhaled deeply then blew smoke into the air, snapping the case shut before slipping it and the lighter back into her handbag. Marjorie was outraged. It was surely only common courtesy to ask before you smoked in someone else's house. She watched the grey ash grow on the end of the cigarette aware it was more than likely to end up on her beloved Axminster. At length Mel tapped her ash into the saucer of her teacup. Marjorie deliberately ignored her. She was doing this on purpose, trying to cause upset. But I won't be bullied, Marjorie thought. Now I'm Chairman of Ladies Circle, those days are over.

'I think,' Sheila Fitzallyn tapped the pad she had been writing on, 'that we ought to bear in mind quite a large group of young people will be attending the Easter Ball, therefore the music should appeal to all age groups.'

'I think so too.' Marjorie agreed, looking at Mel, 'Will Ella be attending?'

'I have no idea, Marjorie.' Mel said with a disinterested shrug.

'Oh I do hope so,' Sheila Fitzallyn said enthusiastically, brushing cake crumbs from the skirt of her lilac dress, 'My Charles thinks she's wonderful. She's really blossomed since she moved here, hasn't she? Turned into real beauty.'

Mel gave a weak smile, stubbing her cigarette into saucer. Marjorie watched the way she was grinding the butt into the bone china, a clear indication she was annoyed. Maybe there was more than just a little jealousy there. After all, Mel liked to think she was the Queen of Abbotsbridge. Perhaps it was time to give her throne a bit of a shake.

'Oh yes,' she replied with an agreeing smile, 'Maurice thinks Ella is lovely too. He's always talking about her hair. He says she ought to be in the shampoo ads.'

'I do so agree.' Nodded Barbara Morris, eager to assist in Mel's discomfort, 'Wonderful hair - thick and curly. Must be from her father's side mustn't it?' She looked inquisitively at Mel, 'Well, it's not like yours is it dear?'

'Not at all,' Marjorie chipped in, 'Yours is straight - and *thinner*.'

'I would just die to have hair like Ella's,' Sheila Fitzallyn said leaning forward as if she was sharing some incredible secret with them all. 'Just die!' Everyone nodded in agreement their gaze automatically going to Mel as if waiting for some response.

'Well,' she gave them all an ingratiating smile, 'Quite a little fan club we have here. I only wish I could stay a little longer but,' she checked her watch, 'I do have to be somewhere else in twenty minutes. Marjorie,' she got to her feet and crossed to where the large woman sat, pressing cheeks with her, 'Thank you so much for the tea. You will call me when the next meeting is due, won't you? I'd be quite happy to assist with the preparations for the ball. No doubt I can tuck an odd afternoon into my busy schedule.'

With a watery smile she backed out of the room, nodding her goodbyes to all and sundry. The door closed, leaving the small group of women looking at each other gleefully.

All the way home Mel smouldered angrily. For the first time in the seventeen months since Ella had moved to Abbotsbridge, she began to wish she had never asked her here. Of course the reasons behind the invitation had been purely selfish. As well as deliberately upsetting her own father, Mel had wanted a pretty daughter to show off; one who would eventually marry into a well off family in the town, thus enhancing her own social connections. It all seemed perfect; Ella had been unsettled by her grandmother's death and her grandfather taking a new wife and was looking to move from Meridan Cross.

On reflection, she had to admit she had no parenting skills. She had left both her children behind when they were small in order to marry Liam and move abroad. What a relief that had been, abandoning the difficult periods of child rearing to her parents. The first years had been awful; smelly nappies and sleepless nights. Her first husband Christopher, had been an airline pilot, on long haul flights and she found herself on her own a lot of the time at Little

Court, the family home. Christopher's mother Laura Kendrick had suggested they hire a nanny but that had been a complete disaster. Mel just could not deal with sloppy girls who answered back and didn't respect their betters. After the third packed her bags and left she called it a day and decided to let her mother Peggy take over. Then Christopher's plane crash changed everything again. She rowed with Laura and left (they had never really got on), moving herself and the children into nearby Fox Cottage which was owned by her father. The move was a good one; she became the brave young widow bringing up her children alone. Peggy supported her need to work, to have some freedom and stepped in again as unpaid nursemaid, much to her father's annoyance. Of course no one knew about the bad investment and lost savings which made her need to work urgent and necessary. But there was another reason too; she wanted to marry again, to get away from the draconian regime of her father. Therefore, when Liam offered her a chance of complete escape she grabbed it with both hands, the children abandoned without a backward glance.

She had returned to find her son a young man at university and a daughter on the threshold of womanhood. Looking at Ella, it seemed fairly simple to invite an eighteen year old to live with them. To all intents and purposes she was an adult of sorts - much easier to deal with than a small niggling child. She had expected Ella to understand what was expected of her; to be the quiet accommodating daughter who knew her place, but instead she appeared to have created quite a reputation for herself. She had friends, fun. Was popular with everyone and turned heads wherever she went. At first Mel had ignored the comments about her beautiful daughter. Now it rankled; she felt second best, treated as if she had no skills or talents that could ever match those of Ella's. Even Liam showed little interest in anything she was doing these days. As she drove away from Marjorie Webster's house she knew she had to remedy the situation and do something that would return her to her rightful place of centre stage.

It was when she turned the car into the High Street that the idea struck her. She was so used to just dropping into Christiana's Boutique to buy her clothes. What if she bought some quality material and made a dress? It was something she used to do as a girl; her mother had been an excellent teacher. Her electric sewing machine, an expensive, unused present from three Christmases ago sat gathering dust in the spare room; she had no excuse.

Finding a parking place she headed for Langley's Drapery Department. Emerging fifteen minutes later with a carrier bag and a confident smile she drove home, dreaming of how they would all eat their words when she wore her stunning creation for the first time.

She found Liam in his den. Suddenly the material was forgotten, she craved attention and spent time hovering in the doorway, telling him about her disagreeable afternoon and the comments of the silly women she had been with. All Liam had done, however, was to tell her not to be so sensitive; that it wasn't a competition. Yes, Ella had great hair and she looked good, but she was young and couldn't be compared with her more mature style, they were two completely different things. Far from having her fears allayed, Mel felt worse. The word 'mature' conjured up images of Marjorie and her cronies. Of spreading hips, false teeth and sensible shoes.

When Ella arrived home from college and they all sat down to dinner Liam jokingly mentioned the comments from the Ladies' Circle. He asked her how she felt being responsible for being the potential cause of heart attacks to half the older male population. Ella had smiled and said she had better brush up on her resuscitation skills, which had made them both laugh. Facing both her husband and her daughter joking with each other across the dinner table at her expense Mel's resentment deepened.

After dinner Ella helped clear the table and stack the dishwasher before rushing off to see Jenny about an English assignment. Watching her leave, Mel felt old and extremely disenchanted with her own life. Even Bob Macayne and the excitement she usually felt when she thought about their affair and the secret meetings, couldn't lift her spirits. Liam, deciding to spend the evening in his den, working on an idea he'd had for a new house design for Bob, left Mel alone in the lounge in front of the TV. Bored with the quiz show she was watching, she changed channels and finding nothing there to entertain her, decided to make a start on her sewing. The lounge floor became the place for her to begin her creation. Pushing back the coffee table, she spread out the expensive silky material and pinned on the pattern.

She was busy cutting when Ella appeared in the doorway.

'Yes, I'm sewing,' She said with a smirk as she got to her feet, clutching the scissors, 'I decided it was about time I resurrected old skills. So as you can see, I'm putting my creative talents to very good use.'

Ella looked at the material on the floor with concentration then said, 'I think you've pinned the pattern on the wrong way round.'

'Rubbish!' Mel glared at the material and then at Ella, 'I know what I'm doing! I was making dresses before you were even born!'

Ella looked at the material again, sensing her mother's hostility, 'I was only trying to be helpful,' she said in a quiet voice.

'Well don't be!' Mel could feel the frustrations of the past eight hours begin to bubble inside her. It seemed to her that all through the day insult after insult had been heaped on her, and now even in her own home she was not safe. This half grown woman in front of her was, underneath that concerned exterior, criticising her. Faces of those in the Ladies Circle loomed out of nowhere at her. *Ella's so pretty! She's really blossomed since she arrived in Abbotsbridge. Her hair is lovely! Not like yours, yours is thin and straight!* With a scream of rage she lunged at her, grabbing at her hair. Ella fell to the floor with a shriek.

Seeing the scissors hovering above her head, Ella screamed again and ducked against the end of the settee.

'What the hell is going on?' Liam was in the doorway, his eyes wide with horror.

'I....' Mel began, then stopped and looked down. She was still holding the scissors in her right hand while in her left she clutched a good nine inch hank of Ella's dark hair. She stared at it for a moment, then at Liam, a look of surprise on her face. A small gasp escaped her lips as she jerked open her fingers, releasing the hair almost as if it had burned her.

Arms over her head, Ella was still pressed against the settee, trying to protect herself. Hearing Liam's voice and sensing safety, she turned just in time to see a cascade of dark curl drop into her lap.

'My hair! What have you done to my hair?' She shouted, clutching frantically at the base of her neck and the ragged ends left from Mel's assault.

Standing there, Mel felt the everything recede in front of her. For a moment the world spun and she found herself engulfed in a fog-like silence. Then everything came crashing back like a sonic tidal wave, and the world was filled with a deafening sound, flooding her senses and echoing in her ears. It took her moments to realise she was listening to the sound of her own hysterical laughter.

THREE

Friday 7th March

Liam sat alone amid the clutter of the breakfast table. He tried to concentrate on his newspaper and the events of the day - the end of the Krays murder trial and the imminent elections in Israel - but his mind kept drifting back to the events of the previous evening.

As Mel had collapsed onto the settee, hysterical with laughter, his first concern had been for Ella and he had quickly helped her to her feet, guiding her past her mother and out of the door. After the initial horrified wail at the sight of her mutilated hair in the hall mirror, he had managed to get her to her room, telling her to stay there while he went back to deal with Mel. When he returned to the lounge he found she had moved into the dining room and was busy helping herself to something from the drinks cabinet. She turned as she heard him enter.

'Would *you* like something while I'm here?' She shook her ice filled whisky glass at him.

'You're having a *drink*?' He stared at her incredulously, 'After what's just happened?'

'I didn't mean to do it Liam,' She shrugged indifferently, 'one moment the scissors were in my hand, the next....'

'Well will you please go and talk to her then Mel. Say sorry. Explain.'

'Oh Liam, I wouldn't know how to deal with an hysterical teenager,' She said bringing the glass to her lips, 'I'd probably make things much worse. I think maybe I'll keep out of her way till everything calms down.'

'Calms down!' He looked at her in amazement, 'Her hair is ruined! She'll have to have it all cut off! How do you expect her to just calm down, as you put it, after an experience like that?'

'Liam please do not shout like that,' She pulled the glass away from her mouth, lips trembling, tears imminent. 'You know I can't cope when you shout at me.'

He knew he was on a hiding to nothing then. When Mel was in this sort of tragic housewife mood the only thing he could do was turn and walk out of the room. And that is exactly what he did, slamming the door behind him.

Now as he sat alone at the breakfast table he could not believe how weak he had been. In the months Ella had been here in Abbotsbridge he had grown to love her as if she were his own daughter. There had been an unwritten rule that they supported each other when Mel was being difficult. But last night when Ella had really needed his help he'd let her down badly. Of course he knew that years of living with Mel had gradually eroded his masculinity. She was used to having her own way and in the past he had always been prepared to give in to her. But not any more; from today things were going to change.

He had returned to Ella moments after trying to deal with Mel, anxious to comfort her. Halfway up the stairs he heard the Mini engine fire and caught the reflection of its tail lights in the hall window as it disappeared up the road. He had left it too late. She had gone.

Work was impossible after that. He spent an uncomfortable night on the couch in his studio, eventually drifting into a restless sleep. He awoke at six and showered, still worrying about her. Now it was eight fifteen and although her car was back she had not yet put in an appearance.

As Mrs Harris, the family's daily, arrived with the teapot and poured him another cup, Ella appeared dressed in jeans and a pale blue shirt, a navy sweater slung around her shoulders. As she said good morning to him and took her usual place at the breakfast table he stared at her hair. Some sort of miracle had taken place; it had now been cut into a short fashionable style. It framed her face beautifully, enhancing her eyes, making her look even prettier.

'Well now there's a change,' Mrs Harris exclaimed with a smile as she moved around the table to pour tea into Ella's cup, 'it really suits you. Toast as usual?'

'Please,' There was Ella's familiar smile. Mrs Harris disappeared into the kitchen leaving Liam staring at Ella.

'I came back to find you, but you were gone,' He said as he folded his newspaper, thinking how lame his words must sound, 'I lay awake most of the night, worrying. Where did you go?'

'To Jenny's. She phoned Sammy Smith at Headlines. He very kindly came out to her house and restyled my hair.'

'It looks lovely,' Liam replied weakly, 'Sorry that must sound pathetic given the circumstances. Ella, I feel so responsible.......'

'It's not your fault Liam,' Ella said, 'this has been brewing for some time. I should never have agreed to come here in the first place.'

'Of course you should, it's been wonderful. You've made such a difference - to me.'

'I know, you told me that soon after I arrived,' She reached across the table to give his hand an affectionate squeeze, 'But as far as mother is concerned, all I've done is annoy her. She hates me being independent and she disapproves of everything I do, everything I wear and everyone I see. What happened last night was deliberate.'

Liam rested his elbows on the table, his eyes filled with concern, 'Ella, you have my solemn promise, this will never happen again. I intend to talk to Mel after breakfast. It's time things changed around here.'

'Liam, please, there's no need.'

Mrs Harris appeared with a full toast rack and took Liam's plate away, halting the conversation for a moment. As she disappeared Liam leaned across the table, his expression serious.

'My darling girl, we have to sort this out, we can't just let it drift.'

'Liam it is being sorted. I'm leaving. I'm going to stay in Kingsford with Issy.'

'Leaving? You can't do that!'

Before she could reply the door opened and Mel appeared wrapped in a quilted lemon house coat.

'Someone has left suitcases in the hall,' she said, staring back towards the door as she took her place at the table. Ignoring them both she reached for the cereal packet.

'They're mine,' Ella replied getting to her feet angrily as she watched her mother sitting there organising her breakfast as if nothing in the world was the matter, 'Issy's parents have offered me a room for as long as I want it.'

'Oh don't be silly Ella. Kingsford? You don't want to live all over there,' Mel smiled pleasantly as she dredged sugar over her cornflakes, 'You're over-reacting. It was an accident. The scissors slipped. It wasn't intentional,' she looked up at her daughter, 'and I have to say looking at you now, it's a vast improvement on what was there before, don't you think so Liam?'

'What!' Ella glared at her mother.

'Well, you must admit darling, your hair was a complete mess,' She said innocently, elbows on the table, hands clasped over her cereal bowl smiling sweetly at her husband, 'Of course in a backwater like Meridan Cross it probably didn't matter what you looked like, but here in Abbotsbridge as I'm sure you realise, standards are slightly higher.' she studied Ella's hair for a moment, 'In fact, I really think you should be thanking me. Accident it may have been, but I do believe I've done you yet another rather large favour.'

'What do you mean another?'

'The Benedict boy,' Mel smiled a self-satisfied smile, 'Back in January his father came here with some cock-and-bull story about an invitation to tea at the Ritz. Of course, I sent him packing. As if people like that would be let in!'

'Mel how could you!' Liam glared at her.

'Liam, Ella is *my* daughter, and I will do as I see fit!'

'*You* did that?' Ella stared at her mother, 'I thought it was Faye!'

'Faye? No it was me,' she said proudly. 'How do you know about it anyway?'

'Matt wrote to me.'

'The Benedict boy and his family are totally unsuitable Ella. Money they may have, class they certainly do not! He's not good enough for you, he never will be. End of subject!' Mel looked at her daughter, her eyes hard chips of blue. 'Now then,' spreading her napkin across her lap she continued with her breakfast, waving a well manicured finger towards the milk jug, 'Pass the milk over will you?'

Leaning across the table, Ella retrieved the jug and paused for a moment, staring thoughtfully down into its depths.

'Ella,' she heard her mother's voice again, saw her hand reaching out impatiently, 'Milk?'

'Coming right up!' Ella smiled and stepping forward threw the contents of the jug straight into her mother's face.

Saturday 19th April

'Liam, the last thing I want to do is get you into trouble.'

'I'm in trouble already. For telling her she deserved it. Well she did! She had no right to interfere like that, it was unforgivable! And now she has a massive sulk on because I've refused to pay for a new dress for the Easter Rotary Ball,' he looked pleased with himself. 'I've put my foot down at last.'

'Well done!' Ella nodded, feeling glad that Liam had started to assert himself but knowing realistically it would not last. Her mother was shrewd and calculating and Ella knew it wouldn't take long for her to have Liam wrapped around her finger again.

She felt no remorse over the milk incident; it was a parting gift for a cold-blooded and callous woman. Once the deed had been done, Ella had simply walked from the room, leaving the chaos behind her. Picking up her cases she left the house and loaded them into the Mini, driving off without a backward glance. A week later Liam had arrived at the Bridge Hotel to see her. At first she thought he had come to persuade her back, but instead he asked her to come and view a flat with him.

'You're not leaving Mother too are you?' She laughed.

'No,' He smiled back, amused, 'This is for you.'

Now sitting beside him in the car, she relaxed as they took a right turn opposite the Esso filling station into Park Street. Half a mile on he drew to a halt outside a row of three storey red bricked houses in a road lined with the dappled trunks of lime trees.

'It looks wonderful,' Ella smiled, surveying the street as she got out of the car, 'Mature, established, I like it already.'

'Good. I thought you would. Don't get me wrong, I'm sure the Bridge Hotel is very nice, but you can't live in a hotel room for ever. You need a proper place, like this.'

They climbed stone steps to a heavy mahogany door inlaid with attractive stained glass. Liam produced a key from his pocket, inserted it in the lock and turned it. The door swung open to reveal a long cream walled hallway carpeted in dark mushroom with an elegant sweep of stairs off to the right. Ella followed him up them, her eyes wide with surprise as she took in the high ceilings and the decorative coving. It had all been lovingly restored; it was elegant and beautiful. On reaching the landing he produced a second key and opened a solid pine door with the brass letters 2B set in it.

'Here we are,' He ushered her through and followed her into the flat, 'Well, what do you think?'

Brightness, that was Ella's first thought as she walked from room to room; all the walls painted in magnolia, blinds or curtains at each window. The furniture, although second hand, was very good quality. Heating for all the flats came from a boiler in the basement; the galley kitchen was compact yet fully equipped the bathroom a pretty yellow and everywhere, the feel of space and light.

She walked across to the living room window. Beyond the narrow stretch of back garden was the park with walkways and fountains, flower beds awash with brightness of marigolds.

'It's wonderful find Liam, simply wonderful,' she turned to look at him with excited eyes, 'How much is the weekly rent?'

'To you nothing,' He said taking her by the shoulders and kissing her forehead, 'it's free, for as long as you want it. Besides, I know since you left your mother has stopped your allowance.'

'Ah, but Grandma gives me an allowance now,' She smiled, 'Please, you have so many other financial commitments; I insist you let me at least put something towards the rent. It's only fair…'

'Hush....' He smiled down into her face, 'I called in a favour from an old friend. The rent is minimal. Please, I insist, just enjoy.'

'I see the Attitude are in Vienna.' Issy said, thumbing through a copy the *Abbotsbridge Times and News* someone had left on a nearby seat. She was sitting with Jenny in the Red Lion waiting for Ella to arrive for a drink before they moved on to Ronaldo's for Issy's 19th birthday meal. She peered at the paper again. 'Oh, and they're in Amsterdam next week, and then Brussels. And they are due back in the UK by the middle of May. Well, well,' her eyes shone, 'It says here that they have had a sell out tour and their last three singles have been No 1 all over Europe. Their debut album is set to go platinum and shows they are not only capable of mainstream pop but also guitar-led rock. It is a clear indication that this band are here to stay, nurtured by the versatility of Matt Benedict's song writing talents. Matt, who celebrated his twenty first birthday earlier this year, recently bought a house in fashionable Chelsea.....' she looked over the paper at Jenny, 'Well, doesn't look as if he'll be coming back to Abbotsbridge in a hurry, does it?'

'Seems not,' Jenny took a sip of her vodka and tonic before resting her glass on the table, 'Of course Ella's still in touch with him,' she said, 'but they've not met up yet - I wonder if they'll catch up next month? Although, of course, things may be different now she is seeing Andy.'

'Andy?' Issy made a face before retrieving the lemon slice from the bottom of her glass, 'That's not a relationship - thank goodness! She just fits him in when she's not busy. She feels sorry for him really. Anyway, if you ask me, I think he's biding his time, waiting for the right moment to get Nina back. Despite what Mick says, the wedding's not going to happen you know.'

'I do wish you were right.' Jenny said, waving out as she caught sight of Ella making her way through the crowded bar towards them.

'I am, in fact I'm so convinced, I'd put money on it,' Issy said confidently.

FOUR

Sunday 25th May

Laura stood on the steps of Little Court watching the red and white Mini as it approached from the east down the curve of gravelled driveway, at the edge of which rhododendron bushes blazed red and purple. The arrangements for Ella to visit over Whitsun had been made weeks ago and now suddenly the day had arrived.

Laura was looking forward to having Ella stay. For a start she wanted to hear all about the new flat, pleased that with Liam's help Ella had at last managed to escape the clutches of Mel. And of course, she had made important plans for the week. Plans which went beyond relaxing, exchanging news and shopping in Taunton. Something so special she had decided to keep it a secret until Ella's arrival.

The small vehicle came to a stop directly in front of the steps. Ella emerged, pulling her suitcase from the back seat.

'Good heavens!' Laura's hands flew to her face, 'What *have* you done to your hair?'

Ella looked at her grandmother's shocked expression. Diplomatically, she decided, the truth was probably best left behind in Abbotsbridge.

'I thought I'd do the whole thing Grandma.' She gave a light-hearted laugh. 'New flat, new image! Don't you like it?'

'Well yes,' Laura said almost reluctantly, 'but it has somewhat ruined my plans.'

'What plans?' Ella said locking her car and joining Laura at the top of the steps.

'I wanted you to sit for a painting.' She said ushering her into the hall.

'A painting?'

Laura nodded. 'That was my surprise; I decided it would be rather nice to have a painting of you to add to the family collection. I wanted it to hang alongside Marcella's at the turn of the stairs.' She gazed upwards at the portrait on the landing. 'The two of you are so similar and yet come from completely different times. I thought it could become quite a talking point.' she reached out and touched the feathered ends of Ella's hair, a disappointed frown on her face, 'But what will poor Hugo make of this?'

'Hugo Monroe-Black is going to do the honours?' Ella smiled.

'Yes.' Laura nodded. 'He wanted to start tomorrow.'

'Well,' Ella thought for a moment, 'That's not a problem is it?'

'But darling, your hair! It's far too short!' Laura said despairingly. 'It won't look right!'

Ella linked arms with Laura and leaned her head towards her. 'Grandma.' she whispered. 'Don't worry! Hugo's a professional; he'll have no trouble improvising!'

Richard Evas was returning from shutting the hens up for the night when he saw Ella's Mini pull up outside the farm house.

'Well, this is a surprise,' He said, greeting her at the garden gate with a tight hug and a kiss on the cheek, 'Laura said you were coming, but I didn't think we'd see you until tomorrow.' His smiled faded as he looked at her again, 'What have you done to your hair?'

'Don't you like it?'

'Well, yes,' He hesitated for a moment. 'Yes, it suits you.' then his smile was suddenly back and he laughed. 'Bit of a shock that's all! Mary!' he called towards the open back door. 'Mary! Ella's here!'

Mary appeared, wearing beige trousers and a turquoise shirt, a navy cardigan over her arm.

'Ella!' Her eyes opened wide. 'Your hair! Goodness what a change!' She stared at Ella for a moment then turned to Richard, 'Actually, I like it don't you?'

He studied Ella for a few seconds more then nodded.

'Well,' Mary said slipping the cardigan over her shoulders and closing the door. 'You've timed your arrival nicely. We were just off to the Arms for a drink. Would you like to join us?'

'Love to,' Ella nodded. 'We can take my car.'

'How are things at the stables?' She asked, glancing at Mary in the rear view mirror as they made their way down the farm track to the main road.

'We're doing well. I've just bought three new horses, I'll take you to see them tomorrow,' Mary replied, leaning between the two front seats of the car, 'Did you know Rachel's with me full time now?'

'Yes, she mentioned it in her last letter; she seems to be enjoying it. And I gather her mother is managing quite well on her own in the shop.'

'Village shops aren't what they used to be you know,' Richard said pensively. 'These new fangled supermarkets have taken away a lot of the local trade with their cheap food. Most people in the village now have a car, so they can get to them quite easily. But Margaret's quite a sensible woman. The shop's become a SPAR grocers now. Dutch or something aren't they? Some of her goods are quite competitive. Mary still gets a few things there, don't you?'

'Ah but Richard,' Mary laughed, 'We all know what that shop really runs on. Village gossip. Now if that were a saleable commodity she'd be the richest woman in Meridan Cross!'

'Grandma told me you have a lodger in Fox Cottage.' Ella said as the village sign flashed past them.

'We have.' Mary nodded. 'It's a three week let; he's been there two already.'

'A poet would you believe?' Richard added. 'From the smoke. Come here for the air, thinks it will improve his *creativity*.' he mimicked.

'Take no notice of your grandfather.' Mary shouted over the noise of the engine. 'Lance McAllister is an extremely nice man.'

'And by the sound of him maybe a successor to Rabbie Burns?' Ella laughed.

'Oh he's not Scottish,' Mary said, shaking her head. 'He's *very* English. And he's got long hair. That's what your grandfather objects to really.'

Catching sight of Mary's amused expression in the rear view mirror Ella smiled. She drove slowly through the village, taking in all the old familiar sights. Then the pub loomed ahead, the cricket field to the rear dotted with white clad figures drifting off the pitch, the match now over.

'The locals will be pleased to see you back,' Richard said as he squeezed out of the car. 'You can sign Doggie's plaster for him, he'll love that.'

'Plaster?'

'Yes, broke his arm. Bit of a set to with one of Mirage Holding's managers who took exception to Doggie's poaching activities.'

'I'll treat him like a hero.' Ella promised, aware that although the land owning consortium was part of village life it showed far less tolerance to Doggie than other farmers in the area.

The Somerset Arms was packed. The two teams were now in the bar extension, helping themselves to a buffet which had been set up on trestle tables while publican Tom Bennett was doing the rounds pouring out free beer from his famous copper jug.

Shouts went up as Ella was spotted and one or two young men in cricket whites, plates in hand, broke away from the crowd and came across to greet her. Rachel also took time out from serving behind the bar for a moment and slipped out to give her friend a welcome hug.

Richard ordered drinks and the three of them found a corner table near Doggie and Toby. Old Doggie related his ordeal with great feeling and offered his arm and a well chewed biro to Ella.

'I love coming back here. Nothing ever changes does it?' Ella smiled contentedly as she finished her message and handed Doggy back his pen.

'No,' Mary said, watching the activity in the bar with a smile, 'You know I loved Meridan Cross from the first day I arrived here and I think I always will. Ah.' her attention was drawn to the bar again. 'It looks as though our lodger's decided to put in an appearance. Over there.'

Ella followed the direction of Mary's nod. 'Well.' she said, smiling. 'What a surprise.'

Matt Benedict stood at the bar waiting to be served. It had been a good day. The creative juices were certainly flowing well. Meridan Cross, he had discovered from discussions with local odd job man-cum-poacher, Doggy Barker, meant "Pretty valley where the road and river cross." It was certainly that; a little piece of paradise; timeless and peaceful. The old cottage had a strange sort of presence, comfortable and settled, despite its remoteness tucked into woods at the end of a lane. The leisurely walk to the pub had taken him ten minutes across the fields and as the shadows lengthened, he was drawn by the beauty of the place. The rich greens of the woods and fields, the wild flowers; the cattle and sheep dotted everywhere and the river meandering lazily through it all. He had glimpsed the Elizabethan chimneys of Little Court on one of his afternoon walks through the village and desperately wanted to visit. But he knew Laura Kendrick would probably wonder who he was if he turned up on her doorstep, for he expected Ella's conversations with her grandmother had never touched on anything as mundane as her relationship with him.

Relationship, he laughed to himself as he ordered a half of cider. What relationship? They had been friends, that was all. He had given her flowers before he left for the band's UK tour and asked her to wait for him. Disappointingly he hadn't made it back for Christmas or the New Year as promised, and her mother had wrecked the invitation to the Ritz in January. However his father had managed to get a regular forwarding address to her and she had corresponded, keeping up a weekly dialog with him, letting him know what was going on back home. He'd been going to write to let her know he was coming here, but there had been no time. He had thought about mentioning it to the Evas's when he arrived, but wasn't sure what their reaction would be. He'd told them he was a poet; changing his story, he knew, wouldn't go down well with Ella's grandfather in particular. He knew prejudice when it looked him in the eye and the once over he had been given on arrival left no doubt in his mind that long hair and scruffy denims were not approved of. He was his daughter's father all right and Matt knew that any connection with Ella would have gone down like a lead balloon.

In the year since the band had become famous many things besides his appearance had changed. He had bought a house in London; an elegant red bricked town house in Chelsea, furnished in creams and beiges with pale Scandinavian furniture. He owned the sleek, red Alfa Spider he had always promised himself. Top designers queued up to dress him and the band and he and The Attitude were the first names on everyone's lips when it came to celebrity party invitations. They mingled with the sixties beautiful people: musicians, photographers, actors, and a sprinkling of titled individuals; hung out at places like Revolution or Speakeasy with all the other happening faces. It was life in the fast lane with a vengeance.

Still he had to admit he loved what he was doing and he knew he had made the right decision. To be able earn a good living from something you really enjoyed must be a rare thing and he counted himself very lucky. He was happy, wealthy and perhaps not quite so shy any more. All in all he was quite content with his lot.

So why had he come here when he could have gone to one of half a dozen other places to write? Was it because Ella's description had left a lasting impression on him? Or that her grandfather had a secluded cottage he was always willing to rent out which would give him the privacy he wanted? Or was it because, a dreamer at heart, he hoped, despite not letting her know he was in Meridan Cross, that she might miraculously have chosen to be here too?

He moved away from the bar, proposing to find a quiet corner for the evening where he could sit and watch the ebb and flow of village life. As he eased himself past the clamour of bodies tucking into the buffet he thought he heard someone call his name. Then all of a sudden he felt a light touch at his elbow.

'Good evening, Mr McAllister.'

Grey eyes looked up at him from a halo of short black curls.

'Ella!'

For a moment he didn't recognise her. He gave himself a secret pinch on the inside of his arm, unable to believe what he had wished for had come true. The pain confirmed she was indeed real. Looking at her sitting with the Evas's, a sudden rush of emotion washed over him as familiar feelings took hold once more.

'You two know each other?' Mary looked at them both in amazement.

'Yes,' Ella was delighted. 'Matt's from Abbotsbridge and I haven't seen him in ages!'

'In that case young man you'd best sit down and tell my granddaughter all your news.' Richard, all smiles, pulled a free stool out from under the table. Matt reached for it blindly, his eyes fixed firmly on Ella.

'I can't believe it.' Ella said as he sat down beside her.

'Neither can I.'

'I've been reading all the magazines, keeping up-to-date with what the band has been doing. I hoped we'd catch up with each other eventually, but this is the last place I thought I'd run into you. What are you doing here?'

'It's a long story. The truth is, this year I've hardly had a moment to myself.' He took her hand and held it gently. 'It's been a mad year, most of it out of the UK so far. Our record company have now grudgingly allowed me time off to write for the next album. I insisted that I would not do it in London. There was too much distraction there, I couldn't concentrate. I wanted somewhere peaceful. And,' he shrugged. 'After the excellent PR job you'd given this place, I thought why not?'

'But why the false name?'

'I use it when I want to avoid fans and the press.' He replied with a grin.

'Well.' She covered his hand with hers, 'I hope I'm one fan you won't be trying to avoid this week.'

'Oh, most definitely not.'

In the days that followed, Ella and Matt were constantly in each other's company. As Hugo required Ella to be available for her portrait until noon each day, Matt used the mornings to concentrate on his writing, tucking himself away at the cottage.

Laura and Hugo had discussed the painting project extensively before he started work. The original painting was formal, showing Ella's great grandmother sitting in a chair wearing a beautiful green dress, the family pearl and emerald choker at her throat.

The new portrait would show Ella in jodhpurs, an open neck shirt and brown riding boots. Holding Merlin's bridle, she would be standing beside an open five bar gate, Hundred Acre wood in the background.

Stiff and cramped from posing in the coach house at Little Court, Ella longed for each morning to end so she could be with Matt again. They took a picnic by the river, walked in Hundred Acre Wood, herded cows, collected eggs, helped with the hay making and took on the Miller boys at darts in the Somerset Arms.

For Matt it was a completely new experience as through their walks and conversations together, the real Ella began to emerge. For this was her proper home; the place where she had grown up. As her childhood unravelled before him, he could visualise her riding through Hundred Acre with the Sedgewick Hunt, tickling trout in the river with brother Nick and taking refreshments out to the harvesters or helping with the milking at Willowbrook.

On evening visits to the Somerset Arms, when bribed with a drink, old Doggie Barker was delighted to entertain them with stories of his life; as a soldier in two wars and finally as a resident of the village. His animated interpretations of events watched adoringly by Toby at his feet. How different this country life had been; still was, in comparison to his urban upbringing, Matt thought as he gradually found himself falling under the spell of this small Somerset village.

And, at the end of the week he was invited to Little Court by Laura. He had never seen such a wonderful old house. History oozed from it, not only in its portraits and tapestries but also the flagstone floor of the great hall, the minstrel gallery and the orangery with its trained fruit trees forming a living arch under glass.

'Where did the name Little Court come from?' He asked, turning to Laura with a curious frown.

'Well,' Laura thought for a moment. 'Jonas Kendrick who originally built this house was, how shall we say, a favoured face during the reign of Henry VIII. Later it had the reputation of being one of Elizabeth's favourite places to stay outside her own royal residencies. Of course in those days when the queen visited her court came with her. Someone jokingly called it Elizabeth's Little Court.' She smiled. 'And Edgar Kendrick who lived here then, remodelled it in Elizabethan style in her honour and renamed it. Much better than Roseberry House don't you think?'

He nodded, his gaze now transferred to one of the portraits.

'She could be Ella's double,' He said, laughing, 'Now I know where her curly hair comes from.'

'Yes, that's Marcella Armstrong. Ella's great grandmother.' Laura nodded, 'I plan to hang Ella's portrait next to hers when it's finished.'

'When will it be ready?'

'In a few weeks. Hugo's work with Ella is finished. He now has to add in Merlin and the background. Shouldn't be too difficult. Mary has taken Polaroids for him. Merlin is such a lively horse he would never had been able to stand still long enough.' she laughed. 'Actually, I'm quite looking forward to the end result.' she turned to look at the portrait again. 'I think the two together will look quite wonderful!'

'But everything here is wonderful Mrs Kendrick!' He said, turning to Laura with amazement. 'The house, its history. You're so lucky!'

'And so is my granddaughter. To have such a good and caring friend and perhaps in time, something more?' She studied him for a moment, fascinated by the strange colour of his eyes and the charm of his smile.

'That's up to Ella.' His face became serious.

'No Matt, it's up to you too.'

'Male egos don't take rejection well,' He smiled shyly, 'They bruise very easily.'

'Ella would never hurt anyone intentionally. If you think there is so much as the smallest percentage of Mel in her you are mistaken. If she favours anyone, it is her father and he was a good human being.'

'I've always been her friend,' He said with a soft lift of his shoulders, 'I'm not sure she's ever wanted anything more than that.'

'Have you ever asked her what she wants?' Laura's bright eyes held his.

He shook his head and stared at the floor, colouring with embarrassment.

'Then perhaps you should; you might have a pleasant surprise. She was very badly hurt you know. She placed an awful lot of trust in someone who failed her miserably.'

'Niall?'

Laura nodded. 'When you've come through that sort of experience, wounds take time to heal and feelings get held back until you are strong enough to trust someone again. You helped her through her bad time. You have been the only person she's talked about ever since. And I think maybe she just might be ready for another relationship. You've been there for her, you've shown you care. My advice is if you want Ella, tell her exactly how you feel about her - and sooner rather than later.' She patted his arm gently. 'Now come along, let's join her on the terrace for some tea.'

As the sun sank slowly in the west, casting a warm glow over the valley, Laura stood on the front steps with Ella waiting for Matt to get the car.

'He's such a nice young man.' She said, watching as the Alfa drew up.

'Yes, he's very special!' Ella agreed, giving her grandmother a kiss on the cheek, before leaving her.

'It's up to you now Matt.' Laura whispered, watching as the car disappeared down the drive way. 'Don't let me down!'

Saturday 31st May

The intermittent wipers of the Alfa cleared the screen of the fine drizzle which had started as soon as Matt left Meridan Cross. In his briefcase on the back seat were the ten songs he had been working on. Ten songs, which realistically he knew would probably condense down into seven, for the new Attitude album which had already been given the unofficial title of *'Back in Business'* by their manager, Sonny Scott who thought it best summed up their return to the UK after a four month absence in Europe.

As he drove, his thoughts centred on his conversation with Laura and his evening with Ella. He had taken her out to the Charlton Cat for a final meal; they had shared a romantic table set in an intimate corner of the restaurant. From the start the whole evening seemed set for success. At first their conversation had been light, highlighting incidents from their week, talking generally about music. Then, for a moment there was silence as the waiter arrived with their meal. As he left, Ella reached across the table and covered his hand with hers, thanking him for a wonderful week. Laura, by insinuation, had opened the door for him and now, with this opportunity, all he had to do was walk through it. But as on previous occasions, his courage had failed him. As he smiled back at her, saying how much he had enjoyed it too, he found he wasn't sure of anything at all. As she withdrew her hand, the urge to stop her, to entwine her fingers with his and declare his feelings was suddenly overshadowed by all his old fears and insecurities.

He bottled out, launching instead into mindless talk about the hard work the band had ahead of them laying tracks down for the new album and their attendance at the forthcoming Isle of Wight Rock Festival at the end of August. Then he had enthused endlessly about being on stage with such names as The Who and the Moody Blues. It was also rumoured that his greatest idol Bob Dylan would be flying in. That fact alone prolonged the conversation for at least another ten minutes as he discussed Dylan's important contribution to modern music.

He groaned, knowing he must have bored her witless. Then at the end of the evening they as they said goodnight, came missed opportunity number two. Slipping her arms around him, Ella had closed her eyes and tilted her face up to his. He hesitated for a moment, wanting desperately to cup her face in his hands and taste the sweetness of her mouth. But instead, his hands moved down to rest on her shoulder and he leaned forward, pressing his lips chastely against her cheek.

He sighed miserably as he pulled up at traffic lights. If only he could arrange for her to come up to London for the day he could take her out to lunch. Do it all differently. But, of course, there wasn't the remotest chance of him having any have time off now. It would be noses to the grindstone straight away, locked in Centaur's Studios until all the tracks were in place and the suits were happy. He calculated this could mean he wouldn't be back in Abbotsbridge until at least the end of the year, as after working on the album they would be actively promoting its release in the autumn and then perhaps rest up for a month before another UK tour in January. In those few precious months, he realised, he might lose her forever. He rested his head against the steering wheel and closed his eyes, cursing his stupidity and wishing at that moment he could be anyone but himself.

The sudden blare of a car horn behind alerted him to the fact that the lights had changed and ramming the car into first he pulled away. Music, that was it; music would drown his thoughts, block out his misery. He turned the radio on, fiddling with the tuner until he reached Radio 1. As the opening chords of '*Yesterday*' drifted from the speakers, he came to the conclusion that everything today appeared to be conspiring to make his life as miserable as possible.

Sunday 1st June

Laura returned from her soft fruit cages carrying a bowl of strawberries. Ted Williams, her gardener, was leaning on his Dutch hoe, taking a break from weeding. Laura smiled and exchanged a few brief pleasantries with him before continuing up the steps towards the kitchen. Ted really was a treasure, she thought. Over the years he had kept Little Court's lawns and flower borders in immaculate condition and under his careful management, the high walled kitchen garden had flourished. He was particularly good with fruit. Gooseberries, raspberries, strawberries and blackcurrants produced succulent fruit inside their safe cages of netting. Apples were grown in espalier runs and in abundant arches which followed the criss-cross of paths from one side of the walled garden to the other. And peach and pear trees were trained against the south facing walls so that by August a variety of ripe fruit would be available for Ettie to bottle for the winter. A well oiled machine Little Court, Laura reflected, taking the strawberries to the sink and washing them carefully.

The sound of tyres on the gravelled driveway told her Ella had arrived. She went to find Ettie to ask her to hull the fruit and bring it out onto the sun terrace.

Ella had returned from a game of tennis with Mary. A tennis court was one of the first things Mary had built at Willowbrook after marrying Richard and she had even persuaded him to take up the game. He had tackled this new venture into sport with vigour and enthusiasm, but the going had been tough and he had complained that if the game had entailed shooting the ball instead of hitting it, there would have been no problem. Co-ordination between ball and racket, Mary had told Ella confidentially, was an area of Richard's game which still had a long way to go.

Taking in the sun on the terrace, Ella, wearing a white tee shirt and shorts, stretched out tanned legs. Tomorrow she would leave for Abbotsbridge but today she would make the most of her last day here in Meridan Cross, cherishing every minute of the peace and stillness of her grandmother's garden. She heard footsteps and opened her eyes to see Laura pulling up a chair opposite her.

'I've just picked some strawberries; I thought we could have some with cream. Just like Wimbledon.' She laughed, 'Did you enjoy your game with Mary?'

Ella nodded. 'Yes. She's very good. Did she tell you she was teaching Granddad?'

'Oh yes, and I understand he's making progress, even if it is slow.' There was humour in Laura's voice.

'Grandfather has gone along with this to please Mary, but I don't think Rod Laver's got anything to worry about!' Ella took off her sunglasses and began to polish the lenses with a tissue she had pulled from her pocket.

At that moment Ettie arrived with the strawberries, a small jug of cream and a sugar shaker, which she lay out on the table. Laura set out the two bowls and offered the sugar and cream to Ella. Ettie then returned with a large jug of iced lemon barley water and filled two tall glasses before disappearing back to the kitchen.

'How did the meal go with Matt?' Laura looked at her eagerly.

'Well,' Ella looked at her grandmother, her spoon, containing a generous portion of strawberry wrapped in cream, suspended in the air. 'It was O.K., apart from the fact that he spent a good part of it rambling on about the new album and the Isle of Wight Concert. And he seemed uncomfortable with me for some reason.'

'Oh dear!'

'You look disappointed.' Ella said, tucking the strawberries into her mouth.

'Well I had this feeling that you two might be on the brink of getting together.'

'After last night I don't think so,' Ella shook her head, 'not in a million years.'

'Now *you* look disappointed...'

'I am.' Ella put down her spoon and looked at her grandmother. 'I always believed we had something special. When he left Abbotsbridge he asked me to wait for him; told me I was really important to him. He's very shy and the last thing I wanted to do was scare him away. So last night I did everything so carefully, trying to encourage him to bring his feelings out into the open. But I guess what I thought I saw wasn't there after all. Sadly we're just destined to be good friends.'

'None of this makes sense!' Laura frowned. 'You see, he opened his heart to me when he was here that day. You're right he is extremely shy Ella. Maybe he didn't feel confident enough. Maybe it was too public a place. Maybe he just fears rejection...I don't know, but what I do know is that he does love you and that love is just waiting for the right moment. Oh dear!' she shook her head with frustration. 'Ella please, promise me you'll give him another chance.'

'You old romantic!' Ella teased. 'All right - but I'm not getting my hopes up. I won't be seeing him for months. You realise anything could have happened by then.'

'It won't,' Laura said confidently placing her spoon neatly in the empty bowl, 'believe me, he'll be waiting.'

FIVE

Monday 16th June

Ella was sitting in the Taylor's' garden under a large beech tree with a cold drink and a pile of revision - British Constitution, the last examination. She gave a sigh, relieved that it was nearly all over. She thought of the summer stretching ahead of them. The plans she had with Jenny for starting their recruitment business; she would be a working woman at last. No more homework and tests and cramming - that would be a thing of the past. She looked forward to the challenges the world of work would bring. She was meeting with Mollie Flannigan, the current owner of Workshop on a regular basis now, learning the processes and meeting clients. Her mind was focused on absorbing as much as she could; feeling a great energy when she thought of what she was going to do with Workshop when it eventually belonged to both of them. True Jenny and herself would both be new and untried, but she was confident they were going to make a real success of it.

Shutting her notebook she leaned back against the tree and smiled as she thought about Saturday and Mick and Nina's wedding. What an event! It had turned up all sorts of interesting scenarios. The church had been awash with the usual rich colour of outfits weddings always seemed to produce. Ella felt a little sad for Nina's mother, Elsie Harrison, who sat picking nervously at the stitching on her jacket, obviously uncomfortable in the fussy peacock blue outfit and black feathered hat she had chosen, a nasty ladder in her tights. Her elder daughter Elaine, wearing a tight suit in powder blue, was by her side, most of her time taken up with pacifying her hyperactive toddler. Beside her sat her husband with Brylcreemed hair and long sideburns, wearing a shiny wine coloured suit and Cuban heeled boots.

Ahead of them, Mick seemed to be suffering in his morning suit, constantly prizing his finger between the collar and his neck with obvious discomfort. Alerted by each echoing footfall down the church aisle, he watched the door nervously. Once or twice he caught Ella's eye and she had smiled at him. He reciprocated with the cheeky grin only he was capable of, then sighed and tapped his watch, raising eyebrows nervously.

The Taylors were sitting behind him. Jack in a charcoal three piece suit,

Peggy a picture in magenta and Jenny in emerald green. How were these two families ever going to adjust to each other Ella wondered? She could hardly see the Harrisons getting regular invites to Westbrook Drive, although she guessed Elsie would now be keen to advertise her new connections all over the Parkway Estate.

When Nina arrived there had been gasps and whispers from the congregation. The organ struck up as she began her walk down the aisle on the arm of a very nervous father, followed by three young bridesmaids in yellow carrying small baskets of white daisies. Ella noticed the way her gaze drifted from one side of the aisle to the other, bestowing smiles on the congregation like royalty, obviously enjoying every minute of the attention she was receiving. Exactly why was she marrying Mick? Could it really be love? Or merely to secure the lifestyle she wanted? It had been a topic heavily debated by Ella and Jenny in the weeks leading up to the wedding and neither could make up their minds.

Ella had to admit that Nina looked quite magnificent in the white lace wedding dress which must have totally bankrupt her poor father, her thick tawny hair draped in one huge plait over her left shoulder. There had been no conventional veil; instead flowers had been plaited into her hair giving her a most delicate and virginal look. Mick had chosen Andy for his best man and Ella found herself watching him, wondering whether despite the fact they were no longer together, he might be feeling just a little regret at seeing his ex-girlfriend marry someone else.

She saw Mick, his eyes shining with adoration, watching as Nina walked the length of the church. He smiled down at her as she arrived next to him. Andy's expression was bland as he watched her approach and there was only a polite, rather disinterested nod as their eyes met.

Later at the Bridge Hotel, Issy was waiting to settle everyone in as they arrived. The banqueting suite consisted of three rooms; a large foyer area with cloakrooms, a bar with pub type seating and beyond that large double doors which led to the main banqueting hall.

The colour scheme throughout was green and gold. The walls were painted magnolia; the foyer and bar area carpeted in thick, green Wilton. The banqueting room, with its green and gold chairs had a wooden floor and a small stage at one end so that receptions could run on into the evening with music and dancing. Today crystal vases of lilies were everywhere, adding that special touch.

Issy stood in the doorway, waiting with a smile as the guests arrived. She was wearing a straight skirted apple green knee length dress topped with a cream matador jacket, her thick fair hair cut in a chin length geometric style with a full fringe which framed her face and accentuated the blueness of her eyes. There was a high colour in her cheeks. She's nervous, Ella thought; this is her first big booking and she wants everything to be just right. As guests arrived, a group of waitresses dressed formally in black with neat white aprons, stepped forward with trays of sherry.

Ella, on her own, had paired up with Jenny who had also come as a single, Nick being unable to make the wedding because of forthcoming finals.

'It looks wonderful,' Ella said glass in hand, looking around the room. 'Issy's amazing, organising all this and managing to fit in revision as well.'

'Yes, it's fantastic.' Jenny agreed, surveying the tables with their gleam of cutlery and glass.

Issy was now busy getting the top table seated, bride, groom, best man, parents and bridesmaids.

'Look at that child!' Jenny nodded towards Nina's sister's toddler who was chasing after a small girl around the empty tables in the banqueting room, pulling at the tablecloths, 'Isn't he dreadful?'

'Absolutely.' Ella winced, watching as he ran into a waitress's legs, almost knocking her over. 'Where's Elaine for heaven sake?'

'Having a smoke somewhere I expect.' Jenny replied, with a wave of acknowledgement to a passing guest. 'Let's face it; her nerves must be shot to pieces coping with an out-of-work husband and a child like that. Changing the subject, did you notice Andy in church? I was watching. He didn't turn a hair when Nina came down the aisle.'

'I know.'

'I expect it's because he only has eyes for you now.' Jenny said teasingly.

'Oh rubbish!' Ella laughed, 'I can tell you now, Andy's interests lie in an entirely different direction.'

She threw Jenny a tantalising smile as she looked over the top of her glass, her eyes following the progress of a tall brunette wearing a micro skirted mauve dress and large cream hat.

Jenny turned to see what she was looking and laughed as she watched the girl disappear into the ladies cloakroom. 'What? Miranda Kelly? Are you serious?'

Ella nodded. 'He was chatting her up in the churchyard in between photographs. I heard him offer to run her home after the reception.'

'But surely he knows her fiancé's an Army Fitness Instructor? If he gets wind of what Andy's up to he'll probably put him in hospital.'

'Not from München Gladbach he won't. I overheard her telling Andy he's just left on a two year posting. Doesn't get leave till Christmas.'

'Ella, Andy is such an awful opportunist.' Jenny stifled an amused laugh.

'I know! But I do like him and I have to say he's always the perfect gentleman with me.'

'He has to be,' Jenny grinned. 'With your mother there's not much option!'

'Hi, sorry I was delayed with the top up, Nick phoned and I stopped to chat. He sends his love and says his exams have gone well.'

Ella found her daydream interrupted suddenly and looked up to see Jenny standing over her with a jug of cold lemonade.

'That's good news. Sorry, I was miles away, thinking about the wedding last Saturday.'

'Yes, I told Nick he missed an interesting day.'

'It certainly was that.' Ella nodded thoughtfully as she lifted her empty glass for a refill. 'Jen, I've been meaning to ask you, did you notice Issy? She came back into the reception around ten; I thought she was looking......' she hesitated, remembering Issy's high colour and the fact that she'd appeared only seconds after Mick. At the time she'd wondered whether they had had been somewhere arguing.

'Come on then, out with it.' Jenny said, lifting the jug away from Ella's glass and beginning to fill her own.

'Oh! Tired.' It wasn't the word Ella wanted, but in time she'd realised perhaps suggesting Issy had been crossing swords with Mick on his wedding day wasn't the most sensible thing to suggest to his sister.

Jenny smiled. 'That's because she'd been up since six that morning. Tired? She must have been exhausted! But she did a brilliant job didn't she? It all went so well.'

'Yes,' Ella nodded, still thinking about what she'd seen. 'It did.'

Over in Kingsford Issy had just finished dealing with the last minute rush of arrivals from a coach party wanting a set lunch in the restaurant. Leaving them in the capable hands of Jean Osborn, the head waitress, to organise drinks, she took their order to the kitchen. She noticed a stack of plates belonging to the banqueting suite and carried them out to the rear of the hotel to return them to their cupboard. Job done, she turned for a moment to look at the room neatly laid out with its collection of long tables and high backed chairs. Suddenly the place was filled with noise and people again; children running back and forth. It was Saturday night; the tables had been pulled back to the perimeter of the room. A five piece band was playing *'Green Green Grass of Home'.* People were dancing and a smiling, inebriated Ron Harrison was standing in the middle of the floor clutching a pint glass to his chest and singing loudly, his small grandson clinging to one of his legs.

She thought of Mick. Maybe she had dreamt it all. But no, it had been as real as Ron's awful singing. She closed her eyes, seeing herself opening the French doors and stepping out into the hotel's garden for a breath of fresh air. The day had gone superbly. Everyone had smiled, shaken her hand and congratulated her. She knew this praise would almost certainly reach her father's ears; he would be delighted and she would be assured of the one thing she wanted more than anything - her place in the family team.

Wine glass in hand she had wandered slowly towards the ornamental pond, breathing in the sweet evening scent of the roses. Above her the sky had just begun to turn deep blue velvet with the first faint indication of stars. There was a stone bench beside the pond, just the place to catch a few quiet moments alone on this beautiful evening before organising the final clearing up operation. Passing through a decorative arch she saw the pond ahead and the seat, which to her surprise, was already occupied.

He was sitting, glass in hand, staring into the water, talking to the Coy Carp. He had slung his jacket over the back of the bench and had rolled up his sleeves to his elbows. His tie had also vanished, leaving his neck open and bare, his sandy hair falling untidily across his forehead.

'Of course I love Nina.' He was saying, 'But it's a different kind of love.' He gave a mirthless laugh as he shook his head, 'Quiet and steady, not passionate. Oh, but I can do passionate you know. Shall I let you all into a secret,' he whispered loudly. 'About my one great passion? It's your Issy.'

'Me?' Issy hissed, watching him disbelievingly, 'He's drunk!'

'But I wrecked all my chances,' He shook his head sadly, 'It was that thing with her teacher that did it. I didn't mean to push the door open like that. And I didn't know she was behind it, or had a plate of food in her hand. I did apologise, but she never forgave me. It has been downhill all the way since then.' He sat back, draining his glass, then looked at the fish again and smiled, 'If she could hear me now, do you know what she'd say? You're drunk Mick Taylor.' He mimicked her accent and laughed, 'But that's just the thing. I'm not. This comes right from my heart.' He brought his fist to his chest. 'I loved her from the moment I first saw her. It's just that we were just never meant to be. Still,' he leaned forward, gazing thoughtfully into the pond, 'I guess I shouldn't dwell on the past.' he got slowly to his feet. 'I've made my choice now.'

Issy turned quickly then, her heart thudding. The last thing she wanted was for him to find her there. Still clutching her wine glass she ran blindly back towards the hotel. Something dark loomed in front of her and she felt the scrape of branches against her face as she almost fell into the Leylandii hedge bordering the foot of the hotel's main terrace. Dashing up the steps and through the French doors she headed for the staff toilets where she removed all traces of hedge and composed herself. Returning to the reception, she was in time to see Mick arrive and make a beeline for his bride to take her out to dance.

Now back in the present, she was still trying to come to terms with what she had heard him say. 'It's not true,' she shook her head. 'It can't be!'

Wednesday 18th June

A gentle breeze lifted the thin veil of curtain covering the balcony doors, allowing a thin finger of pale moonlight to filter into the darkness of the Majorcan hotel bedroom.

Nina lay awake, listening to the gentle wash of the sea on the nearby beach and the night-time chorus of cicadas in the trees outside the window. Next to her Mick lay sound asleep, knocked out by the combined effects of too much sun and cuba libre. His breathing was deep and rhythmic.

Nina looked at the luminous hands of her travel clock. Two thirty. Mick grunted and turned over. She watched the peaceful rise and fall of his chest, and then looked at her wedding band, twisting it around her finger. She had been married five days. Five whole days and this was the first time she had stopped to examine her feelings. The days leading up to the wedding had been filled with anger and uncertainty, had she thought about things then she might well have called the whole thing off. But now.........

She had originally turned to Mick, confident that throwing in her lot with him would bring Andy running back to her. It hadn't. When he had begged her to marry him only weeks after she had started seeing him, she accepted, anticipating the news would yield some sort of reaction from Andy. It hadn't.

And then the wedding; by that time she had got to the stage where she realised maybe Andy wasn't coming back. So she had decided to cut her losses. Life with Mick she convinced herself wouldn't be that bad. In his own way he adored her, showered her with gifts and money. He had paid for driving lessons and bought her a Mini like Ella's as a wedding present. She would still escape from her roots. Live in a lovely home with expensive furniture, wear quality clothes. Maybe she wouldn't be top of the hill in Abbotsbridge, but she'd be living pretty close to the summit.

On the morning of the wedding she had consumed half a bottle of vodka, sneaking it out from the collection tucked away in sideboard. It had been part of her father's special purchase to entertain the neighbours on this grand occasion. It put her in buoyant mood. As she relaxed in the bath that morning she let her mind wander, still convinced that Andy would not let this wedding go ahead. In her alcohol-fuelled daydream Andy would step forward, take her by the hand and they would run from the church to his waiting car, while everyone stood speechless and immobile, just like Dustin Hoffman and Katherine Ross had done in *The Graduate*.

But realistically that wasn't what she wanted any more. She wanted to reject Andy, just as he had rejected her. To make him feel the pain she had felt. To do this she chose the most luxurious dress her father could afford. Let him see me, she thought, let him see what he's thrown away. As she had entered the church, she clearly heard the gasps which rose from the congregation. It made her feel good. High on admiration and vodka she glided confidently down the aisle to Mick side. As she reached him she saw Andy standing there and gave him a gracious smile. His coal black eyes had looked at her from a face showing no trace of emotion. He didn't give a damn.

That made her angry and more determined to throw this wedding in his face. And so she had taken her vows, become Mrs Michael Taylor and continued her reign as queen at the reception afterwards, drinking glass after glass of the Moet Mick's money had bought.

And then the evening was here, more food, more alcohol and another layer of people to meet and greet. She saw Andy, sometimes with Ella Kendrick, but more often than not partnering strangers around the dance floor, hands covering lithe hips, encircling slim waists. He was laughing, having a good time and she hated him even more.

Away in the Med now she found that time and distance had eased things, mellowed the anger. Sex with Mick had not been a disappointment. The earth didn't actually move, but there had been interesting tremors, nothing that given time she couldn't learn to live happily with.

Mick was a generous and honest man, all the things that Andy hadn't been. There would be no battles in this marriage for Mick adored her, put her on a pedestal. She no longer worked (there was no need he had told her). Instead she would become a housewife looking after their beautiful four-bedroom home in Kennet Close, a small established cul-de-sac on the northern edge of Abbotsbridge. The house Jack Taylor had bought them. She would have her own bank account and a regular monthly allowance to spend on herself. Lunching and shopping would be the order of the day. She had dreamed of a life like this and now it had become a reality. She smiled to herself. She couldn't wait to get back. Annabel's sale was imminent; she would make it her first port of call. Driving the new blue Mini of course.

Mick stirred, turning in the bed, his hand reaching for her.

'Nina?'

'I'm here,' she said gently, turning her body towards him. She could just make out his smile in the darkness.

'Happy?'

Stroking his face she leaned over and kissed his lips. 'Yes Mick.' she said. 'I am. I really am.'

SIX

Friday 20th June

Ella, Jenny and Issy sat in the refectory drinking coffee, their exams finally at an end.

'I can't believe it's almost over.' Ella said as she gazed out of the window at the neat flower beds full of red and yellow floribunda rose bushes and the car park beyond.

'So many memories,' Jenny said wistfully, 'We've been here two years and it's gone so quickly.' She made a mournful face, 'Only another week to go.'

'Oh dear, you two!' Issy frowned. 'Am I the only one who's glad to be leaving? For goodness sake lighten up! No more Law, no more Economics and no more bloody shorthand!'

'Issy!' Jenny looked horrified, 'Language!'

'Well! I hate it! And I don't care! We won't use it in the business anyway. All I'm interested in is the diploma.'

'And while we're waiting for the results,' Jenny smiled, 'there are lots of other things to distract us.'

'Our new jobs.' Ella enthused.

'The holiday in Cornwall,' Jenny sat up straight, looking visibly brighter. 'Ella, why won't you come with us?'

'Yes Ella,' Issy leaned forward on her elbows, 'Admit it, you'll only mope around that flat of yours while we're away.'

'No I won't!' Ella argued. 'I've plenty to do. I shall go around all the agents looking for premises and by the time you're back I'll have sorted out a short list for Jen and me to view. Then of course, there's the furniture,' she added, 'Liam said there was a good second hand office furniture store just outside Kingsford. I'll take a trip out and have a look, get some idea of prices. And then there's the decorating......'

'Work, work, work!' Issy shook her head. 'Can't you just squeeze one small week of self-indulgence in before you start all that? It would really do you good, I know it would.'

'I'm fine, honestly Iz....'

'Well if you change your mind.'
'You'll be the first to know.'

Saturday 21st June

'My round I think. Same again everyone?' Charles Fitzallyn got to his feet and surveyed the small group sitting around the table. They were gathered here tonight at the Rotary Midsummer Ball in the Forum, a charitable event held annually for the benefit of the local hospice. Noting the responses and committing everyone's requests to memory he began to load the empty glasses onto a tray.

'I'll give you a hand.' Liam got to his feet, picking up two whisky glasses and following him across to the bar.

'Well,' Barbara Morris looked around the room. 'I see our friend's hogging Bob as usual.'

Marjorie Webster and Sheila Fitzallyn followed the direction of her gaze to where Bob Macayne was whisking Mel expertly around the floor to a fox trot. Mel was in French blue, with high strappy sandals, a burst of colour amongst the muted pastels of the other dancers on the floor.

'He's very handsome.' Marjorie said wistfully. 'Strange he's never married again isn't it?'

'I don't think he will,' Barbara said almost reverently, ' He still carries a torch for his dead wife, you know. She's wasting her time there.'

'You have to admit though,' Maurice Webster interrupted, a slow smile on his craggy face, 'Mel's a fine looking woman. Enough to tempt any man!'

'Maurice!' Marjorie reprimanded. 'How can you say things like that?'

'I have eyes haven't I?' He sounded offended. 'Oh don't look like that woman, I'm not about to go chasing after her. I'm old and wise enough to know that looks are only skin deep. It's what's in here, in the heart.' he patted his chest, 'that counts and I've seen enough of her antics to know that she hasn't got one of those!'

'Hush now Maurice, Liam's coming back,' Sheila hissed, 'He's a lovely man; don't let him hear us talking this way.'

'I wish he would open his eyes and see what we all see.' Said Maurice reflectively, watching Liam laughing and joking with Charles Fitzallyn as they carried the drinks back to the table. 'It will all end in tears you know!'

Mel, in seventh heaven as she danced around with Bob Macayne, watched the heads together talking at her table. Wasn't it wonderful to be speculated about? Because no matter how much chit-chat went on, none of them would ever know the real truth, that she was indeed having an affair with one of the most eligible men in Abbotsbridge. It was her secret. Hers and Bob's. And it was going to stay that way. For now.

The music reached its conclusion and he smiled and bowed in a most charming way before escorting her back to her table. She saw the expressions on the faces of the women as they crossed the floor towards them. Such plain middle aged women, each one eager to be the next dancing partner. Suddenly she stopped, deciding to inject a little disappointment into their evening.

'Can we go to the bar? I think I'd like a drink there if you have the time to sit with me for a while.' She glanced at the three women. 'It's been rather a lifeless evening with those three, all knitting patterns and Woman's Hour.'

'Of course.' He smiled and placing his hand firmly in the middle of her back, guided her away from the table.

At the bar he ordered her a brandy and a whisky for himself. Taking his cigarette case from him she lit up two Senior Service, handing him one before sliding neatly onto a bar stool. She knew without looking that resentful faces were watching and drew great enjoyment from the fact.

Unexpectedly Tad and Faye Benedict arrived, acknowledging Bob with a nod and a smile.

'Another good evening.' Bob said as he paid for the drinks, 'Congratulations Tad, you always manage to find us a first class band.'

Tad smiled at the compliment and ordered two whiskies and tonics.

'How's that boy of yours making out now?' Bob asked, sitting back from the bar so Mel could be included in the conversation.

'Fine, just fine,' Tad laughed, 'I still can't believe it's all happened so quickly.'

'I never did get around to apologising for that fraças last year.' Bob said with a sincere smile. 'Andy tends to get carried away at times.'

'No offence taken,' Tad replied, smiling back, 'Matt's not the first young man to get himself a black eye over a girl.'

'Excuse me!' Mel tapped her cigarette irritably into the nearby ash tray. 'Are you making reference to my daughter by any chance?'

'In general terms, yes.' Tad replied inoffensively, 'It's a fact of life; young men, young women and alcohol can be a potent mixture.'

Mel gave a derisory snort. 'There must be some misunderstanding. I assure you my daughter never had any real interest whatsoever in your son!'

'Real interest is right!' Faye joined in angrily, 'From the start your Ella's been nothing but trouble. Leading him on, playing him off against Andy when the fancy took her. But he's over her now thankfully. In fact he's just got engaged. Her name's Belinda Walsh,' she looked triumphant, 'She works with him in London and she's the best thing that ever happened to him!'

Picking up her evening bag, Mel slipped gracefully from the bar stool. 'Well that is good news Faye, let's hope they'll be very happy.' she replied with a patronising smile and picking up her glass began making her way back to her table, Bob following.

Tad Benedict looked at his wife as they walked away. 'And what possessed you to do that?'

'What?'

'Mention Belinda!'

'Well, I had to say something to shut her up!' Faye replied irritably. 'Besides, I'm still not happy about this business of Matt being with Ella in Meridan Cross. Whatever made him go out there for goodness sake?'

'Peace and quiet so he could write, and before you say anything he said it was a wonderful place. Faye, I honestly think you have it all wrong about the girl. I believe she's good for him. He met the other half of the family. They couldn't be more different from Mel. From what he said, they're lovely people. He came back so happy.'

Faye flapped a hand at him impatiently. 'His career's going well, the band has been number one all over Europe; they're very popular in the Far East and Australia too. He's successful. *That's* what's making him happy. He has it all and more to come but he's still vulnerable where that little troublemaker is concerned.' She gave him a most determined look. 'I won't have her spoiling things for him Tad, I won't and I'm going to do everything in my power to make sure she doesn't.'

Tuesday 24th June

As the curtain fell, enthusiastic applause echoed around the rich red and gold interior of the Queens Theatre in Kingsford. The heavy gold velvet curtain rose again and the actors who had spent the last few hours convincing the audience they were in New York at the time of the Prohibition, took another bow.

Mel smiled and clapped her appreciation. It had been a wonderful evening. A rare opportunity to see a prestigious cast presenting a new play prior to its run in the West End. During the interval there had been drinks in the bar, elbow to elbow with the elite of Kingsford and Abbotsbridge. And with Liam on a visit to his father in the States, who better to have than Bob beside her as her escort, attracting admiring glances from most of the females present.

Mel smiled a self-satisfied smile; how pleasant it was to be envied. Later they ate at a new French restaurant in Castle Street, where the lighting was intimately subdued. Over moules marnière and a finely chilled Chardonnay they discussed the Harrison-Taylor wedding.

'I'd be having a fit if I was Betty Taylor.' Mel laughed. 'Nina Harrison as a daughter in law! What a thought!'

'Don't forget she was nearly mine. I have a lot to thank Mick for.' Bob sounded relieved.

'Oh I'm sure Andy could never have been serious about settling down with someone like her, he was just making best use of what was on offer at the time.' Mel gave a coarse laugh.

'The trouble with Andy is that he never thinks seriously about anything.' Bob said as he refilled both wine glasses. 'You know, this wedding has got me thinking. It seems to me the boys are now at an age where they could take on more responsibility. Young married men, maybe with a family just around the corner; they are more than ready to have their own businesses to run.'

Mel set down her wineglass and looked at him. 'Exactly what had you in mind?'

'Well, I've been talking things over with Jack. We're both keen to keep the business receptive to market needs. I've done some research. There's a demand out there for larger houses in more exclusive areas. Existing housing stock in Abbotsbridge and Kingsford is limited and in big demand. New build could be just the answer; we could clean up quite nicely. So we thought if we set up a completely separate company to cover that end of the market, the boys could run it. It would give them their own identity if you like. They'd feel they were doing something for themselves. We thought about calling it Taylor Macayne Residential.' He said proudly. 'Nice ring to it eh?'

'Sounds an excellent idea.' Mel said approvingly. 'One slight problem though, you talked of them as young married men. Andy isn't married.'

'No, I only wish he was. It's time he stopped running around Abbotsbridge breaking hearts and found himself a wife.'

Mel cocked her head on one side, looking at Bob over the top of her wine glass with an amused smile. 'Had you anyone in mind?'

'Mel, I wouldn't know where to begin.'

'What about Ella? We did discuss her once remember? And I hear on the grapevine that she's been seeing Andy regularly.'

'That's just a friendly thing.'

'Is it? Well maybe if we nurture it, it might easily blossom into something else. After all, look around Abbotsbridge, who's more suitable wife material than my daughter? She's intelligent, attractive, has the right background and the bonus that she inherits a substantial amount of money in a few years time.'

'It's a nice thought.' Bob shrugged his heavy shoulders, his face sceptical. 'But even if Andy did want to marry Ella, we don't know that Ella would be remotely interested do we?'

'Oh she will.' Mel smiled secretively. 'Just leave it to me.'

Thursday 26th June

Ella was browsing in Marks and Spencer. She had dropped Issy and Jenny off to do some last minute shopping before their holiday and was killing time looking at underwear.

'Well, well, fancy running into you.'

Ella turned and found herself face to face with her mother; it was the first time she had seen her since leaving Cambridge Crescent.

'Oh it's you.' She stared at her, immaculate in a green linen suit, her nails frosted beige.

Mel picked up one of the bras from the counter and gave it a cursory inspection before dropping it back. 'Well, I suppose the only thing you can say about this,' she said disdainfully, 'is that it's functional.'

'Is there a reason for you homing in on me like this?' Ella felt annoyed that her quiet browsing had been interrupted by the last person she wanted to see.

'I thought you should know how upset I am.' Mel looked dejected. 'Here I am, all alone, trying to come to terms with losing a daughter and a son.'

Behind her expression a myriad of moods swam around. Although running into Ella was just what she'd been waiting for, seeing her daughter here now brought other emotions to the surface. Ella's leaving home and Nick's involvement with one of the Taylor clan had become a constant source of vexation to her. And she hated the atmosphere which now existed between Liam and her. Liam the easy going and compliant husband stood against her in all of this. It was unthinkable! Where was his loyalty to her? How could he not see Jenny Taylor was totally unsuitable wife material? And why didn't he believe her explanation that cutting off Ella's hair had been an accident during an extremely stressful moment?

'Losing me, as you put it, was entirely your own fault.' She heard Ella say in a voice without pity. 'And you haven't lost Nick, you've just alienated him because of your attitude.' she shook her head. 'I can't understand you; no one else has a problem with Jenny.'

'Well time alone will tell won't it?' Mel said waspishly. 'Believe me I know what I see when I look at that girl. However....'

She placed a theatrical hand to her throat, aware that the moment had come. 'I suppose there is one saving grace. At least you've been spared from going the same way.' She said with a great emotional rush of breath.

'And what exactly is that supposed to mean?'

'Faye Benedict's boy of course, I'm so glad I don't have to worry about you and him any more. Not now he's getting married. Good riddance I say!'

'What *are* you talking about?' Ella said calmly, unaware that Mel had caught the fine ripple of shock in her eyes.

'Matt Benedict is getting married to Belinda........Walsh, I think Faye said.' She waved an impatient hand. 'Works with him in London apparently. She was telling everyone on Saturday night. She was surprised I hadn't already heard about it from you. As you had met up with him in Meridan Cross over Whitsun, she was sure you would already know.' She tilted her head to one side, her eyes bright. 'By the look on your face am I to assume you don't?'

'No, I.........'

Ella looked towards the entrance of the store, her mother's words fading into the background. Suddenly she understood the reason for his strange behaviour on their last night. He was shy and embarrassed by her actions because he was in love with someone else and he didn't know how to tell her. The realisation that she had made a complete fool of herself hit with painful sharpness; but she had been so sure of what she sensed between them, how could she have been so mistaken?

Someone was waving, she saw Issy in the doorway, Jenny beside her.

'Ella, are you all right?' Mel's voice seemed a distant reverberation in her ears.

'I'm sorry. I have to go,' she said abruptly. 'Jenny and Issy are waiting for me. We have to get back to college.'

Leaving her mother standing there she walked towards the door feeling dizzy and disorientated.

'Are you O.K?' Jenny stared at her with a concerned frown as she reached them. 'You've gone quite white.'

'Looks like she's got something to do with it,' Issy glared across to where Mel stood, 'judging by the smug look on her face.'

Taking a deep breath Ella looked at them both. 'It's all right. I'm fine, really I am. Look, about the week in Cornwall. If it's O.K. with you both, I'd really like to come.'

Tuesday 1st July

Bob Macayne, Jack Taylor and their two sons sat around the heavy oak table in the Board Room of Taylor Macayne's head office, its surface covered with plans and financial data.

'So you see from the marketing exercise we've undertaken and the sales projections produced,' Jack was saying, 'we believe very strongly that there is a demand for this calibre of new house in the area and we feel in order to maximise the selling potential of our product, it should be marketed within a brand new company. We intend to call this company Taylor Macayne Residential.'

Bob smiled and leaned forward, steepling his fingers. 'We have hired Liam to come up with suitable designs and Nicholson's, who are old, established and very highly regarded, to handle the marketing for our first development. The first three tranches of land have been purchased, so the whole thing is ready to go.' He shot a glance towards Jack Taylor and smiled. 'Apart from a team to run the business. That is where you two come in.' He cleared his throat, 'Jack and I are both in agreement that we would like you, Mick to front production and you, Andy, to cover sales. Are you interested?'

'Definitely.' Mick was nodding enthusiastically, a grin creasing his face. 'It's a fantastic opportunity, don't you agree Andy?'

'Andy?' Bob turned to his son whose attention seemed drawn by something outside the nearby window.

'What? Oh...yes, great!' He looked at both older men and gave a vague nod.

'Good. Good.' Keeping a tight hold on his temper, Bob surveyed the small group before his gaze landed back on Mick then Andy.

'I think it's important now the structure of the new company is defined that I arrange for all of us to meet with Liam to discuss his designs in more detail.

Then,' he nodded towards Mick and Andy, 'I think you two boys should go out to Haydon Marwick and look at the first piece of land. From then on I'd like us to meet on a weekly basis. Has anyone any problems with that?' He looked at them all for a response, 'No? Good, I'll get Marion to circulate a list of dates and times. The sooner we kick this whole thing off the better.' He pushed back his chair and got to his feet. 'Thank you everyone, see you next week.'

As he collected his papers together Bob looked at Andy. He doubted he been listening to anything they had been saying this afternoon. The pad in front of him was a mass of different shaped biro doodles. That and what lay outside the window seemed to have had the monopoly on his attention while he and Jack Taylor had been talking. As Jack and Mick left the room, their heads bent together in continuing discussion, Bob walked over and closed the door behind them.

'Please tell me you have a good reason for the performance we've all be treated to this afternoon!' He said angrily as he returned to the table and stood facing his son.

Andy, who had by this time got to his feet and was rolling up plans stopped and looked at his father blankly.

'You weren't listening to a damned thing!' Bob pointed to the pad, 'You were either pissing about with that or staring out of the window. Would you care to tell me why?'

'It's Ella,' Andy replied, his face twisted with annoyance. 'She's buggered off to Cornwall on holiday and she didn't even let me know.'

'Ella?' Bob looked at his son and gave a snort of surprise, 'Well, I had no idea you'd formed this sort of attachment to her.' His dark brows came together as he remembered his recent conversation with Mel. 'No idea at all.'

'Well I have! You have no idea how badly I want her, not that it seems to be much use!' Ramming an elastic band over the top of the paper tube in his hand Andy made a face at his father, 'When someone else is always in the way, distracting her!'

'Are we talking about Matt Benedict by any chance?'

Andy nodded, 'She won't admit it, but I know there's always been something going on. He's been gone a year and I thought she'd finally got him out of her system. Then last week she mentioned he'd been staying in Meridan Cross while she was there over Whitsun.' He said bitterly. 'Seems like I'll always be the also ran!'

'Ah but that's where you're wrong.'

'What do you mean?'

'At the Midsummer Ball the other Saturday, Faye Benedict was telling everyone that Matt's getting married soon. To some girl he met in London.'

'Are you sure?'

'Positive. I'm also aware that Ella doesn't know. So when she finds out, she'll probably be looking for a shoulder to cry on.' Bob moved towards the door, his hand hovering over the handle, 'which is just the opportunity you've been looking for to seize the moment. Propose.'

'Marry her?' Andy, collecting up the drawings and tucking them under his arm, gave an amused laugh.

'Yes. I had hoped that Ella might be the kind of girl you'd be looking to settle down with.'

'But Dad, I'm not sure I want to settle down with anybody. I play the field, that's what I enjoy. The chase - the capture. Ella's not long term, Dad. The truth is I want her because I can't have her, that's all. She's a challenge.'

Bob shook his head, 'Is that all you can do? Play games? Live for the moment? Can't you see the bigger picture?'

'What bigger picture?'

'Your future Andy. Jack and I have been talking. Once Taylor Macayne Residential gets going we want it to be run as a completely separate company. And we'd like to hand that responsibility over to Mick and yourself. You'd both become Directors with a substantial increase in salary.'

'Great!'

'No Andy, not so great.' Bob eyed him seriously. 'How can I possibly hand over that kind of responsibility to a self-confessed womaniser who hasn't a shred of commitment to anything that resembles work? Your record is appalling!'

'I could change.'

Catching the glint of avaricious interest in his son's eyes, Bob pressed his case home.

'Could you? Prove it to me then!' He threw the challenge back. 'Put your womanising days behind you and settle down. Perhaps then I might be a little more disposed towards the idea of you as a Director.'

'And settling down,' Andy said quietly, 'means marrying Ella?'

'That's about it...'

'But why her?'

'Because she's perfect.' Bob said enthusiastically. 'She's got the lot. Looks. Class. And a trust fund kicking in on her twenty fourth birthday.'

Andy turned away, shaking his head, doubt creasing his forehead.

'Oh come on!' Bob's voice was soft, persuasive. 'It's not now you've got to think of! Take yourself forward five years. What do you want to be known for? The number of women you've bedded or someone making a major contribution to business in this town? And if you're worrying about Ella, don't! When she finds out about Matt she'll be putty in your hands. She's bound to say yes.'

'But I don't want her to say yes. In fact I don't even want to ask her!' Andy protested, 'How can I? I don't love her!'

Bob walked slowly towards the door, easing it open a little before turning back to his son. 'Andy, who the hell knows what love really is? And who really cares eh? Take your mother and I, well we.....' he hesitated suddenly. 'The thing is, as I said before you have to look at the bigger picture. You'll have your own business. A beautiful wife. A lovely home. In a few years time, great kids. You'll be someone. The envy of Abbotsbridge. And in the end, isn't that what it's all really about?'

Andy thought for a moment, 'I don't know is it?'

'Of course it is Andy.' Bob said, walking out into the corridor and closing the door behind him.

SEVEN

Friday 4th July

The sky was a glorious blue, its colour mirrored in the shimmer of sea below it. Issy and Jenny sat in the pretty garden of the Harbour Heights Hotel, overlooking the small port of Portmeryn where they had been spending the last week. A half empty bottle of white wine sat in an ice bucket on the table and Issy pulled it from the slush of melting cubes and refilled all three glasses. The small harbour below, its walkways piled with lobster pots and fishing nets, was a hive of activity, with boats coming and going, men whistling and the smell of fish and salt on the air.

'Well,' Jenny raised her glass to her lips, 'Here's to the end to a perfect holiday.'

'It's been quite a week hasn't it?' Issy gazed out to sea, 'Swimming, sunbathing and dancing till dawn. A bit of fun before knuckling down to our responsibilities.'

'Ella's happier too; it's done her the world of good to get away.' Jenny said, watching a trawler, heavy with fish make its way slowly into the harbour below. 'This business with Matt; I can't believe he didn't tell her about his engagement. He was supposed to be one of her closest friends. Must have been a bit galling hearing it from her mother.'

Issy sighed. 'Ella made the mistake of thinking he was still the Matt who left Abbotsbridge. He's not. Fame has changed him. He's left us all behind. It's almost like he's shed a skin.' She made a face. 'Excuse the pun but he was a bit of a snake really wasn't he?'

'Yes,' Jenny agreed, 'He was.'

'I'm sure Mr Right will eventually make an appearance.' Issy said as a figure in white tee shirt and jeans appeared out of the shadow of the hotel entrance.

'You said that before Matt arrived.' Jenny replied watching Ella's approach.

'The odds must be shortening,' Issy was confident. 'He'll be here soon, believe me.'

Reaching them, Ella eased herself into her seat and lifted her wineglass from the table.

'Thanks, I could do with this,' She said, looking at both of them and raising her glass. 'Well here's to sun, sea and sand and the Garys of this world. At least he cheered one of us up this week, didn't he Is?'

'He was a bit of holiday fun that's all,' Issy said thinking of the tall blond Australian surfer who had monopolised her for most of the week. 'I'm not interested in relationships' she said fiercely. 'That's a mug's game.'

'Issy!' Jenny glared at her.

'Oh, God, sorry Ella.' Issy winced, wanting to kick herself for being so thoughtless.

'It doesn't matter.' There was just a hint of sadness in Ella's face. 'I lost Matt a long time ago really. I guess seeing him in Meridan Cross made me forget that for a moment. I realise now that he's gone for good. Time for to me to move on; to get on with my own future.'

'You're right,' Issy replied, deciding there was a lot of sense in what Ella was saying. Taking a deep breath she raised her glass to her two friends. 'So, here's to business! May we all become extremely rich and successful!'

The departing sun put on a spectacular show for their last evening at The Smugglers Inn down on the quayside. The three girls sat in the pub's large bay window which faced the sea. As darkness descended and the last chug of incoming boat engines died, the lights came on inside the pub and it began to fill up. Soon it was busy with a press of jersey clad bodies at the bar, a chink of glass against optics and the marvellous aroma of food wafting from the kitchen.

The meal, all fresh seafood, was delicious, washed down with a bottle of chilled white wine. Ella watched continual movement of the beam of the beacon at the end of the breakwater as it circled out into the darkness beyond and back again. Tomorrow they would all be back in Abbotsbridge. College was over; their Diploma results awaited from the Department of Education and now the most important job she had to do with Jenny when they got back was to look for premises.

She was just about to mention this when she thought she glimpsed a familiar face in the open doorway of the pub. She frowned and looked again. Seeing her, he smiled and eased himself through the tightly packed bar until finally he stood at the table looking down at them all, his face solemn.

'Well, well.' Issy rested her knife and fork against the sides of her plate, 'Look what the tide's washed in.'

'Andy!' Ella looked up, amazed, 'What are you doing here? How did you find us?'

'It's a long story.' He said, then glancing uncomfortably at Jenny and Issy. 'Ella, I need to talk to you. It's very important.'

'Bad timing Andy, we're in the middle of dinner.' Issy said pointing at her plate with her fork.

Ella shot her a disapproving look. 'Issy!' Please!'

Andy turned towards Ella again. 'Is there somewhere quiet we can go?'

'Yes,' Ella pushed her chair back and got to her feet, 'there's a bench at the end of harbour.'

'Well,' Jenny made a face at Issy as they disappeared, 'I wonder what he wants?'

Ella looked into Andy's dark eyes, as she sat down beside him on the stone bench under the orange glow of a light on the harbour side, lobster pots and nets stacked around them. He seemed tense, uncomfortable. She puzzled over what had brought him here on the night before they were due to go home.

'So,' she said anxiously, 'Why have you come all this way to see me?'

Looking at her face, caught half in light half in shadow, Andy noticed something different. This wasn't the Ella he knew; she seemed pale, subdued. Her grey eyes caught his, beautiful and sad. Her vulnerability pleased him. It meant the task in front of him was not going to be as difficult as he first thought.

He'd agonised over his father's words for two days. But in the end he realised his choice was no choice. If he wanted the company and the Directorship on offer he had to tow the line. And although giving up his freedom seemed like the ultimate sacrifice, maybe if he had to commit himself to someone, then Ella wasn't such a bad choice.

'Dad told me about Matt's engagement,' He began, psyching himself into the part, looking at the ground, then at her with his well practised brown-eyed embarrassment as he gently took her hands in his, feeling their softness. 'I'm so sorry, I know how you felt about him and I can see how hurt you are.'

Ella hung her head. 'Seems I made a bit of a fool of myself.'

'Well I'm going to make a bit of a fool of myself now.'

She stared at him, perplexed.

'I know I come with a reputation,' He said, still holding onto her hands but manoeuvring himself down onto one knee in front of her. 'And, of course, it's well deserved. But I'm mad about you; crazy in fact. Please, will you marry me?'

'Oh Andy!' Ella sat there for a moment, then her face broke into a broad smile, 'Oh get up please!'

'You're mocking me Ella.' He looked offended.

'I'm not,' She ruffled his hair affectionately, 'You're my knight in shining armour, riding to the rescue and I love you for it. But marriage? That's not you.'

'But it is; with you it is.' He insisted. 'You have no idea how long I've waited to say those words to you. There were times I thought this moment would never arrive and now it has I'm opening my heart to you! I want you for my wife; there is no other direction I want my life to take.' He wiped moisture away from his face with the back of his hand.

Ella sat for a moment thinking of her conversation with her grandmother, about love being trapped, waiting for the right situation to release it. Laura had been talking about Matt at the time, but she realised how it could easily be applied to Andy. Of course, she had lost count of the times he'd told her he was in love with her. She had let most of it drift over her head because that was the sort of patter which she'd come to expect from someone like him. Now she felt guilty that she had treated him with such patronising amusement and even sorrier for the pain she must have put him through. She looked at him sitting there, his eyes moist with tears. He loved her, he really loved her and given time she was sure she could grow to love him.

'I'm sorry,' He got to his feet with a sniff, 'I'm a complete idiot. It's too soon for you isn't it? You need more time.'

'No,' Ella reached out and grabbed his hand as he turned to leave, 'Actually, I don't. My answer is yes; yes I will marry you Andy.'

'Mr Right? More like Mr Nightmare!'

Issy swathed in her blue cotton dressing gown sat on the edge of Jenny's bed, painting her toe nails. 'He's so transparent Jen! He's....'

'Issy, do calm down.'

'Well!' Issy rammed the brush irritably into the nail varnish and screwed the top down tightly. 'Andy has never shown the slightest inclination to settle down with anyone. So why now? And why Ella? I bet his father's behind all this! Wants to get him off his hands!' She stood up and paced back and forth, 'I feel so angry, so helpless.' she looked at Jenny. 'Ella is very vulnerable at the moment! Is there nothing we can do?'

'We can't interfere.' Jenny shook her head. 'We have to accept her decision and support her the way we always have done. It's early days yet but I've seen a difference in him already. He's relaxed, friendly - and he seems genuinely fond of Ella. He's even found us somewhere for the business. We're going to look at it with him tomorrow afternoon.'

'Jen he's buying your approval, like he buys everything else, can't you see that?

'He is not! I'm just keeping an open mind, why can't you?'

'Because his kind of leopard doesn't change spots,' Issy replied, 'I am certain that if Ella goes ahead with this, she will live to regret it. He'll end up hurting her; I know he will, because that's the way he is. And we'll both be left to pick up the pieces.'

Saturday 5th July

'This is wonderful!' Ella walked around the large light and airy first floor office suite, imagining how it would all look once they were up and running.

'It's exactly what we were looking for.' She walked over to the desk and stopped, gazing around the room. 'This will be great for reception and registering and that office over there,' she pointed, 'can be mine and the one next to it yours Jen. The third office can be used for an interview/meeting room and we've a lovely little kitchen and a loo as well - it's absolutely perfect!' She eyed the extravagant use of sunshine yellow on the walls. 'I think we'll have to come in and do a bit of decorating though, tone the place down a bit. I did have specific colours in mind, green and pale grey, just like Liam's studio at home.'

'No need to lift a paintbrush my darling,' Andy interrupted, 'I'll send one of our painters round to see you with some colour cards. You just choose what you want and he'll do the rest. My present to both of you.'

'That is really kind of you.' Jenny smiled

'There's more,' He said, giving Ella an affectionate hug, 'Dad owns the building and as an engagement present he's giving you the first six months rent free.'

'What? Oh Andy thank you!' Ella threw her arms around his neck and kissed him. 'Isn't that fabulous?' she said to Jenny, 'It'll be such a help.'

Jenny smiled and nodded noting the expression in Andy's eyes as he looked at Ella. It was just the way Nick looked at her. She had never seen Matt look at Ella like that in all the time they had been together. Despite Issy's protests she knew she was looking two people very much in love.

'Jen, hey, are you listening?' Ella waved a brightly coloured catalogue at her, 'We need to choose some furniture.'

'But we can't possibly afford this!' Jenny said, taking it and flicking through the pages, 'I thought we were going to look at some second hand stuff over in Kingsford.'

'We were,' Ella said brightly. 'But now we've got six months rent to spend. Unless, of course, you'd prefer to hang on to it.'

'No, no we'll use it. It will make everything look so much better,' Jenny smiled, 'much more professional.'

'I think,' said Ella slipping her arm around Andy's waist and resting her head on his shoulder. 'That you are a marvel. You've saved us both so much money and work. It's wonderful Andy, thank you so much!'

'There is one thing we haven't thought of.' Jenny said suddenly, waving the rolled up catalogue at Ella, 'What are we going to call ourselves?'

'I've got it.' Andy pointed a finger at each of them in turn. 'Ella and Jenny. How about One Plus One?'

The two girls looked at each other and grinned.

'I like it.' Jenny nodded.

'Me too.' Ella agreed. 'One Plus One it is then!'

'Welcome home!' Jack Taylor hugged his son and gave his daughter-in-law a peck on the cheek before opening the boot of his Mercedes and loading their suitcases in the back. 'How was Paris?'

'Very romantic.' Nina enthused, 'I had the most wonderful birthday - Mick really spoilt me.'

'You deserved it.' Mick replied giving Nina a hug as he reached over and opened the back door of the car for her. Settling himself into the front passenger seat he looked across at his father. 'Anything exciting happen while we were away?'

'He means work.' Nina laughed.

'Yes I know he does,' Jack smiled. 'Don't worry Mick, everything's on schedule. There is one piece of news though, quite a surprise too. Andy's only gone and got himself engaged.'

Mick grinned. 'He's a sly one, didn't mention a word to me about it.'

'Engaged?' The word seemed to echo around Nina's head. 'Are you serious? Andy engaged? Never!'

'I'm deadly serious,' Jack replied. 'It's all in black and white in the local rag. You can read the announcement yourself when you get back. Andy Macayne is now engaged to Ella Kendrick and there's a damn great diamond cluster on her hand to prove it.'

'He's engaged to *Ella*?' Nina sat back, closing her eyes against the glare of the sun. The world spun for a moment, she felt stunned and amazed, wondering not only how something like this had happened so quickly but also why the thought of it bothered her so much.

A solemn faced Matt accompanied Baz down the front steps of the Centaur's Recording Studios in Twickenham to where a black limousine was waiting to pick up the band. He threw himself into the back with a tired sigh.

'I thought we'd never finish.' Baz said, stifling a yawn with one of his huge hands. 'You know Chas Monroe might be big in the business, but he doesn't know everything! I still say the bridge on track three needs more bass.'

'I think so too,' Matt nodded in agreement. 'I'll speak to him about it tomorrow. But I have to say,' he said, pushing himself over into the corner of the car. 'Despite all the hassle, I've got a good feel about this album. Chas has put together some great arrangements. I can't wait to hear it.'

'Sounds like you're beginning to bounce back.' Baz gave him a penetrating look from under his heavy brown fringe. 'Am I right?'

'Not really.' Matt shook his head, 'Still, life goes on doesn't it? I suppose at least I know it really is all over now. My fault though; I should have told her long ago how I felt. Just didn't have the courage.' His face creased painfully, and then he looked across at the big man. 'What I can't understand is, why Andy Macayne? And why so soon? She never mentioned anything about it when we were together. Why didn't she tell me?'

Baz laid a large reassuring hand on Matt's shoulder. 'I know it's painful mate, but like your mum said on the phone, it's for the best. She was no good for you really. What you got to think of is the future, what with the Isle of Wight in August, the album to wrap up and the UK tour being brought forward, you won't have time to grieve for long. Give it a few months and you'll look back and wonder what all the fuss was about.' He smiled encouragingly, hoping his words were doing some good, 'Women!' he shook his head, looking bewildered. 'Dangerous lot to get tangled up with. Have your fun and run, that's my motto!'

'Yeah, you're probably right,' Matt gave Baz a half hearted grin, glad to have him there to bounce him out of his melancholy. All of a sudden the other members of the group appeared, dashing down the steps towards the car, eager to make their escape from the building they had been imprisoned in for endless hours each day over the last few weeks.

'Where are we off to then?' Geoff asked, easing himself onto the opposite seat, Paul and Todd sliding next to him. Paddy, the last to arrive, slammed the door shut and settled himself next to Baz.

'Soho, strip clubs......' Todd said, with his usual lustful enthusiasm as the car moved off.

'Sex, that's all you think of!' Geoff sneered, 'If we're going to have a good night out then it's got to be somewhere like Annabel's or Tramp pulling birds with fancy names like Fenella or Pandora.'

'You're pathetic,' said Todd with a snort. 'Most upmarket tarts haven't got two good brain cells between them.'

'It's not their brains he's interested in.' Paddy gave a dirty laugh.

'A tart's a tart.' Paul threw his opinion into the argument, 'What's the big deal? Sex is sex.'

'No it's not,' Geoff argued, 'Given the choice, I'd say a turn with one of them high-class Chelsea birds takes some beating. All that soft skin, glossy hair and legs up to their armpits; Chanel No 5 oozing from every pore. Bit like your bird eh Matt?'

'My bird?' Matt said lightly, 'You mean Ella?' She's not my bird Geoff, never was.' He turned his face to the window, unable to look at them all in case they saw the truth hovering painfully in his eyes. 'Ella,' he gave a humourless laugh, 'was just someone passing through.'

'Never mind mate.' Paddy gave him a friendly slap. 'Cheer up! Plenty more fish in the sea. You stick with me tonight; I'll make sure you have a good time.'

'Oh I intend to,' Matt said grimly, watching the passing traffic as the driver hovered at the junction waiting for a convenient gap. 'Tonight I'm going to celebrate in style. By getting drunk and laid! In that order!'

Saturday 12th July

Laura stood on the stairs in the same spot where only weeks ago Matt Benedict had been with her admiring the house and its paintings. Above her, the finished portrait of Ella hung now side by side with that of the first Marcella. Hugo had done a wonderful job. She only hoped that when Ella saw it she too would be pleased with the finished result.

Ella. She smiled. How wonderful that everything had fallen into place so well after their chat. But why all the secrecy she wondered? She had found out about it accidentally when she called into the village shop at the beginning of the week. Margaret was on one of her visits to her sister in Taunton and Rachel had taken an afternoon off from the stables to hold the fort.

'I expect you're looking forward to Ella's visit this weekend.' She said brightly as she handed Laura her change.

'Yes, I hope she likes the painting. I think it looks wonderful!'

'Is she bringing her fiancé with her?'

'Fiancé?'

Seeing Laura's puzzled expression Rachel put her hand to her face, her cheeks colouring with embarrassment. 'Oh dear, what have I done?'

'Let the cat out of the bag, by the looks of things.' Laura laughed, amused at the horror on Rachel's face.

'Now I feel awful,' Rachel bit her lip, 'Me knowing before you, it doesn't seem right somehow.'

'Please, don't upset yourself;' Laura said reassuringly, 'its obvious Ella wants to surprise me. Well, well.' She gave Rachel a delighted smile as she turned to go, 'Fiancé eh? No prizes for guessing who that is!'

'It's got to be Matt hasn't it?' She said to Mary as they were arranging flowers in the church on Thursday afternoon. 'I mean who else could it be? There isn't anyone else is there?'

'No,' Mary said, busy with a vase of pink and yellow floribunda roses. 'Since Niall he's the only name she's ever mentioned to me. Oh I'm so pleased Laura, he's a lovely young man.'

The jangle of the doorbell below brought Laura back to the present. She saw Ettie cross the hallway, smoothing down the skirt of her navy dress before throwing open the heavy old oak door.

'Miss Ella!' She heard her say, 'How lovely to see you again!'

Laura watched from her eyrie as Ettie stood back and Ella walked into the hall. But to her surprise it wasn't Matt who walked in behind her. It was a young man with olive skin and black curly hair, hands thrust into the pockets of his jacket. He's very handsome, Laura thought as she studied him. Very handsome indeed. But exactly who is he and where has he come from?

Ella's eyes roamed the hallway, and then moved upwards. 'Grandma!' she smiled as she saw Laura.

'Darling!' With a smile, Laura came down the stairs to greet her, arms open wide. They hugged each other tightly for a moment, and then Ella broke away.

'Grandma I have a surprise,' she took Laura by the hand. 'I'd like you to meet Andy....Andy Macayne.' She spread her fingers of her left hand to show the ring sparkling there, 'We're engaged!'

Laura smiled and accepted his polite handshake. The eyes were dark, unfathomable, the mouth full and sensuous. The beauty spot at the edge of his upper lip gave him a rakish look. He really was an attractive young man. But how had this come about so quickly? And whatever had happened to Matt?

Monday 28th July

Ella looked at her watch. Eight forty five, Mollie should be here any moment. She gave a sigh and got up from her desk, wandering leisurely around the room. It was perfection.

True to his word, Andy had sent a painter around with colour cards and the two girls had made their choices. Slowly over the next week the place had become transformed. The pale green walls showed off the pine doors to their best advantage and fitted carpet took away the coldness of the thermoplastic tiled floor.

A week after the decorators had finished the furniture arrived. Black desks and emerald green seating had been chosen for the reception and the interview room, while Ella's apricot and Jenny's French blue office were furnished with pale ash desks and chairs with seat colours to match the walls. A small switchboard was fitted, a photocopier installed and finally a van load of large houseplants arrived to put the finishing touch to the whole thing.

Jenny's projections for the business looked good and she was cautiously optimistic about the future of One Plus One. But for Ella there was no question of failure, she was determined it would be a success; there was, after all, nothing like it in Abbotsbridge. Don had canvassed the business community thoroughly, there was a definite need for an employment agency in the town and with Mollie's guidance and introductions, they were starting out with many advantages.

Next came advertising in the local paper and a flyer sent to every business on Mollie's list, advising of the take-over and re-launch of the business on Monday 28th July. Now all they had to do was wait. And now they were doing just that, with ten minutes to go to opening time, standing at the front window watching people pass by on the pavement below. They were ready - the question was where was Mollie?

At nine fifteen the door opened and a couple of girls arrived wanting to register for temporary employment. They were followed by a woman newly arrived to the area who had seen the advertisement in the paper and was looking for a permanent job.

Two phone calls followed, one from Rich Tate looking for a Clerk/Typist for Octagon's Sales Department, the other from Paul Haskins of Yeoman's Agricultural Merchants with a request for two temps for summer holiday cover. From that moment onwards it became a non stop juggle between people and phone calls.

Ella, seeing they would soon become overwhelmed by arrivals, set up a system of handing out forms and pens and guiding people to spare chairs. In the absence of Mollie, interviews were then booked into a diary for a date and time later that week.

Ella looked at Jenny, eyes bright with excitement. 'Look at this pile of applications; I can't believe how well we've done. All we need now is Mollie to give us a hand to process them. Wherever is she?'

Just as she spoke the phone rang. She answered, finding Mollie on the other end. After a short conversation she put down the receiver and gave Jenny a pinched look. 'Mollie's brother's been involved in a car crash - he's in hospital with bad head injuries. She's travelling up to Peterborough to be with him and his family.'

'For how long?'

'I don't know,' Ella shrugged, 'She didn't say when she'd be back, just that she'd be in touch and that she was very sorry to have let us down.'

'Oh dear, poor Mollie,' Jenny made a face. 'I just knew it was all going too well.'

'Don't panic,' Ella said with a thoughtful smile, 'I've got an idea. I think I know where to find someone who might just get us out of this fix. Can you manage on your own for a while?'

Don Lattimer had just returned from a morning round of golf when he saw Ella's Mini turn into his driveway. He smiled and waved as she got out and walked towards him.

'What are you doing here?' He asked as he retrieved his clubs from the boot of his Cortina. 'Thought it was your big opening day.'

'It is, but I need your help.'

'I thought you had everything organised.'

'We did,' Ella replied, 'But Mollie's had to rush to Peterborough. Her brother's very ill in hospital and for all our enthusiasm and energy, Jenny and I don't possess the expertise she would have provided. We need to find someone to take her place, someone mature and experienced who knows all about shorthand and typing tests.'

'Me? Surely not!'

'No, your newly retired secretary Joan.'

'Ah, Joan! Of course.'

'We need her to shorthand test all the girls. I don't think we'll be seeing Mollie for some time. We're flooded with applicants and quite desperate for some professional guidance!'

'I think,' Don Lattimer said with a smile which lit up his entire face, 'that she'll probably welcome you with open arms. She's enjoying retirement but it might be proving just a little too quiet a times. Come on in, I'll give you her address.'

Jenny looked at her watch. Where had Ella got to? It was five past eleven and through the frosted glass of the door she could see the silhouette of yet another person arriving. She readied herself with a registration form and pen. As she did so, the phone began to ring. She answered it, thinking it might be Ella. It wasn't, it was Andy, wondering how things were going. She had a brief chat to him, only to find as she replaced the receiver there were two more people waiting. Then the phone rang again. It was Liam not only ringing to find out how they were doing, but to given them an assignment to find a tracer for his office. She took details, handed out forms to the queue which had now expanded to three, took back the completed ones, and then the phone was ringing again.

Out of the corner of her eye she noticed a plump brunette in a blue dress who had been filling in a form was watching her closely. Eventually the girl got to her feet and came over.

'Busy isn't it?' She said handing back the pen and her completed form.

'Yes, it's been amazing.' Jenny replied, trying to sound upbeat and enthusiastic.

'You could do with a receptionist,' the girl said with a friendly smile, 'this is far too much to cope with on your own.'

'Oh, there are two of us here normally. My partner was called away. She should be back any moment...' she shot a worrying look at the clock.

The phone began to ring again at the same time as a young woman in a beige trouser suit walked through the door. Jenny looked at the telephone and the new arrival, wondering which to deal with first.

'Here,' said the brown eyed girl, moving behind the desk, 'Let me cover the phone for you - you deal with the customer.'

Jenny was taken aback by this strange girl taking charge, then aware of the woman hovering close by she pulled a form from the tray and found a pen. 'O.K, thank you.....'

'Trudi. Trudi Thompson.' The girl replied, before picking up the receiver. 'Good morning, One Plus One,' she said in a very professional voice. 'How may I help?'

Joan Trimble sat in the sheltered garden of her small cottage finishing off her morning coffee and watching her Siamese cat chase butterflies across the lawn. The appearance of Ella Kendrick through the side gate was sudden and quite unexpected. With a smile she got to her feet and went to meet her.

'Ella, what a surprise.' She said, giving her a hug. 'Come and sit down. How are you? Is that business of yours up and running yet?'

'Yes, we opened today.' Ella replied placing herself neatly on the garden seat beside Joan.

'So what brings you here? Shouldn't you be dealing with your new customers?'

'Yes, but I need your help; it's Mollie - she's been called away, her brother's been taken ill. Without her we're sunk, we just haven't got the experience to test applicants. And if we can't test them there's no way we can place them with employers. Is there any chance you would be willing to step in? I know you've only just started your retirement, but, well, it would only be until Mollie gets back.'

'Um....' Joan hesitated.

'It would only be for a few weeks. And we could work out days and times to suit you.'

Joan looked thoughtfully, and then smiled. 'I have to confess the novelty of retirement is beginning to wear off already. I don't want full time again of course, but I do miss the daily contact with people. Actually I was thinking of coming along to register.' she laughed, 'and now here you are offering me something. Yes I'd love to help out. When exactly did you want me to start?'

'Like right now?'

'I think I can manage that,' Joan said getting to her feet and picking up her cup and saucer. 'Just give me a few minutes to get my things together.'

'Where've you been?' Jenny got to her feet as Ella walked in. It was eleven thirty and the office was empty, although the phone was still ringing.

'Hiring reinforcements,' Ella indicated Joan who followed her into the room, 'Joan has very kindly agreed to come to work for us on a part time basis. Who's this?' she nodded towards Trudi, busy making notes on a pad as she chatted on the phone at the desk in the far corner of the room.

'Oh I've been hiring reinforcements too,' Jenny grinned, 'that's Trudi Thompson, she's our new receptionist.'

'A receptionist?' Ella stared from Jenny to Trudi and back again, 'Just like that? Without any kind of interview or test?'

'Trudi,' Jenny said quite forcefully. 'has been helping me hold the fort. It's been a battlefield in here and as far as I'm concerned, she's passed all the tests she needs to.'

'Well, you can't argue with that Ella.' Joan gave an amused smile as she looked at Jenny. So the quiet studious girl who wouldn't say boo to a goose in class appeared to be quite assertive when she wanted to. Life at One Plus One, she decided, was going to be extremely interesting.

Thursday 18th December

'This is really great,' Nick said, looking around the spare bedroom of Ella's flat as he brought in the last of his luggage, 'Thanks Sis, you're a life saver.'

'Glad I could help,' Ella gave him a hug, pleased that he was back in Abbotsbridge at last, 'Come on through, I'll make some coffee.'

It *was* nice to have Nick home she thought as he followed her down the hallway into the brightness of her kitchen. Since June he had been in the Med, joining in various archaeological digs. He was taking advantage of the three months of freedom he had promised himself before settling down to his chosen career after successfully completing his degree. Realising how much Jenny was missing him, Ella insisted that she take a break from the agency in August so they could spend some time together. It was still early days at One Plus One, but Trudi and Joan (who had now both been taken on permanently) had settled in so well that Ella felt losing Jenny for a week wouldn't be a problem. And so she had joined him in southern Italy where they had wandered Sorrento's narrow streets, taken the ferry over to Capri, climbed Vesuvius and explored the ruins of Pompeii before driving north for a final romantic weekend in Rome.

When he returned at the end of the summer, an old friend of his had offered him a temporary job in Bristol for the autumn term at a private boys' school, covering a colleague's long term sickness. During that brief spell of work he had spent all his spare time applying for permanent teaching posts in the area. But despite several interviews, he had returned to Abbotsbridge only a week away from Christmas with no permanent job and no where to live. Having a spare room, Ella insisted he come and stay with her. The last four years had been punctuated by his visits, but now he was committed to settling down in the area, she longed for an opportunity to recapture the old closeness they had when they lived as children in Meridan Cross.

'So this is where you have your romantic dinners for two with Andy is it?' He joked, lingering by the table in the small dining room.

'No,' she gave an amused laugh as she filled the kettle. 'Actually I hardly eat here now. As I'm *almost* a Macayne, I have the dubious pleasure of dinner at Everdene at least three nights a week. Bob calls them his *en famille* nights.'

'Grim old place isn't it? I've seen it from the road. Looks like the set for a Hammer Horror film. What's it like inside?'

'Strange. Bob has this funny old housekeeper called Mrs Catt. They call her Tabby. Looks like Mrs Danvers from Daphne Du Maurier's *Rebecca.*' She made a face as she pulled two mugs from the rack, remembering her first visit. 'And as for the house, well it's beautifully furnished but I feel it's place of great sadness. Too many trapped memories I suppose.'

'Memories?' Nick reached over and retrieved the coffee jar, pushing it towards her.

'Of Andy's mother,' Ella said as she added a spoonful of coffee to each mug. 'There are photos of her everywhere. Her bedroom's like a shrine. Nothing's been touched since the day she died.' As she retrieved the sugar bowl from the cupboard she looked uneasily at him, 'It's not healthy Nick. I shall be glad when the time comes for Andy to move out.'

'Not set a date yet then?'

'No, not yet. We're in no rush. What about you?'

'May 16th.'

'Wow. That's only six months away. Does everyone know?'

'Yes, we've told Jenny's parents, Granddad and Mary and Grandma. I think Betty will get the organising underway once Christmas is over.'

'And Mother?'

'What about her?' He looked at her as if he didn't understand the question.

Intercepting the kettle just before it came to the boil, Ella poured hot water into the mugs. 'You've not been to see her yet then?'

'After her reaction to the engagement I wasn't going to bother. But,' He said reluctantly, 'I suppose I'd better. I'll drop in and tell her after Christmas. In fact thinking about it, I might really enjoy stirring her up again,' He opened the fridge to retrieve the milk. 'Perhaps it's about time she had a bit of upset after all the chaos she's caused in other people's lives. She was always bloody awful,' he said handing the milk to Ella, 'even when we lived in Fox Cottage.'

'You remember back that far?' Ella poured the milk into the two mugs and began stirring. 'You never said. Why not?'

'Because grandfather said we had to forget her. The memories weren't particularly pleasant anyway.' He took the milk from her and returned it to the fridge. 'She didn't love either of us you know. She was cruel. She enjoyed inflicting pain even then.'

'I can't remember being smacked,' Ella said, handing him one of the mugs.

'Oh, she was too clever for that. It was all psychological. Sending us to bed without any tea, taking our favourite things and saying she'd sell them because we'd been naughty. She even told me there had been a mix up in the nursing home and she wasn't sure if I was hers. And of course she had a hell of a temper. When we were at Fox Cottage she was always irritable, smashing things. And she drank. We were neglected children; all she was interested in was doing her hair, painting her nails and dressing up so she could go gallivanting off into Abbotsbridge to spend time with her friends. I was so glad when we stayed at the farm. Granddad and Grandma Peggy were different. I felt safe with them. Wanted. I prayed she'd leave us.' He stood there looking at her, his eyes moist with emotion as he cradled the mug to his chest. 'Do you remember the day she left?'

Ella nodded. 'Yes, Grandma Peg was taken ill and we had to stay over with the Mitchell's at the Vicarage.'

'That's right,' He smiled, remembering it too. 'And when Granddad came to collect us and told us what had happened, I couldn't believe all my prayers had been answered.'

'But you cried Nick, just like I did. I thought....'

'What? That I was upset?' He shook his head, 'I was. For poor Grandma Peg! But I knew once Mother had gone everything was going to be all right. And it was. But now she's back interfering in our lives again. Well I'm having none of it! She's nothing to me. As far as I'm concerned Peggy was our mother. She was the one who took care of us, tucked us into bed, dried our tears, encouraged us, loved us,' he reached out and caught a wild corkscrew of Ella's hair which now skimmed her shoulders. 'Not the vicious creature that did this!'

'I know, I should have listened to you when you told me to get out. But somehow I was convinced she might change.'

'No chance Ella,' Nick shook his head, 'She's riddled with spite. Still, you're free now, that's the most important thing.'

'Yes,' Ella thought for a moment then laughed, her grey eyes bright with amusement, 'I can run my own life and make my own choices without any interference, It's wonderful! And despite her dire predictions, the business is going well. Talking of which,' she pointed a thoughtful finger at him. 'I've found you a job....'

He ran a hand through his fair hair, 'Teaching?' he looked hopeful.

'I'm afraid not. Office vacancy at Stewarts. But it pays reasonably well and it'll keep the old brain cells from stagnating. I've got the details in my briefcase. Bring your coffee through to the lounge and I'll run through them with you.'

1970

EIGHT

Monday 12th January

Liam, wrapped in a heavy brown overcoat, was busy clearing the driveway when he saw Nick approaching on foot, picking his way carefully between the irregular heaps of snow along the cleared and gritted pavement. Leaning on his shovel for a moment, he watched his stepson as he came in through the gate.

'Hi!' Nick smiled at him over the swathe of wool scarf that surrounded his neck, 'Is Mother in?'

'Yes, I think she's on the phone at the moment; some Ladies Circle thing. Anything I can do?'

'Be ready with the tea and sympathy,' Nick grinned. 'I've come to tell her I've set the wedding date.'

'Well, congratulations!' Liam gave him a friendly pat on the back, 'I'm really pleased for you both. Jenny's a lovely girl. When's the big day?'

'Saturday 16th May. Will you be there?'

'Of course, I will. With or without Mel and that's a promise.'

'Thanks Liam,' Nick looked at the pile of snow his stepfather was moving. 'I'll give you a hand if you like after I've broken the news. It can be my act of penance.'

Mel had been watching the two men from behind her lounge nets. Friendly pats and backslapping, what was that all in aid of she wondered? She heard Nick come in through the back door and walked into the dining room to meet him. She smiled as he came through from the kitchen, peeling off his gloves. How like her he was, with his fine features and vivid blue eyes, yet how disappointing he should be so easy-going, like his father. A dangerous flaw in his personality, she decided, making him easy prey to scheming little tarts like Jenny Taylor.

'Nick, how nice to see you.' She approached him warmly, reaching up to kiss his cheek. 'My you are cold,' She stepped back to look at him, 'Would you like some coffee? I was just about to make myself one.'

'No thanks, I'm fine.'

'Well,' she clasped hands together in anticipation, 'I gather from all the congratulations that were going on out front that you have come to tell us you have a job at last.'

'Not yet,' He shook his head, 'I'm still at Stewarts.'

'I really don't understand why you're there at all.' She tutted disapprovingly. 'Work as an office clerk - it's very demeaning for someone with a degree.'

'Don't knock it Mother.' He tried to sound patient, but already she was beginning to irritate him. 'It was good of Ella to find it for me. It's short term. Six months and it brings me in some money while I'm applying for teaching jobs. Besides, I have to pay my way. It's kind of Ella to let me stay with her but she's not a charity.'

'I suppose you know what you're doing,' Mel said reluctantly as she turned to look at herself in the gilt framed mirror over the sideboard, distracted from their conversation by the demands of her own reflection. 'It just seems a pity you can't find a proper job after all that education. So,' she said with forced cheerfulness as she turned back to him, 'exactly what has brought you here?'

'Jenny and I have set a date for the wedding. May 16th. I came to let you both know. Invitations will follow shortly.'

Mel did not answer. Instead she crossed to the dining room table and selected a cigarette from the silver case lying there. Lighting it she moved back towards him, blowing smoke into the room. 'You still intend to go ahead with this folly then?'

'I'm an adult, I make my own choices.' His tone was uncompromising. 'I love Jenny and she loves me. If you don't agree with this wedding, that's a problem you'll have to deal with. I merely came to tell you my news out of courtesy.'

'Courtesy!' She gave a harsh laugh. 'Is that what you call it?'

She picked up a small brass ashtray on the table by the window, stubbing out the cigarette with red nailed anger, 'You are such a selfish young man, you know. You take after the Kendricks for that.'

Nick stood there regarding her for a moment. He had known this would be the reaction and that somehow the Kendricks would get dragged into it. On the way here he had prepared all sorts of responses to anything she might come up with. Right now he would really have liked to tell her if she thought him selfish then it was traits of herself she could see in him, not his father's family, but something stopped him. Arguing with his mother, he had learned very quickly, only added fuel to a strongly burning fire. She thrived on confrontation. But this time she was going to be disappointed.

'Cross you off the list then shall I?' He said as he pulled on his gloves and turned to go.

'What?' She glared at him.

'The wedding,' He was hovering in the dining room doorway now, anxious to leave, 'I gather you won't be coming.'

'I didn't say that!' She looked flustered for a moment. 'I may not agree with your choice of wife, but as mother of the bridegroom, well I'm expected to be there aren't I?'

'Unfortunately,' Nick said under his breath as he turned and left.

Friday 16th January

Nick stood at the bar in the lounge of the Red Lion. It was lunch time and the pub was gradually filling up. Each time the door opened with a wheeze his gaze would drift towards it, only to find yet another unfamiliar face catch his eye. He checked his watch then turned to look again, just as Ella appeared. He waved. She saw him, acknowledged him with a smile and began pushing through the crush of bodies to reach him.

'Hi, sorry I'm late. I had a phone call from you know who.'

'Still mad at me is she?' He grinned, raising a hand to attract the attention of the barmaid.

'You'd better believe it!' Ella said as she unbuttoned her sheepskin. 'She just went on and on and on!'

The barmaid arrived and Nick ordered wine for Ella and another half pint for himself.

'Well it's about time she learned she can't have the world her own way all the time.' He said as he handed over a pound note. 'I did think of suggesting a double wedding, now that really would have stirred things up.'

'She wouldn't have bitten.' She smiled as she picked up her glass of wine. 'We now have a date.'

'Twisted Andy's arm did you?' He laughed.

'Nothing to do with Andy. Bob's decided we should have an August wedding.'

'What's Bob got to do with anything?'

'He thinks it would be best that the wedding coincides with the start of Andy and Mick's new business venture.'

'The old romantic!' Nick gave a cynical smile. 'New venture eh, what's that all about?'

'Bob's formed a separate company, Taylor Macayne Residential. Andy and Mick are going to run it. Bob says it's to cover the exclusive end of the company's house building operation. Small infill developments of half a dozen or so large houses, mostly in village or semi rural settings.'

'Is there that sort of money about?'

'He seems to thinks there is. He's already got three lots of land lined up. One on the southern edge of Abbotsbridge, and two in outlying villages. Mick's going to look after production and Andy sales.'

'A sort of coming of age present then?' Nick suddenly envied Andy and Mick, having a business created for them and not having to write endless letters or fill in application forms.

'Yes,' Ella nodded. 'I think he's recognised it's time the boys had their own independent responsibilities.'

'And a lot of responsibility ahead for you too, Sis. Church, dress, flowers, cake, reception.'

Ella stood running her finger around the top of her wine glass thoughtfully. She looked up at her brother and smiled. 'Actually it's all done; there's just the guest list left.'

'Goodness, you're organised. Funny.....' He frowned, 'Mother never mentioned anything when I saw her. I'm surprised she was so upset about me, considering she's had your wedding to organise.'

'She doesn't know anything about it.'

'What?'

'I've organised it myself, with help from Grandma.'

'You'll be in worse trouble than me when she finds out.' He couldn't resist a laugh. 'Imagine. Your wedding being organised, here right under her nose. She'll be furious. It's a wonder it hasn't leaked out. Jenny says Bob Macayne knows everything that goes on in Abbotsbridge.'

'I expect he does, but I'm not getting married here, I'm getting married back in the village.'

Thursday 23rd April

Bob Macayne crossed the car park of Abbotsbridge Urban District Council Offices, black briefcase in hand. It was nine thirty and darkness had fallen in a subdued hush, the town now stippled with the glow of street lights.

He had just come from the monthly Planning Meeting; on the agenda tonight the project he had been eagerly awaiting. The proposed shopping precinct and multi-storey car park. But all had not gone well. Chief Planning Officer Miles Anderson had headed a lively debate which concluded with an agreement in principle for a new shopping precinct and connecting multi storey car park. Discussions on the termination of leases and temporary re-housing of businesses affected by the redevelopment would be on the agenda for next month's meeting.

Bob sat expectantly, waiting for the next announcement - the Committee's choice of contractor for the project. It had always been a foregone conclusion in the past that Taylor Macayne would get new build work. These matters had become so routine, almost a matter of course. But not tonight. Miles had been adamant that when the time came for a contractor to be appointed, on this occasion it would be done with sealed bids. Bob was disappointed, realising just how many others like himself saw the importance of getting this project.

He slid behind the wheel of his Rover, easing the briefcase onto the passenger seat. Closing his eyes, he pinched the bridge of his nose, feeling tired. It was a setback but one he knew he would overcome by fair means or foul. The contract was incredibly important; it would enable him to leave his mark on Abbotsbridge for all time. He wanted it and he was determined he would have it, by whatever means. As he turned the key in the ignition there was a tap on the window and he turned to see Miles Anderson peering in at him.

Pale eyed, charismatic, Miles, although well into middle age, showed no evidence of any grey in his thick brown hair. This, together with his slim frame, gave him the look of a man at least ten years younger. Tonight, as always, his expression was bland. A mask behind which lurked a razor sharp mind. He was a key player in local politics in Abbotsbridge and everyone respected him. It was unwise not to, for Miles could make or break anyone he chose, such was his power and ability to influence.

'Miles?' Bob wound down the window.

'Glad I caught you Bob; can you spare a minute to talk about the new precinct?'

'What's to discuss?' Bob looked surprised. 'It's sealed bids, every man for himself.'

'Look,' Miles replied, turning his gaze to the car park for a moment and raising his arm casually to one of the departing vehicles before leaning back into the car, 'I know you're disappointed that you haven't automatically got the contract this time, but I thought you ought to be aware that things aren't quite as bad as they seem.'

'In what way?' Bob eyed Miles thoughtfully.

'There is a certain amount of room for manoeuvre.'

'What are you getting at?'

'I can probably swing it. For a favour.'

'Bribery Miles? Didn't think that was your style.'

'Needs must when the devil drives Bob.'

'Get to the point please.' Bob said irritably.

'Liam Carpenter's wife.'

'What about her?'

'Close friend of yours is she?'

'Yes Miles and so is her husband Liam.'

'Oh come, come now Bob, don't be so defensive. I've seen you dancing together. The way she is with you.'

'And since when have you been an expert on heterosexual behaviour Miles?' Bob looked amused.

'Oh, I may not like women in that way Bob, but I know what I see, and I think the lady definitely has a bit of a thing for you.'

Bob gave a strange laugh. 'Miles, exactly what do you want?'

'Are you aware that Mel Carpenter's father owns a farm in Meridan Cross?'

'Yes.'

‘I want to buy the cottage there and some of his land.’

‘Early retirement Miles?’ Bob laughed.

‘Not just yet.’

‘You want it for a project then?’

Miles nodded. ‘Richard Evas is, by reputation, a difficult man, I’ll probably get the door slammed in my face if I approach him. So I thought maybe his daughter might be the best person to persuade him to sell me Fox Cottage and a section of land next to it. And the person to talk to her is you.’

‘Is it? I would have thought you’d been better talking to Liam.’

‘Liam’s a green belt man. He wouldn’t want any part of this.’

‘So it’s a building project.’

Miles studied him for a moment then gave a reluctant nod.

‘But if as you say it’s green belt, you must know you’ll never get planning permission.’

‘We shall see Bob.’

‘And what’s in it for me if I perform this miracle?’

‘You’ll get not only the contract for the precinct and the multi storey but also the new civic hall. The Grand Slam eh?’ He laughed.

‘This project must be something pretty big and important.’

‘It is,’ Miles nodded, ‘Very.’

‘Well,’ Bob scratched his chin, ‘if my bid comes in just under everyone else’s, someone is sure to smell a rat. Everyone knows I’m usually expensive, they’ll soon be shouting foul and demanding some sort of enquiry.’

‘Is that no then?’ Miles looked disappointed.

‘Not necessarily,’ Bob eyed Miles speculatively. ‘It can be done; it just means the package will need to be adjusted slightly.’

‘Go on.’ Miles leaned closer into the car.

‘I’ll throw in the multi storey for nothing, that way my bid will come in well under everyone else’s and no one will be suspicious.’

‘Well,’ Miles’ face lit up with a smile. ‘I think the Committee will be pleased with that. I must say that’s a very philanthropic gesture, Bob.’

‘Don’t be silly Miles,’ Bob tutted, ‘You know I never do anything for nothing.’

‘Meaning?’ Miles eyed him suspiciously.

‘Your project. Guarantee me the contract for the build and I think we might have a deal.’

‘Mmm.’ Miles scratched his chin thoughtfully, his pale eyes warming slightly. ‘Yes, I think when the time comes we can probably work something out between us.’

‘Can we shake on that then?’

‘Sure, let’s call it a Gentlemen‘s Agreement,’ Miles smiled, extending his hand towards the open window of the car.

Tuesday 28th April

Mel faced Bob across their usual table in the dining room of the Ragbourne Grove Hotel. She had been looking forward all week to their illicit evening together. Liam had gone up to Oxford to meet a group of old friends for dinner and planned to stay overnight. She felt excited at the thought of spending another night with Bob, whose demands on her body had been a breath of fresh air in comparison to her brief once a week coupling with Liam. But now a cloud had been cast over the whole evening.

It seemed straightforward at first. Listening to Bob telling her about Miles' need to buy Fox Cottage and a small part of Hundred Acre for a project but when he asked if she could use her influence on her father to persuade him to sell, everything changed. Her father was hard; unforgiving. They had been at odds with each other as long as she could remember. Her return had opened old, festering wounds and after enticing Ella away she doubted it would be safe to show her face in Meridan Cross for the foreseeable future.

'You must realise what you're asking is impossible.' She said, once Bob had finished. 'We don't have any sort of relationship. He positively hates me.'

'Oh come on Mel, it can't be that bad.' Bob protested.

'You don't know my father. He bears grudges long term,' She shook her head, 'sorry, it just can't be done.'

Bob reached across the table and stroked the back of her hand.

'Mel, please, it's not just Miles; I need you to do this for me. It's very important.'

'You're involved in this project too?'

'I will be, but only on the condition we persuade your father to sell.'

'Just a minute,' She sat bolt upright and withdrew her hand from his. 'If that's the case, shouldn't there be something in it for me too?'

'What?'

'Well, you can't expect me to put my head in the lion's mouth for nothing.'

Bob was taken aback, he hadn't expected this.

'Then you can do it.'

'I can probably do anything if there's money involved.' Mel said graciously.

'I'll have to talk to Miles.' He refilled his glass began to raise it to his lips then stopped. 'What's that look for?'

'There's a payphone in reception.' Mel said placing her napkin on the table.

'You want me to do it now?'

'Well, no time like the present is there?'

'She wants what?' Miles shouted down the phone, annoyed at being called out in the middle of an important dinner party he was holding for the local MP and his wife.

'She won't budge otherwise,' Bob said calmly. 'It's a state of war between them at the moment apparently. I've worked damned hard on her this evening but she's not stupid. She knows where you're concerned there's bound to be money involved and on reflection perhaps we should offer her some incentive for helping us both.'

'Has she mentioned a figure?'

'No, but taking all things into consideration, a grand should do it.'

There was muttering at the other end of the phone, then Miles said.

'O.K., one thousand pounds it is. But only on completion of the job. No land, no money.'

'I think I can safely say she'll go with that,' Bob sounded pleased, 'Excellent!'

'Bob,' Miles' voice was silky smooth, 'Don't get too excited. You're the one who's going to be paying her. Goodnight.'

Saturday 16th May

'Forasmuch as Nick and Jenny have consented together in holy wedlock and have witnessed the same before God and this company.....'

The Reverend Hubbard, sunlight streaming through the stain glass window behind him, made the final pronouncements over the two figures kneeling at the altar.

Ella and Issy, side by side in electric blue, their hair pinned up and secured with woven circlets of white daisies, watched quietly. As the couple rose and walked back towards the congregation, Ella thought how beautiful Jenny looked; small and dark in a simple sheath of white, her hand firmly in Nick's, glancing up at him with an unspoken message of love in her eyes. She looked across to where her grandmother sat and received the benefit of a contented smile. In the pew in front, sitting beside Liam, Mel looked tight lipped and uncomfortable, her glance occasionally wandering to the back of the church where Bob Macayne was sitting with Andy.

On the other side of the church Betty Taylor, swathed in shocking pink, dabbed her eyes gently, overcome with emotion. Jack, strong and solid by her side, slid an arm around her shoulder and whispered something into her ear which made her stop suddenly, a smile breaking through her tears. Mick, sitting next to his father, watched his sister with an expression bordering on awe. Nina, however, was the exception, looking for all the world as if she had no idea what she was doing there.

Despite wanting a quiet affair, the church was packed with well wishers, and when the couple eventually stepped out into the bright sunlight of the late spring day, they were greeted with a snowstorm of confetti from those gathered outside in the churchyard. It seemed as if the whole of Abbotsbridge had descended on St Marks.

Ella watched her mother, all smiles as she chatted to Mary and her grandfather. Despite her opposition to the wedding, she seemed to be using it as an opportunity for bridge building. Could it be that in some areas at least she was mellowing?

'She gave in eventually then.' Issy nodded her head towards Mel as they posed for photographs moments later.

'Not really,' Ella responded, relaxing her smile as the photographer reloaded his camera, 'She's here because she feels she has to be. She still doesn't agree with the wedding. In fact, she said some pretty awful things to Nick. She thinks he's let the side down, marrying Jenny.'

'God, she's such a snob.'

'I know,' Ella teased out the skirt of her dress and took up her pose again. 'The only plus is that Andy is exactly what mother had hoped for in a son in law so that rather balances things out.'

'Oh no!' Issy groaned.

'What?'

'Your mother, she'll be organising your wedding soon, bossing us all about, trying to make everyone feel inadequate.'

'Ah....'

The photographer was organising all the guests, getting them compacted into a space small enough to get a good shot of everyone.

'What?' Issy hissed, moving a little to the left.

'She isn't organising it, I am, with the help of my grandmother.'

'And she doesn't mind?'

'She doesn't know, I haven't told her.' Ella smiled again and stood still as the photographer leaned into his camera and waved at the assembled crowd.

'Big mistake Ella.'

'I know, but there hasn't been a good time to break the news. She's been impossible lately and so wound up about today I just couldn't risk mentioning it.'

'So what will you do?'

'I don't know. What do you suggest?'

Issy thought for a moment, and then she said. 'You'll have to cut her in. Give her something to do.'

'I can't, everything's organised.'

'Everything?'

'Except the invitations.'

'Wonderful! Just hand it all over to her.'

'Will it be enough?'

'It's a power thing, she'll love it. She'll be so involved with who to invite and who to leave out that the incidentals like the dress and the reception probably won't even cross her mind.'

'You know I think you might be right.' Ella replied. 'Thanks, I owe you one.'

'Mind if I call the favour in now then?' Issy relaxed as the photographer gave the thumbs up and everyone started to disperse.

'What had you in mind?'

'Your flat. Any chance of putting a good word in for me when you move out?'

'Flying the nest at last?' Ella couldn't resist a smile

'Yes. It's not that I don't get on with Mum and Dad, but I think it's time I lived somewhere totally separate from the hotel. I need my own space, away from work.'

Ella gave an understanding nod.

'I'll have a word with Liam,' she said as they moved off towards the waiting limousine, 'he'll be able to put you in touch with the landlord.'

Wednesday 10th June

Ella was lunching in Ronaldo's with Andy when she saw her mother standing outside peering in through the window.

'Oh no!' She heard Andy hiss under his breath as he spotted her.

'Perhaps she hasn't seen us.' She said hopefully.

'Oh but she has.'

Andy watched her come in through the door only to be pounced upon by Ronaldo himself. There had been one brief moment when he actually admired Mel Carpenter. Not many young women in the town had mothers as elegant and glamorous as her. However, over the months since his engagement to Ella he had drastically changed his opinion. She had settled herself upon them like a leech. She was ingratiating and patronising and he had also come to recognise her as manipulative, obsessive and hell bent on interference. Hadn't she got a life of her own? Obviously not. And now she was seating herself down beside them, smiling and interlocking scarlet tipped fingers. Suddenly he found his appetite had vanished.

'So, what are you two up to today?' She gave them both a generous smile.

'Oh, just having lunch.' Ella said casually.

'That's nice. Mel nodded, gazing at their plates. 'I'm glad I caught you both. As you know time is marching on. One wedding's over and we haven't even started to organise the next one yet have we?'

'It's all under control Mrs Carpenter.' Andy said, pushing his plate away and signalling for coffee.

'Au contraire, Andy, as far as I am aware absolutely nothing has been done and that's where I come in, isn't it Ella?'

She looked at her daughter for confirmation.

'Actually mother I've been meaning to talk to you.......'

'There's absolutely no need.' Mel raised a confident hand. 'I've been in touch with Chantal's Bridal Shop in the High Street and chosen some quite exquisite dresses for you to try on. Fresh in from London. And of course I've had preliminary discussions with the Reverend Hubbard at St Marks.'

'But I have already chosen my dress.'

The waiter arrived with two coffees which he placed before Ella and Andy. He hovered at Mel's elbow asking her if she would like something. She waved him away like a minor irritation and leaned forward, her face creased into a frown. 'You've done *what*!'

'I said I have already chosen my dress, it's being made.'

'You've done this without my permission?'

'Permission? I don't need *permission.*' Ella laughed. 'This is my wedding.'

'Which, you've obviously forgotten, is being paid for by myself and Liam! Therefore as the bride's mother *I* should be taking charge of the organisation.'

'Not this bride's mother. As I said, I was meaning to talk to you, but there never seems to have been a good moment. The fact is, I'm getting married in Meridan Cross, I'm organising the wedding myself and Grandma's paying for it.'

'Not again!' Mel spluttered under her breath, 'I might have known Laura Kendrick's hand was in this somewhere! The interfering old busy body.'

'She's not interfering, I asked her to help me.'

'Did you now? And where does that leave me? What will the Ladies Circle say?' The famous Carpenter pout surfaced immediately, trying to make Ella feel guilty.

'You can have the guest list Mother.' Ella said brightly, crossing her fingers under the table.

'The guest list! Well I suppose it's better than nothing.' Mel sat for a moment contemplating the offer, and then she smiled. 'On second thoughts, yes, I think I would like that Ella.' She paused, 'After all, there are so many influential people in this town, who just have to be there, although I still don't like the idea of Meridan Cross. The thought of the great and good of this town descending on the land of the great unwashed….'

'Actually, most of the great unwashed are coming.'

'The villagers? You can't be serious!'

'Yes I am. You're free to invite anyone you like from Abbotsbridge but the list must include my choices from the village.'

'Bridesmaids!' She raised a finger in the air. 'That's something else I can do! There are such charming children about. Sylvia and Rupert Beckton-Abbot from No 24, now their little Sophie-Louise - what an absolute poppet!'

'No Mother! It's the guest list or nothing. Do you want it or not?' Ella took a sip of her coffee, watching her mother carefully.

'Oh! I suppose so!' Mel got to her feet impatiently with the look of a small child who had been denied its dearest wish, 'You just don't understand Ella do you? You're making a grave mistake handling all this yourself. It is so important to create the right impression.'

'Don't you worry about a thing,' Ella said, looking at Andy and trying not to laugh, 'All the impressions created at my wedding will certainly be the right ones. You just get on with that guest list and come back to me in a fortnight.

Numbers are irrelevant, the reception's being held at Little Court so there's plenty of room for everyone.'

'Little Court!' Mel gave an indignant snort, 'This whole thing is going to descend into a complete fiasco. You'll regret this Ella, you really will! When I think of what it could have been.' She said, waving a finger at her as she turned and left them.

As the restaurant door closed and Mel disappeared into the street, the waiter arrived with the bill. Reaching into his jacket Andy pulled out his wallet. As he drew a sheaf of notes from its depths he smiled across the table at Ella.

'Well done for standing your ground. Sylvia and Woopert Beckton-Abbot.' He mimicked, 'God she can be so tiresome at times.'

'Your father doesn't seem to think so.' Ella replied. 'He has a very obvious soft spot for her.'

'Don't be silly Ella,' Andy frowned as he tossed the notes onto the small brass plate in front of him. 'Dad's just incredibly tolerant. He says all that touchy feely she does is to keep him sweet so he'll continue to use Liam's business. It's self interest - Dad uses Liam. Liam gets paid. And your mother can continue living in the style she's grown accustomed to. Simple as that!' He gave a dry laugh. 'What did you think then? That they had some torrid affair going on? Dad's not like that. My Mother may be dead but she's still very much the centre of his life. Always was. Always will be.'

Saturday 25th July

'Here we are, this is it, Tennyson Avenue!' Ella turned her Mini into a tree-lined avenue of mature Victorian semi detached houses.

'There's 18!' Issy pointed up ahead on the right. 'Looks as if we're the first to arrive.' Slowing, Ella indicated and pulled across the road onto a neat tarmac driveway. The two girls sat looking up at the three storey redbrick Victorian semi, its solid stone steps leading up to a white front door with a heavy black knocker. The front garden, a riot of colour, reminded Ella of Willowbrook. Borders of delphiniums, sweet William and lupins circled a large square lawn, while floribunda rose bushes sat like a multicoloured guard of honour under the front window.

As they got out of the car the front door opened and Jenny stood there, wearing jeans and a short sleeved shirt, her hair loose around her shoulders.

'Hi!' She called out as Nick appeared behind her.

'Happy housewarming.' Ella said, reaching the top of the steps, kissing Jenny and handing her brother two bottles of wine, 'Andy's been delayed. Got called into a meeting. He'll be here in half an hour.'

'I can hold lunch, it's not a problem,' Jenny said, finishing hugging Issy and turning to follow Nick. 'Come on in both of you!'

The front door closed on a long carpeted hall punctuated with pine doors.

Ahead, Ella could see gleaming white kitchen units nestled against rich Mediterranean blue walls and she paused for a moment to breathe in the delicious aroma of roast lunch. Then they were moving again, ushered through into a large airy room with walls of pale cream and an explosion of house plants.

'Have a seat,' Jenny indicated one of the comfortable settees facing the honey stone fireplace, 'I'll show you the rest of the house after lunch. Dad and Mick have made such a good job of it. We're really pleased, aren't we?'

She looked up at Nick who smiled and nodded in agreement.

'Right, let's get us all a drink then.' Nick brandished the two bottles he was still carrying. 'Red or white?'

Committing their choices to memory he left the room.

'I'll give you a hand,' Ella said, following him.

'Your own place at last.' She said admiring the kitchen as he put the bottles on the worktop and searched for the cork screw.

'Yes and even better, I've got a job!' He said, cutting the plastic from the top of the bottle of red wine. 'They phoned me yesterday afternoon; I start in September.'

'That's such good news Nick. Where?'

'Park Street Prep School.' Inserting the bottle opener, he extracted the cork with a healthy pop. 'You know, the one with the royal blue and green uniform?'

'I'm really pleased for you.' She gave him a sisterly hug, 'everything's coming good at last.'

'Great news about Nick's new job!' Ella said enthusiastically as she returned to the lounge carrying two glasses of wine.

'Yes, I've just been telling Issy about it.' Jenny said, taking one of the glasses. 'It really couldn't have happened at a better time.'

'Oh?' Issy shot Ella a knowing look. 'And why's that then Jen? Pregnant are you?'

Cheeks flushed, Jenny looked across at Nick, who had just appeared in the doorway with the remaining two glasses. They both smiled conspiratorially.

'Yes,' Jenny said, her eyes still fixed on her husband. 'We didn't want to wait. Baby Kendrick will be arriving in the spring.'

NINE

Thursday 27th August

'Hello stranger.'

Nina swung around from her contemplation of Langley's front window to find herself face to face with Andy Macayne.

'Oh dear!' He made a face. 'You don't seem very pleased to see me.'

'Should I be?' She looked at him calmly, desperately trying to ignore the fact that just standing next to him her pulse had gone into overdrive.

Ever since his engagement to Ella last year she had deliberately kept herself away from him when social gatherings brought them into each other's company. She had tried to persuade herself that Mick was her life now, but there was part of her that wouldn't listen. A small part that was still convinced her destiny lay with Andy, no matter which direction it was taking her in at the moment. Of course, she had tried very hard to put the past behind her, to concentrate on all the things her mother had said. That Mick was an honest, caring, reliable man, who worked hard and would give her everything she had never had in her own marriage. All of that was true of course and she had tried so hard to count her blessings and settle into a life many would envy. At first she loved it; a relaxed existence, looking after the house, driving into Abbotsbridge to shop; to stop for lunch if she wanted to. She loved her blue Mini, the way her bank account was regularly topped up each month with her allowance. Then there was the account the Taylor's kept in Langleys where she could buy things for the house. It was all so exciting at first; she thought the feeling would last for ever. Only it hadn't.

It occurred to her that being independent wasn't just down to money. It also meant having a life outside the four walls of the house in Kennet Close. Without that, she felt out of step with everyone else. She missed her job, the ups-and-downs of office life, and the day-to-day gossip. There was only so many times a room could be dusted, a shirt washed and ironed, a window cleaned. Ironically, Bryony, Ella and Annabel, the very people that Mick wanted her to emulate, all had their own careers. But Mick didn't care about that; they could all do what they liked. He was a traditionalist and his wife, like his mother, did not work and that was that. And so she remained at home, a lady of leisure while Mick was on site, sometimes well into the evening, leaving her alone with just the TV for company. This morning over breakfast she had complained about her loneliness and tried again to persuade him to let her work, even if it was only a part time job of some sort. But Mick wouldn't budge.

'You don't understand.' He said, 'You've left that life behind now. Why don't you have a chat to Mum, she can give you a few pointers on time fillers. She always has plenty of things to do.'

'Such as?'

'I don't know. Charity stuff. Committees.'

'But that's for older women.'

'Well speak to her anyway,' He'd shrugged, pulling on his jacket, 'I'm sure she could get you involved with something.'

Their breakfast conversation had left her feeling depressed and so she had taken herself into Abbotsbridge. At least there she could at least be amongst the bustle of everyday life. And now dark brown eyes were looking at her with interest; she wondered what he wanted.

'Nice dress.' He looked at the display in the window. 'You'd look good in that.'

'Really?' She gave a careless shrug, her eyes deliberately avoiding his. Then looking up, she saw the Town Hall clock and an excuse to escape. 'Sorry, I can't stop,' she said, 'I'm meeting Mick for lunch.'

'I'm surprised he has the time.' The smile was there again; eyes full of mocking amusement. 'Normally, no one can prise him off the site during the day.'

'Well today he's made an exception!'

'Dear, touched a nerve have I?'

'Just go away Andy!' She turned to leave but he blocked her way.

'Oh come on, there's no need to be like that!'

'Leave me alone!' She was angry now. His words, his nearness made her even more aware of her disenchantment with her own life. She wanted him so badly, but it was impossible. He was with Ella now. The wedding was due to take place on Saturday. Pushing him away she began to run back towards the High Street to where her car was parked.

Watching her, an amused smile crossed Andy's face. There was no doubt about it, Nina's current home situation made her ripe for an affair. He remembered how much fun she had been; the sex had been incredible. Such a shame he was committed now, looking forward to a life with Ella, otherwise he might well have been tempted to start things up again.

Friday 28th August

Mick Taylor parked his new blue MGB GT in the Red Lion car park. He checked his watch. 8.30. It was boys' night out tonight. Andy Macayne's stag party and he had the dubious job of acting as minder. Why did he always get the jobs no one else wanted he wondered? And why was it that Bob Macayne had to go to the lengths of calling him in to talk to him, making him feel as if he was a small boy in charge of a friend on a school trip? Watch his back. Don't let them spike his drinks. Keep him away from women and get him home by 1.00.

He knew it was going to be a tall order, because everyone else in the party was hell bent on making sure Andy got a good send off. It was what stag nights were all about, a good laugh and a bit of fun at someone else's expense. He remembered his own, that had been an absolute riot. A pub crawl through Abbotsbridge, finishing up at the Roundabout Strip Club where he had ended up on stage in the clutches of a voluptuous brunette, holding the pieces of her outfit for her as she had gradually peeled down to the buff. It had, of course, predictably nearly got out of hand, as egged on by his crowd the stripper, whose name was Imogen, began helping him out of his own clothes. He had been so drunk that he had very little recollection of what was going on. Thankfully the bouncers had been quick to react and he had been promptly escorted off the stage clutching his trousers. He laughed to himself as he thought of it. He had woken up with a dreadful hangover the next day, but it didn't matter. He was sensible enough to have arranged his stag night the week before the wedding, not the night before like Andy. Everything about this evening made him feel uneasy, because he knew from experience that anything connected with Bob's only son ultimately spelt trouble.

'Are you going to the big bash tomorrow then Tad?'

Tad shook his head. 'How about you?'

Tad was sitting at the bar of the Mill having an early evening drink with Tony Rutherford, his accountant. It was around eight thirty and people were beginning to drift into the club, ordering drinks and finding seats. The Kinks '*Till the End of the Day*' was playing, a song which had become the Club's anthem, used regularly to kick off each evening's entertainment, ever since it had opened its doors to the public. Tapping his feet, Tad felt relaxed, a whisky in his hand watching the club, his baby, gradually come to life.

'Yes, Fiona's keen to go.' Tony replied, his elbow on the bar. 'It's an out of town do. The reception's being held in the grounds of some big house near the church. Huge marquee. They're really pushing the boat out.'

'Typical Mel Carpenter, everything to excess.' Tad gave a derisory snort. 'What's wrong with St Mark's for the wedding for heaven's sake?'

'Nothing to do with Mel,' Tony shook his head, 'Ella's done it all with her grandmother. Apparently she wanted to get married in the village where she grew up. As you can imagine, Mel was very put out, but I gather Ella did let her put the guest list together.'

'Ah that's why we've been left off.' Tad understood now. He gave an amused laugh. 'Can't see Andy Macayne as the marrying type, can you? Do you think he'll turn up?'

'Well,' Tony looked at his friend, 'if I was marrying a girl like Ella I'd sure as hell turn up.' He looked at Tad for a moment. 'Am I right in thinking she was involved with your boy before this thing with Andy?'

'Yes, for a while, but it was a matey thing. Of course Faye saw trouble there, you know, what with Mel being Ella's mother. Thought some of her charming habits might have rubbed off on her daughter. I think she was relieved when Matt left with the band.'

'I've always liked Ella,' Tony tipped back the last of his whisky and set the glass on the bar, 'Apart from her obvious physical charms, she's a got an old head on young shoulders that one. She's certainly worked hard with her sister-in -law to get their business going. Ask around and I think you'll find that unlike her mother, people have a lot of time for her.'

'Don't get me wrong,' Tad shook his head. 'Personally I have no problems with Ella. She's a great girl. I would have been quite happy had romance blossomed with Matt, but,' there was a hint of regret in his voice. 'It obviously wasn't to be.'

Tony looked at his watch. 'I'd better get back, we've an early start tomorrow, the wedding's at 11.00 and I did promise Fiona I'd be home by nine thirty tonight.' He picked up his brief case. 'I'll have those costings ready for you next week.'

'Thanks.' Tad raised a hand in farewell. 'Night Tony.'

He watched him leave, then immediately focussed his attention on a noisy group of arrivals crowding around the far end of the bar. He saw Mick Taylor among the sea of faces. Andy's stag party had landed here with Mick looking tense and worried. Minding Andy he expected, under strict instructions from Bob Macayne. A cheer went up and he saw the crowd part and Andy climb up onto one of the bar stools. He looked as if he had had quite a few already, his eye on a couple of girls who had just come up to the bar to buy drinks. One of them, a small brown haired girl in a tight red dress leaned towards him to say something and they all laughed.

Tad turned away for a moment, watching the dance floor as the disco geared up a notch and the strobe cut in. Although this was a young scene he enjoyed it, watching everyone coming together to have a good time. Out of the corner of his eye he caught sight of Andy Macayne and one of the others in the group, coming onto the dance floor with the two girls. Tad watched with interest. The music was fast, but Andy and his partner immediately clung to each other, moving slowly round and round, his hands cupping her buttocks tightly. He was gazing down into her face as they chatted.

Tad felt movement at his arm. Faye had joined him.

'What's he doing with her?' She nodded out into the half light.

'It's his stag night.'

'Oh yes, the wedding.'

'Looks as if he's had a few already.' Tad watched Andy thoughtfully. 'Let's hope we don't get any trouble.'

'Looking at that behaviour, I think the only one who may be heading for trouble is Ella.' Faye said as she raised her arm to attract the barman's attention. 'Have a drink with me?'

'Sure, I'll have another Glenfiddich.' Tad eased his empty glass along the bar.

They sat together drinking and talking for a while, eventually making their way up to the first floor office which over looked the dance floor. There they spent the rest of the evening discussing their forthcoming holiday in Switzerland, renovation plans for the Blue Lion Hotel and Faye's interest in an empty baker's shop in Gane Street which she thought had potential for a new retail project she had planned.

Just before midnight they went back downstairs; the club was thinning, about half full. Waitresses were clearing tables; the music had softened as a prelude to the end of the evening.

Suddenly Mick Taylor was at Tad's elbow.

'Have you seen Andy?' He sounded frantic.

'No, we've been up in the office all evening,' Tad looked at Faye with an expression which spoke of the inevitability of becoming involved with this problem, 'When did *you* last see him?'

'About fifteen minutes ago - he was here at the bar. I was feeling quite pleased with myself. I've managed to keep him reasonably sober and upright and now this!' He held his hands up in a gesture of helplessness. 'Bob will kill me!'

'Is anyone else missing?' Faye looked towards the bar where the rest of the party sat. '

'No, apart from Andy everyone is there.

'Looked in the gents?'

Mick nodded.

'What about the two girls who were with you?'

'Sharon and Linda? I think they went around 11.30.'

'Stay here with Faye,' Tad said firmly. 'I'll just have a look around outside, he can't be far away.'

Letting himself out by a side door Tad walked out into the floodlit car park. There were only a dozen or so cars dotted around and a coach tucked into the far corner. He stopped and listened. The night was warm, a soft breeze blowing; a full moon hung in the willows. He could hear the rush of the river and not far away the unmistakable murmur of voices. Silently he moved across the grass towards the river where two poplars stood close together.

Between them was a deep cleft in the bank frequently used by fishermen. Tonight, however, he could see the outline of three figures, two female, one male and the sound of soft laughter. As he watched the silhouettes he knew instinctively from their movement and the accompanying giggles that clothes were being removed and some sort of three way sexual activity was about to take place.

Tad moved away, wondering how he could abort Andy's ménage à trois without the panic stricken Mick getting involved. An idea came to him and he began walking quickly back towards the Club. Minutes later he reappeared with the Mill's canine deterrent, Bruce, holding tightly onto his collar. Reaching the edge of the car park he bent down, found a discarded piece of wood and hurled it towards the trees. 'Fetch!' He hissed, and watched as the dog launched himself eagerly across the grass towards the river bank.

Saturday 29th August

'Darling you look absolutely radiant!' Laura, standing in her bedroom at Little Court, smiled and stood back to look at Ella as the dressmaker zipped her into her cream silk wedding dress.

'I think the veil now Sonia.' She said to the dressmaker as she continued to gaze appreciatively at her granddaughter.

Sonia Gregory had come highly recommended and she had been worth every penny. She watched the small blonde as she fixed the veil and pinned it gently to Ella's hair before walking around her teasing it out and arranging corkscrew tendrils of hair around her face. Pleased with the overall result, she joined Laura, nodding with satisfaction.

'We haven't quite finished,' Laura walked over to the dressing table and pulled out a long black velvet box. Opening it, she lifted the choker out gently, a large square antique cut emerald set in gold as the centre piece with two strands of perfectly matching pearls attached, finished with an unusual circular gold clasp.

'Can you lift the veil please?' She asked Sonia, as she stepped behind Ella and draped the pearls around her neck.

'Turn around.' A contented sigh escaped from Laura's lips. 'Absolutely wonderful! Take a look at yourself in the mirror.'

Ella crossed the bedroom and stood in front of the cheval mirror, unable to believe she was looking at herself. Cream had been a good choice; it complimented her colouring exactly, as did the pearls.

There was a knock on the door and it opened slightly.

'Can we come in?'

A small, dark head peaked around the door. It was Jenny, Issy and Rachel behind her. They walked into the room and stood there. Wearing matching green full length empire line dresses - Issy and Rachel in eau de nil and Jenny in emerald - their hair was pinned up in a similar fashion to Ella's and decorated with small white flowers.

'Wow!' Jenny's eyes were wide.

'Ella!' Rachel's mouth hung open.

'You look....incredible!' Issy was, for one of those rare moments in her life, struggling to find the words.

'It's fantastic!' Ella laughed. 'Thank you so much!' she said, kissing both Sonia and her grandmother.

'We came to say the car's arrived for us.' Jenny said. 'And that Liam is here.'

'Send him up.' Laura was eager to show Ella off. 'And Mel too if she's there.'

'She isn't; she went straight to the church.' Issy answered. 'You wouldn't want her here anyway Mrs Kendrick, not the mood she's in.'

'You're quite right my dear,' Laura agreed. 'I probably wouldn't. Now shoo the lot of you and please, send Liam up.'

The three girls disappeared downstairs. Ella stood at the window watching as Little Court's gardener Ted Williams, who was chauffeuring for the day, helped them into the back of Laura's black Bentley. As the car slid gracefully away down the driveway, she turned away from the window and saw Liam standing in the doorway, splendid in his grey morning suit, a bouquet of cream roses in his hand.

'You look like a fairy tale princess.' He said, smiling.

'She certainly does.' Laura nodded in agreement.

Crossing the room he gave Ella a light kiss on the cheek and handed her the bouquet. 'Are you ready?' he asked.

'Oh yes,' she said as she took his hand and they made their way out of the room, down the stairs and into the waiting limousine.

Villagers and invited guests were packed into the small church of All Hallows. At the front of the church Mel sat peevish and irritable, trying her best to ignore her father and his wife sitting beside her. This was to have been *her* big day. The day when she showed all of Abbotsbridge how weddings were done properly. Instead she had been denied that and dragged out here to Meridan Cross to sit cheek by jowl with every piece of local riff raff imaginable.

Hearing a noise she turned to look back up the aisle, wondering if Ella and Liam might have arrived, but all she could see was the vicar, silhouetted against the strong sunlight as he stood waiting in the church porch. She frowned, noticing Jenny, Rachel Sylvester and Isobel Llewellyn were now standing with him. Whatever had possessed Ella to choose those three great lumps for bridesmaids, she wondered, when there were so many small delightful children in Abbotsbridge. Small flower girls would have looked quite exquisite. It just was not fair that besides the invitations, she had been shut out of every part of this wedding. Still, at least there she had managed to get some of her own back, excluding those she felt were not suitable, like the Benedicts. Especially the Benedicts.

She took her gaze from the porch, scanning the pews. Her eyes rested on the Miller clan. Nelson Miller and his two lads Ash and Rowan looked strange in their grey suits, dark hair curling around their collars. She tried to tear her mind away from the fact that more than likely underneath his jacket Nelson had his trousers tied up with string. They were didicois, uneducated yobs with olive skins and black hair. She remembered that Nelson had been the first generation of his family to have given up the nomadic life to live in a house. Oh yes, she knew all about him and his petty thieving, and his womanising which had resulted in at least half a dozen illegitimate children dotted around the county. How embarrassing it was to have such a cultured gathering rubbing elbows with the likes of him and his two loutish sons.

Mel then looked across at Andy, with Nick as best man, sitting beside him. She was glad Ella had suggested her brother for the role as that had given her the opportunity to leave Mick Taylor and that tarty wife of his off the guest list. She was a dreadful creature and she was sure Andy must have had a momentary lapse of sanity to have ever been involved with anyone like that. Still, it had all worked out well in the end. She'd ended up marrying the gullible Mick instead. A far better match, Mel concluded, given Jack Taylor's working class background.

The sound of voices at the entrance to the church caused her to turn and look back again. She saw Laura and a small blonde woman making their way down the aisle. She stood up to let them in as they reached her pew, frowning at the stranger. Who was she and why had Laura brought her into the family pew? Another local intruder she guessed as she sat down with an indignant sigh.

Then the organ came to life, the sound of Mendelssohn filling the church. She saw Andy look round, saw the rapt expression on his face, and turned, following his gaze. Her daughter was coming towards her on Liam's arm looking like a Hollywood movie star in the most beautiful dress she had ever seen. She heard the gasps and murmurs from the congregation and then Ella were standing facing the vicar, Andy by her side. Bob turned in his pew, looked across at her and smiled. How handsome he looked in his morning suit, she thought. And seeing him now, with his crown of black hair, deep brown eyes and sensuous mouth she realised how foolish she was. True, she might have lost the opportunity to organise the wedding of the year, but in missing out on this she had accidentally discovered something else; something far more important and relevant in her life.

It was when she complained to him about being sidelined in all the arrangements that it happened. Bob was annoyed at her attitude, saying her father would be there and she should be concentrating her energies on how best to approach him. His lack of sympathy made her irritable. 'If this is so important to you Bob!' she had shouted at him. 'I would have thought that my services would have been worth more than a bloody grand!'

'Is that all you're doing it for?!' He'd said, gripping her arms tightly, his face flushed with anger. 'The money? What about…' he hesitated for a moment, 'What about us?'

She'd been taken aback. 'Us?'

'You and me Mel,' His face had become serious, 'and a life together once all this comes good.'

'You really mean that?'

He'd nodded and pulled her to him, his mouth tender on her own. She felt tears threatening. She'd had no idea this is what he wanted. It had always been her secret dream and now it was going to become a reality. She was overwhelmed; her hands went to her face to staunch the wetness. Seeing her distress, he'd smiled and stroked her hair. 'You silly woman. Don't' you realise what an important part of my life you've become? I can't let you go. Not now, not ever.'

His revelations made the job of persuading her father to part with Fox Cottage and a parcel of woodland even more vital. For the sooner it was completed, the sooner she could abandon Liam to start her new life. With Bob.

As she heard the first notes of *'Love Divine All Love's Excelling'* the smile returned to her face and she picked up her Order of Service and began to sing.

TEN

Sunday 30th August

Laura stood at the water's edge feeding the birds. It was late morning on the day after the wedding and everyone had now gone. The house had been full of bustle for a while as people surfaced and took breakfast before saying their goodbyes. Now it was quiet, back to normal.

Throwing the last of the bread she stood for a moment watching the sparkle of sun on the clear water as it flowed by, agitating the soft green tendrils of weed just below its surface.

She turned to walk back to the house. The men were dismantling the marquee, pulling out tent pegs, rolling up canvas. Soon, apart from a few scars on the grass it would be as if it had never happened. It had been a wonderful day; the caterers had done a splendid job - champagne chilled to perfection, food in abundance. The cake quite spectacular. The expense, like that of the dress, had been well worth it. Ella had been one of the most beautiful brides she had ever seen. In fact they made a striking couple. Ella the pale skinned English rose and Andy Macayne, with his olive skinned Mediterranean looks. But where had he come from? That he appeared to have been in Ella's life all along and yet not worth a mention until the engagement seemed very strange. And what of Matt? Ella's engagement to Andy had come within weeks of her stay here. Too quickly. Something had happened and she wanted to get to the bottom of it. There had never been a chance to ask before. A time alone with Ella when she had she felt comfortable enough to broach the subject. The opportunity eventually arose when Ella went up to change. Following her to her room, she knocked the door and opened it, discovering her granddaughter struggling with the zip of her wedding dress, her veil tossed across the blue counterpane of the bed.

'Here let me help you,' she said reaching out to gently ease the zip downwards. While Ella freshened up in the bathroom, Laura returned the choker to its velvet box and covered the dress in a polythene wrap before hanging it in the wardrobe.

Emerging from the bathroom Ella took her going away outfit, a beige linen dress and matching jacket, from the back of the door and slipped them on, then sitting in front of the mirror she brushed her hair and reapplied her make up before slipping her feet into pale green leather shoes.

As she retrieved the matching bag and checked her hair in the mirror, Laura broke the silence.

'Ella, my darling, before you go, can I ask you something?'

'Of course,' Ella turned from the mirror, a curious half smile on her face.

'What happened to Matt?'

'Matt?' Ella gave a soft laugh as they stepped out onto the landing. 'We all got him horribly wrong, you know. All that business about being shy, about having his feelings locked away.'

'Meaning?'

'He already belonged to someone else. I heard about his engagement a week after I returned to Abbotsbridge. It was to some girl in London who worked for his record company.'

'Oh Ella!' Laura put a hand to her face, 'But when I spoke to him, he said….' she shook her head, 'I was so sure.....'

From somewhere below came the sound of Andy's voice, calling to say their taxi was waiting.

'It doesn't matter,' Ella's hand was on her arm, she was smiling, 'I'm glad it did happen. I'd been friends with Andy for a long time. As soon as he heard the news about Matt he came to find me. Told me he wanted to marry me; that he'd always loved me and wanted to spend his life making me happy! You said sometimes love was waiting for the right opportunity to show itself. Well you were right! Even if it wasn't in the way you thought!' She leaned over and kissed Laura's cheek. 'Thank you *so* much for everything. I promise I'll phone as soon as we're back.' Then she was gone, dashing down the stairs into the arms of her new husband. Laura stood and watched as the taxi disappeared down the driveway, followed by a flurry of confetti from pursuing well-wishers. Now in the silence of an empty Little Court the day after, she still remained stunned at what Ella had told her. 'I was so sure about that young man.' she said to herself as she walked back to the house. 'How could I have got it so wrong?'

'Tad why ever didn't you tell me this before?'

'It went completely out of my mind, we've been so busy.'

Faye laughed softly. 'Sounds typical of the way Andy would spend his last night of freedom.'

'Yes,' Tad couldn't resist a smile.

They were having a relaxing evening drink on the patio, watching the sun setting behind the trees at the end of the garden and discussing the week's events at the club. It was when Faye mentioned Andy's stag night that Tad remembered.

'So what happened after you found them?' He had Faye's full attention now.

'Well I had to do something. If Mick had found out, all hell would have broken loose, wouldn't it? So I went back into the club and let Bruce out. Threw a stick for him.' He looked pleased with himself. 'It did the trick. He flushed the three of them out just like that!' he said with a snap of his fingers, 'The two girls fled along the river bank carrying their clothes, and I have to hand it to Macayne, he wandered into the club five minutes later looking as if butter wouldn't melt in his mouth. Said he'd gone out to get some fresh air.' He laughed. 'Do you know he even asked what all the commotion along the river bank was about. Make no mistake; he's a cool bastard, that one.'

Faye raised her wineglass and drank, savouring the taste of the wine. 'Seems to me he and Ella are a match made in heaven.'

'Faye what is it about her that rankles you so much?'

'Oh I don't know,' she replied, reaching for the wine bottle to refill her glass. 'There was something about her right from the start. She was too good to be true, all smiles and prettiness. Of course, you men were all taken in, but after a while I could see what she was up to. She was a trouble maker, just like her mother and I don't regret doing the things I did to part them, even though it went against everything I believe in.'

Faye realised the wine had loosened her tongue, that she was admitting to things Tad knew nothing about. But perhaps now was the right time to get it out of her system. She hated deceit and this secret had been festering for too long now. She knew he would be angry, but not for long. He loved her, he would forgive her; she knew he would. After all, she had only been protecting their son.

'What sort of things?' Tad was taken aback by the savageness in her expression. For the first time in all the years they had been married it appeared she had kept something from him and it hurt him to think this could happen in a relationship others envied for its closeness and honesty.

'You didn't see it, did you? How she was trying to make a fool of Matt?' Faye's eyes met his without a trace of guilt or embarrassment. 'Playing him off against Andy Macayne. I saw it one night at the club. Letting Andy kiss her and then looking up at Matt to gauge his reaction. He was about to be handed the opportunity of a lifetime. I couldn't let her wreck that for him with her silly games. I had to act Tad; I had to put a stop to it!'

Tad looked at her curiously. 'And exactly how did you do that Faye?'

'Oh it was just little things really. Like forgetting to pass on her congratulations to Matt when the band reached number one. And leaving her off the VIPs guest list for the celebrations here afterwards.'

'And Cassandra, was that you too?'

She nodded. 'I thought if she saw Matt enjoying himself with someone else she'd take the hint. Unfortunately it wasn't enough. When I learned they'd been in Meridan Cross together I knew I had to do something to finish it once and for all, so I created Belinda, the fictitious fiancée. I knew Mel would be itching to tell Ella. She wanted to split them up as much as I did. It was just the news she'd been waiting for.'

'Faye, ' Tad closed his eyes. 'How could you?'

She looked at him, the fierceness in her expression returning. 'Believe me I'm not proud of myself, but it was the only way I could think of to get her out of Matt's life permanently. She was playing dangerous games and I couldn't let her interfere with his future. I did it for him, you must understand that. For him.'

Tad was just about to reply when a figure materialized from the shadows of the wisteria covering the side of the house. Carrying a guitar case, and clad in dusty denims he stopped on the edge of the patio, regarding them both silently.

'Matt!' The surprise on Faye's face, melted into a smile. 'Well! This is a surprise! Where have you come from?'

'The Isle of Wight Festival - it finished last night,' He said. 'The others went out by helicopter, but I wanted to come home so I had to take my chances with everyone else queuing for the ferry. It's been a nightmare!'

'Darling it's wonderful to see you,' With an uncomfortable smile, Faye got to her feet and pulled up another chair, 'Here,' she patted the seat, 'Sit yourself down. Are you hungry?'

'No, ate on the way.' He said, dropping the case and sinking wearily into the comfort of the patio chair.

'How about a drink? There's lager, or wine.'

'Lager please.' He gave her a tired smile then turned his attention back to Tad. 'It took me an age to get here. Even after I'd got a place on the ferry, the snarl ups in Southampton were dreadful.'

'So, how was the festival?' Tad looked at him, wondering whether he had heard any of the conversation going on prior to his arrival, but unable to see anything in his son's face other than tiredness.

'Much better than last year!' Matt grinned, 'We were due on Friday night, just before the Who, but everything was behind schedule and we actually ended up on stage just before midnight. The atmosphere was fantastic!' he smiled thoughtfully, deciding perhaps it was better his father didn't know about the a permanent smell of dope that wafted across the site or the two girls who had stripped off and clambered onto the stage, offering themselves quite blatantly to Geoff before security guards despatched them back into the crowd.

'How many people were there?'

'Over half a million they reckon.'

Tad whistled.

'There was trouble though. Some people thought it should have been a free concert, so they wrecked the perimeter fence and got in. There were so many of them they couldn't be stopped. In the end the organisers just had to let them in. It was chaotic!' He shook his head, 'We had a great time though! The music. Everyone coming together. I heard because of the gatecrashers the organisers made a big loss. They reckon there's a chance some bands probably won't get paid. Don't worry though, we were OK.' He gave an amused smile. 'Our new label Scorpio wouldn't dream of doing anything for anyone without cold hard cash in their hands.'

They were still laughing when Faye appeared with a glass and a cold bottle of lager which she placed on the table in front of her son. Matt pushed himself up from his chair, half filled the glass, took a long drink then relaxed, tilting his head back and closing his eyes.

'Boy, I needed that,' He looked at them both and grinned for a moment. Then his eyes settled themselves on his mother and the smile suddenly died.

'So, how long are you staying?' Faye said brightly, pleased that he was home.

'Flying visit. I'll be off first thing tomorrow,' He said abruptly, 'back to the smoke. Scorpio are setting up a Far East tour, we'll probably be spending Christmas in Australia.'

'Oh Matt!' Faye was disappointed, 'I was hoping you'd be here for Christmas this year.'

'Mother, you know what I do doesn't come under the category of a regular nine to five job,' His eyes met hers and held them, 'And if I remember rightly you didn't mind in the beginning, in fact you were keen for me to go.'

'Yes, I know I was, darling.' She asked, ignoring the irritation in his tone. He was tired she decided, what he needed was a good night's sleep.

'Well, when can we expect you back for a longer visit?' Tad asked.

'Um, January, then a rest, then into Europe again, but only France and Germany this time.'

'You'll wear yourself out.' Tad laughed.

'We won't be flavour of the month for ever.' Matt said in a very matter of fact way as he poured the remaining lager into his glass. 'We have to grab every opportunity now. And sometimes that means having to let go of the things that really mean a lot to you.' His eyes met his mother's again as he brought the glass to his lips. 'Or having other people do it for you. In your best interest of course.' He drained his glass and got to his feet, picking up his guitar case. 'I think I'll turn in, if you don't mind. I'm absolutely wrecked.'

'Of course,' Faye smiled, getting to her feet. 'It's good to have you back Matt, even if it's a flying visit. You know I've missed you so much.'

'Yes, I expect you have Mother,' Matt replied, a chill in his eyes as he looked at her. He turned to his father. ''Night Dad,' he said giving him a gentle pat on the shoulder, 'see you in the morning.'

Pushing open the French doors he disappeared into the house, leaving Tad and Faye staring at each other in silence.

'He heard us didn't he?' Faye said, her voice barely a whisper.

'Unfortunately,' Tad said with a sigh, 'I think he did.'

Matt carried the holdall into his room and dropped it onto the floor, tucking the guitar under the bed. He pulled his curtains and turned on the light, walking over to the mirrored wardrobe doors to look at himself. This was the room where long ago she had stood so close to him and where he had resisted the urge to kiss her. In the silence that now surrounded him, he could almost feel her still there standing in his room in her blue dress, admiring his record collection and his guitars on the day she had come to lunch. Telling him how his eyes reminded her of Paul McCartney's. He had been different then. Tall, slim, a youth. Unsure of himself. He looked at his reflection now, shoulders broader, his body filled out, no longer a naive boy.

He had travelled a long, hard road full of disappointments. Disappointments brought about partly by fate and partly by missed opportunities triggered by his own lack of confidence. The news of her engagement had taken him completely by surprise. She had never mentioned anything of it when they had been together in Meridan Cross and the realisation he had lost her to Andy of all people was more than he could bear.

That evening he went out with the band, got very drunk and finally lost his virginity. He had been saving himself for Ella, turning down all the offers and opportunities fans and willing groupies presented him with. Why should he bother with milk when he could have the cream he used to joke with Baz. Now he'd been cheated of that experience, there didn't seem much point holding back. The sex, which took place in the hallway of his house with a nameless redhead, amounted to no more than a frantic shedding of clothes, followed by five minutes of swift coital activity. He could hardly remember anything of it the next morning when he woke alone with a banging head and one hundred pounds missing from his wallet. Women, he confided miserably to Baz later that day, were bad news.

'You've still got your music.' Baz had said, slapping him on the back in an effort to cheer him up. 'That's one love that will never let you down.'

And Baz had been right. In the end music was indeed his salvation. He threw himself back into the new album. They completed well ahead of schedule and were invited to play at the Isle of Wight Festival. Once released *Back in Business* sat at number one for five weeks; three singles from it would dominate the charts well into the New Year. Six months later, their contract with Centaur came up for renewal; but because of the company's reluctance to send them Stateside, they signed to Scorpio, a label with American connections, instead. There was talk of a tour to the Far East at the end of the year, followed by an American tour in 1971. Everything was coming good again and he found his positive outlook returning. Then quite by accident he let Ella back into his thoughts. He wondered how things were back in Abbotsbridge, whether the engagement was still holding. Of course, common sense told him he should leave well enough alone, but some sixth sense kept telling him he should go home, that things might have changed between her and capricious, unreliable Andy. But Europe beckoned and he had to put such thoughts on hold. Before he left however, he promised himself that once the Isle of Wight Festival was over and his time was his own, he would return to Abbotsbridge to find her.

He had been true to his promise, driven home, tired but hopeful. But that hope had died when quite by accident he had run into Mick Taylor as he stopped to buy petrol in Green Street. As he stood filling up his car, listening to Mick break the news of Ella's wedding, he couldn't believe he was too late. Leaving the filling station he had driven back through town to his parents' house in Portway in a daze, his dreams in ruins.

At the front door, unable to make anyone hear, he skirted around the back of the house, only to stumble into the second great shock of the evening. His mother's confession.

The wretchedness he felt on hearing the news of the wedding had slowly turned to anger as he heard her admissions. As he stood listening, the blame for his current situation took a sudden subtle shift. Ella slipping through his fingers hadn't been down to his shyness alone. How could he have ever stood a chance with her when his mother, someone he had loved and trusted, had been at work behind his back, deliberately keeping them apart?

He pulled the toilet bag from his holdall and walked into the en suite bathroom. As he squeezed toothpaste onto the brush thoughts of Ella and his mother swam around in his mind. He felt betrayed, empty. He realised he didn't belong in this small provincial West Country town any more. It had become a place where memories brought only pain and sadness. Maybe it was time to move on. To close the door on yesterday and say goodbye to Ella and Abbotsbridge for good.

Monday 7th September

Andy Macayne stretched out on his sun bed feeling the sun's warmth on his face. This was bliss. Two weeks in Corfu - sun, sea, ouzo and sex. He opened one eye and looked at Ella, long, golden limbs glistening with sun oil, relaxing beside him. From behind his sunglasses he watched three young men walk around the pool towards them, their gaze lingering quite blatantly on his wife's body as they passed. He smiled to himself. It was great to be the subject of such envy. To have something others wanted.

All in all it had been pretty good so far. This might not be the way he'd planned things, but he had to admit he liked Ella. She wasn't given to tantrums or sulking like the over indulged Annabel. Neither was she like the weird arty-farty caftan wearing Bryony. No, she was a normal, sensible girl and her family were loaded. He thought of his new red Mercedes waiting back at home; a gift to him from her grandmother. Yes it certainly was all good stuff so far and there had been some interesting moments too. For a start she was a virgin. He had been so sure that Benedict had got there before him. He had an instinct for these things, but on this occasion he had been proved wrong. In some ways being the first had made things more exciting. However the sex had been disappointing. There was no fire, no participation. She was virginal, compliant and gentle. The new wife wanting to please, expecting her husband always to take the lead. If this was what married sex was going to be like, he was bored already. His thoughts immediately turned to Nina. He remembered her face on the day they had met outside Langleys. Oh yes the old chemistry was still there. And the way things were currently between her and Mick, she was his for the taking. He smiled; if he played his cards right he just might be able to have the best of both worlds.

Wednesday 16th September

'Welcome back Ella!' Sitting behind her reception desk, Trudi looked up and smiled as Ella walked into One Plus One on her first working day since returning from honeymoon.

'Thank you! I gather from Jen that everything has been fine while I've been away.'

'Yes, I think we all managed to keep the ship afloat in the captain's absence.' She laughed as she picked up a handful of green slips. 'These are the messages which were left for you personally. There's one from Don. He called on Monday morning, asked if you'd contact him as soon as you'd settled yourself back in.'

'I wonder what he wants?' Ella said, collecting up her handbag and walking towards her office.

She was on the phone when Trudi tapped the door and entered with a cup of coffee. As she left the College switchboard put her through to Don's office and she heard his familiar tones.

'Hello there. Glad to be back?'

'Yes.'

'You didn't worry about the place while you were away I hope.'

'Certainly not. The girls have done a great job. '

'Good.'

'So what can I do for you?'

It's more what I can do for you. I wanted to talk to you because I wondered whether you would be interested in looking at another agency with me.'

'Oh Don,' Ella hesitated, 'I'm not sure whether we're ready to expand yet.'

'Come on, where's your sense of adventure?'

'Alive and very well thank you, but I really think we need to learn to walk before we can run.'

'All I ask is that you take a look. The present owner is in his fifties, wants to slow down, open a small chain of stationery shops instead. Says it's a less energetic occupation and the profit margin is higher. This is a going concern, in profit. You could quite easily run with it for a while. Sit back and plan your moves, ease any changes in and that way it would be less disruptive to both the business and the staff.'

'And exactly where is this place Don?'

'It's two places, actually. Taunton and Wellington. Are you game?'

'Two! Well yes I'll take a look but I'm not promising anything. Can I bring Jenny?'

'Of course. How about Friday morning?'
'Fine. I'll pick you up from home at 9.30.'

Friday 18th September

'What do you think then?' Jenny asked as she looked out of the front window of Derek Emerson's office, watching people as they passed back and forth along Taunton High Street. Don Lattimer and Derek had left them to talk it over and headed for the Castle Green Hotel where they were all to have lunch together, with a table booked for 12.30.

Ella walked around the room making a mental note of what she had seen and heard that morning. She nodded.

'Both places have all the right ingredients. Centrally placed. Good client base.'

'What about the staff?'

'Seem very capable. It feels good.' She smiled then her expression clouded. 'Only one drawback though.'

'What?'

'I'll need to work between here and Wellington. Get to know the staff, get a good feel of how the place runs. I'm not sure Andy will like me being on the road a lot.'

'Does that mean a no then?'

'Not at all,' Ella said confidently. 'It just means I'll have to work that little bit harder to keep him happy.' She looked around the room once more before turning back to Jenny and giving her an enthusiastic nod. 'Let's go for it shall we?'

'I think so!' Jenny grinned. 'I'll get Tony Rutherford in to check over the books and set up a meeting with Mike Langdon of Lloyds next week to discuss finance. We'll take it from there.'

Wednesday 23rd September

An enthusiastic round of applause accompanied the fall of the curtain at the Queens Theatre in Kingsford. As the lights went up people began to leave their seats, heading for the bar, eager to make the most of the fifteen minute intermission.

Evening bag tucked under her arm, Mel headed for the cloakroom, leaving Bob to retrieve their pre-ordered drinks. As he sat waiting in a window seat for her return, Miles Anderson appeared around a corner and cut through the chatting groups of theatre goers to join him.

'Bob. Enjoying the play?'

'Yes, there's nothing like a good tragedy Miles, puts life in its right perspective don't you think?'

'And how's my little negotiator? Is she here tonight?' Miles scanned the room.

'Powdering her nose,' Bob replied, savouring a mouthful of whisky. 'And if you're looking for an update; progress, I'm afraid is still very slow.'

'Problems Bob?'

'Problems,' Bob nodded. 'I did think the wedding might be a turning point, but unfortunately not. Even a recent family lunch doesn't seem to have done much to melt the ice. You were right, he's a stubborn old sod, but I have to say Mel's working really hard to gain his trust! There will be a breakthrough, I'm sure. It will just take a little longer than planned.'

'Bob,' Miles said reproachfully, 'I hope you're not dragging your feet!'

'And why would I do that?' Bob hissed indignantly.

'I can think of one thousand good reasons can't you? I know you're unhappy about having to pay her yourself.' Miles said, his ice cold gaze switching between Bob and something across the room behind him. 'All I will say is, if this lack of progress continues it could put an entirely different complexion on our arrangement. Just remember, you have to speculate to accumulate. And a grand against the benefits I'm offering you is chicken feed!'

'But Miles I'm telling the truth!' Bob got to his feet angrily as with a curt nod Miles turned and walked away.

'Bastard!' He swore under his breath as he sat down, then switched to his warmest smile as with a waft of perfume, Mel pulled up the chair next to him and picked up her drink.

ELEVEN

Tuesday 6th October

'Oh I do love all this Ella, it's so now!'

Annabel Langley gazed around the dining room, her eyes shining partly from admiration, partly from envy as she took in the French blue Hessian covered walls. In the middle of the room sat a large circular white table set for dinner with deep blue Poole pottery and co-ordinating place mats and napkins. A matching white unit ran the length of one wall, its surfaces dotted with pieces of glass and porcelain. 'Very chic, don't you think so Nina darling?'

Nina nodded, glass in hand, watching Ella, Annabel and Bryony as they stood together; a mutual admiration society.

'I just love the paintings in the lounge,' Bryony was saying. 'Such vibrant colours. Where did you buy them?'

'Actually they were a wedding present. A friend of my grandmother's paints. He did them for me.'

'Yes, they're really gorgeous,' Annabel joined in, 'Would he paint something for me if I commissioned him? Daddy would just adore something like that for his birthday.'

'Of course, I'll give you his telephone number.'

Nina closed her eyes and turned away. Looking at the three of them standing there she felt as if she had landed on another planet. In fact Annabel's plummy approval for everything Ella was beginning to irritate her. Of course she had expected this. She had not wanted to come in the first place, but realised getting out of Andy and Ella's house warming dinner party wasn't an option. She had gazed at Chelwood Lodge in amazement as they drove through wrought iron gates and up the gravelled driveway. Elegant and red-bricked it was fronted by a stone portico, Virgina creeper clinging to its walls, while around it lay two acres of beautiful gardens. In comparison with their four bedroom home, it was a small stately home.

'Grand isn't it?' Mick gazed at the house as they pulled up outside.

'It's enormous.'

'Envious?'

'Just a little.' She nodded, wondering if she would have been mistress of this had she married Andy.

'Would you like an older place then?'

'Why? Are you planning on buying something like this?'

'Yes.' He smiled secretively.

'Where is it? Tell me!' She was full of girlish excitement.

'You know the site at Bracken Down?'

'Yes. But I don't want one of those, they're.....'

'It's not one of those,' He interrupted, 'It's the old farmhouse on the site. Bob wanted to knock it down, but I could see what it could be turned into. It's beautiful Nina...'

'But Mick...'

'Nina darling,' He took her hand, his blue-grey eyes full of excitement. 'I've bought it and I intend to spend all my spare time doing it up. I'm going to make it into something special, just for you! I want it to be a place where we can be really happy. A real home for you, me and eventually our kids. What do you think?'

'I think.....I think it's wonderful Mick.' She said looking at him, knowing it wasn't what she meant at all. A project like this would take months, even years and that meant she would be spending even more time alone, feeling even more isolated than she already did. Unless, of course, she could turn this to her advantage, use it as a lever.

'Mick, if you're going to be involved with this, then I insist on doing my bit too.' She said as they got out of the car and walked towards the front door.

'In what way?'

'By going back to work......'

'No Nina, definitely not,' He shook his head. 'We've been through all this before. I don't want you working. There's absolutely no need.'

'What about part time, like I mentioned,' She insisted, 'then I could use my own money to buy things for the house.'

'Oh Nina, you're so sweet, you really are. But Dad's been very generous, there's money already set aside for the furnishing. And when the time comes,' he squeezed her hand affectionately, 'you can go out and buy exactly what you want. Now,' his finger hovered over the doorbell, 'Come on, we'd better not keep everybody waiting.....'

Ella, elegant in a cream silk pants suit, welcomed them into a warm, inviting lounge where glasses of wine were handed round and they joined Rich Tate and fiancée Annabel who was busy showing and Gareth and Bryony Stewart her emerald and diamond engagement ring. Almost immediately Nina was aware of Andy watching her; his attention constantly straying between her and the conversation he was having with Rich and Gareth. He's playing his stupid games again she thought. Still irritable from her discussion with Mick, she decided to ignore him and joined the three girls' conversation, boring as it was, about current fashion trends and Annabel's boutique.

The meal, a fondue followed by an enormous Pavlova, was like everything else in Ella's house, absolutely perfect. As the table was cleared and they moved back into the lounge for coffee, Nina excused herself to find the bathroom, a huge glass walled cavern where she locked herself in and stood miserably amongst the fronded palms reapplying her make up and wishing the evening was over and she could go home.

On her way back downstairs she paused at the landing window, gazing out across the open fields beyond the garden at the lights of Abbotsbridge in the distance, groping desperately for some seed of inspiration which might make Mick change his mind about her return to work.

'Ah there you are.'

She turned from her preoccupation to find Andy beside her.

'The women are talking kitchens, the men cars.' He said quietly, 'I thought I'd leave them to it for a while, come and look for you. Thought you might have got lost.'

'Lost?' She said tartly, 'Do you think I'm stupid or something?'

'Not at all Nina my darling.' He said, moving behind her and pushing the long curtain of her hair back over her shoulder to expose her neck.

'What are you doing?' She felt a ripple go through her as his fingers touched her.

'I want to smell your hair, feel the softness your skin,' He replied, kissing her earlobe and making her shudder again, 'It's been such a long time.'

'Stop it Andy.' She twisted her head away from him. 'Someone might come.'

'Only me if I'm not careful,' He gave a soft laugh, placing his hands on her shoulders and turning her around to face him.

'Nina, look at me,' He lifted her chin with his finger, 'You ran off that day. You should at least have listened to what I had to say.'

She felt weak, unable to resist the blackness of his eyes, the curve of his lips.

'Poor little neglected Nina,' He stroked her face, 'and now it's even worse isn't it? Now he's going to be working on that dream home of yours. The neglect, the loneliness. I know, it will drive you slowly mad. But never mind my darling,' he eased her gently back down the landing, 'Fortunately, I have the answer to all your problems.'

Friday 9th October

'I hear you're off tomorrow.'

Miles Anderson appeared suddenly at Liam's elbow as he was standing at the bar of The Red Lion ordering a round of drinks. Away in the far corner of the bar his small team of architects and support staff sat talking animatedly and passing around the lunch time menu.

'Yes, can't wait. We delayed our holiday this year because of the weddings.' Liam gave Miles a tired smile. 'I have to say I'm really ready for it. Two weeks of relaxing and forgetting about work. I've been turning night into day to get those plans for the Precinct to Bob on time. I hope it's all worth it.'

'Where are you going?'

'Barbados.'

'Abroad eh? Thought you might be spending time with your wife's family in Meridan Cross. Pretty place isn't it?'

'Yes, it is, but I don't think Mel would relish the thought of two weeks under the same roof as her father.'

The barmaid put the last drink on the tray and took the five pound note Liam was holding.

'Oh?' Miles looked at him curiously.

'Don't get me wrong, we see them socially, which is really good. But there are still areas where Richard and Mel agree to disagree.' Liam gave an embarrassed smile. 'Richard's a good sort, but he has very traditional views about women and I'm afraid Mel doesn't fit into any of them.'

'That's a shame.'

'Yes it is, especially as she seems to have been making a real effort lately. She's very keen to patch up their differences you know. Says she wants peace in the family for the new generation who'll be coming along. Jenny's pregnant now and, well, Ella may be soon. I'm proud of her, she's really committed.'

Taking the change from the returning barmaid Liam picked up the tray and eased himself away from the bar. 'Richard's not going to be a pushover,' he laughed. 'It may take time, but Mel's very determined. My money's on her.'

So Bob had been telling the truth after all, Miles thought as he watched Liam handing round drinks to his team. Of course, there was no question of him not getting the bid, but then it wouldn't hurt to let him sweat for a little longer would it?

Tuesday 27th October

'What do you think?' Faye Benedict asked as she locked the door of Sherrington's Bakery in Gane Street and stepped out on the pavement, pushing her hands deep into the pockets of her camel coat.

'Yes,' Tad replied, looking at the double fronted shop with its Dickensian style bow windows, 'it will do very nicely.'

'I thought,' Faye studied the windows, 'that we could have handbags, shoes and tights as the main feature in the left window and perhaps the gloves, scarves and costume jewellery in the right. I've seen some really good bag and shoe samples, unusual coloured leather, we could co-ordinate the window each week, make it more interesting.'

'What are you going to call the place?' He asked looking up at the faded lettering above the door.

'*Handbags and Gladrags*.'

'I like it.' He nodded approvingly. 'And when are you planning to open for business?'

Faye did some calculations on her fingers. 'In around three months.'

'Great. That gives you plenty of time to talk to Marianne O'Donnell.'

'Marianne?' She frowned.

'I'm sure anyone buying clothes in Christiana's boutique would be interested in your shoes and bags. Teaming up with her would give the business a cracking start.'

'What a good idea!' Faye was delighted. 'I could take some samples round, we could swap items, make our windows more interesting.....'

Tad looked at the enthusiasm in his wife's face. He knew Matt's brief visit and hasty departure had unsettled her and was pleased she was channelling her energies into a project like this. Hopefully it would fill her day and stop her brooding until he eventually came home to Abbotsbridge again.

Monday 2nd November

Ella turned her Mercedes through the gates of Chelwood Lodge. A day of frustrations, she reflected, which had started from the moment she arrived in the office that morning. First of all she found herself unexpectedly pulled into a meeting with Jenny and Tony Rutherford. Then she sat in on a short listing exercise with Joan to select candidates for the post of Managing Director's Secretary at Stewarts, to replace Oliver's very capable Pam Dimmock whose husband's job move meant she was leaving the area.

By ten thirty she found herself desperate for a coffee and finding the filter empty she had gone to the kitchen to make herself a cup of instant. It was as she pulled a cup and saucer from the cupboard that she noticed the cake. A substantial chocolate fondant topped arrangement sandwiched together with butter icing, one slice already gone.

'Whose birthday?' She called out to Trudi.

'No one's. Helen brought it in.'

'Who's Helen?' She frowned, pushing her head around the kitchen door curiously.

'Our office cleaner, Trudi smiled. 'And I thought you knew everyone here! She does this occasionally, just as a treat for us all.'

'Well if this cake tastes as good as it looks,' Ella said cutting herself a slice, 'I'd say her talents are totally wasted.'

'Oh the cleaning's only a temporary thing. She's new to the area.' Trudi said as Ella emerged from the kitchen. 'Multi-talented too. Cordon bleu cook /housekeeper/nanny with loads of experience. I suggested she register with us.' she said brightly. 'Someone with those skills is bound to be snapped up quickly.'

The conversation with Trudy had been her one brief moment of respite in the madness of the day. After snatching a sandwich at twelve thirty and resisting Jenny's attempt to drag her out into town shopping for baby clothes, she left for Wellington. The journey was frustrating, hampered by road works, slow tractors and a herd of temperamental cows. Then when she eventually reached her destination she found Manager Adrian Lennard had been called away from the office due to a family emergency.

Turning the car around she drove home, deciding to have an early finish and a good soak in a hot bath. But the bad day had not quite ended. On a lonely stretch of country road five miles from Wellington a tyre blew. It took her twenty minutes to change it, a dirty job on a wet, grimy road. As she continued her journey, more slow traffic conspired to delay her and she eventually drove into Abbotsbridge at six thirty.

Pulling up outside the garage now, she dragged her briefcase from the back seat, locked the car and made her way slowly to the front door. Andy opened it just as she reached the top step.

'God, Ella, where've you been? I was so worried.'

'Changing a tyre.' She indicate the dirt on her clothes.

'We're due at Rich's place for drinks at eight.'

'Damn!' She closed her eyes, realising the long hot bath she'd been dreaming of wasn't going to happen. 'I completely forgot.'

'Better get your skates on.'

'Have you eaten yet?' She asked dumping her briefcase in the hall and pulling off her jacket.

'I did myself some beans on toast. Kitchen's a bit of a mess I'm afraid. Burnt the toast -and the beans'

'Don't worry; I'll sort it tomorrow morning.' She ran a tired hand through her hair; right now it was the least of her worries.

'Ella,' Andy shook his head, 'Since you took over the other two businesses, it's been chaos here. You're late at least three nights a week, sometimes more. Most of my meals come out of a tin. Sorry, but you're going to have to do something about it.' He looked unhappy. 'And, I've just looked in the laundry basket.....'

'Oh God, shirts!' She closed her eyes.

'It's O.K. I rang Rich. It's casual; I'll wear a jacket and a polo neck.....'

Ella stood there feeling the whole world was collapsing around her. The juggling act wasn't working; she couldn't be in two places at once, keeping the house and business running together smoothly. She needed help.

'Andy,' she said as they were getting ready, 'How do you feel about having a housekeeper?'

'What? A live-in like Tabby you mean?'

'No, a daily.'

'I suppose that might work.' He didn't sound convinced. 'But the chances of getting someone just like that....'

'Are pretty good actually!' Ella said eagerly, 'I know someone who might just fit the bill.'

Tuesday 3rd November

Helen Barker was not at all what Ella had expected. She was in her late thirties, slim and brown haired with clear skin and blue eyes. Her smile surfaced regularly as they chatted and her manner was warm and friendly. Ella showed her over Chelwood Lodge, talked her through the support she needed - cooking, cleaning and laundry and discussed the hours involved. She offered a generous salary. Helen stood in the kitchen, ran her hand over the worktops, gazed at the ceiling and smiled yet again. Yes, she would be more than happy to start. Would a week's time be all right?

They shook hands at the door and Ella watched her climb into her green Austin A40 and drive away. She had cleared the first hurdle; she had found someone. Of course she still had to convince Andy that a housekeeper was the right solution. Still, she thought, that wasn't such a problem. Once he'd tasted Helen's chocolate cake she knew he'd be completely sold.

Friday 18th December

'I wonder what 1971 will bring?' Jenny said standing at the window of Ella's office, watching the snow falling into the courtyard outside.

Ella stopped writing and looked up at her sister in law. 'Oh new opportunities, new challenges I guess and of course,' she pointed with her pen at Jenny's stomach, 'a new baby.'

Jenny smiled. 'I can't wait. I hope it's a boy. I think Nick would like a boy.'

'I think he would too. He'll make a good father.' Ella went back to writing.

'Isn't it strange?' Jenny said turning from the window. 'Me about to become a mother. Seems like only yesterday we were at school.'

'Yes, time's flown, 'Ella laughed, 'Just look at us now, you and me, running a successful business. Who'd have thought it?'

Jenny nodded in agreement. 'We have done well. The two new agencies have really come into their own and now, of course, there's the printing. George Martock was a brilliant find.'

'Wasn't he just?' Ella laughed. The retired printer had initially approached her for some temporary work to get out from under his wife's feet. It soon became clear, however, that his skills could be put to use running a small printing outlet in the basement of the Wellington branch to supply stationery for the three branches. It had, however, expanded very quickly to serve other small businesses, another gap in the market she had recognised and capitalised on.

'Do you know something,' she said joining Jenny at the window. 'Three years ago when I came to Abbotsbridge, my mother completely changed the direction my life was taking. However, I was determined something positive would come out of it and it has. Now here I am, twenty one, surrounded by good friends. I own a thriving business, have a lovely home and a gorgeous husband who adores me. Family rifts are healing with Liam and mother going to Willowbrook for Christmas.' She looped her arm in Jenny's, 'I have to pinch myself Jen but I'm beginning to believe that life is absolutely perfect.'

As usual, a key to Room 305 at the Highcrest Motel had been left on reception. Andy Macayne unlocked the door and walked in. The geometric patterned curtains were pulled, shutting out the fading light and the snow falling silently outside. The room was in semi darkness, lit only by the golden glow of two matching bedside lights - removing his jacket and easing off his tie he sat down on the bed. Noticing an opened lingerie box, its tissue spilling onto the bedspread, he smiled.

The bathroom door opened and she stood there. His breath caught in his throat. The cream basque she was wearing moulded itself to her body like a second skin, full, round breasts spilling enticingly out of the half cups. Her hair, thick and tousled and the red wetness of her lips made her look wanton. His eyes wandered down past the suspenders to the sheer stockings, then back up to the tiny vee of lace g-string. He got to his feet as she approached, eager to touch her; to feel the softness of her skin.

'Thank you for my Christmas present.' Nina purred, slipping her arms around his neck.

'My pleasure,' he whispered in her ear, hardly able to control his need for her, 'and have you got a little Christmas something for me?'

'Right here,' she pushed her body enticingly against his, 'I hope you like it.'

'Can I unwrap it now?'

She nodded. 'I hope you'll be able to stay long enough to enjoy it.'

'That won't be a problem. She thinks I'm in Taunton - black tie function.' He smiled. 'And if I drink too much, well, I'll just have to book myself into a hotel and stay overnight won't I?'

'You think of everything Andy.' Nina laughed.

'I know, clever bastard aren't I?'

1971

TWELVE

Wednesday 6th January

Bob Macayne sat at his desk gazing out on a cold sleety morning wondering how a conversation back in March last year, which had triggered so many expectations, had finally come to such an empty and disappointing conclusion. The bids for the new precinct and multi-storey, he knew, with their noon deadline of Monday 4th January, would now have been opened and the successful contractor notified. He looked at the clock. Two fifteen. Despite the offer to throw the multi-storey in for free, it obviously hadn't turned out to be him.

He cursed Miles for dragging him into this fiasco with Mel, which because it had not yielded results, had now wrecked his chances of the biggest contract ever in Abbotsbridge. But perhaps, he thought, he should also blame himself just a little, for having the arrogance to want to leave something of himself in Abbotsbridge for posterity. He had put his fingers in the fire and this time he had got well and truly burned.

Watching the slow trickle of melting sleet against the window, he felt reluctant to venture out, but knew that getting out of the office was the only sensible thing to do on a day like this. What he needed was to be totally distracted from his disappointment. He decided maybe he'd take a trip out to the village of Middle Morton to look at some land someone had tipped him off about. Taylor Macayne Residential was always looking for new development land and this had sounded ideal.

Throwing on his raincoat he told Marion Westwood, his secretary, that he would not be available for the rest of the afternoon and left their suite of offices. The journey downstairs to the main foyer, found him still wrestling with his anger and disappointment. As the lift doors opened with a soft sigh he walked out past the carpeted reception area towards the rotating glass door and the cold wet January afternoon beyond.

Someone was coming into the building as he was going out, lowering and shaking out an umbrella. Someone familiar, wearing a black cashmere coat and carrying a briefcase. Unable to stop he went with the revolving door then stood outside on the pavement for a moment looking back into the building. The figure stayed in the glass cylinder, eventually joining him where he stood on the pavement under the shelter of the iron portico.

'Bob.' Miles was beaming at him, 'Just in time.'

'What for Miles?' Bob eyed him warily.

'The contract.'

'A phone call would have been sufficient.' Bob said abruptly

Miles patted his brief case. 'But I need you to sign it.'

'What?' Bob raised his eyebrows in surprise.

'Yes, for the precinct and the Civic Hall.' Miles was still smiling.

'But I thought....'

'What? That you wouldn't get it?' Miles couldn't resist a smile. 'That's not like you Bob. You're normally the confident one, taking everything in his stride,' he gave Bob a firm pat on the back. 'Relax. The wood isn't an urgent issue any more. It's on hold indefinitely.'

'What?'

'Don't look so angry,' Miles beamed, 'You've just landed a very prestigious contract.'

'And the bill for the multi-storey!' Bob countered angrily, 'You set me up Miles! You know I'm the best there is, you just didn't want to pay my price!'

'Nonsense Bob,' Miles was quick to contradict him. 'As Head of the Planning Committee I have to look after the ratepayers' interest. See that they get good value for money. And as for the project, well it does exist, it's just that currently the timing's wrong.' He stared at Bob's angry, disbelieving face. 'It really does exist. Bob and I can prove it. After the contract's signed we'll go back to my office and I'll show you.'

Friday 8th January

'Gentlemen, a toast!' Bob Macayne raised a glass of pale bubbling liquid to the small group gathered in his board room. 'To our success with the new precinct, oh and of course, the Civic Hall,' his features set themselves in a self-satisfied grin.

Jack, Mick, Liam and Andy touched glasses and raised them to their lips.

'Well,' Jack Taylor said with a smile as he turned to Liam. 'We have done well haven't we? The new shopping precinct and Civic Hall will really put Abbotsbridge on the map and I have to say your designs for the new site at Bracken Down are wonderful. The houses blend so well with the village, they're going to look as if they've been there years.'

'Infill in villages is a very emotive subject,' Liam replied, casting an eye in the direction of his plans which still lay open on the boardroom table. 'I knew if we were to get these past the Planning Committee then design was going to be as important as the materials used. Fortunately I seem to have hit the all right buttons and everybody's happy.' he smiled. 'When does everything start?'

'Infrastructure's going in next month,' Jack said refilling his glass. 'Then Mick will take over; get the foundations in for plots four and five at the top of the site. We've had quite a bit of interest already, especially on The Bridport.

'Good.' Liam smiled and stared across the room where Andy stood with Mick discussing tile and brick samples. His original qualms about Ella's choice of husband were gradually beginning to fade. Andy seemed a different man these days, happy, settled and showing a huge amount enthusiasm for his job. Ella had worked her magic on him, just like she had on her business. I was wrong, he decided, I take it all back. Despite my misgivings, this marriage looks as if it's going to work after all.

Sunday 10th January

Mel picked her way carefully across the snow covered park. The call from Bob had come yesterday afternoon. It had been brief, giving only the time and place. Wearing her camel wool coat with its thick brown fur collar, matching fur hat and brown leather boots, she felt like Tatiana Romanova on her way to a secret meeting with James Bond in *From Russia with Love.* There was a small sheltered seat with a tiled roof and half glass sides behind the bandstand he'd said. Could she get there at three thirty? It would be quiet and the light would be fading then, they'd be less likely to be noticed.

Pacing up and down, blowing on gloved fingers, he turned and smiled as she approached.

'Bob?' She frowned as she reached him. 'Is everything all right?'

'Yes, yes.' His cold lips touched hers briefly before he pulled her into the shelter and settled her down beside him.

She could feel the cold seeping up from the concrete floor and through the soles of her boots as she sat there, sheltered from the cold northerly wind amongst the scratched words of wisdom and declarations of unrequited love littering the wall behind her. She hoped this would not take too long.

'Well?' She said pushing her gloved hands deep into her pockets and tucking her chin into the fur collar of her coat.

'It's about Willowbrook. Miles says the project's shelved for the time being.'

'After all the trouble I've gone to!'

'I'm angry too,' He gave her arm an understanding pat, 'Miles has been very devious. He knew I wanted the Precinct, the multi-storey and the Civic Centre contracts. Bids were sealed, so I offered to build the multi-storey for nothing, knowing my loss would have been covered by him guaranteeing me the build for his project, which he did. We shook hands. A gentleman's agreement, he said. Now he's back-pedalled on the deal so currently I'm looking at a substantial loss on the Abbotsbridge project.'

'So he never really wanted Fox Cottage at all? It was just a ruse?'

'I thought so too first. But after the contract was signed we went back to his office. I saw the plans. It's a holiday village. Do you know Sedgewick wood?'

She nodded.

'Well that's where it's going to be built. But it is land locked. Fox Cottage and several acres of Hundred Acre are essential to provide access for the site and to create an entrance for the whole development.'

'Butlins in Meridan Cross?' Mel laughed. 'I don't think so.'

'Ah but we're not talking Butlins, were talking something completely different.'

'What sort of different?'

'A unique holiday experience was how Miles described it. Wooden cabins and a luxury holiday centre where people can come to relax and be pampered or be active with loads of different outdoor and indoor pursuits. He said these centres are very big in Scandinavia. He gave me this,' he pulled a brochure from his overcoat pocket and handed it to her.

Mel sat for a moment, turning the pages, taking in the detail.

'It's very different.' She looked up at Bob and smiled.

'It's a big project. Perhaps too big for them at the moment, that's why they've shelved it.'

'Who's *they* Bob? I thought we were talking about Miles.'

'No. Mirage Holdings. Martin Templeman and Gavin Briggs-Howe. Old friends of Miles' apparently.'

'Well this is all very interesting,' she said handing him back the brochure. 'But I hardly think it warranted dragging me out in the cold to tell me you'd been made a fool of and I've been wasting my time.'

'But the thing is Mel, we haven't. I still want you to continue working on your father.'

'Why?'

'Because,' He tapped the brochure. 'This project is revolutionary. It won't be shelved for long. It has to happen. And when they resurrect it, I want to be the one calling the shots! Oh the cottage and the wood will be for sale, but by then I'll own it and they'll be paying my price!'

Monday 5th April

Joan Trimble sat in the small interview room with its sunny apple green walls and white Venetian blinds, stop watch in hand. Opposite her, a neat brunette in a blue blouse and black skirt was taking down shorthand on a pad as Joan dictated a passage from the business page of one of the daily papers left in reception.

'This country's reputation as an international centre of innovation for engineering has taken a terrible blow with the recent collapse of Rolls Royce....'

Her concentration was broken by a sudden burst of voices beyond the door in the reception area. Despite the continued noise she finished her dictation and after settling the girl down to type the test back, went to investigate.

A small group had gathered around Trudi, who was on the telephone.

'Girls, please.....' She began, 'Someone is trying to type back a speed test; do you think we could keep the noise down?' She gazed at all of them in turn. 'And if I may say so, I don't think Ella would be very pleased to see you all congregating like this in reception.'

Placing her hand over the receiver, Trudi smiled up at Joan. 'I think Ella will let us off on this occasion Mrs Trimble,' she said, her face flushed with excitement. 'I'm talking to her now; she's just phoned to let us know that Jenny's had her baby..... It's a 7lb 4 boy and mum and baby are both fine! Would you like to have a word?'

The serious expression on Joan's face vanished immediately; she took the receiver, all smiles. 'Ella! Wonderful news! Yes Trudi just told me. What? Where? Right, I'll get it organised. Two thirty? Fine, we'll see you then.'

'What did she say?' Trudi looked puzzled as she took the phone back.

'Apparently there's champagne chilling in the fridge. Come on, everyone let's get organised, she'll be back in twenty minutes.'

Wednesday 7th April

'I just called in quickly; all the girls send their love. Issy said she'd be here later on this afternoon and Trudi said she'd call in this evening. Ooh, let me look at him again.'

Ella walked to the end of Jenny's bed and looked down at the downy haired baby sleeping peacefully in his crib beneath a neat blue blanket. Beside the bed, the small wooden cabinet was covered in cards, a huge bunch of red roses from Nick eclipsing all the other flowers in the room.

Jenny sat up in bed, cradling her arms around her knees.

'You know this motherhood thing's a job in itself, all I seem to be doing at the moment is feeding him. Goodness knows how I'm going to fit everything else in when I get home.'

'I expect you'll handle it brilliantly, just like you handle everything else.' Ella said confidently. 'Besides you've always got your Mum. I saw her in town yesterday, she was in her element. You ought to see the baby clothes she's been buying! How are you feeling now?'

She winced. 'Still a bit sore, I had to have stitches. Lizzie,' she nodded towards a pale faced girl with curly blonde hair, lying in the bed opposite, 'had a caesarean. She hardly knew a thing.'

'Has Mother been in yet?'

'Don't be silly Ella.'

Ella looked thoughtfully at the baby, letting the tip of her finger run gently over the back of one of his tiny pink hands. 'You know I really did hope that this baby would bring her to her senses. Still, I hear Barbara Morris's daughter in law is about to produce, perhaps that will give her the incentive she needs.'

'Please, if that's the only reason she's going to show her face here, I'd rather she didn't.' Jenny shrugged, 'I'm tired of all her pompous attitudes and so is Mum. If she isn't interested in Christopher that's fine, she's going to be the one losing out in the end.'

'You're calling him Christopher? Jen that's great!'

'Yep, Christopher Michael Kendrick.'

Ella's face lit up. 'Even better, Granddad will be pleased.'

'Nick's already told him. And Laura's delighted too. She's coming to see me tomorrow.'

'And I'm sure she'll find Christopher as adorable was we do.' Ella said noticing the clock over the door and getting to her feet. 'Sorry, I'm going to have to go. I've a meeting with Leon Brookfield at two.'

'As in Brookfields of Kingsford?'

'The very same. He's only been there nine months and he's expanding already. Knocking through into the old electricity showroom next door. Says he needs to recruit at least half a dozen people. They're having a big new china section and opening a record and hi fi department. It seems Kingsford's first big store is going down a storm. Which is all good news for us!' She leaned over the bed and kissed Jenny on her cheek, 'I'll see you tomorrow, same time.'

As Ella left, Jenny climbed out of bed and retrieved Christopher from his cot. It was time for his feed and his small face was puckered, his pink mouth gnawing at his tiny fist.

'There goes your Auntie Ella,' Jenny whispered to him as Ella disappeared through the swing doors at the end of the ward. 'She thinks she's got the best job in the world. But we know different, don't we?'

Saturday 8th May

'Happy Birthday Dad!'

'What's all this then?' Richard Evas said gruffly as Mel placed a large package in his lap.

'Open it. Go on!' Mel stood back, clasping her hands enthusiastically.

Richard tore at the wrapping.

'A new Harris tweed jacket!' He exclaimed, 'Well, well. How did you know I wanted this?'

'Oh a little bird told me.' Mel gave Mary a knowing smile. 'Here, let me help you on with it.'

Richard stood up, allowing Mel to pull away what was left of the wrapping paper and ease the jacket over his shoulders.

'It's a perfect fit,' she said, smoothing her hands over the back. 'Come along, turn round. Show Mary.'

'It's lovely Richard,' Mary nodded, 'just the right colour too.'

'I'll just take a look at myself in the bedroom mirror, if you'll both excuse me.'

As Richard left the room, Mel turned to Mary.

'Does he *really* like it?' She asked anxiously.

'Of course he does.'

'It means a lot to me - having his approval. We've not got on in the past. I want to make up for that if I can. It's important - being part of the family. Nick and Ella are married now. The first baby has already arrived. I don't want grandchildren growing up with this rift between Dad and myself.'

'I can understand that.' Mary replied. 'But he's a proud man. He'll go at his own pace.'

'But with your intervention I know we can speed things up.' Mel said brightly. 'You know, make him see reason.'

'Of course, I'll do all I can.' Mary promised. 'But in the end, it's down to your father. Surely you've known him long enough to know that?'

Mel nodded, tight lipped and annoyed. Why was Mary being so awkward?

'Ah come on, don't look so down,' Mary rested a gentle hand on Mel's shoulder. 'I've set a wonderful tea. Stay with us. He'd really appreciate that.'

'I'm not sure I have the time!' Mel said, brushing Mary's hand away irritably.

'But Mel, making time for him is very important. If you're trying to win back his heart it's simple things like caring and being there for him that matter the most.'

'That jacket cost me a small fortune!' Mel said tartly. 'I resent you dismissing it as if it's nothing! Telling me sitting here over tea and cake is more important!'

'I didn't say that at all,' Mary said gently, 'I merely said that actions are as important.'

'Are they really!' Angrily Mel snatched up her handbag from the chair and swept out of the room.

The closing of the front door coincided with Richard's return from the appraisal of his new jacket.

'Lovely,' He enthused, patting the front of it as he entered the parlour and found Mary staring out of the window. 'Where's Mel?'

'Gone.' Mary said, watching the Spitfire bump its way down the farm track towards the road.

'Didn't want to stay for tea then?'

'Sadly no. We were talking, she took exception to something I said, lost her temper and just upped and left.'

'Oh dear, pity. Same old Mel.'

Monday 14th June

Nina Taylor stood at the kitchen sink drinking coffee and gazing out of the window. It was mid afternoon and the sky was blue, large white clouds pushing by on the same brisk wind which blew the washing on the line in her garden. As she stood there she reflected on the frustrations in her life.

The farmhouse was progressing well. It had a new roof, the dry rot and damp had been cured and Mick was spending long hours working evenings and weekends on the inside. He updated her weekly on the progress of the work. Currently with the help of Dave Mason, the site's plumber, he was busy installing two new bathrooms. Of course he was hardly ever home now, but that didn't bother her much, in fact it had worked to her advantage. It meant she could meet Andy without having to make excuses for her absences from the house.

That evening in September when he had found her on the landing looking out of the window; when he had touched her, confronted her with her unhappiness, told her about his own - she realised how fate, intervening to part them, had now brought them back together again. And so she had gone willingly with him into one of the guest bedrooms where he had pushed her gently onto the bed. Of course it had been quick, but the thrill of having sex with Andy in a room anyone could have walked into added spice to the occasion. Afterwards, it seemed only natural that they made plans to meet again.

Their meetings were irregular; arranged at short notice to fit in with the busy working and social life he now had as Sales Manager of one of his father's companies. Their usual meeting place was the Highcrest Motel. However, on nights when Mick was working late, he came to the house, undressing her with impatient hands as soon as he was inside the front door. Of course, her one secret wish was to go to Chelwood Lodge while Ella was away on business; to sleep with him in his and Ella's bed. But she knew without asking, that Andy would never agree to that. His own life had to be kept completely separate. Whilst she agreed to this, she had laid her own long term plans for their relationship, determined to get them both out of their unsatisfactory marriages for good.

To begin with, her plans had been on course. Andy was insatiable; he couldn't get enough of her. Her strategy for the future also had a knock on effect in her own life; the boredom of being married to Mick became more bearable now that she could see an eventual ending in sight. And then a fortnight ago, Andy said he wouldn't be able to see her for the next four weeks, due to pressure of work and other commitments on his time. Her spirits dipped through the colourless days that followed as she began to realise she did not have as much influence or control over him as she had first imagined.

Finishing off her coffee she set the mug to one side and picking up the potato peeler, retrieved one of three large potatoes which sat in the blue plastic bowl in the sink. Resentfully she pulled at the potato with the peeler, showering thin slivers of skin across the draining board. With Andy gone she was back to square one, stuck here in a boring marriage with no way out and she hated it.

The phone rang, interrupting her thoughts. She dropped the potato and the peeler into the bowl and wiped her hands on her jeans. Mick, she suspected, saying he'd be working late again. Bloody men, she thought as she picked up the receiver.

'Hello Nina.'

'Andy!' She couldn't believe it.

'Nina, 'His voice was smooth, mesmerising. 'I'm so sorry I haven't been around. But I'm free now and thought you might like to meet me out at Bracken Down this afternoon.'

'With Mick there? Are you mad?'

'You're cross, I'm sorry. I've missed you too. Mick's not here. He's off site all afternoon.'

'I don't know. What about the workmen? If they see us.........'

'They won't. I want you to meet me at the house.'

'Which house?'

'The farmhouse. Your new home.'

'Mick said it's off limits to me, till it's finished.'

'He's a real party pooper isn't he Nina?' She caught the mockery in his tone. 'That's not very fair is it?'

'No, it's not.'

'I know just how you feel.' There was a moment's pause, 'And that's why I think it's time you had a guided tour. Come up to the site and turn left just before the main entrance. It's down a short track, quite secluded. No one will see us. You can park in the field opposite, I'll leave the gate open.' he whispered. 'Oh by the way, he's just finished the bathrooms. There's a shower room too. Bring some towels, we might as well christen it while we're there'

Nina smiled. One phone call had changed everything - her plans were very much on again. Christen the shower? She'd show him what he'd been missing. 'Give me half an hour.' she said and hung up.

Out at Bracken Down Andy relaxed back in his seat and smiled to himself. Sex in the shower was one of his biggest turn-ons. Doing it in Mick's shower with his wife even more of a turn on; for this was also to be a secret act of revenge against his boring workaholic partner.

Ever since he had bought the house, Mick was always going on about the work he was doing. Someone on site only had to mention it and he'd bang on for hours about how far he'd got with his grand project and how much it was costing. Andy had found the whole thing tedious and boring, but now his father had started to take an interest and had joined Mick's fan club, making regular visits to the site to see how the work was progressing. Andy resented this. He had applied himself well to his job, had achieved the sales targets set him, yet there was no praise for this from his father, only for Mick and his bloody farmhouse.

Andy had harboured evil thoughts of setting fire to it, demented thoughts of blowing it up, preferably with Mick inside it. But sensibly he knew none of this was realistic. However, what he was about to do today, was very real and the nearest he would ever come to getting his own back. The thought was warm and comforting.

'Well, what do you think?'

'Very nice. Very expensive. Very you.'

Bob smiled, watching the way Mel ran her red tipped fingers over the cream leather seats of his new pale blue Jaguar XJ6.

'Wanted a change from the Rover,' Bob grinned, looking appreciatively at her legs as she slid into the passenger seat, 'Did you know old Charlie paid over the odds for this very model last year so he'd be one of the first owners.'

'Yes Liam told me.'

'That sounds as if you don't approve.'

'Not at all, I'm just a little envious of that sort of spending power.'

'And what would you do if you had the money then?' He laughed. 'Buy a new wardrobe of clothes I suppose?'

'Oh no, nothing so frivolous.' Mel replied, her expression serious. 'I'd put my money into bricks and mortar. A new home, somewhere exclusive, like Portway. That's *my* dream Bob.'

Andy stood at the open door of the farmhouse watching Nina park her Mini safely behind the hedge in the field opposite. Watching the swell of her breasts as they strained against the material of the bright yellow dress she wore as she walked up the small track towards him he realised how much he had missed her body. How despite putting her on hold because of work commitments, he found without her there was no fire; no spark in his life if she wasn't there to provide the sexual excitement he so much needed. Without Nina all he had was his pleasant, comfortable life with Ella. Beautiful, clever Ella. A woman who thought sex was something that was man driven, who was responsive and affectionate in bed, but who lacked the most important ingredient - passion. Of course she was capable of passion, but only, it seemed, where her business was concerned. He often imagined what the whole, complete Ella might be like. One, who put as much energy into sex as she did work. The thought was quite intoxicating. One thing he was sure of, if she had existed, he wouldn't be here now. He'd have had no need for Nina. No need at all.

She was at the door now; he felt the smoothness of her arms as she slid them around his neck.

'I've missed you.' She said, her green cat's eyes looking directly into his.

'I've missed you too,' He said breathlessly. And lifting her into his arms he kicked the door firmly shut with his foot and headed for the stairs.

'It's really good of you to give up an afternoon for me.' Ella said as she walked out of Sutton's builder's merchants with Mick.

'It's not a problem. Any excuse to get involved in someone else's project and I'm there,' He grinned, 'I'm only surprised Andy didn't want a say in your new kitchen.'

'I did ask, but he said he'd leave it all to me - and Helen, of course. She's going to choose the appliances.'

'Seems to me the appliances are going to be the easy part,' Mick said as he slid into the passenger seat of Ella's Mercedes, 'I don't think you've been very impressed with what I've shown you so far.'

'I wouldn't say that.' Ella said, slotting the car into reverse and backing out of the parking space. 'The quality's been excellent. But that's the problem Mick, I don't just want quality. I want something that's going to hit me between the eyes when I see it. I don't want what everyone else has; I'm looking for something completely different.'

'Liam,' Mick grinned, 'you need to talk to Liam.'

'Why Liam?'

'Because he's designed the kitchen for me in the farmhouse I'm doing up at Bracken Down. It's out of this world. Fancy taking a look?'

'Well...yes!' Ella nodded enthusiastically.

'Take the next left then, we'll be there in ten minutes.'

Looking at the old stone farmhouse Ella was immediately struck by how similar it was to Willowbrook. Situated at the end of a short driveway it was fronted by small dry stone wall, beyond which was a riot of perennial floral colour. To the rear she glimpsed lawn and mature apple trees.

'*This* is going to be your new home?' She asked as she stopped the car.

'Yep!' He looked affectionately at the house. 'Bob wanted this demolished you know. Said we could get two new houses in here. But I could see what it could be like, so I persuaded him to let me buy it off him and restore it. Liam was great. Gave me some really good ideas - and designed a brilliant kitchen.'

'It's beautiful Mick. What does Nina think?'

'She's not been out here yet.' He said as he got out of the car. 'This is so special I want to finish it first.' he looked at the house then turned back to Ella with an enthusiastic grin. 'This is going to be a fantastic home you know, just the place for raising kids! Won't be a minute, I'll just go to the site hut and get the keys.'

Ella walked slowly up the driveway, enjoying warmth of the sun on her shoulders and the peacefulness of a summer's afternoon on the edge of a quiet village. The stillness, broken only by the purr of a distant tractor immediately resurrected memories of Meridan Cross. But this was a totally different countryside. There was no sheltered valley, no glistening trail of river or dark band of railway track. Bracken Down was set in low, open countryside; a patchwork of fields stretching out towards a shadowy impression of hills on the horizon.

She reached the front door, solid stained oak with a heavy round black ring handle. Instinctively she slipped her fingers into the handle and twisted it. To her surprise it opened. Her first thought was to wait for Mick to return, but curiosity about the kitchen drew her into the house. She found herself standing in a long narrow flagstone hallway, a bare staircase directly in front of her. The place should have been silent, but above her she caught the sound of running water. Frowning, she began to slowly climb the stairs, wondering whether someone had been in and left a tap running. As she reached the top she stopped. Ahead of her clothes lay strewn along the length of the landing. A shirt, a dress, trousers, underwear.

She crept slowly back down stairs, deciding she should leave this to Mick. Obviously someone on site had decided this place was remote enough to use for an amorous encounter. Cheeky, she thought, but knew Mick would not see it that way. Neither would Bob. It would be instant dismissal for whoever was up there.

Moments later, as she stepped outside the door and closed it, Mick appeared, his face creased with annoyance.

'The keys are missing.' He said irritably. 'They haven't been booked out and no one knows who's got them. They think it's a subbie. Andy's nowhere to be found so I can't ask him. I'm sorry Ella, dragging you all this way for nothing.'

'You haven't, it's open Mick,' she said quietly. 'And I think someone's using the shower.'

'What!' Mick quickly pushed past her into the hallway

'I got as far as the landing,' she said, following him as he took the stairs two at a time, 'There are clothes everywhere.'

Reaching the top of the stairs he stopped, staring at the scatter of clothes in front of him. Bending down slowly, he picked up the dress, taking the material gently in his hands and lifting it to his face.

'What is it?'

'This is Nina's dress.' He held it out. 'It's her perfume too.'

'Are you sure?'

'Positive.' He dropped the garment and moved towards the bathroom door.

Ella stood there watching him fighting with his emotions.

'You'd better come too,' He said. 'If you're there maybe I won't feel so inclined to kill the bastard who's with her!'

The bathroom was full of steam, towels littering the tiled floor. The murmur of voices and soft laughter came from beyond a glass door totally obscured by condensation.

Walking up to it Mick threw it open.

Ella heard the woman's shriek of surprise as the door swung back; saw the water cascading down over the naked bodies of the two individuals who stood there, the man dark, the woman red headed, hair plastered to their faces. As the man brushed his out of his eyes her hand went to her face in horror.

'Andy!'

Memories long ago of catching Niall and Rachel in Fox Cottage flooded suddenly into her mind. But this time it was worse. This was her husband. The man who had kissed her goodbye this morning and reminded her, as he always did, how much he loved her. Betrayed; she had been betrayed again. Stifling a sob she turned and ran from the room.

Andy felt he was in the middle of a nightmare. He had found soaping Nina's body totally erotic, so much so that any potential danger attached to the location he had chosen for these activities had receded somewhat as things progressed. When the shower door was thrown open and he had seen Mick and Ella standing there somehow the whole situation seemed unreal. After all Mick was off site all afternoon and Ella was supposed to be looking at kitchens. Then the penny dropped.

He saw the horrified expression on Ella's face, watched as she ran out of the room and knew he had to stop her. He saw everything slipping away; his marriage, his job. He saw his father's outraged face and his stomach churned with fear.

Pushing out of the shower, he dodged a punch from Mick, grabbed a towel and ran from the bathroom. He could hear Mick shouting and Nina screaming as he gathered up his clothes along the landing. He ran downstairs, quickly pulled on his clothes in the kitchen and then headed for his car.

As he drove he tried to work out where she would go. Jenny's maybe? He stopped at the next phone box and called her. He could hear the sound of Christopher crying in the background as she answered. He tried to sound light hearted as he asked her if Ella was with her. Jenny was her normal friendly self. No, she hadn't seen her all day, but she'd said something about being out with Mick looking at kitchens. He finished the call and phoned the Lodge. Hearing Helen call out to her, he put the phone down and ran back to his car.

As Andy rushed out of the bathroom, Mick turned off the shower, grabbed Nina and pushed her against the wall.

'Dry yourself and get dressed!' He shouted, picking up a towel and throwing it at her. When she seemed reluctant to move he opened the door and wheeled her out by her elbow onto the landing.

'Come on, hurry up, your clothes are there!' He pushed her to the floor.

'What are you going to do?' She looked at him fearfully as she began collecting up her clothes.

'I know what I ought to do! Give you a bloody good hiding!'

'You wouldn't do that. Not to me Mick, you know you wouldn't.'

'I ought to! How could you do this? With him! And in this house?' His face crumpled, he seemed on the verge of tears.

'It's not just my fault!' She said miserably, pulling on her underwear. 'You're never at home any more. I hardly see you. I'm bored and unhappy. I keep trying to talk to you and you don't listen. I ran into Andy quite by accident. He made me laugh, showed me all the things I was missing.....'

'Shut up! I don't want to hear any more!' He shouted angrily. 'All this,' he waved a desperate arm around the landing, 'Was for you! I wanted to give you the best! So this is where I spent my time, building a dream home. Not out drinking, or having a good time with the boys. If I had maybe I'd be able to understand why you've done this to me.' He bent his head, his fingers stemming the wetness that threatened in his eyes.

'Mick,' she put her arms gently around his neck, her voice choking, 'Please.......'

He felt the warmth of her body, saw the rise of her breasts, soft and round, cradled within the confines of her low cut bra. She kissed him, her lips damp against his own, wriggling her body persuasively against his and he responded, finding, that despite his anger, his desire for her was as strong as ever.

'I love you Nina,' He whispered in her ear, holding her tightly to him, 'I couldn't bear to lose you.'

'You won't Mick.' She broke away from his embrace to look at him seriously. 'but you have to treat me right. I feel so neglected because of this farmhouse and the time you spend on it. I've been so miserable.' Her mouth wobbled as her eyes filled with tears. 'I don't think you love me any more.'

'But I do Nina,' He pulled her close again, 'I'd do anything for you.'

'Anything?' She sniffed.

'Anything! Just name it.'

'Get rid of this place then. I hate it!'

'But this is our home. A place to live. To grow. To have kids.' He pulled away from her, frowning.

'But I can't have kids.' She said looking at him bleakly.

'What?'

'It happened when I was fourteen. I got beaten up by a gang of girls on the estate. One of them kicked me in the stomach. I ended up in hospital. Took them ages to stop the bleeding. I nearly died. The doctor told me I'd never be able to have a baby. So, if you bring me here it will just be us two,' she said, tears welling up in her eyes. 'We'll be lost in all these rooms and all I'll ever be thinking about is how disappointed you are and how I've let you down, not being able to give you what you want.'

'My poor darling Nina,' He touched her face tenderly, her misdemeanours totally obliterated by the tragic revelation he'd just heard. 'I had no idea. Why didn't you say something when we first talked about this?'

'I don't know. You were so excited. Somehow I couldn't,' She looked at him, still tearful, 'but now it's all out in the open I want you to get rid of it, sell it. Please! I just want to stay in Kennet Close.'

'If that's what you really want Nina,' He said, cradling her like a small child and kissing her face. 'Then that's what we'll do.'

Ella was in the hall with her suitcase as Andy came through the front door.

'Ella darling, stop!'

He tried to intercept her but she elbowed him out of the way and ran for the door. The emotional vulnerability of tears which he knew he'd be able to handle weren't there any more. Instead she was dry eyed and full of anger.

'Leave me alone you bastard!' She shouted angrily as she ran across the gravel towards her car.

'Ella, please, listen to me!' He ran after her, reaching the car just as she heaved the case onto the back seat and climbed in.

He put his hand around the door pillar and leaned in.

'Take your hand away!' She looked up at him venomously.

'No, not before you hear me out.'

'I'll break your fingers!'

'Come on Ella, be reasonable,' He gave her his best sad little boy look, guaranteed to warm even the hardest heart.

The door swung shut with amazing force, giving him only seconds to extract his hand. The click of the lock followed immediately, and then the engine fired. He banged on the glass with the flat of his hand, pleading with her, promising her anything, but she refused look at him. Instead, her foot came down hard on the accelerator and she shot down the driveway leaving him standing there in a cloud of flying gravel and dust.

THIRTEEN

Tuesday 15th June

Instinct had told her Meridan Cross was the place to come. That here she would find the support she needed from those who loved her, in order to help her out of this nightmare. But now she was here Ella found she was unable to confide in the very people she had thought she could turn to.

After phoning Jenny and making emergency arrangements for the business to be covered by Joan for a week, she left Abbotsbridge, arriving at her grandmother's with the story that on impulse she had decided to give herself a well deserved break from the office.

'Hadn't you better ring Andy to let him know you've arrived safely?' Her grandmother had said when she had finished unpacking.

'Oh he's away on business with his father,' she stalled, wanting to pick the right time to sit down and discuss her troubles, 'He'll be back at the weekend.'

'Like you isn't he?' Laura had said with an approving smile, 'Wants to make a success of things. I think he's a grand young man! Handsome, hard working. You're so lucky Ella!'

Half heartedly returning her grandmother's smile, Ella sensed somehow that discussing the flaws in Andy's character might not be as easy as she first thought. And it suddenly occurred to her if she couldn't seek advice from Laura, neither would she be able to talk to Mary. Laura would expect to be consulted first on all family issues. She was caught and for the time being would have to put her marriage problems on hold until she found an appropriate time and place to discuss them with her grandmother.

In the Somerset Arms that evening she tried to leave her troubles behind as she met old friends and caught up with the gossip. The Miller boys were there; Rowan had been going out with Rachel for six months now, whilst it was rumoured Ash, a man in the same mould as his father, was involved with two different married women over in Morden. Doggy, grey and dignified occupied his usual corner by the fireplace; Guinness in hand and Toby asleep at his feet as he chatted to Jake Carr. And then there was Rachel. Watching her waiting at the bar chatting to Tom as he refilled their glasses, Ella noticed how happy and relaxed she looked.

The reason for this, beside her relationship with Rowan, Ella guessed, was due to her involvement in Mary's new business. Since the spring Willowbrook Farm had been running a small trekking centre. Mary had now extended the block where Merlin and Buster were stabled, bought in new stock and advertised in Dalton's Weekly and the Somerset County Council's tourist office for business. An enthusiastic Rachel had volunteered to help and Mary had been so impressed by Rachel's boundless energy and organising skills she had now handed the day-to-day management of the business over to her.

The enthusiasm for her new job had spilled over into their conversation as they sat talking that evening. For the first time everything in Rachel's life seemed to be going in the right direction.

'Oh yes, I knew there was something I had to tell you!' Rachel said excitedly as she returned with their drinks and sat herself down again, 'Your friend's back in the village.'

'Which friend?'

'The one with the band...Matt - what's his other name?'

'Benedict.'

'Yes, him. He came in for a drink last night. Said he'd come here to write and have a break before they tour America at the end of the month. And do you know something! Well,' she raised her eyes dreamily. 'Ella he's gorgeous, a real hunk in fact!'

'Is he now?' Ella looked at her friend sceptically. All she could remember were the cheesecloth shirts and scruffy jeans. His hair had been shoulder length, thick and untidy, his body greyhound lean. Both Mary and her grandmother had been very forthright about the difference a few good meals might make.

'What are you thinking about?' Rachel eyed her suspiciously.

'Your hunk. When I last saw him two years ago he was a six foot string bean.' Ella gave an amused laugh. 'In fact Mary said he needed fattening up.' She gave a far away smile and looked at Rachel. 'I always thought we were close, you know. It wasn't until I returned home that I found out he was getting married. To someone from his record company. And he'd never even mentioned a word of it while he was here.' She looked curiously at Rachel. 'So, what's she like?'

'Oh there's no one with him.'

'Probably back home in London.' Ella said as she looked at her friend and raised her glass, 'Still, he's history now, just like Niall!'

Rachel didn't reply she simply stared beyond Ella, her teeth tugging at her bottom lip.

'Rachel?'

'It's all right.' Rachel's looked at her, blue eyes filling with tears, 'Ignore me, I'm just being silly.'

'I'm so sorry, after all this time I'd thought.....'

'Oh I know! That I should be happy with Rowan. I am. Very. He's so good to me. But somehow the memory of Niall is always there, in the background. Remember the letter? He left the village so my mother wouldn't send me to Taunton as Aunt Ethel's housekeeper. He said he loved me and I know now he really did,' she said in a small, quiet voice. 'I wish I could get over him, give myself a chance with Rowan. But it's not happening.'

'Not yet maybe Rach. But I've been there too and it will, believe me, it will.'

Wednesday 16th June

Bob Macayne paced the floor of his office, cigarette in hand, pausing briefly to look out of his second floor window towards the site of the shopping precinct, watching the booms of the two yellow cranes swing back and forth, lifting and depositing materials as the building works progressed. Everything was going so well, he had even made the regional T.V. news, being interviewed about his vision for the town by that newly-arrived brunette presenter everyone was talking about. This feeling of being on course, of everything in his life finally falling into place had been short lived, however, when, on the evening of the interview he had received a telephone call from an almost hysterical Mel, telling him Ella had left Andy and gone back to Meridan Cross because she and Mick had caught Andy and Nina Taylor in the shower in Mick's farmhouse. The story seemed totally unbelievable, having definite undertones of a Brian Rix farce. And now he stood here waiting for Andy to arrive so that he could satisfy himself as to what had really happened.

A knock interrupted his thoughts and he turned from the window to see the red suited figure of Marion Westwood opening the door to let his son through. Andy crossed the room to one of the leather Chesterfields and eased himself quietly into it.

'Up!' As Bob seated himself behind his heavy mahogany desk, he motioned for Andy to get to his feet. 'Stand over here where I can see you properly.' he pointed to the empty area in front of his desk. Making eye contact with Andy for the first time he was met with a steadfast gaze from a face that was a daily reminder of his dead wife.

'Now,' Bob reached over and stubbed out the cigarette into the brass ashtray. 'What the fuck is this all about Andy?'

'All what Dad?'

'You and Nina Taylor,' Bob tilted back in his leather chair, watching his son impassively. 'What's been going on?'

'Nothing's been *going on* as you put it.'

'Bullshit Andy. I want to know!' Bob stabbed a finger at his son, 'and you won't leave this room until I get some answers.'

Met with silence he stood up angrily and paced towards the window. Hands in his trouser pockets he turned and stood there, waiting.

Andy shifted uncomfortably. 'It was a stupid thing I did which got out of hand,' he said with a shrug, 'It shouldn't have happened but it did. I'm sorry.'

Bob nodded, his expression sour, 'Details Andy, details please.'

Andy took a deep breath. There was no escape, he'd just have to improvise as he went along and hope his father believed him.

'Well, you know Mick's been doing up that old farmhouse at Bracken Down?'

Bob nodded.

'For some reason he wouldn't let Nina see it until it was finished. Wanted it all just right before she stepped over the threshold. I got a phone call from her yesterday afternoon, said she was tired of waiting. She knew Mick wouldn't be on site so asked if she could come up and have a sneaky look. I had a quiet afternoon so I though why not? I couldn't see the big deal in keeping it all hush-hush. She arrived and I let her in, showed her round. When we got upstairs she made a pass at me, she wouldn't leave me alone.' he gave a hopeless shrug of his shoulders, 'I tried to push her away Dad, but she just wouldn't let go. Then she was kissing me, pulling my clothes off and, well, I just gave in. It was just a one off, honestly. And I had no idea Mick would turn up with Ella like that. It made me realise how sordid it all must have looked.' He stared quietly at the floor for a moment, and then raised his head again, 'But it wasn't like that, it was a mistake. I blame myself for being so weak.' He said miserably. 'Mick and Nina seem to have managed to patch things up. I only wish I could do the same. But Ella's gone to Meridan Cross and I don't know how to go about getting her back. Maybe if we could get away from Abbotsbridge for a few weeks, spend some time together, we could sort things out, make it all right again.'

Bob Macayne, now back behind his desk, looked at his son's distress. Nina Harrison, he concluded, had been the worst thing that ever happened to him. A common, pushy little tart with an eye on getting herself up the social ladder. He thought marriage to Mick Taylor had sorted all that out, but obviously not.

'Sit down please.' He gave a weary sigh and waved a hand towards the couch, noticing the relief in Andy's face as he settled himself onto the Chesterfield.

'You mentioned getting away for a while.' Elbows on his desk, Bob steepled his fingers, bringing them to his lips thoughtfully. 'I think I may have an idea......'

'This problem with Ella and Andy, it is sorted now isn't it Bob?'

Mel Carpenter sat opposite Bob Macayne in a discreet corner of Ronaldo's. Liam had gone to London for three days on a RIBA Conference, leaving Mel as mistress of her own desires, with no need for excuses or pretexts to get her out of the house for secret meetings. Coffee had just arrived along with Bob's customary after dinner brandy and he looked relaxed and happy.

'Everything's under control Mel,' He gave her a confident look, 'believe me, a month in the sun with Lucia's family and they'll be new people.'

Mel stirred her coffee and brought the cup elegantly to her lips pausing for a moment, her head on one side, staring beyond him. 'Of course,' she said, returning her concentration to him, 'I blame Ella for most of this. Her and that blessed business. She's never home. It's about time someone reminded her of her wifely responsibilities.'

'Yes, well I think that may be taken care of too,' Bob replied, swirling the brandy around in his glass, 'I've also told Andy it's about time he thought about starting a family. A spot of motherhood should finish off Ella's great yen for work; bring her down to earth, back to reality. But,' he smiled, 'Not leaving anything to chance, if that doesn't work I have a contingency plan.'

'What sort of contingency plan?'

'I'm Ella's landlord. I now own all the buildings which house her businesses. Which means I can lean on her if necessary.'

'Lean on her?' Mel looked horrified, 'I'm not sure I like the sound of that Bob!'

'Renegotiate the lease Mel, put up the rent.' Bob laughed, 'What did you think I was going to do? Send in thugs with baseball bats?'

'I was a little concerned that was all.' Mel gave a shrug, trying to conceal her embarrassment.

'Well don't be; now about the holiday. My sister in law and her husband are away this week, visiting his family in the south. But they would be happy to have them from next Monday. So I have arranged a flight to Pisa for them. It leaves Heathrow early on Monday evening. Andy will collect Ella from Meridan Cross around lunch time that day and......'

'Just a minute!' Mel set her cup down noisily in its saucer. 'Are you telling me that you're leaving the responsibility for getting Ella on that plane to Andy?'

'Why not? I think he's more than capable of sorting out his own marital problems Mel; he's had the fatherly guidance bit from me and I'm now providing the means for him to carry it all out. We have to treat him as a man. We must not interfere otherwise he'll feel totally undermined.'

'Bob, how can you be so naive?' Mel's eyes sparked. 'Have you any idea how wilful my daughter is? Aided and abetted by that dreadful grandmother of hers, your son would almost certainly end up with the door shut firmly in his face.'

'So what do you suggest?'

'That we *all* go to Meridan Cross. As concerned parents we're merely turning up to add weight to Andy's plea for her to return and then of course we want to wave them off at the airport don't we?'

Bob could see the devious mind at work behind her cool expression. Mel had only one thing in mind; she was going there to drag Ella screaming and kicking out of Meridan Cross if need be.

'If we go, I don't want any heavy handedness,' He warned, 'We have to do this properly, otherwise Andy will end up living with the consequences while they're away and it could also wreck any prospects of you making peace with your father.'

'Oh don't worry, I will be perfectly lady-like,' She assured him with a wave of crimson tipped fingers, 'All I want to do is to ensure my daughter gets on that plane because believe me if you leave it to your son, she won't.'

'All right,' Bob caved in, partly because of the look he was getting and partly because he felt Mel's worries were possibly a little justified, 'but the last thing I want is Andy compromised in any way. We are merely there to support. Now then,' he leaned across the table to look into her flawless face, 'as Liam is away I don't suppose you'll be in a hurry to get home tonight.'

'Not especially,' She pulled her compact from her handbag and viewed her face in the mirror, 'Had you something in mind?'

'I thought you might like to come back to Everdene, maybe stay overnight.' He grinned. 'Tabby's away for a few days.'

'But I haven't brought a nightdress.' She said wickedly, reapplying the brilliant red to her mouth before snapping the compact shut.

'For what I've got planned Mel.' His dark eyes scanned her face, 'You won't need one.'

Thursday 17th June

It was mid afternoon and Ella sat relaxing in the garden at Willowbrook with Mary.

'This is the life!' Mary looked across at her and smiled, 'A brief moment of relaxation before we get on with the rest of the day. Oh, by the way, there's a folk singer on at the pub tonight. Richard and I thought we might pop down, would you like to join us?'

'Yes, I'd love to,' Ella laughed, finishing off her tea. 'I don't think I have any other pressing engagements.'

'Are you missing work?'

'Not really. I should have done this ages ago. It's nice to have different distractions for a change.'

'Does Matt come under that heading?'

'Matt? What made you think of him?' Ella turned to look at Mary. 'Rachel told me he was back in Fox Cottage, but I haven't seen him yet, nor do I intend going to seek him out. We parted company a long time ago.'

'On fighting terms by the sound of it.'

'Not quite,' she sat up, tucking her empty glass under her chair. 'Although I have to say, he was less than honest with me.'

'Are we talking about the same Matt? Your close friend?'

Ella nodded. 'Remember when he was here two years ago? That week we spent together, it was so good, it made me feel that after all the years of friendship we might be on the brink of something much more. Matt was always very shy, the last thing I wanted to do was scare or embarrass him. On the last night, when we went out to dinner, without actually saying so, I made my feelings very clear.' She gave a hopeless shrug, 'But it didn't work. As usual, at the first sign of intimacy he seemed to turn off like he always has done in the past. I felt totally confused. We seemed to be getting on so well until then. When I got home, mother told me he was involved with someone in London. She said he was about to get engaged. And his mother told her, so it must have been true. Of course it explained everything. But why didn't he mention a girlfriend? We told each other everything, there were no secrets, why hide that?'

'I have no idea Ella. But you've just said yourself how shy he was. When he sensed you wanted to be more than just his friend maybe it was the only way he could cope with the situation.' Mary said sympathetically. 'Sometimes saying and doing nothing seems the least harmful option.'

'Mary,' Ella looked amused, 'why are you making excuses for him?'

'I like him. I always have done,' she said with a serene smile. 'And as you're married to Andy now, don't you think it's time to put the past behind you?'

Ella stared out into the distance towards the hills which stood grey-green in the heat haze of the afternoon.

'I don't think I have the energy to sort the past out,' She replied softly. 'I've enough trouble coping with the present.'

'Ella what is it?' Mary leaned forward and gently touched her arm. 'What's wrong?'

Ella found herself caught by a sudden temptation to open up to Mary then quickly changed her mind. The potential rift between Mary and Laura, should her grandmother ever find out she had sought help for her problems at Willowbrook rather than Little Court, thrust itself to the front of her mind again.

'Problems at work, that's all,' she turned to Mary with a reassuring smile. 'Nothing for you to worry about.'

Matt could hear the sound of music as he got out of the car. As he walked towards the front door of the pub strains of Simon and Garfunkel's *'The Boxer'* could be heard coming through one of the open windows. He pushed open the half glass blue front door and stepped inside.

The pub was packed with people. In the far corner a young man in scruffy denims sat on an empty table, his feet on a chair, playing an acoustic guitar. He reminded Matt of Donovan with his dark unruly hair. The voice was pure and clear - this boy had star potential Matt thought, yet knew fame was the last thing he would want. Celebrity status would merely cheapen him; turn him into a money making circus act. Just like The Attitude had become, he thought cynically, knowing first hand about the constant manipulation of record company executives. Scorpio were just as bad as Centaur.

Easing between the push of bodies he stood between two older villagers leaning on the bar and ordered a cider. As he waited for Tom Bennett to serve him he looked around through the gaps in the crowd, trying to locate old Doggie Barker who had promised him a chance to win back the money he had lost at dominoes yesterday.

Tom placed the glass on the bar, smiling as he took the money from him.

'Over there in the corner,' He grinned, gesturing in the direction of the dart board. Matt moved away from the bar, sipping his drink. Now where was that old rogue?

Ella sat in rapt concentration, watching the young singer who had introduced himself as Dominic Sartain. There was an aura about him, a unique quality to his voice and simplicity in his singing. Her grandfather said he had been travelling the country over the last year, staying in one location for a few weeks and doing the rounds of the local pubs. He had a small notebook with an alphabetical index in which was written his repertoire and the audience were invited to choose songs from it during the evening's performance.

As the last chords of *The Boxer* faded away, followed by loud applause, Mary cast a glance across at Ella, watching as she whispered something to her grandfather before adding her hands to the appreciative clapping. She's hiding something I know, she thought, and it has absolutely nothing to do with work.

Old Doggie, sitting off to their left, had been thumbing through Dominic's songbook. Slowly he got up and approached him with his request. The young man nodded and after a mouthful of tonic water, picked up his guitar.

'The young man from the old country. He's very good isn't he?' Mary whispered to Ella as the first chords of *The Carnival is Over* filled the room.

Ella nodded, 'His voice is beautiful and there's so much emotion in each song he sings.' Looking at him she found all her tenseness gradually fading. Her world was crumbling, but that was twelve miles away, part of her other life. Tonight she would just relax and enjoy the evening. She closed her eyes and rested her head against the rough stone of the wall, carried away by the music. When eventually she opened them again she found someone in a battered Levi jacket, jeans and a white tee shirt, standing over her with a familiar grin on his face.

'Ella!' Matt said with a polite smile, sitting himself down beside her, with not so much a hint of surprise. 'Tracked you down at last. Rachel told me you were staying over at Little Court.'

'Yes,' she realised her tone sounded anything but friendly. 'Sorry, I haven't had time to call round; I've been busy helping Mary.' It was a lie but she desperately wanted to stifle his curiosity.

'Andy not with you then?' The question sounded innocent enough but Ella sensed intrusion. If Rachel had told him she was here, he also knew she was alone and he obviously wanted to know why.

'No. I understand you've left your fiancée behind as well,' she responded quickly, 'Or is it wife now?'

'Not yet,' He laughed, pausing to stare back to where Dominic was just coming to the end of his song. 'I'm here on my own because I didn't want any distractions while I was out here writing.'

Ella bristled at the casualness of his remark. Distraction indeed! This was supposed to be the woman he was going to spend the rest of his life with. Men, they were all the same she thought irritably.

'Can I get you all a drink?' She heard him say and saw him reach into his back pocket for his wallet.

Richard and Mary nodded, offering their empty glasses with a request for cider.

'Cider for me too please.' Ella looked into his face as she handed him her glass. He took it with a lazy smile, gathering up Richard's and Mary's at the same time. She watched him go; Rachel's description had been right. Matt Benedict had turned into an incredibly handsome man.

Now the evening was drawing to a close, almost time for everyone to go home. Last orders had been called and Dominic, finishing a medley of Springfields hits, raised his head to the crowd, catching sight of the clock above the bar, 'I have time for one more song before I bid you all good night,' He said in his lilting Irish accent, He held the book aloft, 'Are there any last requests?'

Matt got to his feet, leaned forward and took the small dog eared book from the young singer. Turning the pages slowly, he stopped before handing it back to Dominic, pointing.

He sat down again beside Ella just as Richard returned with a round of drinks. The room fell into hushed anticipation as guitar tucked into his lap, Dominic began strumming.

'What have you chosen?' Mary whispered as she picked up her glass.

'My father's one and only claim to fame,' He said picking up his glass, *'The Londonderry Air.'*

As if on cue, Dominic cleared his throat, put down his guitar, stood up and began to sing.

Oh Danny Boy, the pipes, the pipes are calling……

By the time he had eventually finished, everyone was singing along with him. All the older villagers, who remembered the song so well, had been caught by the clarity of his voice and the spell he had cast over the lyrics, each one plucking their own personal memories from the lines as they sang. Even Doggie sitting in his corner, wiped moisture from his eyes.

As the song came to an end, everyone clapped and cheered. Someone commandeered an empty beer glass, which was passed around for the audience to show monetary appreciation. When handed the glass, Dominic bowed and thanked everyone then began packing away his guitar. His actions signalled the end of the evening and gradually the bar emptied and one by one Tom's customers began to drift homeward.

'Well, that *was* beautiful,' Mary looked at Richard, reaching for his hand and holding it tightly. 'Didn't you just think so?'

'It certainly was,' He agreed, giving her an affection peck on the cheek, 'Ready for home now?'

'I am. Busy day tomorrow.'

They both stood up, Mary slipping on her jacket, Richard searching for his keys. 'Goodnight Matt,' Mary raised her hand in farewell as they moved towards the door, 'I'll see you in the morning,' she called to Ella, 'Jonty Michaels isn't due till nine thirty, you can have a bit of a lie in if you like. '

'No way,' Ella shook her head. 'I'll be up at six thirty as usual to take Merlin out; I couldn't bear to miss the best part of the day.'

'There you are, 'Richard said to his wife, slipping his arm in hers as they made their way towards the door, 'She may have been away for a while, but she's still a country girl at heart.'

'Mind if I come with you tomorrow morning?' Matt asked as they said their goodnights to Rachel and the Miller boys and followed the Evas's out of the pub.

'You don't ride.' She said abruptly.

'Yes I do.'

'Since when?' As they stepped out into the darkness she was eager to be gone away from this conversation and him.

'Last year in Australia,' He continued, pulling his car keys from his pocket, 'Jeff wanted to visit a cattle station. We had a few days resting up between concerts so the promoters fixed us up with a break on one up in Northern Territory,' He laughed, 'Wall to wall cows and you should have seen the dust....'

'Actually Matt,' Ella interrupted as she watched him unlock his car, 'If you don't mind I think I'd rather be by myself. I'm not very good company first thing in the morning.'

'Ella, what is it?' His face creased into a frown as he leaned on the open car door.

'Nothing; nothing at all,' she said calmly as she backed away from him, eager to go, 'It's as I said, at that time of the morning I like my own company. Maybe I'll catch up with you later in the week. Bye.'

Moments later he passed her in the lane, hooted and roared off into the darkness. She smiled. The easiness with which she had got rid of him pleased her and left her feeling confident that he had got the message and she could now concentrate on more important matters; like what to do about Andy.

As she walked she ran her mind back over that day and the events that had preceded her leaving. She saw the bathroom thick with steam, Mick opening the cubicle door. The horrified surprise on the faces of its two occupants, wet and naked, wrapped in each other's arms. She felt sick. How could he have done that to her behind her back? Was it the first time? Or had they been seeing each other regularly? She had expected resistance when she told him about the extra hours she'd need to put in travelling out to Wellington and Taunton. Instead, he'd been un-typically agreeable. Now she knew why. It gave him the perfect opportunity to......she couldn't think about it without feeling angry. As she passed the shadowed walls of Greystone Lodge and walked through the gates of Little Court she knew almost certainly that he would be coming for her soon. Perhaps, she decided, it might be better not to mention anything to her grandmother until he arrived. Let him do the explaining. It would make for a much more interesting scenario.

Friday 17th June

Ella arrived at Willowbrook at 6.35 the next morning, looking forward to her ride. She passed Richard and his foreman Jake Carr on the road up to the farm, border collies Gaffer and Laddie trotting behind them as they headed towards the south pasture in the brilliance of the early morning to collect the herd for milking.

Twenty minutes later she was riding back down the lane, breathing in the cool, clear country air. Childhood memories came rushing to meet her; the hay bale houses she played in with Nick, bottles of tea for the thirsty farmhands, the village fête held in the grounds of her grandmother's house. But things had moved on. She was an adult now. She had a business and a husband; a husband who just might turn up any day, probably with his father in tow, to try to persuade her to come home. Let them come, she said to herself fiercely. Just let them come. They'll have to explain everything to my grandmother first. Let's see how Bob gets out of this one!

The sun was coming up behind Hundred Acre, filling the wood with shafts of smoking light as the night's dampness met early morning warmth. Above her the sky was a clear vivid blue as she turned Merlin towards the edge of the barley field. Yet another hot day was promised. Perhaps this afternoon she would relax on the terrace at Little Court and sunbathe. A whisper of breeze caught the ends of the wild dark hair which tumbled loosely down her back and over her shoulders. Already she could feel the warmth of the sun through the back of the scarlet polo shirt she wore over her jodhpurs.

The pathway she took around the field led her steadily upwards towards the dappled green shadow of the wood. It was a longer route but she wanted to avoid passing Fox Cottage, where Matt was staying, at all costs. Reaching the edge of the trees, she took a deep breath and relaxed. This was truly the best part of the day, fresh and untouched with half the world still sleeping. Suddenly she heard the two tone blare of a diesel and saw what she realised must be the Penzance Express pass at speed along the valley bottom past the empty station buildings. She reined in for a moment and sat looking at the view, the multicoloured green patchwork of fields bordered by darker hedges, cows and sheep dotted over the hills to the west and east, the entwining ribbons of road, rail and river running the length of the valley floor.

'Fantastic isn't it?' The sudden intrusion of a voice into her daydream startled her and she turned in the saddle to see Matt sitting only yards from her on Mary's black mare Cassie.

'What are you doing here?' She kneed Merlin closer to him.

'Waiting for you. See, I can ride.'

'O.K., you've proved your point,' she said, un-amused, 'Now I think you'd better take Cassie back before Mary finds her missing and phones the police.'

'No need, Mary knows. I come up here every morning before breakfast. To get my inspiration for the day. That's why I wanted to join you.'

She studied him for a moment, tanned and finely muscled, sitting astride Cassie in white tee shirt and jeans. Physically, the old Matt had completely disappeared, only the tormenting cognac eyes remained unchanged. Those eyes, which had once smiled into hers now looked adoringly at someone else. A faceless blonde, brunette or redhead living in London. The sudden thought of his emotional commitment to another woman blew ice cold through her, immediately extinguishing the small flame which had been fluttering.

'So,' he broke into her daydream, 'now I'm here, where are you taking me?'

'No where.' She replied, nudging Merlin forward into the wood. 'I told you, I ride alone.'

'Ella,' He called after her, 'please, don't go.....'

But Ella simply ignored him and rode away without a backward glance.

Matt watched as horse and rider were swallowed up by the wood. He had sensed her hostility the moment he met her last night. Something had happened. He wondered what it could be. And what gave her the right to be angry at all? Shouldn't he be the one nursing a grudge? After all she had been the one who only a month after being here with him in Meridan Cross had announced her engagement to Andy Macayne. They had never had secrets from each other. Why then? Nothing made sense any more. He turned Cassie's head and pushed her eastwards in the opposite direction to Ella. Now was not the time, but he was not going to let this drop. One way or the other he was determined to get some answers out of her.

FOURTEEN

Saturday 19th June,

Andy was having breakfast when the telephone rang. Taking his coffee with him he moved over to the kitchen wall, lifting the receiver.

'Andy.' It was Bob, 'How are things?'

'Fine, Helen's been looking after me really well. What's the latest?'

'Lorenzo's expecting you Monday evening. I've booked the flight. We'll drive over to Meridan Cross and pick Ella up on the way to Heathrow. He'll send the boys to meet you at Pisa. Oh by the way, Mel's coming out to see you this morning.'

'Mel? Why?'

'She's covering your job while you're away.'

'Mel selling houses? Are you mad?'

'No Andy. I think she's perfectly capable of looking after site sales in your absence. She's good with people, likes to chat.'

'That's about it, Dad, chat! She'll just turn it into a big social occasion, she won't sell a thing!'

'Andy, she's very keen and I think you under estimate her powers of persuasion. In fact, I'm so confident of Mel selling at least one property while you're away that I'm prepared to put fifty pounds on it.'

'That's totally crazy Dad! Still, if you're prepared to lose that kind of money.'

'I think you'll be the one losing, son.' Bob laughed, and then his tone softened slightly. 'Look, I know you've had a bit of a rough time of it lately, but with what I've set up for you now, all you need to do is to go away, relax,' he gave a rough laugh, 'and start planning that family of yours. Not much else to think about while you're soaking up the sun is there?'

'No Dad,' Andy knew arguing was useless, given the mood his father was in. He had broken out in a cold sweat when the discussion in his father's office turned to family planning. It was far too early to complicate his life with talk of babies. All he wanted was things to go back to being safe and boring as they had been before. As he said goodbye and put down the phone he suddenly realised his father had missed out one vital component in all these arrangements; the fact that Ella might not want to go with him.

Ella skirted the barley field, slowly edging Merlin into the wood. After several restless days wondering what was going on in Abbotsbridge she had decided to delay her ride until after breakfast to put in a call to Jenny first.

She felt the emotion in Jenny's voice as she spoke to her. Her normal calmness had been completely abandoned. All these events were close to home, they affected members of her family and what Bob Macayne had done had left her seething.

'I can't believe it Ella,' She said bitterly, 'Andy's caused all this trouble and what does he get? A month in Italy with his Aunt and Uncle. Bob's sweeping this all under the carpet, getting him out of the way for a month so that by the time he comes back you'll have returned from Meridan Cross and everything will have calmed down. It's so cowardly!'

'What about Mick? How's he coping?'

'Don't ask! Would you believe he's taken her back?'

'What?'

'Yes, Dad saw him last night,' Jenny said, her voice quiet exasperation, 'He told him he's forgiven her, that it was partly his fault and he's going to make sure it never happens again. He said he hoped you and Andy sort things out soon!'

'How could he do this?' Ella felt the anger flooding through her as she realised how isolated that made her position, 'Oh Jen, what am I going to do?'

'Why don't you come home Ella? You can stay with us for a while.'

'I can't. Not yet. I need to think things through properly first. I'll call you Monday......'

The conversation haunted her as she turned Merlin into the wood, following her usual path. On the lower edge of the hill where Hundred Acre and Sedgewick Woods merged she came to a small flat clearing full of lush grass and flowers, sheltered by a circle of heavy oaks but open enough to let the sun's rays through. She dismounted and tied Merlin loosely to a low branch, leaving him to crop the grass. Pulling a bottle of lemon barley from her saddlebag, she unscrewed it and took several mouthfuls then, clasping it tightly in her hand, began pacing back and forth across the clearing, running her mind over recent events. There was no justice, none at all. Andy and Nina had got away with it, aided and abetted by Bob's protection and Mick's spinelessness. It was more than she could bear!

Angrily she threw the bottle across the clearing then sat down on a nearby log, covering her face with her hands, voicing her frustration through her fingers, with a scream that sent wood pigeons scattering noisily into the air from the trees above her. In the stillness that followed she heard the soft nicker of a horse. A rider was coming, probably drawn here by her scream. Now she'd have to find an excuse for her outburst. Merlin raised his head as he heard the sound of approaching hooves. A rider on a black horse entered the clearing. Ella watched them approach; knowing Matt Benedict was the very last person she wanted to see.

'I heard a scream.' He said with a look of concern as he dismounted and tied Cassie next to Merlin. 'Are you all right?'

'Yes, fine.' She shrugged as if nothing in the world was the matter.

'You don't look all right.'

'What's that supposed to mean?'

'It means I'm concerned.' He looked at her for a moment. 'I'd say you're upset about something.'

'If I am, it's my business!' She said tartly, getting up and walking past him, nudging a gap between Cassie and Merlin, her fingers releasing his reins from the branch.

'Is that it? You're just going to leave? I thought someone was murdering you. Don't you think you owe me some sort of explanation?'

Checking Merlin's girth, Ella could feel the anger burning in her face, 'Actually Matt, I think you're the last person I owe any explanation to,' she said irritably, gathering up the reins and slotting her foot into the stirrup. She swung herself up into the saddle, eager to be gone, only to find strong hands were around her waist pulling her from Merlin's back. She cried out in fear as she felt Merlin move away from her and found herself in mid air with the prospect of landing between him and Cassie and being trampled on. But Matt held onto her, swinging her around until she was clear of both horses before releasing her effortlessly into the soft grass.

She was up in an instant, brushing herself down, facing him indignantly.

'How dare you manhandle me!'

'I'm not letting you go until I get some answers.' Anger and hurt mingled in his face as he spoke.

'You're wasting your time,' she said, walking back to her fallen tree trunk and sitting down, crossing her arms defensively, 'We've nothing to discuss.'

'Oh yes we have,' He replied as he re-tied Merlin's reins to a nearby tree, 'I want to know why all of a sudden I've become public enemy number one. What exactly have I done? I thought we were friends.'

'We were........once.'

Giving Merlin an affectionate pat on the rump he turned to look at her.

'Were?'

'I thought I knew who you were,' She replied, staring at the ground, 'but I don't think I do any more.'

He walked across the clearing, stopping in front of her, frowning. 'Me? I haven't changed.'

'Yes you have,' On the brink of tears, she found herself confronting the subject she had wanted so badly to avoid. She looked up at him. 'You're no better than him really.'

'Andy,' He grimaced, 'I might have known! That's why you've come back here on your own isn't it? What's happened?'

'Nothing that concerns you!'

'Ella I only want to help.' He leaned forward and pulled her to her feet.

'I don't need your help!' She shouted, pushing him away, 'Just leave me alone!'

Turning away from him she ran as fast as she could across the clearing, ripping the reins from the branch and pulling herself into the saddle.

Once she had reached the safety of the wood she stopped. Oh God, she thought, what have I done? Slowly she swung Merlin round and rode back towards the clearing, taking shelter behind a group of ash trees. Beneath the curtain of leafy branches she looked for him, saw him sitting on the upturned log, wearily resting his head in his hands.

She studied him for a moment. She had let her temper get the better of her. Her grandmother would be horrified. Worse still she had her anger explode over the wrong man. Hadn't she been saving that for Andy?

She hesitated, remembering that last evening together. What if Mary was right? What if he had read her signals and had not been able to respond to them, scared to tell her about Belinda because he didn't want to hurt her feelings. Was that really such a crime? Wasn't that caring in a strange sort of way? After all he had never lied to her, never led her on or made her feel there could ever be anything but friendship between them. Her pain had been all about confronting the truth, realising that her dream of being with him was over, because he was going to marry someone else. It had absolutely nothing at all to do with him.

She nudged Merlin forward and back out into the clearing. Matt watched her as she approached his expression tight.

'I'm sorry,' She said quietly, 'that was totally unforgivable of me. Can we talk?' And sliding from Merlin's back she joined him on the log.

Matt leaned across the table to look at Ella, a contented smile on his face.

'Thank you for this evening.' He said as the waitress brought their coffee.

'It's the least I could do. I'm still horrified that I could have behaved so badly.' She felt light headed from the wine as she smiled back at him, watching as he added cream and sugar to his cup.

'Understandable under the circumstances. Still let's not dwell on the negative side of life. We've had a great time, caught up with each other at last.'

He was right, of course, it had been a marvellous evening at their old haunt The Charlton Cat, complimented with good food and wine, as they sat together unravelling the last two years of their respective lives; she with One Plus One and he with his life in the music business. There had been no mention of Belinda, but Ella expected that was because, sensitive to her situation, he didn't want to upset her.

Occasionally when their eyes met she felt the old familiar pull of attraction, but deliberately ignored it, telling herself to behave. He was just a friend; a very good friend she had sat for an hour with up in Hundred Acre wood talking about her problems with Andy. A friend who had advised her that no matter how angry and hurt she was, she should pick up and phone and contact Andy and make arrangements to meet somewhere neutral to try and resolve the problem. It wouldn't be easy, he said, but she couldn't simply run away from it. Andy was after all her husband.

She smiled to herself; Matt had always had a sensible and logical approach to problems, but now he seemed worldlier too. With his fame he had travelled extensively, seen and done things those left behind in Abbotsbridge could only dream about. The changes to his physique were he said, down to Sonny.

'We were sitting round in one of the hotel rooms drinking and he came in. He looked at us and shook his head. 'What a bunch of layabouts you are!' He said, mimicking Sonny's Cockney accent. 'Look at Roger Daltrey. He's one fit geezer. And if you lot think you've any chance of coming within a whisker of being as good as the 'Orrible Who, then it's time you got off your backsides and did some exercise!'

That had been the beginning and Matt had been amazed at the changes it had brought all of them. 'No one kicks sand in my face these days,' he said, making Ella laugh.

It was 10.30. A few tables were still occupied, taped music drifting from the speakers. The waitress returned to refill their cups, leaving the bill on a small silver dish.

'We'll have to do this again,' He said, watching as she dropped a fan of notes onto the bill. 'My shout next time.'

'Yes, I'd like that,' She said, closing her bag, 'You know, I forgotten what good company you are.'

'Flatterer,' He smiled, his hand reaching reassuringly for hers across the table, his eyes warm. As his fingers closed over hers, she trembled slightly.

'Cold?' He frowned.

'It's nothing,' She said feeling the ripple again as she got to her feet, 'Shall we go?'

They were both silent during the five mile drive back to Meridan Cross which took them through unlit country lanes, the headlights of the car bathing the overgrown banks with an eerie brightness.

Ella looked out of the window feeling relaxed and sleepy as she watched the moon which hung round and bright above Hundred Acre, veiled by a single fine pale finger of cloud.

The road took them downhill, clipping the edge of the wood, where over the years branches had laced like fingers to make a roof high above the overgrown banks. Passing Collins Barn and the derelict station, they soon reached the outskirts of the village.

'Fancy a night-cap before I take you back?'

Ella nodded and the car accelerated quickly through the village and back out into the darkness of the countryside. A moment later, it swung sharply to the right and up the track towards Fox Cottage.

The Alfa eventually came to a standstill outside the cottage; Matt killed the engine and got out. Ella eased herself from the passenger seat and followed him carefully over the uneven ground towards the front door of the cottage. The coolness of the night air made her feel quite light headed. How much red wine had she drunk? Four glasses? Five? She couldn't remember.

In the darkness of the porch, they paused while he pulled the front door key from his jacket pocket.

'Damn!' He swore as it slipped from his grasp, falling with a metallic ring onto the stone slabs of the porch floor. They both laughed and squatted down, running their hands over the rough flagstones. It was Ella's fingers which eventually touched metal.

'Got it!' She said triumphantly, getting to her feet slowly and leaning against the door as she handed it to him. The strange tingling sensation began again almost as soon as his fingers closed around hers.

He smiled, leaning across her, feeling for the lock and quite unexpectedly something intruded into the silence of the dark countryside surrounding them. A sound which came from nowhere, triggered by the touch of his fingers and the way his body was now pressed closely against hers; the unmistakeable rhythmic thud of her heart.

As he twisted the key and pushed, his cheek almost touched hers and she was suddenly overcome by a great desire to turn her face to his and kiss him. Then the door opened and she almost fell inside.

'I think I've drunk rather too much red wine,' She said as he caught her and took her into the front room, settling her unsteadily on the arm of the settee, 'Thank you, I'll perch here for a moment.'

'Better just make it a coffee then,' He laughed, disappearing into the kitchen.

She sat there for a moment, dazed and muzzy not only from the wine but also from the sudden and unexpected return of feelings left behind long ago. This was silly, very silly, she thought. It shouldn't be happening; it's the wine. The wine! She sat bolt upright, her hand going to the base of her throat, feeling nauseous. Then clamping her hand over her mouth, she got to her feet and ran for the front door.

'Ella, are you O.K.?'

She was aware of his hand on her back as she knelt in the grass afterwards, wiping her mouth with the handkerchief she had found in her pocket. She nodded silently her mouth tasting vile.

'Come on,' He pulled her gently to her feet, 'I think I'd better get you home.'

Sunday 20th June,

The blue and white pleasure cruiser, *Lord Nelson*, cut smoothly through the water carrying just over one hundred passengers to celebrate Bryan Tate's fiftieth birthday. On board with Bryan and his immediate family were friends and business colleagues from both Kingsford and Abbotsbridge. A jazz band on the lower deck was playing *Alexander's Rag Time Band*, while couples danced enthusiastically around an open area in front of the small stage. On the upper deck under a broad canvas canopy, Jenny and Issy, drinking Pimms in long tall glasses sat together watching the river wash past the boat as they left Kingsford far behind.

Issy, who had successfully won the catering contract for Bryan's birthday bash, was taking advantage of a quiet moment, her gaze drawn occasionally towards the beautifully decorated table at the end of the deck. There lay the remnants of the sumptuous buffet which had just been consumed by Bryan's guests and she watched as her waitresses stacked plates and cleared away. Below deck fresh preparations were going on for the champagne toast and the cutting of the cake, scheduled for later, when the boat was on the journey back to Kingsford. For the moment however, there was time to relax. Below among the dancers, Betty and Jack Taylor were enjoying themselves, while Liam, who had come alone - Mel having one of her famous migraines - was with Nick, heads together as they leaned on the rail, deep in conversation.

'Well,' Jenny said gazing out into the green, open countryside, 'This *is* an enjoyable way to pass a Sunday afternoon.'

'Very relaxing,' Issy agreed, closing her eyes and tilting her face towards the warmth of the sun. After a moment's silence she opened them. 'Have you heard from Ella?' she asked.

Jenny nodded. 'Spoke to her yesterday.'

'How was she?'

'Angry. She can't believe what's happened.'

'Neither can I. Andy's got away with it again, hasn't he? Like he always does! What's she going to do?'

'She wants more time to think. Said she'd call me tomorrow.'

'I told you this would happen didn't I?'

'You did,' Jenny nodded, her attention caught by something behind Issy.

'Of course that brother of yours hasn't exactly helped the situation,' Issy gave the ice in her glass a gentle shake, ignoring the fact that Jenny was looking directly at her and shaking her head. 'In fact I'd say kissing and making up with Nina has made things a lot worse for Ella. I mean who in their right mind....what is it?' She frowned at Jenny then swung around to find Mick looming over her.

'Go on then!' Mick glared down at her, 'Finish what you've got to say!'

'I.....' Issy's blue eyes moved nervously from him back to Jenny and then she suddenly glanced over the side of the boat, 'Oh, we're slowing down! That means we're at Chatley Weir. If you'll excuse me both, I must check on how things are below deck.' And with an embarrassed smile, she slid out of her seat and away from them both.

Mick turned to follow her but Jenny caught his arm.

'Mick, don't!' She shook her head.

'She had no right Jen! Absolutely no right!'

'She's only saying what a lot of people are thinking. Ella has friends in Abbotsbridge, many of whom feel things would have been a lot better if you'd made a little more fuss over what happened.'

'I couldn't do that Jen,' He said stubbornly, 'Not when what happened was partly my fault.......'

'Mick, how exactly was it your fault?'

'I neglected Nina. You know she likes going out, having a good time. I was so busy involved with other things. Work, the farmhouse. I see how easy it was for Andy to take advantage of her. But from now on things will be different, she'll have my undivided attention,' he gave a determined smile, 'Seems I lost my way a bit, but it won't happen again.'

'So where is she today?' Jenny's gaze wandered to the lower deck, realising she hadn't seen her sister-in-law on board.

'She felt a bit under the weather,' He said quietly, 'I left her in bed.'

'So how come you're here? Where's all this *undivided attention*?'

'She wanted me to come, said it was important that I enjoy myself. Said she didn't mind spending the day alone. Of course I had to make it up to her. I know she was bitterly disappointed so I've promised to buy her the diamond bracelet she's had her eye on in Kendals.'

'She's very lucky having you,' Jenny said gently, keeping a firm grasp on the angry frustration she felt welling up inside, 'I hope she realises that, Mick.'

'Of course she does, Jen. Like I know I'm very lucky having her,' He paused to glance down at the dancers below. 'Better go, I only came up here to get Mum another drink. Catch you later eh?'

Watching him walk away down the deck she knew he was happy now. Issy's deprecating words had left him unsure of himself and so he had looked to her for sisterly support. And she, being the sister she was, had sacrificed her feelings to protect his. But this will all end in tears she thought as he disappeared from sight. I know it will.

The *Lord Nelson* had now reached the weir and some of the crew had jumped off to tie it to the bank, letting the passengers disembark while they manoeuvred the vessel around for the return journey. Jenny left the table and went in search of Issy, finding her leaning over the side of the boat watching the gang plank being lowered.

'Sorry,' Issy said quietly as she joined her. 'Me and my big mouth again. Is he O.K?'

Jenny nodded her head wearily. 'I've patched up his ego for the time being, but I've had to compromise my real feelings. I hate doing that, you know Iz, but what else is there? If I tell him I feel exactly the same as you do, he'll probably never speak to me again.'

'Fancy stretching your legs while they turn this thing around?' Issy said, looking longingly at the bank. 'It might cheer you up a bit.'

'Yes, why not?' Jenny forced a smile, 'I don't know. Brothers! Just be thankful you haven't any!'

They walked together along the lower deck where the band was now playing *Hernando's Hideaway* and a general scramble for the gang plank was taking place. Out on the river bank someone had started a conga and the sway of bodies stretched far out along the well worn dirt path, laughter floating out across the water.

As Jenny stepped off the gang plank she was immediately claimed by her father as the end of the conga chain went by, and was carried off.

Issy managed to escape and headed towards the narrow Victorian footbridge which straddled the weir just a few hundred yards from the boat. Walking to its middle, she stopped and leaned on the balustrade, her gaze switching between the activity on the *Lord Nelson* and the conga line which had now disappeared up into the thin wood which bordered the river. As the sun broke through the trees she smiled, feeling relaxed. Reaching up she pulled her sunglasses down from their perch up in her thick fair hair to shield her eyes from the brightness.

'I want a word with you!'

She hadn't heard him coming and the force with which he grabbed her arm and spun her around almost made her cry out with shock as the sunglasses fell from her hand and clattered onto the boarded walkway.

'Let go of me!' She wrenched herself free, 'What do you think you're doing!'

'Over there, just now!' A red faced Mick gestured angrily in the direction of the *Lord Nelson*, 'Exactly what were you insinuating?!'

'Oh for goodness sake!' Angrily she bent down to retrieve her sunglasses, 'Does it really matter?'

'Yes it does!' He looked at her, his face full of indignation.

'O.K.,' She faced him fearlessly, 'If you must know, it's been puzzling me for days now. I can't quite work out what makes you tick.'

'What are you talking about?!'

'You catch your wife in the shower in your own house with another man and do nothing about it.'

'Ah!' He gave her a triumphant smile, 'That's where you're wrong. I have done something about it. It won't happen again. It's sorted.' He hesitated, 'What are you looking like that for? Why are you smirking?'

'Sorted?' She gave a disdainful snort, 'How, exactly?'

'I've made some changes.'

'What sort of changes?'

'Well for a start I've put the farmhouse on the market.'

'What?'

'Don't you see? That was part of the problem. I was never home. I neglected her, that's why it happened.'

'Now let me get this straight,' Issy gave him a thoughtful look, 'She took all her clothes off and got into the shower with Andy simply because you weren't paying her enough attention?'

'There's more to it than that, but, well, yes.'

She raised her eyes skywards, 'I can't believe you just said that! Can't you see? She's made a complete fool of you!'

'She has not!'

'She has,' Issy argued, 'She's turned it all around; got you taking the blame. And what's even more incredible is that you are actually stupid enough to believe her!'

'And you're so smart I suppose!' He countered, 'Don't you understand what she did was a cry for help! Can't you see how desperate she must have been to do what she did?'

'Desperate!' She almost shrieked, 'I think she probably enjoyed every minute of it! And if the opportunity presents itself, she'll do it again! And next time it will be a whole lot easier, because she's got the measure of you now! She knows just how to play you and get away with it!'

'Issy,' Mick said with a patronising shake of his head, 'You obviously don't see the same woman I do.'

Issy glared at him, 'See! I can see perfectly well thank you! You're the one who's in obvious need of a guide dog!' And with a parting huff of indignation, she pulled on her glasses, pushed past him, and ran back across the bridge towards the boat.

FIFTEEN

Sunday 20th June

'I thought I'd find you here,' Matt climbed onto the five bar gate in the paddock at Willowbrook, watching as Ella schooled an enthusiastic four year old perched precariously on a chunky brown pony, 'I came to see how you were feeling.'

'I'm fine now thanks,' Ella replied, adjusting her grip on the pony's halter as she circled the paddock, 'I'll just have to remember to take my alcohol in moderation next time.'

'I didn't think you'd drunk that much.'

'Neither did I, but there you go.'

He watched her as she slipped a long leading rein on the pony and after a few words with the small boy stood back to let him show the skills he had learned so far.

'If I promise not to ply you with too much alcohol would you come out with me again this evening? I'd like to see Otter Falls'

She turned around with a frown, 'Why?'

'Well, for starters, I've never been there. Rachel says it's very pretty and that sometimes at dusk you might actually get to see an otter. I thought we could have a drink in the Arms and then take the short cut across the fields.'

'Fine,' she turned and smiled at him, 'but don't pin your hopes too much on Tarka appearing. He's very shy species.'

'Takes after me then,' he said with a laugh as he slid from the gate. 'I'll be in the Arms at eight, see you then.'

It was after six when Ella pulled up outside Little Court. As she got out of her car she saw her grandmother coming towards her across the front lawn with a trug of lilies over her arm, secateurs in her hand.

'Finished for the day?' She asked as Ella reached her.

'Yes, I stayed on to help Mary and Rachel stable the trekking ponies.' Ella replied, kissing her cheek, 'Rachel took a group of eight out today. This trekking thing really seems to have caught on.'

'Mary's always had a good nose for a gap in the market.' Laura said as they made their way towards the house. 'And, of course, Tom provides the packed lunches, so it's good for local business too.'

Entering the back lobby, Laura pulled off her cotton gloves and dropped them into the basket.

'Would you like me to find a vase for those flowers?' Ella asked sliding her jacket from her shoulders and hanging it up.

'Please. There should be a tall cut glass thing in the cupboard over there, under the sink.'

Ella found the vase and half filled it with water, setting it on the draining board in front of her grandmother.

'So what are you up to this evening?' Laura asked as she began carefully arranging each of the pure white blooms.

'Oh, nothing exciting; just a drink with Matt.'

Laura lifted the vase and carried it through the kitchen and up the passageway which led to the hall, Ella following behind. 'Ettie left some cold meat and salad for dinner if you're interested,' she called over her shoulder, 'I'm eating out tonight - Higher Padbury; my bridge evening.'

'It's OK, I'll just grab a sandwich; I have to be at the Arms by eight.'

Laura placed the vase on a highly polished mahogany table set under a small window and altered the position of each bloom slightly to show them off to their best effect.

'Ella,' She turned to look at her granddaughter, her face serious, 'I don't want to interfere, but whatever you're up to with Matt you will be careful won't you?'

'I'm not up to anything Grandma. We're good friends, that's all.'

'I'm glad to hear it.' She looked at Ella, her blue eyes solemn, 'The reason for my concern is you've been here nearly a week and there hasn't been one phone call from Andy.'

'I told you he's away on business.'

'Then I thought at you at least might have called him. Forgive me for asking my dear, but here's nothing wrong at home is there?'

Ella paused for a second and then shook her head firmly.

'No. Everything is fine, it really is. Oohh!' Suddenly she sucked her breath in sharply.

'What's wrong?'

'I was sick last night,' She winced, 'And my stomach's been upset today too. I thought it was the wine, but it must have been the prawns I had at the Charlton Cat,' she rubbed her stomach gently. 'I'm still getting the odd twinge.'

'Milk of Magnesia, that will settle your stomach,' Laura declared. 'Go and see Ettie.'

'But Grandma!'

'Ella! Please go!'

Laura watched her leave the room. Upset stomach indeed! More like a deliberate distraction to avoid awkward questions. Something wasn't right, she was sure of it. Something Ella obviously did not want to talk about. Whatever it was, perhaps a quiet moment together tomorrow afternoon might just get to the bottom of it all.

Matt walked into a half empty Somerset Arms to find Ella sitting by the dart board talking to Rachel who was playing darts with Rowan Miller. She looked up at him with a smile as he approached, her long black hair caught back with green combs, exactly matching the colour of the halter neck top she wore.

As he had driven down to the village tonight his thoughts had been of nothing but her. Last night the invitation back to Fox Cottage was just the opportunity he needed to ask the question that had been niggling at him ever since he had run into her again. Unfortunately too much wine had wrecked his chances. But tonight was different; they would have a quick drink and then walk up to Otter Falls. There he would have her undivided attention.

As he joined them, the game finished. Rowan, pulled his darts from the board and walked to the bar to hand them over to Tom. Rachel got to her feet, slipping her blue cardigan over her shoulders.

Matt checked his watch, 'You two off already?'

'Yes.' Rachel cast a look of pure pleasure in Rowan's direction. 'Rowan's taking me out to dinner. We've a table booked at the Castle Hotel in Kingsford.'

'Big bucks job eh? Must be something special.'

'It's Rowan's twenty fifth birthday. Hey! Why don't you both join us?' Rachel said, looking quickly from Ella to Matt. 'It would be like a proper birthday party then. I'm sure there wouldn't be any trouble seating two extra. You wouldn't mind would you Rowan?' She asked, eyes wide like an excited child.

Matt could see from Rowan's dark-eyed expression that extra company was the last thing on the agenda for that evening.

'It's a kind thought,' He replied, looking at both of them, 'But we already have plans for the evening.'

'Yes,' Ella nodded in agreement, 'Matt wants to see Otter Falls.'

'Oh!' A flicker of disappointment crossed Rachel's face.

'Never mind Rach,' Rowan said with a smile, hugging her tightly and winking his thanks to Matt over the top of her head. 'We'll just have to drink all that bubbly ourselves. Come on....'

Watching them leave, Ella slipped off her jacket and sat down.

'I thought we were off to Otter Falls,' Matt frowned.

'We are, there's plenty of time, sit down and finish your drink,' she patted the seat beside her. Obediently he joined her.

'So what exactly are these Falls?' He said after a mouthful of cider. 'I'm intrigued; no one ever mentioned them before.'

'Oh they're nothing special. A place in the wood just over the hill out of the village, where Hundred Acre ends and Sedgewick Wood begins. The land falls away quite steeply, there's a waterfall and a large pool then the river continues west,' she raised her eyes thoughtfully to the ceiling. 'Nick and I used to swim there as children. There's also a legend attached to the place.'

'Is there?'

'Yes. A young Saxon noblewoman called Enna threw herself off the falls and drowned when she heard that her husband had been killed in battle by the Danes. She loved him so much she couldn't live without him.'

'Love and tragedy,' Matt said with a grin, 'Just the right ingredients for a song I'd say, wouldn't you?' He began humming.

'Don't you ever switch off?' Ella laughed.

'Of course not! You never know when inspiration will strike.'

'Come on, finish up your cider,' She said, smiling, 'You can sing to me on the way up to the wood.'

The sun was lowering itself towards the horizon as they made their way along the road and over the railway bridge in a southerly direction. Half a mile out of the village, just on from Collins Barn they climbed over a stile and into a field littered with rich tussocks of grass and dried cow pats. Following a well used footpath they made their way towards the wood, a small herd of heifers scattering nervously in all directions as they passed by. They stood for a moment, watching as the sky turned a vivid blue, before making their way into Hundred Acre's cool, leafy interior. Eventually, as the departing sun turned the under belly of the evening cloud to candy floss pink, they emerged into a small valley where rough, grey stone pushed intermittently through a rich undergrowth of ferns and grasses and the smell of wild garlic hung on the evening air. Below them a small river rushed nosily away from a large deep pool, at the head of which, a pretty waterfall cascaded, its curtain of liquid interrupted in several places by the protrusion of rocks. Ahead, an intricate lacing of ageing beams and planks straddled the river, joining the two sides of the clearing at their narrowest point.

'It's beautiful!' Matt ran ahead onto the bridge and stood there, watching the water pour down over the rocks, 'Looking at the wood from the road you would never imagine a place like this existed,' He turned as Ella joined him. 'Did Enna's husband have a name?'

'Cerdic,' she said, leaning her hip against the railings and staring into the water. 'And he was tall, fair and very handsome.'

'Oh yes,' He laughed. 'Who says?'

'My other grandmother, Peggy Evas,' Ella smiled, 'when she told me the story I think she modelled Cerdic on my grandfather. He was her ideal man.'

Matt paused for a moment, leaning forward, his elbows on the wooden railing watching the water's energetic flow with silent concentration. Ella's words had quite innocently pushed the conversation in the direction he wanted. Slowly, he inclined his head towards her.

'And was Andy your ideal man?'

'What?' She frowned.

'I mean,' He studied her thoughtfully, 'Would you have married me if I'd hung around long enough to ask you?'

Her eyes widened in amazement and she laughed as she twisted her body, leaning her back against the handrail of the bridge, letting her wild dark hair fall out into the void, 'Oh come on, that would never have happened would it?'

'Why not?' He looked offended.

'Because,' She pushed herself up from the rail and moved closer to him, 'you never ever wanted that sort of relationship with me, Matt. We were friends. Just good friends.'

Dusk hovered, casting its shadows in long fingers down the small valley and two bats appeared, like fragments of black chiffon moving in and out of the trees overhanging the river.

'Is that what you thought?'

'Well, what else was there to think? In all the time I knew you, you never attempted to make a pass at me.'

He looked at her for a moment then said quietly. 'You sound disappointed Ella.'

'No I'm not!' She protested, suddenly feeling very vulnerable. 'I always wanted Andy really.'

'Ella,' His hands were on her shoulders. 'You're an awfully bad liar.'

She could feel it beginning again as soon as he looked down into her eyes; the tremor through her body, a feeling of breathlessness and the thunder of her heart in her ears. Common sense told her to push him away and she pressed her palms against his chest in a half hearted gesture. Her fingers felt the warmth of his body through the tee shirt he was wearing and then she was suddenly aware of something else. His heartbeat; continuous and heavy, matching the pace and intensity of her own.

There seemed no point then to do anything but stand passively as he gently pushed her hair back over her shoulders and brought his lips to base of her neck. She gave a little gasp as his mouth worked its way slowly and deliberately upwards to her earlobe.

'Matt,' She said hesitantly, 'This isn't very sensible.'

'Ella!' He whispered fiercely, cupping her face in his hands. 'To hell with sensible!' Bringing his mouth to hers he kissed her slowly and deliberately. She closed her eyes, almost drowning in the great flood of emotion which swept through her. This is what she had been longing for him to do from the first moment she saw him, and now it was actually happening, nothing in her life had ever felt so right. For one brief second she thought of Andy, then as Matt swept her up into his arms and carried her across the bridge into the darkness of the wood, she realised he was probably the last person in the world who mattered.

SIXTEEN

Monday 21st June

'You haven't listened to a word I've said have you?'

For the last half hour Ella and Rachel had been sitting together on the top of Lancombe Hill chatting, the horses tied to one of the wind blown Scots Pines which clung to its summit. Ella was stretched out on a weather-beaten wooden bench, while Rachel sat just above her on a grassy outcrop, reliving the high points of Rowan's birthday meal.

'Sorry?' Ella shook her head and took her gaze away from the horizon.

'See, I was right,' Rachel said, joining Ella on the bench, 'Come on then. Out with it! What's the matter with you this morning?'

'Me?' Ella frowned at her friend then stared out across the valley again 'Nothing, I'm fine.' She turned back to her with a smile. 'Do you want me to prove it? Right - one action replay coming up! The sparkling wine, the duck, the little fondant creams you had with the coffee afterwards. Oh and the proposal.'

'Proposal? I didn't say anything about proposal!'

'I had a feeling he might though. It was quite clear he didn't want us tagging along last night.'

Rachel rubbed her palms together then clasped her hands and looked at Ella with some discomfort.

'Actually he did, you know - propose.'

'And?'

'I had to turn him down,' she said with a sad shake of her head. She paused for a moment and then turned to look at Ella, her eyes bright with tears. 'You know if things had been different I'd be shouting yes to the rooftops and rushing out to buy the big white dress! But they're not.' She hung her head and stared at her hands. 'Last night made me realise I do actually love Rowan in a funny sort of way; but not enough to marry him. He'll never replace Niall and it wouldn't be fair to make him believe he could. Or that he could offer me something as good.'

'So what are you going to do?'

Rachel gave a casual shrug, 'Wait.'

'For Niall to come back? But he's running a cattle ranch in Australia with his brother Martyn. The likelihood of him returning to Meridan Cross must be very slim.'

'That's a chance I'm prepared take,' she said determinedly, 'in order to have what I really want. Believe me, sometimes, despite everyone telling you you're mad, you have to go with your instincts. And mine say he will be back one day. And when he does, I'll be waiting.'

Ella nodded silently, absorbing Rachel's words as her memory drifted back to last night and the seclusion of that small valley; the sun gone, darkness falling, a slight humidity hanging in the air. It was so quiet, nothing moved; the only sound the rush of water over the falls. Then as the sky darkened the sounds of night creatures began to fill the wood.

Slowly and almost reverently he'd undressed her, lowering her gently down into the soft grass beneath the spread of a large oak tree. She remembered the damp coolness of the grass on her back; then in an instant it was forgotten as she watched him slowly take off his own clothes. Naked, he was beautiful, dark hair covering his chest; his eyes like pools of melted amber, soft with love. Instinctively she reached for him, drawing him down into her arms. Memories lingered. The hardness of his body against her own. His hands, firm and yet gentle; his mouth persuasive, teasing. The great shudder of pleasure that drove through her as she felt him enter her for the first time. And afterwards, lying together in each other's arms, a canopy of stars overhead, feeling that she never wanted this night to end.

'Ella, 'He whispered in her hair as the stars faded and faint strands of light filtered into the wood. 'Will you come to America with me next week?'

'America?'

He nodded.

'For how long?'

'Ten weeks.'

'*Ten weeks?*'

'Yes. Just think of it. San Francisco, Denver, Dallas, Tulsa, Boston.....'

'Matt it's impossible.' She interrupted him, as the reality of what that meant hit her quite forcefully. She could never leave the business for that length of time. And then what about - a host of figures paraded by in her mind, mouthing silently, fingers pointing accusingly, among them the faceless Belinda.

'No it isn't,' He rolled towards her and leaning over kissed her face, unaware of her concern. 'When you're in love' he laughed, 'Anything's possible.'

'Is it? While I may be happy to leave Andy there's your fiancé to consider. I know what it's like to have the man you love betray you with another woman.' Her heart felt heavy as she thought of the innocent Belinda sitting in his house in Chelsea, waiting for him.

He threw back his head and laughed. 'Ella, there isn't a fiancée. There never has been.'

'But you said.....'

'Stop it!' He put his finger to her lips to silence her. 'Ella, I love *you*. There's never been anyone else.' He looked down at her, his face serious, 'Look, I want you with me on the tour. It's important.'

She looked up into his face, feeling the warmth in his eyes begin to melt her resistance.

'Oh Matt,' she shook her head and laughed at him. He was impossible, but somehow she knew he was going to get his way. 'All right, but I must be crazy.'

'I hope you are, about me.' Propping himself up on one elbow he grinned down at her.

'Matt, seriously,' She said, her eyes on him again, 'if I'm going to come with you we have to do it properly. No running away like my mother did with Liam. We have to face everyone. Together.'

'Together.' He echoed, taking her hand and kissing the tips of her fingers.

'Matt,' She said, withdrawing her hand from his. 'This is deadly serious.'

'I know.'

'You do mean this don't you?'

He thought for a moment then said, 'Ella, remember Dad's song. There's a line in it. '*For I'll be there in sunshine or in shadow*. That's my promise to you.' The humour had gone from him now. 'I'm here now and I'll never ever leave you, I swear, no matter what happens.'

She reached out and stroked his face, 'And I'll always be here for you too. But what we're planning to do is so complicated and affects so many other people.'

'OK, how about we discuss it over lunch tomorrow?'

'Why not now?'

'Because at this very moment,' He said with a smile as he traced his hand over the curve of her hip and lowered his mouth to hers. 'There's only one thing I want to do and it doesn't involve talking.'

Back in the present once more she patted Rachel's hand. 'Rach,' she said, 'I think you're right you know. We only get one life after all don't we? We have do what's right for us. We owe it to ourselves. Come on,' she got up and pulled a smiling Rachel to her feet, 'time to go. I'm meeting Matt for lunch. I mustn't keep him waiting.'

As they rode back down the track away from Lancombe Hill, Ella felt strangely at peace with herself. Quite unexpectedly, Rachel had given her the solution to all her problems. What use was second best? A life spent pretending. Just as Rachel was physically and emotionally bound to Niall, so she knew she was similarly bound to Matt. Going to America with him was the right thing she decided. It's what she had to do.

Matt was just picking up his car keys when the phone rang.

Expecting Ella, he was disappointed to find Sonny's gruff Cockney voice echoing down the line. 'Blimey Matt, I've had a terrible time findin' you. What you doin' there?'

'Resting up Sonny, recharging the batteries before next week and getting in some song writing. What's the problem?'

'Todd. Can you get yourself on the next plane to Malaga? He's only gone mad, wrecked 'is hotel room and assaulted two policemen. He's in custody at the moment. If we can't sort things out no one will be going anywhere next week. As you can imagine, Scorpio are not happy. They've sunk a lot of money into this tour, if it goes belly up, I guarantee we'll all be joining the dole queue!'

'Can't you go?' Matt felt irritable at being drawn into something he felt wasn't his responsibility, 'The Spanish Police will listen to you. You're mature, respectable, wear a suit. I'm young, long haired and irresponsible. Besides,' he hesitated, 'Something's come up here. Something important. I have to sort it today.'

'Oh come on Matt!' Sonny grumbled. 'You've sorted this sort of thing out loads 'a times before on tour. Besides, I've got my work cut out pacifying Scorpio! As I said, there's a lot of money riding on America.'

'Tomorrow then. I'll go first thing tomorrow.'

'Sorry Matt, it's gotta be today. With the tour starting next week, twenty four hours could make all the difference,' His voice became soothing. 'Everything's taken care of; there's a ticket waiting for you on the Iberia desk at Heathrow. The flight goes at five. Geoff will meet you at the other end. Got yer passport?'

'Yes,' Matt groaned inwardly, realising he wasn't making any impression on Sonny. He would have to go and hope that Ella would understand. Damn Todd Graham! How many times before had he done this? But it had been different then, travelling between cities, giving high octane performances at each venue, the adrenaline close to overload. It was almost inevitable something would tip Todd over the edge. But now was a different matter, they were supposed to have been relaxing, unwinding, having a good time.

'I'm not walking into anything involved with drugs am I Sonny?' He asked suspiciously.

'Nah, it's booze, just like all the times before.'

'Well that's something I suppose.'

'Look Matt, I'm sorry to land you with this but look on the bright side. You should be able to turn this round in 48 hours max, and then I'll leave you in peace to get back to your unfinished business.'

'Wonderful!' Matt put the receiver down then picked it up immediately and dialled Little Court. The line was engaged. He swore, ran upstairs and packed his clothes. This was going to be his last day here now. A quick lunch with Ella instead of the day they had planned, to talk about their future. He felt angry and cheated. Once packing was finished he tried Little Court again; it was still engaged. He phoned the farm, no reply. He checked his watch. 11.45.

He realised he had been optimistic about lunch as he mentally plotted his car journey across country to London, half motorway, half A roads. He would need to leave almost immediately. Hastily he pulled a piece of paper from his song writing pad and began to scribble. If he couldn't tell her in person, he would leave something to reassure her that he would be back. It was important she knew that what had happened between them last night meant he loved her and no matter what obstacles lay ahead in the future, from now on they would face them together.

Margaret Sylvester was adding packets of biscuits to the display stand in her shop when the door opened with the usual accompanying jangle of the bell and a tall, brown haired man walked in. He had strange honey coloured eyes and although he could not be described as conventionally handsome, there was something in the make up of his features and his athletic physique which she acknowledged, most young women would find very attractive. One woman in particular she realised. Wasn't this the young man staying at Fox Cottage, the one Ella Kendrick or whatever she called herself now had been seen with. The one Rachel was always droning on about.

'Hello.' He smiled and pointed to the cold cabinet behind her, 'Can I take a couple of cans of Coke please.....oh and a Mars Bar....yes and a pack of envelopes if you have them.'

She put the cans and Mars Bar in front of him and found a pack of envelopes. She noticed he seemed agitated, checking his watch before he pulled out his wallet and handed her a pound note.

'You're staying in Fox Cottage aren't you?' She said as she handed him his change.

'That's right. I'm leaving today actually. Got a plane to catch,' he fished a bunch of keys from his back pocket, 'and these to return to Willowbrook.'

'Oh I'll take those back to Mary for you if you like.' Margaret volunteered with a friendly smile. 'Save you the journey back up to the farm.'

'That's kind of you. I've got a letter too,' He said, producing a piece of notepaper from his pocket, 'that's why I need the envelope.'

'For Ella is it?'

He gave an embarrassed nod and pulled one of the envelopes from the pack and sealed the note inside.

'It's all right,' She said reassuringly, 'Rachel mentioned you and Ella were friends. I can deliver that too if you like.'

'Thank you.' He finished writing on the envelope and handed it to her. 'I'd appreciate that. I'm in a bit of a rush I'm afraid.'

'No trouble.' She smiled pleasantly, 'The girls are out riding this morning. I'll make sure Ella gets the note as soon as I see her.'

'Thanks again, I'm very grateful. Oh and apologise to Mary Evas for me will you? An emergency has called me away.'

He picked up the Coke and Mars and turned to go.

'Safe journey.' Margaret's bright eyes gleamed as following him to the door, she watched him make his way down the steps to the car. As the Alfa pulled away towards Taunton she slowly unsealed the envelope and began to read.

Moments later, she tucked the letter into her overall with a smile; this was better than she could ever have anticipated. Remembering her threat to Ella all those years ago, she smiled, deciding that revenge was indeed a dish best served cold.

A slamming door followed by the sound of hurried feet heralded Ella's arrival back at Little Court. Laura left the drawing room where she had been reading and caught sight of her granddaughter on the stairs.

'Ella do slow down, you'll have an accident.' She said, watching in amazement as Ella took the stairs two at a time.

'Sorry Grandma, I'm late for lunch, I can't stop. Has Matt phoned?'

'No he hasn't, but I must admit I have hogged the phone somewhat this morning.' Laura called after her. 'I'm organising the August Fête so I've been extremely busy calling in favours and summoning my usual helpers to assist.'

Moments later Ella appeared on the landing above, tugging herself into a pair of white trousers.

'Darling, we really need to set aside some time to have a chat.' Laura's expression became serious as Ella reached the bottom of the stairs. 'I've hardly seen you since you arrived and there are things we need to discuss. Perhaps some time this afternoon?'

'Of course, sorry.' Ella smiled apologetically, 'I'll be back by three thirty.' she said as she headed for the front door. 'There's something important I need to talk to you about too.'

As she pulled into the pub car park Ella could see no sign of the Spider. Inside she found the usual lunchtime regulars with their pints and cheese rolls. Rachel was at the bar, having a drink and discussing tomorrow's order for packed lunches for her trekkers.

'Has Matt been in?' Ella asked as she reached her.

'No.' Rachel shook her head. 'Why?'

'He was due to meet me for lunch fifteen minutes ago.' Ella said checking her watch against the clock above the bar.

'Why don't you ring the cottage?' Rachel suggested.

'Could I use the phone Tom?'

Tom Bennett smiled. 'Of course you can.' he said lifting the flap and letting her through to the back of the pub.

There was no response from the cottage. Replacing the receiver, Ella looked uneasily at Tom. 'This isn't like him.' She said. 'Something's happened, I know it has.'

'Maybe he's had a puncture,' The publican suggested, letting Ella back into the bar, 'It's a rough old track up there mind.'

'Yes,' Ella gave a distracted nod. 'Yes it is. Maybe I should go up and check.'

Watching Ella go, Tom turned to Rachel. 'Think you best go with her Rach, just to keep an eye on her. She's beginning to get herself in a bit of a state.'

Rachel nodded and ran to catch Ella up.

Fox Cottage looked silent and empty when they reached it, Matt's missing car adding to Ella's sense of unease. Leaving Rachel in the Mini she ran to the front door, banging her hand against it before bending to shout through the letter box. When there was no response she turned and ran around to the back of the house calling his name, causing a flock of pigeons to rise noisily from the nearby wood.

'Damn!' Ella said angrily as she walked back to the car. 'Where is he?'

'What about the farm?' Rachel called out. 'Do you think he might have gone there?'

Andy Macayne was enjoying his drive to Meridan Cross. What he was not enjoying, however, was having to be accompanied by his father and his mother in law. It was obvious they did not trust him to collect Ella and get onto the plane for Pisa by himself. He was being chaperoned and he felt resentful.

The countryside sped by and he checked occasionally in his rear view mirror to see what they were up to in the back of the car. They had been exceptionally quiet for the last five miles. He sensed collusion.

'How much farther?' Bob Macayne broke the silence. Dressed casually in grey slacks and blue open neck shirt, he stretched out in the back of the Jaguar, enjoying being chauffeured by his son.

'About three miles.' Mel leant forward, the sweetness of her perfume overpowering as it wafted from the rear of the car. 'Drive to Little Court first. I doubt she'll be at the farm at this time of day.'

Andy sighed. His insides were in knots. Over the last few days he had set out a careful strategy for today, his main goal being to retrieve his wife, settle his marriage back into its normal pattern and get back into his father's good books. This morning he felt confident he had every angle covered, counting her grandmother as someone he could easily charm and not as Mel Carpenter was insisting, an interfering old witch who would stand between them and what they wanted to do. He needed Laura's assistance to help him persuade Ella that he was serious about sorting their marriage out. And the whole exercise stood a much better chance if it was carried out diplomatically. Ella had to be coaxed, convinced, but with Mel along he knew now it stood precious little chance of that. She had been in confrontational mood ever since she got into his father's car and he knew she was capable of wrecking the whole thing if they weren't careful. He prayed his father would keep her under control.

Mary opened the front door of the farmhouse as the two girls arrived.

'I saw the dust, whatever's the matter?'

'We can't find Matt.' Ella said, her face tight with worry.

'Neither can I.' Mary said irritably. 'He pushed the keys to Fox Cottage through my letter box some time between eleven and one when I was out. There's no note of explanation, nothing! Whatever's going on?'

'I was supposed to meet him at the pub at one. He didn't turn up.' Ella replied, her anxiety worsening at Mary's revelations.

As they stood there, Richard's old green Land Rover appeared, pulling up next to them. In the back with Laddie and Gaffer were Doggy Barker and Toby. With a flash of uneven teeth Doggy smiled and raised his cap to them as he clambered out.

'What a delight!' He smiled as he greeted them. 'Not only free lunch but the company of three lovely ladies. What more could a man want?'

'Where did you find Don Juan?' Mary eyed Richard suspiciously, knowing with certainty that Doggy had probably been helping them out in the fields on the promise of food.

'He's been doing a bit of hedging for me down by Lockleys. Made a good job of it too.' Richard looked back at the old man, 'I promised him some sandwiches and a cold beer. Seemed a fair exchange at the time....' Seeing their serious faces, he frowned. 'What's the matter? What's happened?'

'Matt's gone and no one seems to know where.' Ella said as a sick feeling began seeping into her stomach.

Doggy stood there silently, dark eyes watching the quartet.

'Looking for your friend with the red car Miss Ella?'

Everyone's attention immediately turned to him, standing there clutching his cap, Toby sitting solemnly at his side, one ear cocked.

'Yes, have you seen him Doggy?' Ella walked over to the old man, bending to ruffle Toby's ears, as she looked eagerly into his face. His black eyes regarded her solemnly. 'Passed me about twelve o'clock, going that way.' He pointed east. 'Like the devil hisself were after 'im.'

'Gone?' Ella shook her head in disbelief. 'He can't be.'

Mary frowned. 'I think I hear the phone,' she said, turning back into the house.

'Maybe it's Matt,' Rachel said hopefully. 'Don't worry Ella; I'm sure there's a simple explanation to all of this.'

Moments later, Mary appeared in the doorway, her expression solemn.

'Ella, Laura's on the phone. Andy has just turned up at Little Court.'

'Oh brilliant! Well, he'll just have to wait!' Ella replied angrily. 'Right now finding Matt is my priority.'

'I'm afraid it isn't,' Mary shook her head sympathetically. 'His father and your mother are with him and Mel's insisting you return there immediately.'

SEVENTEEN

Tuesday 22nd June

Ella opened her eyes. She was lying, fully clothed on an elegant brass bed, the sun streaming through the window. She raised her arm to shade her eyes against its brightness as she looked at her watch. 9.02. Sitting up, she pushed her hair from her eyes and stared at her surroundings; marbled floor, elegant furniture and white walls. Lying back on the bed again, she stared at ceiling, her mind running over the events that had brought her over a thousand miles from home to Tarvaggio and the Hotel Bella Flora.

After dropping Rachel back to the Arms, she had driven straight to Little Court where Laura stood waiting for her on the front steps. She expected to go through into the drawing room to meet the visitors straight away. She was fully prepared for confrontation and was more than ready to do battle. Of course it would have been better to confront them all with Matt at her side, to see their expressions when she told them her marriage was over and that he was the one she loved and was going to spend the rest of her life with. Instead, she was being left to fight it out alone not having any idea why he had disappeared or where to. Despite this setback she was determined to be positive and stand her ground over the issues that faced her. She wanted to end her marriage; Andy's behaviour was intolerable and unacceptable, there was no way she could go back to him now. And she wasn't quite alone; she had a valuable ally. Here in Meridan Cross her grandmother held power and whatever persuasive tactics might be employed by her mother and Bob it meant nothing here within the walls of Little Court. Once Laura knew what Andy had done she knew she would be safe. Then once they had all left she would resume her search for Matt.

However, as soon as she was inside the house, Laura showed her straight to her small sitting room and closed the door, her expression grave.

'What's wrong?' Ella settled herself in one of the chairs, watching her grandmother closely.

'Ella, why did you lie to me?' Laura asked calmly as she stood in front of her, hands clasped.

'Lie?'

'Yes, about you and Andy. You told me there were no problems at home, do you remember?'

Ella nodded, biting her bottom lip nervously. 'Yes, I did. I'm sorry Grandma, I was going to sit down and explain everything this afternoon, when we had our chat.'

'I see!' Laura looked at her frostily. 'Do you realise how embarrassed I have been today? Faced with three people who think I know all about your reasons for being here; who think I have colluded with you when in reality I know absolutely nothing.'

'Oh Grandma, I am so sorry.' Ella hung her head miserably.

'Is it true what they're saying, that you've run away from Andy?'

She nodded defiantly. 'Did they tell you why?'

'Yes, they did.' Laura walked over and sat down beside her, taking her hand and squeezing it affectionately.

Ella relaxed. Everything was going to be all right.

'Now you know why I couldn't tell you, oh Grandma, it's been so awful.'

'Ella you have to go back.'

'What?' Pulling away from Laura's grip, Ella was suddenly aware that the safety she had taken for granted wasn't there after all. Panic seized her; she had to make her grandmother realise just what had forced her to come here. 'Grandma you can't expect me to return, you must understand....'

'I understand,' Laura looked at her impassively, 'that problems should be faced, not run away from.' She shook her head. 'Ella this isn't some sort of game you can change the rules to if you don't like it. Marriage is for keeps; if you hit a bumpy patch you have to hang on.'

'Why are you being like this?' Ella bristled tearfully, angry that her grandmother appeared to have made a decision without considering all the facts. 'You haven't even asked me for my side of the story. What happened to make me run away? What have they told you? Did they tell you about Andy and her....?'

'Ella, please listen.' Laura gripped Ella firmly by the shoulders. 'I cannot allow you to stay here. You have to talk to him, sort out your differences. Andy has told me he loves you. He is ashamed of what he has done. I believe him. He is desperate for a second chance. Darling, you must give him that.'

'But I don't want to - Grandma, please!' Tears welled up in Ella's grey eyes. 'I thought you at least would be wise enough to know who was telling the truth. Can't you see, this is all my mother's doing, she's evil.'

'Hush now,' Laura pulled Ella close, letting her head rest in the well of her shoulder. 'Please listen. Your mother and Mr Macayne have not influenced me in any way. Your mother did start her nonsense but Mr Macayne made it clear I was to speak with Andy alone. Look, I sympathise with you my darling, but I also see his point of view. I cannot keep you here. You must go back. There is no alternative. You are a married woman. Your place is with your husband. He's a good, caring young man Ella. He says if he's to blame for anything, it's for letting you work too hard in your business. He says you see very little of each other.' she pulled back and smiled radiantly at her. 'He wants to change all that, but he needs help. That's what we're all here for....yes, surprisingly even your mother! Mr Macayne has arranged a holiday for both of you in Italy, staying with Andy's mother's family.'

'But the business......'

'Joan and Jenny have stepped in,' she smiled gently. 'Forget about the business. Go away and relax. Enjoy the sun and please, try and find some common ground.'

Sitting there in her grandmother's embrace, listening to her soothing words, Ella held on tightly to the impulse to scream. Laura, her greatest ally, the one person she thought she could count on, was treating her as if she was a silly little girl who didn't know what she was doing. She was planning to hand her straight back to Andy. The believable Andy, with eyes like melted chocolate and the ability to charm even the hardest heart.

For a moment she thought of defying them all, of taking a stand, but realised how impossible that was. She was alone now, with no one to fight her corner. She cleared her head, trying to think logically. Wherever Matt was he did not currently figure in the picture. She had to act as if he didn't exist and see the consequences of any decisions as they affected only her. Logically she saw her life was centred in Abbotsbridge and she knew her ability to continue living and working there normally would depend on being with Andy. Bob was not a man to cross, if she left his son now he could and would make life impossible for her, aided and abetted by her mother. Releasing herself from her grandmother's embrace she got to her feet, knowing right now, until Matt returned, there was only one option open to her.

The next few hours seemed unreal. First the reunion where they all seemed to treat her as if she'd had some sort of mental breakdown; speaking to her in a gentle but almost patronising manner. She stood impassively while they all hugged and made a fuss of her; false displays of affection she knew were purely for her grandmother's benefit. Afterwards she was taken upstairs to her room, where she sat on the bed watching as her mother packed her clothes into her suitcase.

Three hours later, after a fast car ride and more artificial demonstrations of affection as they parted at the check in desk, she sat silently in the departure lounge closing her mind to anything Andy attempted to say to her. She bought a magazine; reading made it easier to ignore him and his current need to play the attentive husband.

Eventually the voice saved her, coming out of nowhere. The echoing of the tannoy, announcing that their flight was ready to board. She was on her feet immediately, eager to find her seat on the plane, shrugging off Andy's attempt to help with her hand luggage as she moved forward alone down the corridor towards Gate 7 and a distant foreign country.

Now, twenty four hours later, here she was. Miles away, isolated from all her friends. Alone. Getting up from the bed she walked to the window and pushed back the shutters, refreshed from a night in a room where surprisingly, after locking Andy out, she had slept very soundly. The view that greeted her was breathtaking. A brilliant blue sea fringed by tree clad rocky slopes and a coastal road which wound far into the distance like a tarmac ribbon. Houses were dotted here and there, along the road and up in the hills; light brown roofs over white and pale terracotta walls, with colourful gardens of bougainvillea, hibiscus and oleander.

She realised that twenty four hours had not only changed where she was in the world, it had changed her whole perspective. She was now able to think clearly, away from the hysteria which had surrounded the events of yesterday. As she showered she thought of Matt. Her heart told her that although he had gone, there had to be a good reason. After all, hadn't he promised to be with her for always? As the refreshing jet of water from the shower head massaged her back she considered her situation logically. She was stuck here for a month and there was nothing she could do about it. It was too lovely to be miserable, so why not just enjoy it and take each day at a time? The time to look for answers to Matt's disappearance would have to be left until she returned home. And what was a month out of the lifetime they had to look forward to together?

She towel dried her hair, changed into tee shirt and shorts then headed for the door, thinking of breakfast. It was as her hand touched the door handle that she remembered and turned back towards the bathroom. Finding her toilet bag, she unzipped it and tipped its contents into the wash basin. 'Damn!' She swore out loud, realising her precious contraceptive pills were probably still sitting in her bathroom cabinet at Little Court. No need to ask who had been responsible for that. Ah well, on reflection perhaps it didn't really matter. She had no intention of allowing Andy anywhere near her ever again anyway.

Standing in front of the bathroom mirror Ella gave her damp hair a final tease through with her fingers and smiled at her reflection. Time for breakfast - time to meet the family.

EIGHTEEN

Tuesday 23rd June

Matt felt the whole world had gone mad. He had cleared Malaga Airport a little before nine the night before, tired and exhausted. Jeff had met him in a rented Mercedes and driven him along the coast and up into the hills where the band were now staying, eager to get away from the press who had homed in on them once the news of Todd's arrest had broken.

Throughout the journey, which took just under an hour, Jeff explained how Todd, with alcohol on tap twenty four hours a day had gone on a real bender. This, aside from the regular procurement of willing groupies, had been the usual format in the weeks they had been here, but on this occasion, instead of becoming completely comatose and collapsing onto the bed, he had decided to pick a fight with a group of young Germans sitting out on the pool terrace below. Insults were hurled back and forth then Todd, not to be bested had managed to throw most of the contents of his bedroom into the swimming pool. When the Manager had arrived with the police, verbal insults turned to physical violence and one of the Policia and the Manager had followed the furniture into the pool below. The local Policia had called up reinforcements and eventually six hefty Spanish Guardia arrived and dragged him out to the police van, still howling abuse.

'We ought to get rid of him, he's a bloody albatross!' Jeff said, as large wrought iron electric gates parted to let the car in. They closed behind a wide driveway lined with palms and other tropical shrubs, at the head of which stood a large, imposing brilliantly-lit villa.

After a brief meeting to reassure them all that the American tour was still very much on, Matt had fallen into an exhausted sleep. He had woken the next day to a typical Spanish morning, warm and clear with the sparkle of blue sea in the distance. After breakfast Jeff had driven him to the local Comisaria, an imposing stone building with barred windows and vast marble floored entrance hall. There they were supposed to meet with Manuel Garcia Ortega, a Spanish lawyer Sonny had managed to procure to arrange Todd's release. Now, forty five minutes later here they were, still sitting on a stone bench outside the

Comisaria with no sign of him. Jeff reminded an impatient Matt that this was not England; the pace of life was slower - here everything was manaña.

'I'm not prepared to waste a perfectly good day sitting here.' Matt protested irritably. 'If the guy hasn't shown in ten minutes, we'll just have to go in and sort it out ourselves, OK?'

Jeff nodded silently, wondering if Matt realised this course of action might not be a simple as he imagined.

Eventually after twenty more minutes had elapsed, Matt got to his feet and headed for the front door. He had everything planned out in his mind, a whole strategy to get the ball rolling. All he had to do was walk up to the heavy mahogany counter, be polite, explain the delay with the lawyer and discuss the issue with them in a professional and adult way.

The young dark haired policeman, smiled, obviously keen to help, but his English was very basic and an appeal to those more senior to him for assistance only brought responses in bursts of rapid Spanish accompanied by energetic shakes of the head. Jeff looked on sympathetically.

'We'll just have to find an interpreter.' Matt said, deciding that when he eventually got Todd out of incarceration he was going to kill him.

'Where are we going to do that?' Jeff frowned.

'Surely you've run into someone during your stay who speaks Spanish well enough to make us understood here?'

'Can't say we have. We've kept away from the locals. Anyway, most of the local senoritas are heavily chaperoned by their grandmothers. All the contact we've had since we've been here has been with British girls oh and a couple of Australians and I had trouble understanding one of them!'

Their conversation was interrupted suddenly by the trip of high heels across the marbled floor and both men turned to see a young blonde woman coming down the corridor towards them. She was wearing a low cut blue sundress and strappy white stiletto sandals. Thick curly hair bounced around her shoulders as she walked, her bag tucked tightly under her arm. As she reached them she removed her sunglasses and pushed them up into her hair, revealing heavily mascara'd blue eyes. She gave them both a smile as she passed.

Placing her bag on the counter she addressed one of the policeman in fluent Spanish.

Matt saw that Jeff was spell-bound, unable to take his eyes off her.

'Put your tongue away.' He said with a grin.

The young policeman was animated, smiling. He left the counter, returning with a small package which he handed to her, pushing some paperwork forward and offering her a pen. As she bent her head to sign, the policeman leaned forward and said something quietly in her ear, causing her to stop and look towards Matt and Jeff for a moment. Taking the package with a flutter of eyelashes and a smile, she turned and came towards them, slipping her bag over her shoulder and unhooking her sunglasses from their perch above her forehead.

'Hello boys.' She said in a strong East End accent. 'I understand you got a bit of a problem with the lingo; anything I can help with?'

'Well, yes......' Matt got to his feet with a smile

'Matt Benedict ain't it?' The coral pink lips parted in a smile, her blue eyes scanning him appreciatively, 'I'm Shandy Flynn.' She offered him her hand. 'I just love your songs. I'm a singer myself y'know, at the Flamenca Playa here in town.'

Letting go of Matt's hand she turned her attention to Jeff. 'And you must be Jeff Davis. Sex on Legs my friends call you.' she laughed.

'Really?' Jeff said weakly, overcome by her directness and the soft brown cleavage which was being thrust into his face.

'So, what you doin' here?'

'Todd our drummer's in here. There was a spot of bother at the hotel.' Jeff was on his feet immediately, 'Matt here's flown in to try to settle things, but our lawyer's not turned up. We need to get Todd out. We're due to fly to America in less than a week, and right now we'd do anything for someone who can speak Spanish.'

'Anything eh? Well,' She raised her eyebrows and gave Matt a sexy smile, 'a few interesting possibilities spring to mind,' she moistened her lips and smiled at both of them. 'but first, let's see what we can do shall we?'

Mary Evas adjusted the girth on Merlin's saddle before swinging herself up onto his back. She had spent the morning at Little Court with Laura going over plans for the summer fête and was now preparing to ride back to Willowbrook. The conversation had touched on many subjects; the layout of the field, which local farmer would be likely to donate the animal for the bowling for the pig event, who would run the tombola and which minor local celebrity they should choose to open the fête and present the gymkhana prizes.

Now it was time to go, and business over, both women had paused to discuss the events of the last twenty four hours. Mary had been keen to find out what had made Ella leave so willingly.

'She lied to me Mary,' Laura said with an angry shake of her head. 'She made an absolute fool of me! She said everything was fine between them and it wasn't - I felt like a complete idiot when they all turned up on my doorstep like that. I didn't know what to say. Poor Andy, I felt really sorry for him. He said he loved her desperately and wanted her back. Mary, why didn't she tell me what was really going on? Why was she so secretive?'

'I don't know,' Mary replied, leaning down from the saddle. 'I had a feeling something was wrong but when I asked her, she just said there were problems at work. At the time I didn't believe it. But,' she shook her head, 'Andy and another woman you say? I can't say I'm surprised. On their wedding day I caught him flirting quite outrageously with Tasha, Brigadier Hesketh-Morris's daughter. I thought then he had the potential for trouble. Still,' she looked at Laura thoughtfully, 'I think Bob Macayne's had the right idea. Sending them away is quite sensible really. No external influences, just the two of them, sorting out their differences.' she laughed. 'I expect Ella will knock some sense into him, don't you?'

'Well at least she's concentrating on her husband now.' Laura nodded in agreement. 'To be quite honest, I was beginning to get a little concerned about her friendship with Matt.'

Mary gathered up her reins. 'Ah yes, Matt. Now there's another funny thing.'

'Oh?' Laura looked at her curiously.

'He left Meridan Cross yesterday morning without so much as a goodbye. Ella was pretty upset; she was supposed to be meeting him for lunch. I don't suppose that helped the situation, you know, with Andy arriving and her having to leave, not knowing what had happened to him.'

'No, I don't suppose it did,' Laura said thoughtfully, 'Strange isn't it though? You'd have thought if he hadn't the time to speak to anyone at least he'd have left a message somewhere.'

'Well he didn't,' Mary sounded aggrieved, 'He simply pushed Fox Cottage keys through my front door and disappeared. I have to say I was not amused.'

'Such bad manners and not at all like him,' Laura shook her head pensively, 'How very odd.'

'I'd better be off,' Mary said kicking her heels into Merlin's flanks, turning him towards the driveway. 'I'll give you a call in the week, I'm sure I can twist Richard's arm to sort you out a pig for the fête. That will be one less thing for you to think about.'

'Thank you, I'll put a note on my list,' Laura said cheerfully, with a parting wave.

She watched Mary trot Merlin slowly down the gravelled driveway until she disappeared out of sight behind the rhododendron bushes. Walking back into the house and closing the door her thoughts drifted to Matt. What a funny business. It looked very much as if he had run away from something. But what and where was he now?

Friday 25th June

Matt sat in a comfortable chair on the villa's verandah. To the west, the sun was going down, turning the surrounding hills a deep purple. The evening was warm, the smell of jasmine in the air. Receiver in hand, he was about to make a second phone call. Thanks to Shandy's help, he had been able to contact Sonny to reassure him that after two days of careful diplomatic negotiation with local police and hotel management, Todd was now a free man. Added to that, he was also completely sober with damages paid to the hotel from his own pocket. It had also been agreed that his share of the proceeds of their last single should be donated to a local orphanage. Now that he had managed to forestall a disaster and reassure Sonny all was well, Matt decided he needed to call his mother; to make his peace with her and tell her about his future plans.

'Matt, oh Matt is it really you?' He could hear the emotion in her voice on the other end of the phone. 'I've missed you so much. Where are you?'

'Watching the sun go down, just outside Marbella.'

'Whatever are you doing there?'

'It's a long story.'

'Involving Todd, no doubt.'

'Who else?' He laughed. 'Wrecked his hotel room and ended up in jail, could have put the whole American tour in jeopardy. However, it's all sorted now and I'm due on the afternoon flight out of Malaga tomorrow. I'll be home by early evening.'

'You're coming home! Oh Matt, that's wonderful!' There was a sudden pause; he knew she was reaching for her handkerchief. Then she was back, her voice choked with tears. 'I know why you left and I'm so, so sorry for the things I did.'

'It's O.K., it doesn't matter,' He said gently. 'Look, the reason I'm ringing is because I need to come and talk to you and Dad - about Ella.'

'Ella?' The warmth in her voice immediately dropped several degrees.

'Yes. I love her and I'm going to marry her.'

There was a sharp intake of breath, and then Faye was back on the line, her voice uneasy. 'Matt have you gone completely mad?'

'Mum, I know this is going to be hard for you to come to terms with, but we really do love each other.' He laughed. 'I was with her in Meridan Cross last week. She's left Andy.....'

'No Matt.'

'Mum, I'm sorry, but once you see how much in love we are, I know you'll understand......'

'I mean no, she hasn't left Andy. She's gone to Italy with him.'

'That's impossible, she's still in Meridan Cross!'

'She isn't - Matt, I'm telling the truth,' Faye sighed. 'I had the misfortune of being in the next chair to Mel at the hairdressers today. She was full of it. Apparently Andy and Ella have gone to stay with his mother's family somewhere in northern Italy for a month. They had a bit of a spat a couple of weeks ago - Mel said it was bound to happen they were both working far too hard. Ella apparently had taken herself off in a huff to her grandmothers and Andy decided the remedy to the situation was to book this trip for them as a break and an opportunity for her to meet his mother's family. Mel took great pleasure in telling the whole salon that everything was OK now and they were like a couple of lovebirds when she and Bob saw them off at the airport.'

'There must be some mistake.'

'Matt, listen. I'm telling the truth, I really am. I only wish for your sake I wasn't.'

'When did they go?'

'Monday evening I think.'

'Are you sure about that?'

'Yes, it was definitely Monday. There was a bad accident at Stowford Cross and she was complaining that they were stuck in traffic for over an hour coming back from the airport. It made her late for a drinks party at the golf club, poor thing. Matt, are you still there?' She called out anxiously in the silence that followed, frustrated at the distance between them, longing to give him a hug and ease the pain she knew he must be feeling.

'Sorry,' He was back on the line again almost immediately. 'Had to put the phone down; the boys have just arrived back; we're going into town tonight to celebrate Todd's release.'

Noisy voices and laughter drowned him out for a moment. Thank God for the group, she thought; right now their mad chaos was just what he needed.

'Mum, sorry, I'll have to go,' He was shouting over the high spirits going on in the background. 'Please, try not to worry about me. I'm not the only man who's ever made a fool of himself over a woman and I doubt I'll be the last. It's painful but I'm an adult, I'll get over it. I'm only sorry I didn't listen to you in the first place.'

'Oh Matt, are you sure you'll be all right?'

'Positive. The tour's my main focus now – it will be good therapy for me. I'll call you next week when we've reached the States. And when it's all over I'll be home – that's a promise.'

'You will?' Faye was on the verge of tears again.

'I will. Take care of yourself and give my love to Dad.'

The line went dead and she was left standing alone in a silent house with only the tick of the clock for company.

'That bloody girl!' She came to life, shouting her frustrations at the receiver before slamming it down, 'I hate her - how could she?'

By 11.30 Matt and the band had reached the Flamenca Playa, their regular hang out since meeting Shandy. Owned by a wealthy Moroccan, the club was one of the premier night spots on the coast. Not only was there drinking and dancing till the early hours, but also a casino, something which had drawn Todd like a magnet. To be able to play the tables like a character from a Bond film was new and exciting territory for someone who did everything to excess.

Tonight, however, gambling was off the menu for Todd had something far more exciting to involve himself with - getting Matt drunk. Not that Matt needed much encouragement. For the first time he seemed to have totally let go, abandoning the moderate stance he always took and joining in with the rest of the group. Once in the Flamenca Playa, Todd had called the waitress over and ordered twelve single shots of tequila. These were then lined up on their table. He then challenged Matt to a head to head with Baz, who could drink anyone under the table. Matt threw himself enthusiastically into matching his friend's consumption.

Sitting at the bar, Shandy watched Matt with interest wondering what had turned this rational individual into a man on an alcoholic suicide mission.

All of a sudden she was aware of someone at her elbow. A sharp faced, black haired man in blue cords and a denim shirt was leaning on the bar next to her ordering a rum and coke.

'On a bit of a bender tonight isn't he?' He said with a smile, turning in her direction and nodding towards Matt, who face-to-face with Baz was downing yet another tequila slammer in one swallow. 'Isn't he supposed to be the sensible one out of that lot?'

Each emptied glass brought the stamping of feet and howls of approval from the band members, clustered in a corner of the club, surrounded by an audience of glamorous young girls.

'Maybe he just feels like being one of the boys for a change.' Shandy shouted over the boom of Bob and Earl's *'Harlem Shuffle'*.

The man took his gaze away from the corner of the room and turned it on her, 'Shandy, isn't it?' He said as if rekindling an old acquaintance, his gaze going straight down the front of her dress. 'I enjoyed your performance just now.'

'Thanks,' She stared blatantly at him, 'and you are?'

'Oliver Rix,' He smiled, 'I'm a freelance journalist, although currently I'm on contract to Scorpio.'

'The band's record company?' Sandy's eyes widened with interest.

'Yep.' He glanced across at the group again, 'They sent me out here looking for something to keep them in the public eye as the US tour kicks off. I think Todd's little escapade would have sold papers by the bucketful but they thought it was too passé. However, seeing Matt there letting his hair down, it looks as though my journey hasn't been in vain,' she noticed he'd turned his attention to her breasts again, 'Although I have to say I'd hoped perhaps for something with a sex angle.'

'Well you're wasting your time looking at me,' She held his violet-eyed gaze coolly, 'I'm a singer not a hooker.'

'Oh come on love, don't give me that,' He gave a syrupy smile. 'I've been here every night this week watching them - and you. I've seen your face, the way you look at him. Admit it, you'd kill for a night in the sack with him, wouldn't you.'

Shandy shook off the blush she felt rising in her cheeks. 'What's it to you what I want Mr Rix?'

'Maybe what I want and what you want aren't so far apart.'

'Meaning?'

'Well the truth is Scorpio's getting a little worried. They feel Matt's image....this clean cut celibacy trip he seems to be on is at odds with the rest of the band. In fact some people are beginning to question his sexuality. Sex, drugs and rock and roll is all part of the game, but a queer in the middle of that lot?' he shook his head, 'Not good! However, if you could help me prove these rumours wrong, you'd not only be getting what you wanted and being paid well for your story, you'd be doing us a favour by silencing all that malicious gossip.'

'I don't know,' She shook her head hesitantly, gazing across the room to where Jeff was pulling Matt to his feet, pushing him into the arms of one of the attending girls for a dance.

'I'm here to set up and sell a story Miss Flynn,' Oliver's voice was smooth in her ear as Matt and the girl came out onto the dance floor. 'Who does the deed and who gets paid is immaterial. I'm sorry, I've obviously been wasting my time with you. Still, never mind.' He smiled as he watched the girl put her arms around Matt's neck and bring her mouth to his, 'As you can see I won't have to look far to get what I want.' He slid gracefully from the bar stool. 'Good night.'

'Wait!' She said, grabbing his arm. 'O.K., you got a deal.'

'Wonderful!' He smiled, slipping back onto his seat again, 'Now let's have a drink shall we? And discuss exactly how we're going to do this.'

Monday 28th June

It was the seventh day of Ella's stay in Italy. Ever since her arrival the weather had been classic Mediterranean; cloudless blue skies and dazzling sunshine. This morning was no exception. She stood at the window, breathing in the morning air, feeling the sun warming her shoulders and face. The brilliance of the flowers, the spill of green cypress trees to the blue water's edge, it was all so beautiful.

She closed her eyes, feeling relaxed; how easy slipping into life with the Merlini family had become. Uncle Lorenzo, tall and broad shouldered with eyes as black as Andy's spent his day with his two married sons Vincenzo and Marco at the family's boat building business an hour's drive down the coast in Viareggio. Their well established company had a reputation for producing the most luxurious yachts for those with the money to pay for them. This left Aunt Martina to manage their small hotel, organising the restaurant and reception, while Andy's grandmother Illaria, with amazing energy for a woman in her seventies, managed the maids and laundry room with ruthless precision.

The hotel itself, square and elegant, with its rendered walls of golden ochre and deep brown shuttered windows fringed with cream, nestled comfortably into the side of a wooded hill. A small winding single width tarmac track linked it to the main road. Its fifteen rooms were furnished in simple Italian country style and guests were an international mix of independent tourists, all wanting to experience the spectacular Riviera di Levante with its romantic medley of tiny fishing villages, resorts, pine forests and mountains.

The dining room was light and airy with huge windows giving stunning views of the coast. Its walls were painted with pastel murals of entwined garlands of flowers, its floor pale Italian marble. And the amazing thing was that everything here not only looked wonderful and welcoming, it was. Every member of staff was polite and friendly, every need catered for.

She looked at the date on the face of her watch. Twenty two days to go, she thought, raising her head to gaze out across the blue sparkle of sea, wondering which American city the band had now reached. Although his disappearance still puzzled her, in her heart she held the memory of their one night together and that more than any one thing kept her believing there was some sensible explanation. And of course, he must know what had happened to her by now. He was bound to have contacted either Mary or Grandma. And he'd be as angry and frustrated as she was that he hadn't been there to stop them taking her away. *Only twenty two days left here* she whispered to the breeze which teased the curtains. *I vow as soon as I reach home I'll find out where he is and fly out to join him. We'll never be apart again.*

Her thoughts were interrupted by a sudden knock at the door. She turned away from the window immediately.

'Hi.' Andy stood hovering in the doorway. 'I've decided to take the hotel car up the coast into France, spend the day in San Remo. I thought you might like to come.'

'I'm sunbathing.' She gave him a cold look.

'Ella you can't keep avoiding me. We have to.....'

'What? Pretend nothing has happened?'

'Don't be like that. I'm very concerned about you.'

'Are you?' She mocked. 'Well it's a pity you weren't so concerned when you got into that shower with Nina!'

Andy gave her one of his hurt looks; it was more than she could cope with. 'Oh for goodness sake, just get out and leave me alone!' she said, turning away, back to the window.

He went, closing the door quietly behind him.

Ella watched the ancient black Mercedes depart. Relieved that she was at last alone, she changed into her bikini, pulled on a turquoise silk over shirt, found her suntan lotion and a towel and went downstairs. As she passed through reception she noticed the daily papers laid out on their usual table. Martina routinely bought in a selection for her guests to read and today Ella noticed the *Daily Mail* was amongst them.

She picked it up. She didn't usually read newspapers but decided it would give her something to do other than lie in the sun for most of the morning. Then she changed her mind. The tan was the most important thing. If it was still there she could read later when she took her siesta.

Finding a bed, she stretched herself out by the pool and relaxed, enjoying the warmth of the sun on her limbs. Then, as usual, when she heard the village church clock strike one she gathered up her things and retreated to a secluded corner of the terrace for a cool glass of wine and a light lunch with Martina.

'So, what shall we talk of today?' The older woman's dark eyes smiled as she twisted her fork into her bowl of pasta.

'I think we've covered everything,' Ella said thoughtfully as she buttered a piece of freshly baked bread. 'I know all about your delicious Italian food and wine, Hotel Bella Flora; your family. And you know all about me and my life in England,' She hesitated, 'although, there is one thing I know very little of and would like to know more about.'

'Tell me of this thing.' Martina picked up her glass of wine, watching Ella curiously.

'Bob and Lucia. It must have been a great love affair.'

'Love affair!' Martina's voice was filled with scorn as she put her glass down heavily.

'Yes,' Ella said dabbing her mouth with her serviette, shocked at her companion's outburst. 'He keeps her room just as it was; he carries a torch for her still - he's never remarried.'

'That Ella is guilt, not love.' Martina replied, resting her fork on the edge of her bowl. She looked across the table at Ella, her eyes narrowed, dark and flinty.

'Let me tell you how it was. I loved my baby sister. I watched her fall in love with the handsome English Captain who was here in the War. Dada gave her the most wonderful wedding. It was a great family occasion. She looked so beautiful,' she shook her head. 'And then we had to let her go. To a strange country, with her new husband. He told us he loved her. He promised he would look after her.' Her mouth tightened, 'And we, fools that we were, believed him. But all he really wanted was her money.'

'Money?'

Martina nodded. 'Mama's brother, Uncle Pietro had property - hotels. When he died Lucia and I inherited everything. Dada say sell the hotels; best to have money. So all were sold, but we kept Bella Flora. It was very special place for us as children,' she smiled. 'Dada opened bank accounts in Switzerland. This was very wise, for soon came the war.'

'But I thought Bob had his own money?'

Martina shook her head, 'That is what he told us too. In truth the war had killed his father and destroyed the business in England. When they returned, he used my sister's money to rebuild his company. Her money, his hard work and a beautiful baby son.' She gave a sad smile, her eyes fulling with tears, 'For some that would have been enough.'

'So what went wrong?'

'Who knows?' Martina wiped the wetness away with her finger tips, 'What makes a man who has everything take another woman?'

'A mistress?'

'Amante,' Martina nodded. *'Segretaria.* - his secretary.'

'Secretary?'

'Yes. He was with her when he should have been meeting Lucia at the house. That is why the accident happen. As soon as we heard, Dada flew to

England. Roberto was there in a terrible state. He had not washed, his clothes were filthy. At first Dada thought this was grief, but then Roberto told him what had happened, begged forgiveness on his knees. But Dada would have none of it. To see this man crawling on the floor crying like a baby as he confessed to unfaithfulness; to being responsible for Lucia's death. It was too much! Dada said he was bringing Lucia home. That she would be buried in Italy and that Roberto should stay away. The Merlinis did not want him here.'

'So that's why he's never visited.' Ella nodded, understanding.

'Yes. Dada died five years ago but nothing has changed,' Martina continued, 'Roberto will never be welcome here.'

'I'm so sorry Martina,' Ella stretched a sympathetic hand out to the older woman, letting it rest for a moment on her arm. 'I had no idea about any of this. He still seems so dedicated to her. Does Andy know of this?'

Martina shook her head. 'He was a child. He saw his father's tears as grief. Better it is kept that way I think. But what of Andrea? You have come with your own problems, this much I know. Is it also because of a woman?'

'Yes,' Ella nodded.

Martina shook her head sadly and picked up her fork again.

'It is in the blood. He is his father's son.' She paused for a moment. 'And yet I see much of Lucia in him. There is hope, but it is you who must dig deeply to find this other Andrea, and work hard to make him the man he can be,' she said enthusiastically.

Ella smiled and nodded in silent agreement, watching as Martina finished eating.

'That was delicious,' she said, finishing her own meal, 'What are you planning for your guests this evening?' Tactfully she steered the conversation away from Andy.

'Tiramasu,' Marina's face brightened at once. 'It is a wonderful pudding. It means pick me up!' she said proudly, getting to her feet and collecting up their bowls. 'You like cooking?'

Ella nodded.

'Good! I teach you after siesta.'

Siesta left the whole valley strangely still in the shimmering heat of the summer afternoon, broken only by the constant gentle chirrup of cicadas. Finding the *Mail* still in reception, Ella retreated to her room taking it with her. Casually dropping it onto the bed, she showered, then changed into pink shorts and a white tee-shirt. A cool breeze teased the curtains as she settled herself on the edge of the bed, opened the paper and began to read. The news as usual was mixed; trouble at Upper Clyde Shipbuilders, cholera in Bangladesh, the great debate that seemed to be raging everywhere about whether or not to join the Common Market. She sighed, feeling it was all such serious stuff for holiday reading. She skimmed through the rest of the paper looking for the horoscopes, then stopped suddenly.

'Shandy's Got Attitude.' the article announced over a photograph of a leggy girl with tumbling blonde hair, spread along a leather couch, her half naked breasts thrust at the camera. Ella's eyes were immediately drawn to the block of text accompanying it.

Top British Group The Attitude were relaxing in Marbella last week prior to flying out for their forthcoming coast-to-coast US tour. Joined by their Tour Manager/Songwriter Matt Benedict, the lads are pictured below at their favourite haunt, the Flamenca Playa, one of Marbella's top night spots.

The club's resident songbird, Shandy Flynn has spoken exclusively to us about her whirlwind romance with the group's backstage genius.

'It was crazy.' Shandy said when we caught up with her yesterday just before rehearsals. 'He walked in, our eyes met and that was it! Instant chemistry! He's an amazing guy both in and out of bed. He never left my side while he was here.'

Ella froze, staring at the second photograph below the text; the five band members on the dance floor, arms wrapped around various shadowy girls, while to the far right, Matt stood, his mouth locked on Shandy's, one hand moulded tightly around her left breast. Blinking back the tears she felt an urgent need to scream. She had believed everything he had said about their future together - but it had all been lies; he had made it up, just like the lyrics to one of his songs. She had been naive enough to believe he was someone who still remained untouched by a business where willing groupies and casual sex were considered the behavioural norm; her Matt. But he wasn't any more was he? Ella gazed down at her picture and read the last piece of text beneath it.

Asked if there are any plans to rekindle the romance once the band returns to the UK, she said. 'I know we have something really special. As soon as the tour is over he's promised to fly back and join me here. I'm counting the days till we're together again.'

So was I,' Ella said, closing the paper, 'so was I!' and hanging her head she began to cry.

Later that afternoon, sitting on the sun terrace gazing out to sea, Ella was deep in thought when a shadow fell across her. She looked up to see Andy, a serious expression on his face.

'You're back early.'

'Sight seeing for one, I have discovered, is bad news. Felt I'd be better off here, even with you ignoring me.' He dropped the car keys onto the low table next to her, eased himself into the chair opposite and studied her quietly for a moment.

'Are you O.K?'

'Yes, fine.'

'I'd say you've been crying.'

'You'd be right then.'

'So, not O.K.?'

'No.'

'It's all my fault,' He shook his head, 'I'm a complete shit aren't I?'

'If you say so.'

He reached for her hand. She didn't resist, allowing him to hold it in the warmth of his own.

'Ella I don't want to fight any more. Please, all I want is for things to be as they were.'

She looked at him, wondering how anything could possibly be that after Nina. The fear of it happening again would remain in the back of her mind for a very long time. But what other choice was there now? Her one and only option was to go back and try and make her marriage work. It could be different though, she reasoned. After all, the one thing he got from Nina, the one ingredient which appeared to be missing in their marriage was something she was perfectly capable of providing him with. Weighing up the situation she decided to offer him an olive branch.

'Could we talk over dinner?'

Letting go of her hand, he sprang to his feet immediately, his face full of hope.

'Darling of course we can. I'll book a table. How about Portofino?'

She nodded, 'In that romantic little restaurant below the Castello Di San Giorgio. You know, the one overlooking the harbour.'

He nodded. 'I'll go and make a reservation right away.'

The delicate chimes of Tarvaggio's Town Hall clock striking seven drifted across the valley. As they fell silent, Ella appeared in the doorway of the hotel. Her dress was red silk, low cut; her sandals high, black and strappy. Diamonds glistened in her ears and her hair tumbled dark and luxurious over her shoulders.

She saw Andy waiting in the Mercedes and noted the expression on his face as his eyes scanned her from top to toe. From the lazy smile which crossed his face she knew he was liking what he was seeing. She smiled back, then slipping her small evening bag under her arm she made her way to the car with the same graceful, exaggerated steps as a catwalk model. As she walked, her mind was running over her game plan for the coming evening. She was single minded, resolute and totally ruthless in what she had to do; determined that by the time the night was over, she was going to be the only woman in Andy's life. He would never need or want anyone else ever again. In her mind there was no question of failing in this task - she *had* to make it happen - it was all about survival.

NINETEEN

Wednesday 21st July

'Darling you look so well!' Mel said brightly, crushing Ella tightly to her in a great display of motherly affection for the benefit those around her in Heathrow's arrival hall. She held her daughter out at arms length, surveying her, liking what she saw; the new yellow dress, the healthy tan. 'The holiday appears to have done you the power of good! Hasn't it Bob?' she turned to look at him as if needing his endorsement.

Bob Macayne, standing apart from the little group nodded, his face lighting up with a smile of approval. He stepped forward, kissed Ella's cheek and slapped his son on the back. 'Welcome home both of you.' He said, smiling broadly as he picked up their suitcases and led the way through the crowds and out of the terminal building.

'Darlings, while you've been away I've had a wonderful time in sales,' Mel said as they reached the car. 'I bonded with so many delightful people while I was showing them around. I've had a dinner invitation from Mr and Mrs Conner-Day from Taunton and I've a lunch date with Marguerite Blake, a top-flight civil servant retiring here from London - I'm going to show her around Abbotsbridge! Oh and Dr and Mrs Thomas who live in Bishops Lydiard have invited Liam and myself over for drinks next Sunday.'

'You've sold three plots Mel? That's pretty good going, don't you think Andy?' Bob was jubilant and couldn't resist giving his son a reminding nudge over their bet.

'Oh I haven't sold anything Bob.' Mel said with a careless shrug as she slipped into the front passenger seat. 'Was I supposed to?' she frowned up at him. 'I thought I was just there to hold the fort; you know, flick a duster over the show house, keep people sweet, give the whole place the right sort of ambience.'

Bob gave an annoyed grunt as he shut the passenger door. Andy began to laugh. 'I'll take cash.' he said, holding out his hand, 'But if you haven't got that much on you, I'll be happy to take a cheque.'

Later as the car sped westwards down the M4, Mel turned to look at them both. 'Oh I completely forgot,' she said, 'Don't think you're going to be allowed to curl up in front of the TV like an old married couple tonight. You're both needed.'

'What for?' Ella asked sleepily, her eyes shut.

'Bob's birthday party.'

'But his birthday was last month.' Andy laughed.

'I know,' Bob interrupted testily, 'It's all Mel's idea. She thinks my 50th is such a landmark that it needs to be celebrated publicly. At the Mill. We decided to delay it until your return.'

'The Mill?' Ella was fully awake now, sitting bolt upright in the rear of the Jaguar, 'How many people have you invited?'

'Oh just a few.' Mel said casually.

'How many Mother?'

'Two hundred and fifty.....but it will be very informal. Tad and Faye have promised to put on a splendid evening for us and as the Mill is one of your old haunts, I know you'll both enjoy it.'

'But Mother, we've been travelling all day.' Ella protested as she sank back into the seat, turning her view to the window and the traffic passing on the London-bound side of the M4. Far away in Italy she had felt strong enough to cope with anything, but suddenly faced with an evening at the Mill surrounded by everyone she knew, she realised it was the last place on earth she wanted to be.

'Ella, my dear,' Bob said, his voice cold but firm, 'I'm afraid avoiding this is not option. It may be my birthday but it goes far beyond that. Your presence is crucial to the whole event. You see, we need you together tonight to make it clear that all is well. To scotch any of the ugly rumours which have been circulating in your absence. I trust I'm making myself clear.'

In the silence of the back seat as Ella opened her mouth to respond, Andy reached for her hand and gave her a warning shake of his head. Keeping her eyes on Andy's worried face she took a deep breath. 'Yes,' she said quietly, 'Perfectly.'

Andy stared thoughtfully out of the window into the garden below where the reds and yellows of a line of beautifully manicured rose bushes skirted the stone pathway to the covered swimming pool. After dropping Mel in Cambridge Crescent, his father had whisked them back to Everdene insisting they stay there the night, and return to Chelwood Lodge the next morning. After the guest room door had been firmly closed, leaving him alone with Ella, he feared his father's comments in the car would result in him having to bear the fallout of her temper. Instead, however, she seemed to have accepted the situation, calmly unpacking her case and hanging up her clothes before going to take a bath.

Her absence had left him with time on his hands. Time to stand here by the window, to admire the garden and contemplate the last weeks of his life. For the first time since his return he thought about the events that had taken him away for the month. He felt lucky he had escaped so lightly and wondered what Nina was doing and whether she would be at tonight's reception. Suddenly he realised she was no longer relevant.

'Andy.'

She gave him a start; he had not heard her, barefoot across the carpet. He swung around to look at her with a smile.

Wrapped in a large white bath sheet she handed him a bottle of Chanel body lotion.

'Could you rub some of this into my shoulders and back please?'

She turned, loosening the towel so the whole of her upper back was exposed.

He lifted her hair gently, dropping it over her left shoulder so that it cascaded down the front of the towel. Upending the bottle, he squeezed a small amount into his palm, transferring the lotion onto her brown skin in small circular motions.

'Mmm, that feels so good.' She said, lifting her shoulders slowly and sensuously.

Suddenly finding the combination of scent, touch and the flimsy barrier of the towel provocative and erotic, Andy bent forward. Gently he brushed his lips over her shoulders, letting his mouth linger on her skin before he turned her around to face him, removing the towel and admiring her body appreciatively.

'I think we may be a little delayed.' He said with a grin.

Ella smiled up at him seductively as she began to slowly unbutton his shirt. Andy closed his eyes, in warm anticipation of what was to come. What had brought Ella back into his bed he had no idea, nor exactly where or how she had developed her new found talents as a skilful seductress. Not that he was going to complain. Nina was gone; a pleasant memory, but he had no regrets. Feeling the teasing softness of Ella's body against his as she eased him out of his clothes, he smiled. Some sort of miracle had happened and his wish had been granted; he now had absolutely everything he could wish for in one woman.

Turning into Kington Road later that evening, Ella had her first glimpse of the Mill, partially hidden by the thick wall of willows which sprung from the bank opposite. It was the first tangible reminder of Matt and she steadied herself against the emotions which welled up inside her. Determined, she concentrated her mind on her new self. She had gone away from here four weeks ago as an unhappy young wife. She had experienced so much in that time, but she had survived and learned, returning home strong and confident, armed with an awareness of what she wanted and where she was going in life.

Bob Macayne, all smiling benevolence now, helped her out of the car and escorted her into the club, Andy walking just slightly behind, slim and tanned in a linen suit and green shirt.

Tad and Faye stood in the foyer in front of an enormous framed colour print of Matt and The Attitude, waiting to greet them. Tad's smile was warm and welcoming, but Faye's eyes were chips of ice as she watched Ella silently. Ella deliberately diverted her eyes from the almost life size colour figure of Matt lurking behind his mother's right shoulder. As glasses of Moet were handed around, Mel stepped through the main doorway, causing a sensation in clingy silver and green evening dress which sparkled as it caught the light. Liam trailed in behind, pale suited, a smile on his face. He came straight to Ella, reached for her hand and kissed her softly.

'How are you darling girl?' He whispered into her hair.

'I'm fine,' She said with a reassuring smile, seeing concern in his eyes, 'Fighting fit and ready to meet everyone.'

He sighed and shook his head, 'This is all totally over the top you know. Bob's birthday was weeks ago.'

'I believe it has a hidden public relations angle. Mother and Bob need the acceptance of the great and good of Abbotsbridge. Our spot of bother, they feel, rather reflects on them; they are keen to set the record straight. Tell me,' She took two glasses of champagne from a nearby tray and handed him one, 'who is here this evening? Anyone I should know about?'

'Mick and Nina you mean? Yes, they're coming with Jack and Betty. Is that going to be a problem for you?'

'Not at all,' Ella said tilting her glass to her lips, her eyes wandering around the guests, searching for Andy. Eventually she saw him, deep in conversation with his father. 'Andy and I have sorted out our differences.' She turned to Liam with a dazzling smile, 'I don't think Nina will hold much interest for him from now on.'

By nine, guests had begun to arrive and the club gradually filled with people. Music started and a few energetic individuals began to drift onto the floor, eager to dance. Nina, dressed in a pale lemon trouser suit arrived with a solemn faced Mick and the Taylors. They were shown to a table to the right of the stage next to the carpeted walkway which led back to the main foyer. Once seated and served drinks, Nina found herself ignored by the rest of the Taylor clan, Mick immersing himself in conversation with his father, while Betty spotting Charles and Sheila Fitzallyn near the bar, left for a chat. Bored, she watched the room, noticing Andy surrounded by a group of overdressed Abbotsbridge matrons laughing and talking, the centre of attention. She wondered how things were now after a month away with Ella. He had singled out Barbara Morris for special attention, bending his head close to hers, hanging on her every word. With a smile on his lips he raised his head, his gaze momentarily leaving Barbara and roaming the room as if he was trying to locate someone. Then he stopped, he was looking in her direction and he was smiling. Nina felt her pulse quicken. Extracting himself from the gaggle of ladies he began to cross the floor to where she sat. She couldn't believe it. He was coming over to say hello. She knew how much it was going to cost him to do this. His father would be furious, but that was Andy all over. He didn't give a damn and that, she realised, was part of his attraction. Then, feet from the table he stopped. He wasn't looking at her at all; he was looking past her down towards the foyer, his arm out in greeting. She was aware of a figure passing her table, someone in blue with a cloud of unruly hair cascading down her back. She looked in dismay as she recognised Ella. Andy's hand slipped around her waist, his smile was radiant and for her.

'Darling,' She heard him say, 'Barbara's been looking for you; do come and chat, she wants to hear all about Italy.'

Watching them walk back to the waiting women, Nina felt foolish. How could she have been so naïve as to think she actually meant something to him? But he was so bloody plausible and she was looking for something beyond the boredom of life with Mick. Now she realised all she had done was to fill a void, a moment of tedium in his life.

Looking across the room once more she saw that Ella and Andy were laughing and joking with the Abbotsbridge matrons as if they didn't have a care in the world.

'Bastard!' She said under her breath.

Saturday 31st July

Issy was gazing in the window of Miller and Thomas's Estate Agents when the door opened and Mick stepped out onto the pavement.

'Issy!' He looked surprised to see her.

She took her gaze away from the window for a moment. 'Hello Mick,' she said, eyeing him warily.

'If you're after for the farm house, you're too late.' He grinned, nodding towards the window where photos of the property had a prominent position. 'I've just taken it off the market.'

'Had a change of heart then?' She tilted her head inquisitively.

'No, nothing like that. Dad said he'd take it off my hands. I think he might have a buyer lined up.'

'Really?'

'Iz,' He said quietly after a moment's embarrassed silence, 'About the other day, on the river bank. I'm sorry we had words. But you must realise, Nina's my wife. I stood up in church and made vows. Serious stuff. It's my duty to work at it and make it right. And I don't want to rub it in or anything but things are really good between us now.'

'And, of course, that means more business for Roy Kendal.'

The smile on his face faded immediately, 'What's Jenny been saying?'

'Jenny?' Issy frowned, 'Why nothing. Old man Kendal and his wife were in the hotel for Sunday lunch last weekend. I overheard him telling her about the bracelet you were buying. White gold and diamonds isn't it? And he says Nina's got her eye on a solitaire too.' She shook her head. 'If you really want to sort things out, that's not the way to go about it you know.'

'Mind your own business Issy!' He snapped, pausing for a moment to brush his hand through his hair in a gesture of frustration before launching himself at her again. 'Ever since I was seventeen years old, I've had to put up with you rubbishing me. And what's at the bottom of it all? Two people in the wrong place at the wrong time. No malice, nothing deliberate, just an unfortunate accident!'

Shocked by his outburst, Issy opened her mouth to speak but he silenced her.

'Let me finish! I know about your crush on Mr Davies, Jenny told me. OK, you ended up sprawled in the guy's lap. But I apologised, admitted I was stupid. I could understand your anger then, but to still be holding onto it now, after seven years is utterly pathetic!'

He seemed to run out of steam then, his cheeks red with indignation. Issy stood her ground, watching him steadily.

'Mick this has nothing to do with Mr Davies,' She said gently, 'I'm just being sensible; if you try to buy Nina's affection, she'll only end up despising you.'

'Enough!' He raised an angry finger towards her, and then turning, strode off down the street. eventually disappearing among the crowds of Saturday morning shoppers.

Monday 2nd August

'Sally, I really can't believe you've done this! It really isn't good enough and it reflects extremely badly on the agency!' Ella tossed aside the letter she was reading and looked up at Sally Monroe, one of her best temps, her expression as sharp as her voice.

Sally's dark eyes widened. In the two years she had worked for the agency she had never been spoken to like this, Ella had always been approachable and fair; if something was wrong it was talked through.

'But Ella, I thought.......' She began, trying to embark on an explanation of the circumstances which had made her late for the first day of a new assignment.

'You're not paid to think Sally, you're just paid to turn up on time and do the business. Mr Cadthorpe was not happy.'

'But he knew all about it. I got Trudi to ring him and let him know I'd be late.'

'I run this company, not Trudi. Any problems, you tell me first, not the receptionist.'

'But you weren't here, neither was Jenny or Joan. I had a doctor's appointment for Mandy, it was the only one I could get. She was very poorly, I couldn't leave it any longer....'

Ella picked up the next item on her morning's post pile and began to read it, flapping a dismissing hand at her. 'Please Sally don't argue with me. Just go away and get on with whatever you've got to do.'

Sally Monroe turned to leave, her curly fair hair bouncing off her shoulders, biting back the anger she felt at being dismissed like some silly schoolchild. As her fingers closed over the handle of the door she turned. 'Do you know something Ella, there's been a change in you since you came back from Italy. You're not the boss we all used to know. In fact you're beginning to act and sound just like your mother.'

Slowly Ella got to her feet and walked around the desk to face Sally. 'If you don't like the way I run my business, you don't have to stay.' she said tartly.

'You're right. I don't. I quit!' Sally turned and left the room, slamming the door behind her.

Ella closed her eyes and gave a deep sigh; for a moment she yearned to go after Sally, to give her a hug and tell her she was sorry. Tell her that she was one of her best temps and she realised how difficult it must be coping as a single mother. But the whole issue - Cadthorpe's complaint and Sally's outspoken comments, comparing her to her mother, made her feel even more irritable and angry. So instead she returned to her desk, snatched up the Philips Pocket Memo and began to dictate a letter.

Sunday 15th August

'I thought that was your car in the car park. What are you doing here?'

Nina, sitting at the bar of the Red Lion, a cigarette on her finger and a large whisky and tonic in front of her, unexpectedly found Rich Tate standing next to her. She appraised Rich's blond college boy looks and long denim clad legs as he leaned on the bar beside her. Quite a dish really, she thought giving him a welcoming smile. Not man enough though, she decided, reflecting on the biggest defect in his character, letting that uppity Annabel run him around like a pet poodle.

She sighed inwardly. Men, they were all flawed. Rich was henpecked, Andy a womaniser, and Mick....... well that had been a complete waste of time hadn't it? Although that day at the farmhouse the anger in his face had been frightening, it had been easy enough to take control again. Mick was soft and she had played on that softness with her arguments, some of which, of course, she felt were justified. She left the farmhouse that day feeling confident that not only had she escaped a very damaging incident as far as her marriage was concerned, but had also managed to persuade him along another path. One of balance; of getting his priorities right And for a while that had happened. First he had got rid of that awful old farmhouse; then he had begun coming home at normal time. Their new life saw them spending the evening together watching TV or going to the cinema, or ten pin bowling or a out for meal. He showered her with presents and something told her everything was going to be fine, she had him where she wanted him and from now on she would be the focal point in his life. But then gradually, work on the site had started to intrude. A snatched hour here and there, sorting out problems stretched to two. And then today a phone call had taken him away early. He'd called from the site at four, saying he'd be home by six and they'd eat out. Not good enough she thought and left the house leaving him a note saying she'd gone to her sister's for the evening. And now here she was in the Red Lion in search of someone to amuse herself with.

She turned to Rich again. Well he almost fitted the criteria. She gave him a teasing smile as she stubbed her cigarette butt into the ash tray.

'I'm drowning my sorrows,' She said, 'Care to join me?'

'How much have you had?' Rich replied noticing her glazed expression as he pulled himself onto the bar stool beside her.

'Not enough,' She gave a quiet little laugh, 'Four I think.' She licked her lips, 'I *like* whisky.'

'Why are you doing this Nina? Is it Mick? At work again is he?'

'You'd better believe it.' She said as she brought the glass carefully to her lips, 'He phoned at four to say he'd be back by six and I thought sod it, I'm not hanging around!'

She emptied her glass and looked at him. 'I thought he'd changed, but he hasn't. He's still a bloody boring workaholic. How I envy Annabel being engaged to someone like you. I bet you give her a good time. Make her feel special.'

'Making someone like Annabel feel special, now that's a laugh. She already thinks she's special. She's been ruined by her father that's the trouble. And she's absolute hell to be with at the moment!' His face took on a sour expression. 'Every day's a crisis! The boutique, her hair, her figure, the wedding! And now today Bryony really put the cat among the pigeons when she phoned to say that they have booked to go to Barbados for three weeks!' He raised painful eyes to hers, 'Well you can imagine what a rumpus that's caused. We were at my flat when she started on about it. Then she got really stroppy and started to throw things. I couldn't stand it any longer. I just bundled her in the car, dropped her home and came here for some peace and quiet.'

'She threw things?' Nina looked amused.

'Oh yes. Mostly crockery; got a deadly aim too,' He lifted his fringe to show the angry graze on his forehead, 'Poole Pottery tea plate.'

'Ooh, poor Rich!' She reached up and touched the spot tenderly. 'How could she do such a thing?'

'Very easily I assure you. Familiarity breeds contempt.'

'Yeah, well I know all about that,' She gave a bitter smile. 'Still, never mind as fate's thrown us both together for the evening, perhaps we should make the most of it.'

'Yes, perhaps we should.' He nodded, his eyes watching her intently.

'Like a drink?'

He nodded absently and watched her wave out at the publican who was talking to a customer at the other end of the bar.

'Here, let me get these.' He said taking his wallet from his jacket pocket and handing a note to the barman as the drinks arrived.

'A toast!' Nina lifted her glass to his, tossed the thick, straight curtain of hair off her face and re-crossed her legs, rocketing the hemline of her dress half way up her thigh. 'To me and you and a bit of fun eh!'

'I'm all for that!' Rich smiled as their glasses touched, his eyes drawn to breasts pushing invitingly out the top of her dress. What was it Gareth had said the last time they were all together and she was wearing that awful yellow and white striped top that showed her nipples? That she might be married to Mick but she had available written all over her. Well sitting in front of him now with all the goods on display she certainly was that he decided. All at once he found her closeness quite disconcerting.

'A bit of fun eh?' He grinned. 'You're a naughty girl Nina.'

'One more drink Rich,' She laughed, leaning towards him, 'and maybe I'll show you just how naughty I can be.'

Monday 23rd August

'Are you O.K. in there Ella?' The sound of Jenny's anxious voice could be heard on the other side of the cloakroom door.

'Yes, I'm fine.' Ella replied, leaning over the basin, patting her face with cold water, taking in her pallid expression in the mirror. Picking up the towel she dabbed it gently against her cheeks.

Jenny stood waiting anxiously as the door opened and Ella emerged looking pale and drawn.

'Too much alcohol last night?'

'No,' Ella shook her head, 'I haven't touched a drop all week.'

'Seafood then? Shellfish can be a bit dodgy.....'

'No,' Ella shook her head again, 'It must be something I've eaten, but I can't think what. We had pasta last night, could be the cream in the sauce I suppose. But I felt dreadful yesterday too, and I had eaten completely different food then.'

'Sit down. I'll get you a glass of cold water.'

Ella returned to her desk and swivelled her chair round to look down into the courtyard below. She had been like this for several days; feeling sick and nauseous. Her emotions had been up and down too, she was irritable and irrational one moment, close to tears the next. What was going on?

She watched the sun dancing though the leaves of the cherry trees, making shadowed movements over the cobbles below. They'd be harvesting the barley in Meridan Cross now. She saw Jake behind the wheel of the big red combine which moved effortlessly through the sea of gold, cascading the grain into the back of the old Bedford truck, driven by her grandfather, which kept pace at its side. Monty and Gaffer would be in the cab with him, tongues lolling, ears pricked, ever watchful for the odd rabbit who might decide to burst from the cover of the barley to head for the safety of the wood. At the thought of all this she felt a lump come to her throat, a great choking mass that threatened to overwhelm her completely, followed by a rush of tears. She bent her head and sobbed uncontrollably.

How she longed to be back there now with her grandfather, Mary and Laura. She had been so happy then, riding through the fields on Merlin, Rachel beside her, both of them without a care in the world. Meridan Cross had been the one shelter from the storm. No matter how bad things got in Abbotsbridge, there was always the safe haven of the village. But a dark cloud hung over it now, created by the events earlier in the year. Meridan Cross and Matt had become entwined. If she returned now with the leaves on the trees and the warmth still in the ground it would tear her apart. She couldn't face going back, not yet, despite the invitations she had received from Mary, desperate for her and Laura to make peace. Of course she kept in regular touch by phone but any visits would have to wait until the end of the year. Then it would be a different place; Hundred Acre brown and leafless, the barley field black and bare and the rich greens of the pasture diminished to the dull beiges of winter. Only then would she feel safe. It had been so easy far away in Italy to convince herself that she could move on from this; put it all behind her. But it wasn't true, was it? It was no good telling herself he was a complete bastard and not worthy of her affection. What she felt for him had been pile driven into her soul, it could be easily suppressed, but erasing it was something quite different. Time, she knew, was the only thing that would help mellow the pain she felt now. All of a sudden she was aware of Jenny hovering in the doorway.

'Ella, whatever's wrong? '

'It's nothing,' Ella pulled a tissue from the box on her desk and dabbed her eyes. 'Work's got on top of me a bit, that's all. Losing Nigel from the Taunton branch has meant I've had to spend more time there making sure everything runs O.K.'

'Then slow down - delegate. I'd be quite willing to do alternate weeks with you until we get a replacement.' Jenny said, handing her the glass of water she had been carrying. 'I'm sure we could work something out.'

Ella looked up at Jenny, caught in a sudden moment of wanting to unburden herself, then realising how impossible that was she simply said. 'Jen, I only want our business to be the best.'

'It is - so stop trying so hard!' Jenny eased herself onto the edge of Ella's desk, 'Ella there's something else isn't there?' She said gently, 'It's been noticeable since you came back from Italy. You seem to have lost touch with us all. Look at that business with Sally. You know what an old woman Mr Cadthorpe is, you can give him 110% and he's still not satisfied. Just as well I stopped her going. We'd have lost one of our best temps otherwise.'

Ella pulled another tissue from the box and blew her nose. 'I know, I was so stupid.' she said.

Pushing herself off the desk Jenny walked over to the window. 'Ella,' she said thoughtfully, 'when was your last period?'

'Why?' Ella made a face.

'It might explain an awful lot.'

'Yes, I suppose you're right, it would explain why my hormones seem to be running riot. It's all been a bit chaotic hasn't it? When mother and Bob came for me and everything was packed, my pills got left behind. I've only been back on them since coming home. Andy had to buy condoms while we were in Italy, and.......'

'Yes?'

'Well,' Ella looked up cautiously, 'One split. But Andy didn't seem to think there was anything to worry about.'

'Ella,' Jenny said hesitantly, 'I think you should book an appointment to see Dr Savage as soon as possible.'

'Do you think I might be pregnant then?' Ella frowned, 'No Jen I can't be.'

'I think it is very possible you are.'

'Damn.....'

TWENTY

Thursday 9th September

With loud applause from the crowd ringing in their ears, the five members of The Attitude bowed out of New York's Madison Square Gardens and with Matt, were bundled quickly into the back of a large white limousine. The tour had ended on a high note - America loved them!

Arriving back at the Waldorf Astoria, the group gradually drifted into Baz's suite to unwind before they got ready for the lavish Tour End Party in the hotel that evening. This had been organised for them and two hundred celebrity guests by Scorpio Records as the grand finale prior their return to the UK.

'Well!' Baz said, handing out cans of beer from the fridge. 'We definitely haven't lost our touch have we boys? It's taken two years to get over here, to show the Yanks what they've been missing! Now the really big money will start coming in! I bet the guys at Centaur are kicking themselves.'

'Serves the bastards right!' Paddy grinned, relaxing back on the pale beige leather settee, 'They should known we'd sell here big time. And what about American women eh? Are they something else or what? Did you see some of the girls the bouncers were pulling off the stage? I had a hard on all evening!'

'There'll be plenty more like that hanging about at the party tonight,' Jeff grinned. 'We can all go out with a bang, if you'll excuse the pun.'

Matt stood silently by the window, looking down into the street, watching the flow of traffic on the wet, dark road below, somehow removed from the other occupants of the room and the conversation which was going on.

'Here,' Baz joined him pushing an opened can of Budweizer into his hand.

'Thanks,' Matt turned, took the can and tilted it to his mouth.

'Have you phoned Sonny yet?' Baz asked. 'You know what he's like; he'll be dying to hear how *his boys* did.'

'I'll call him later.'

'You all right mate?'

Matt felt the weight of Baz's big hand on his shoulder.

'Fine. Bit of a headache, that's all,' he said as the door opened and Paul arrived, Todd behind him.

Todd squatted in front of the TV, scanning the channels for something that would hold his interest. Unable to find anything, he turned it off and slumped impatiently into one of the leather chairs. He wore a petulant look; Baz watched him, anticipating trouble and hoping he was wrong. Todd was like a bored, spoiled child, if the world wasn't going his way he looked for a reaction from others. He thrived on upset. Usually the rest of them were able to contain him, but on this tour he had totally exhausted everyone's patience with his behaviour both on and off stage.

Watching Matt, whose gaze was still fixed somewhere out into the darkness, Baz realised a lot of their on tour problems had been caused as a direct result of his sudden loss of enthusiasm. True the whole thing had run smooth as clockwork, but it had all been presided over in a rather soulless, mechanical way. Usually Matt was central to each tour, demanding, nagging, encouraging them to make each new performance better than the last. But this time it hadn't been there and neither had the firm hand which kept Todd in check. He knew the root of the problem was Ella and that it was long term; it would not go away in a hurry. Now the tour was over they had been promised a three month break before returning to the recording studios early in the New Year. Baz had planned to use that time to take time away with his girlfriend Caroline. To see Europe properly, not from a hotel window or the inside of a tour bus or plane but first hand, driving himself, stopping wherever the fancy took him, meeting real people, tasting the local food and wine. He wondered whether Matt might be interested in tagging along. A few months freedom on the open road with no distractions might be just what he needed to cure his ills.

'Did you see that girl in the green hot pants one of the bouncers pulled off me?' Jeff grinned at Paul. 'Tits to die for! Wouldn't mind waking up next to that!'

'Actually I think American women are shit!' Todd gave Jeff an insolent stare, relaxing back in his chair, cowboy booted feet resting on the coffee table. 'Trouble with you lot is you got no taste. Me? Can't say I've had good shag since I bin here.'

'Maybe you're the one with no taste then Todd,' Jeff reacted angrily. 'The rest of us have had a bloody good time, haven't we guys?'

They all nodded.

Ignoring him, Todd finished off his can, crushing it in his fist before consigning it to the carpet. Getting to his feet he went to the fridge and pulled out another. As he opened it his gaze travelled the room finally landing on Matt.

'Matt!' He raised the new can in mock toast. 'Come on! Cheer up you miserable bugger!'

'Shut up Todd!' Growled Baz.

'Yeah, shut up Todd,' Paul joined in. 'You're a real arsehole at times.'

'What d'you mean at times?' Paddy said irritably. 'He's like it all the bloody time.'

Todd, annoyed that he was being ganged up on, faced them all determined to have his say.

'You boys got it all wrong.' He waved his can dramatically at them and sidled over to the window to stand beside Matt. 'Matt's here's my friend,' he said placing a hand on his shoulder. 'And because he's my friend I'm going to give him some brotherly advice.' 'Listen to me!' he tugged at his shoulder. 'You're a poor sad sod, d'you know that? Women? They're all shit - especially the ones with money. Wake up Matt!' He hissed as he took his hand away. 'You ain't the first and you sure as hell won't be the last to be shafted. Anyone with any sense knows she only let you 'ave her to get back at 'er husband.' He waved a knowing finger in Matt's face. 'You ain't nothing to her mate, you probably never was. Still,' he grinned. 'It wasn't all bad. You got to shag Shandy, which is more than we all did!'

Matt stood there for a moment, his eyes fixed on the lit silhouette of the Chrysler Building, his mind returning to that night in Spain. He remembered lying on his bed, groggy from drink, a moonless night making everything in the room dark and indistinct. Then suddenly out of blackness she had appeared. He heard the soft rustle of material as her clothes fell to the floor, felt the movement of the mattress as she joined him, stretching her long, soft naked body against him. He couldn't see her, but he touched her hair, smelt her Estee Lauder Youth Dew and knew instinctively. It was Ella.

'I don't believe this,' He said tears blurring his vision as he tenderly stroked her face, 'I thought you left me, that you'd gone with him.'

'Who wants second best?' She whispered.

'But how did you find me?'

'Simple,' She gave a low laugh, 'I just walked down the hallway.'

'No, I mean how…..?'

'Ssh…..' She touched his lips with her finger, 'That's enough. I'm here now, that's all that matters.'

He crushed her closely to him, kissing her lips, his hands running over the sweet softness of her body. He made love to her slowly, wanting these feelings, these wonderful sensations to last for ever. Afterwards, he had fallen asleep in her arms, happy in the knowledge that she had finally left Andy and their new life together was about to begin.

But in the morning when he woke, a vile taste in his mouth and someone with a hammer banging in his head, he found it wasn't Ella lying next to him at all. The tumbling hair he had run fingers through in the darkness the night before wasn't black, it was peroxide blonde and the body he had caressed was full and voluptuous, not gently curved. He gasped in horror, grabbing a sheet from the bed and wrapping it around himself.

Shandy smiled, bleary eyed from sleep as she rolled over and looked at him.

'What you doin' that for?' She laughed at his modesty, 'There's nothin' I ain't already seen.' She reached out and tugged teasingly at a trailing corner of the sheet, 'or touched come to that.'

'Get away from me!' He shouted, scrambling from the bed and taking himself off to a corner of the room with his sheet, brushing an uneasy hand through his hair, wanting this to be a bad dream, but knowing it wasn't. Shandy sat up, dangling long legs over the bed, totally naked and unashamed, her breasts thrusting forward in typical Playboy model pose.

'Now that's not nice Matt,' she said watching him from under the thick cascade of her hair. 'As I recall last night you had absolutely no complaints. No complaints at all.'

'You tricked me! I had no idea it was you!' Matt stood up angrily.

'Is that so!' She looked put out. 'You were giving me the old come-on on the dance floor. Yer 'ands were everywhere,' She paused for a moment, 'Who d'you think I was then?'

He turned his face away, feeling nothing but guilt and revulsion at what he had done.

'Oh yes,' She put a finger to her mouth. 'What was the name? Ella. That's it. Ella. Thought that was just you and the booze. Who's she then? Some frosty little virgin with a padlock on her knickers?'

'None of your business!'

Seeing his anger Shandy hesitated. 'Well whoever she is,' she said with a toss of her head. 'She ain't a patch on me!'

'No?' He gave a cynical laugh. 'Well right now I'd say there's not a lot between the two of you.'

'What d'you mean?'

'Deceitful. Conniving!'

She looked at his angry face for a moment, then pushed herself off the bed and began to pick up her clothes. 'I'm not staying to listen to this crap!' She said sullenly, 'You're a user, just like the rest ain't you? And just when I had you down for someone halfway decent!'

Matt turned away, unable to look at her any more. Eventually he heard the door close quietly and knew she had gone. He thought for a moment. How he could have got himself into this situation? Of course, she was right, he had danced with her. But that was only because she'd come out onto the dance floor and pushed the girl he was with out of the way. She'd settled herself on him like a leech and in the end, coming to his senses, he'd pushed her off and wandered back to his seat. After that she'd homed in on Todd and it was him who had brought her back with them to the villa after the club had closed. He thought for a moment. Todd had organised the drinking bout, got him drunk. Could Shandy have been part of Todd's mischief making as well? Knowing Todd, she probably was, he decided.

He remembered gritting his teeth. Fighting the urge to march into Todd's room and punch him, angry that he had made everything worse than it already was. But wasn't it just typical of his moronic mind to think that what he'd done was nothing more than harmless fun?

And now here he was again, his face unpleasantly close, his breath reeking of alcohol, spoiling for some sort of reaction. The memory of what had happened that night at the villa coupled with Todd's wingeing complaint about Shandy told Matt that maybe the time had come to do something about it. And so without another word he simply turned, smiled and slammed his fist straight into Todd's face, sending him sprawling onto the floor, his half empty can of beer spraying its contents across one of the settees, narrowly missing Paul.

'That's it!' Matt turned around to look at all of them, 'It's over! I quit!' And without another word he left the room, closing the door behind him.

'You dick head!' Baz hauled Todd to his feet and pushed him into a chair, 'You've really blown it for us this time. Don't you realise we owe him everything? If he goes we're finished! You and your big mouth!'

'He'll be back,' Paul said, retrieving the can from the floor, 'This has been building all through the tour. I think he's needed a bit of space for some time. Give him an hour, he'll probably be a right as rain.'

'You hope.' Jeff replied sceptically, watching a dazed Todd wiping the blood from his mouth.

'Blimey,' Todd said with a grin, looking at the dark stain on the back of his hand and then at the others, totally immune to the chaos he had caused, 'Matty's got a belting right hook ain't he?'

A serious Paddy turned to Baz, 'And what are we going to do if he doesn't come back?'

'I don't know Pad.' The big man said quietly, 'That's not really an option I want to think about.'

Matt sat in the corner of a small bar he had found. With a constantly replenished glass of bourbon he spent his time watching people come and go. All of life was here; two garishly dressed women who obviously knew Louie the barman well, an off duty policeman, a couple of weary businessmen, together with a smattering of locals. The interior was dark and smoky with a heavy wooden mahogany bar, matching tables and dark green seating.

Matt decided he liked this place, it suited his purpose; he was faceless here and the shadowy interior mirrored his mood. He had walked out of the Waldorf Astoria into a world full of brightness and activity. New York was a city which never slept; it was a permanent living thing, a world of garish neon, yellow taxi cabs, hotels, clubs and bars. He had walked for over an hour before he had come to this place of refuge - Kawalski's Bar. There he had ordered a Jim Beam, taken a seat and contemplated his options. Of one thing he was certain; he really had finished with the band. It had not been just empty words thrown at them; he meant it.

As he sat there he reflected on the three short years of their collective fame. It had been a blast; but it had also changed many things. To make big money you had to tie yourself into the treadmill life of recording and touring with a few snatched moments of respite in between. They had done this successfully with his musical guidance changing their style to meet current pop trends and the tastes of the ever fickle record buying public. It was a case of continually re-inventing yourself and it had paid off; they were all wealthy now, owned property, fast cars, expensive clothes with a lifestyle far removed from the old days when they toured in a second hand Transit van.

Miraculously he had kept them out of the drug scene, ensuring Sonny had tied them into a contract which dictated that anyone who got involved with illegal substances would be sacked immediately. It was unique and perhaps a little harsh given the lifestyles of other rock bands, but he had told them they had to make choices and sacrifices, just as he had. If they wanted to remain at the top, they had to concentrate on being the best, and to be the best, the drug scene was out.

Booze and birds, on the other hand, were considered a natural part of their way of life. It went with the territory, and although in some ways a drunken Todd became a one man publicity machine for the band with reports of his outrageous behaviour keeping them firmly in the limelight, he was also a walking hand grenade with the pin partially pulled. Drink always made him aggressive and confrontational, just like tonight. Matt had seen his destructive personality at work and on most occasions had been on hand to defuse potentially dangerous situations. Tonight, however, it was he who had been on the receiving end.

He knew had it been any other time he would have ignored the derisory comments, but tonight was different. Ella had changed everything. Somehow all his energy and enthusiasm for the band had gone, his life soured by a woman who had abandoned him to go back to a husband she had sworn she did not love. Of course he knew the reason he had hit Todd was because his words had held just a little too much truth. A truth he had done his best to brush under the carpet while the tour was on. But now it was all out in the open again, in full view of the band. He remembered the sympathy in their expressions in the silence that followed his punch. And something worse - pity. Pity, for someone who had been foolish enough to let a woman make a fool of him, not once but twice. Poor bastard their faces said and he couldn't cope with that because somehow it diminished him as a man. And seeing that he knew he could no longer stay with them.

He checked his watch. Eleven fifteen. Time to return to the hotel, phone Sonny, then pack and get the first available flight back to the UK. Exactly what was going to happen after that he wasn't sure.

He passed the bar, leaving his empty glass with a 'Thanks' and a 'Goodnight'. The barman frowned at him and in a thick Brooklyn accent and a smile which almost cracked his round face in two, said.

'Hey, I know you. You're that guy with that English band on tour here ain't you? Whatta they called? The Attitoode, that's right, The Attitoode.'

Matt nodded and smiled, almost embarrassed at the attention the man's words were drawing from those around him.

'Hey Doug!' The barman waved out a shadowy figure sitting at the end of the bar. 'Look who's here, that Limey songwriter.'

A stocky, middle aged man in a dark grey suit, black hair slicked to his head, slid off his stool and walked past the onlookers to where Matt stood.

'Well!' He said with a look of surprise, 'What brings you here? I would have thought Kawalski's was about the last place in town a famous face like yours would have wanted to hang out. Shouldn't you be partying somewhere?'

'I didn't feel like it,' Matt smiled, feeling strangely relaxed under the friendly dark eyed gaze of this stranger, 'I wanted to be somewhere quiet.'

'I was at Madison Square Gardens this evening, I enjoyed the performance,' His dark eyes smiled warmly, 'The material you write for them is somethin' else.'

'Thanks. Do you see many bands?'

'You could say that. I'm in the business.' He reached into his jacket pocket and pulled a business card from his wallet, 'My name's Doug Henderson, I own Maverick Records,' he said handing the card to Matt, 'Ever heard of them?'

Matt shook his head, 'Can't say I have.'

'It's a pity you gotta go,' Doug looked disappointed, 'It would have been great to have talked to you.'

'I guess I can stay a while longer,' Matt smiled as he leaned on the bar.

'Great!' Doug was all smiles, 'Whatta you having?'

Saturday 11th September

Tad Benedict walked into his house and threw his car keys onto the hall table. What an awful day he thought as he hung up his coat and it wasn't over yet - he still had to break the news to Faye.

She appeared from the kitchen where she had been in the throes of preparing their evening meal.

'Tad? Whatever's wrong?'

'Come and sit down,' He pulled her towards the drawing room, 'I'll tell you when I've a drink in my hand and not before.'

Faye took a seat and watched while he poured out two glasses of best malt, then crossed the room to hand her one.

'Sonny rang me late this afternoon. The band's tour has just ended in New York.'

Faye smiled, that meant Matt would be home soon. He had been away for so long, keeping in regular touch, with her. All his calls had been upbeat and positive with laughter and jokes about the tour, and not one mention of Ella. Secretly she hoped this meant the events of June were well and truly behind him.

Tad took a mouthful of whisky, savouring its taste. 'The good news is,' he said eventually, 'that the tour's gone well; they've gone down a storm - the Americans love them. Sonny says it's just like The Beatles; they've done TV, radio, interviews and played to packed stadiums. He says the new deal with Scorpio's just what they needed.'

‘So, why the long face?’

‘Because,’ He took another mouthful, ‘after their last show there was a row between Matt and Todd. Matt punched Todd and then promptly announced he was quitting the band. He phoned Sonny this morning to tell him.’

‘So is he on his way home?’ Faye asked anxiously.

‘No, he’s still in New York.’ Tad said slowly, taking another mouthful of whisky, ‘He told Sonny that he’s been talking to a record company there, with a view to working with them for a while.’

‘And exactly what was this row about?’ Faye asked, feeling upset that it looked as though she was going to be deprived of her son’s company yet again, ‘No, don’t tell me! It’s Ella isn’t it?’

Tad took a deep breath, ‘I’m afraid so. Todd made some derogatory remark and Matt hit him.’

‘What!?’

‘He loved her Faye, probably still does. I think we have to accept that. And the kind of love he’s experienced takes time to get over.’

‘That’s it!’ Faye pushed herself out of the chair angrily. ‘I can’t just stand back and do nothing, I’m going to fly out to New York to find him and bring him home. I would think right now he needs us more than ever.’

Tad shook his head sadly. ‘Right now I think the farther he is away from Abbotsbridge the better. Ella’s pregnant. If he comes back to find that, God knows what it will do to him. I would suggest for now that we leave well enough alone. We’ just have to accept that he’ll come home when he‘s ready.’

‘Oh Tad!’ Faye felt the sting of tears in her eyes, ‘Not again! That bloody girl! How I hate her!

Monday 13th September

The yellow taxi came to a halt outside a large grey stone building.

'Here we are Bud.' The cab driver called over his right shoulder.

Matt hauled himself and his guitar case out of the back of the taxi and paid the driver. As the cab disappeared around the end of the block he stood looking at his reflection in glass of the front doors. Last week he had been part of a famous band, someone who mattered, who called the shots. Now he was on his own, a virtual unknown, arriving at a strange record company with a brief to revitalise the flagging career of one of its stars. Feeling both apprehensive and excited, he ran his fingers through his thick brown hair, straightened his jacket and entered the building.

‘Mr Henderson's in the studio at the moment Sir. Would you like to take a seat? I'll tell him you're here.’

The immaculately made up brunette on reception gave him a warm smile as he stood in the pale marble floored foyer, its walls adorned with photographs of Maverick's record stable. He wandered over to look at them; some faces were familiar, others totally unknown to him. All had one thing in common. They were country and western acts and the last thing he was, was a country and western song writer. In fact, he positively hated country and western. Why hadn't Doug mentioned this? And what was Maverick doing here anyway? Shouldn't it be in Nashville? A little worm of worry started to niggle in his brain.

He turned as the ping of a bell and accompanying sigh of parting doors announced the lift had arrived. A young woman dressed from head to foot in tight green leather and wearing red platform boots stepped from it and headed towards him, clutching a clipboard.

'Matt Hi!' She reached him breathlessly and extended an enthusiastic hand. 'Sorry to have kept you waiting. I'm Marcie Maguire. Doug's Personal Assistant.'

'Pleased to meet you,' Matt got to his feet slowly, and shook her hand. Slim and sexy with skin the colour of pale amber, her eyes were deep brown, her small heart shaped face encircled by a mass of wild black hair.

She looked at his guitar case and smiled, 'Like to bring your things and follow me? Doug's in the studio at the moment, he'd like you to join him.'

She kept up a torrent of small talk as the lift descended into the basement of the building. She knew about the Attitude, had been to London, loved the boutiques and 'Buck House' and wasn't he lucky being a Brit because that was where it was at these days. Mr Henderson thought he would be just the thing, bringing in new material, an exciting departure for the company, taking them in a totally different direction. It was all good, for Maverick and for him she said, her unruly hair bouncing energetically around her shoulders as she talked.

With his head ringing from this barrage of chatter, Matt followed her out of the lift and down a narrow passageway towards a half glass door over which a red light declared 'QUIET, RECORDING '. Bringing a cautionary finger to her lips Marcie opened the door and showed him in.

As he followed her into the room, he was aware of the voice; a voice which filled the whole room with its richness and clarity. A voice trapped and marginalised by the weakness of the song it was in the process of singing. He stared into the recording booth. There, perched on a high stool, clad from head to foot in white sat a woman. A woman with a long tumble of gold blonde hair. The spotlight which shone down on her from above gave her an ethereal quality.

The power from her voice was awesome, but the song was dreary, repetitive. In fact it was awful. A touch on his sleeve dragged his concentration back into the studio. Doug was there smiling, grabbing his hand and shaking it enthusiastically.

'I've spent all weekend sweating.' He whispered, 'Thought you might change your mind.'

'No fear of that.' Matt hissed back. 'Who's the blonde?'

'Kendal Conway. Have you heard of her?'

'Vaguely.''

'The Galveston Pearl. Maverick's Queen of Country. She's the act I want you to work with.'

Matt gave a silent groan.

As the song came to its conclusion, Doug leaned forward and pressed down the intercom button.

'Can we take a break now Kendal? Matt's here, I'd like you to meet him.'

The woman removed her headphones, slipped from the stool and came back into the studio. She was smaller than Matt had first thought, about five feet four, and older. Underneath the lights he had thought her somewhere between twenty five and thirty, but as she joined them, hands tucked into the front pockets of her tight white jeans, he could see she was well into her forties.

'Kendal, I'd like you to meet Matt Benedict.' Doug said enthusiastically. 'Remember Honey, I was telling you about him over dinner on Saturday night?'

'Sure do.' She drawled, appraising him with her vivid blue eyes. 'Pleased to meet you Mr Benedict. Doug here tells me you're gonna work miracles, revive my career.' She gave Doug an amused look. 'Make me a big star again.'

'I'll do my best.' Matt smiled back, suddenly feeling defensive. This failing singer was laughing at him, sceptical of his abilities. He opened his guitar case and pulled out a sheaf of paper, scanning through the individual sheets until he found what he was looking for.

'As soon as I came into the studio and heard your voice, I knew this was just right for you.' He said, handing her three sheets of penned music and lyrics. 'It was something I worked on during the tour with the Attitude, needs a little fine tuning but I think it's good.'

She took the wad of paper from him and scanned each sheet in turn; suddenly she began to hum the tune.

'Very impressive,' she said, handing it back to him with a disdainful flourish. 'But I don't do this stuff.'

Matt held his breath, appalled by the woman's arrogance. He had heard about American stars, treating people like dirt because they believed themselves the centre of everything, but he never thought he'd be on the receiving end.

'This stuff, as you put it.' He said, shaking the music at her, 'Would do real justice to that voice of yours, which is something that certainly wasn't happening when I came in.'

'What d'you mean?'

'That song you were singing. It was awful.'

The blue eyes narrowed. 'That song Mr Benedict, was my song. I wrote it. And I think it's great. How dare you talk to me like that! Doug,' she turned to looked at her confused manager. 'I don't want this guy anywhere near me, do you understand?'

'But Honey, he's penned loadsa number one songs. His band's albums have sold world-wide.'

'I don't care if he's walked on the moon, just put him on the first goddam plane to England, that's where he belongs.'

'But Angel.'

'Are you arguing with me Doug?'

'Kendal all I'm just asking........'

'Enough!' She raised a regal hand. 'I don't want to hear another word. I am going back to my apartment now. You do what you want, but understand this, I do not intend to set foot in this studio again until he is gone! Do I make myself clear?'

And with a toss of her head, she marched out of the studio slamming the door heavily behind her.

TWENTY ONE

Friday 17th September

Doug Henderson sat behind his office desk, staring out across the Hudson River, the New York skyline a pastiche of muted shades. His concentration, however, was not taken up with the clear blueness of the day, but rather the dreadful situation he was in. His star act had boarded herself up in her Manhattan penthouse and refused to come out and Matt Benedict was on the point of returning home. The whole plan to revive the company's flagging fortunes was in tatters and he had no idea what to do.

Of course, with hindsight he knew he should never have encouraged Kendal to write, it was the worst possible scenario. But she had been quite confident that as she had spent years singing other people's lyrics and music, it would be relatively simple to pen a song herself. He knew Matt had been right; as soon as he had heard the first few bars of *'Sunset Canyon.'* he knew it was awful. But for Kendal, already bruised by a recent panning in the press, Matt's comments had been one insult too many.

The sound of his door opening turned him away from the window. Marcie stood there smiling uncertainly, orange button fly flares clashing heavily with her green and yellow skinny rib sweater, unruly black hair falling around her face,

'What is it?' He asked tiredly.

'Can you come down to the studio?'

'What for?' He gave an unenthusiastic sigh.

'Matt wants you to show you something.'

'Matt? What's he doing down there?'

'He's been working on the song he offered Kendal. He asked me to bring you down to listen to it.'

'Not now Marcie, I'm not in the mood.' He flapped a disinterested hand in her direction.

'Oh come on Doug! You'll be impressed. Honest!'

'Will I?' Doug looked up at her wearily.

'Yeah, you will. Now please.....!'

Matt was in the studio with the technicians when Doug arrived; all were smiling.

'Marcie's just dragged me out of a warm office to see you,' Doug raised warning eyebrows at Matt, 'for your sake I hope it's worth it.'

'It is. You can have it as a parting gift from me.'

'So you are leaving.'

'First thing in the morning.' Matt nodded.

'Shame.' Doug gave a heavy sigh.

'I have to. It's the only way you'll get Kendal back.' Matt offered him a chair.

Now, prepare to be wowed! 'Marcie said looking a Matt with a grin as Doug settled himself down.

As the first chords came through the sound system Doug's eyes opened wide. The melody was beautiful, haunting and then it broke into something faster paced, causing feet to tap and heads to nod.

'Who's this?' Doug frowned, 'I don't recognise the voice. What a range!'

'It's me.' Marcie looked amused.

'I didn't know you sang.' Doug looked at her in amazement.

'I did some session work, way back. Backing vocals.'

'You been moonlighting?' He looked aggrieved.

'It was years ago! Doug, just shut up and listen will you!?'

Suitably chastised he sat there quietly, closing his eyes, immersed in the music, until the song eventually came to its conclusion, Marcie's voice carrying it onward and upward to a dramatic ending. As the studio fell silent someone at the back of the room began to clap.

Matt turned to see Kendal Conway standing there, swathed from head to foot in fur. 'Congratulations,' she said coolly as she stared at him, 'I owe you an apology, it's a very good song.'

'Yes it is,' Doug said, dancing around her like a boisterous dog. 'and it's just what you need to put you right back on top again.'

'On top of where Doug? This isn't country music, it's some sort of hybrid that doesn't really fit in anywhere,' She was dismissive.

'The American Billboard of course.' Matt interrupted.

'But I'm not a mainstream singer. I've only ever had hits in the country chart.'

'Perhaps it's time you changed direction then Kendal.'

'Miss Conway to you.' Her tone was sharp, 'And if there are to be any changes in the way I do things, I'll decide.'

'Fine by me,' Matt shrugged indifferently, 'If you don't want it then I'll just take it elsewhere.'

'You can't do that, you're working for me!' Doug frowned at Matt.

'Yes but this song is my property, I can do what I like with it. The question is, do you want to revive this company's fortunes or not?'

'He knows what he's saying Doug,' Marcie tugged at his arm, 'We have to listen to him.'

'Kendal,' Doug swallowed hard and faced her, 'You know the current situation. We just don't click with the public any more. Everything has moved on but we haven't. Sweetness, I am convinced this song could be our salvation.'

Kendal began to laugh. 'You're so damned dramatic Doug, you should be in the movies.'

'Is that a yes then?' He looked at her hopefully.

'If it keeps the boat afloat, then yes, I guess so.' She gave a reluctant sigh, casting disapproving look in Matt's direction. 'But if it backfires on me and my career, he's dog meat! Understand?'

Saturday 30th October

'Happy?' Bob Macayne smiled at Mel as he handed her a gin and tonic. They were alone at the time, all the others from their group on the floor, involved in rather an energetic fox trot.

Tonight the Forum was guest to Abbotsbridge Round Table's Halloween Ball and the place had been decorated out in black and orange - pumpkins, witches, spiders and bats adorning the walls and the ceiling.

'Thank you.' Mel took her drink and watched him lower himself into the chair next to her. 'Yes, I am actually Bob. It's good to see Ella's decided to embark on motherhood at last.' she studied him for a moment, 'and I can see you're pleased too. Another Macayne to continue the family business - if it's a boy of course.'

'No question of it being anything else. Macaynes don't produce girls.' He smiled, 'You know I'm very proud of Andy, he's done everything that's been asked of him. Sorted out his marriage, got his wife pregnant. He's had a few false starts but I think he's grown up a lot in the past few months. I'll make a Macayne of him yet!' He relaxed back in his chair and then raised his eyes to Mel again. 'We should savour rare moments like this you know. It's not often everything in life is almost perfect.'

'My life's not perfect Bob. Far from it!' Mel was indignant, 'Take my father. He changes like the weather. One moment he's friendly and I think I'm getting somewhere with him and then suddenly he freezes me out. I feel totally confused!' she gave a frustrated sigh, 'You know sometimes I think he's playing some sort of spiteful game with me. And enjoying it!' she frowned into her glass. 'My great worry is he'll have one of his negative strops on when this holiday village thing comes back to life again. And if he does, what are we going to do?'

'Perhaps,' Bob said soothingly, 'it's time we went to see him together. Put our cards on the table.'

'When?'

'After Christmas.'

'Then what?'

Bob grinned, 'I make him an offer he can't refuse.'

'My father will never accept money.'

'Don't be silly Mel. Everyone has their price. It's just a matter of finding out how much.'

Friday 31st December

Matt stood with his back to the picture window of Maverick's penthouse entertainment suite. Behind him in the darkness, the lights of New York shimmered against the night sky, while in front of him, a party was beginning to rev up.

Doug had really pushed the boat out this evening. Huge vases of red roses were everywhere, while waiters in scarlet bow ties and cummerbunds weaved their way through the high profile guests, handing out glasses of Veuve Cliquot and canapés. Conversation and the chink of glasses filled the room; he glimpsed famous faces, glamorous women dressed to kill, handsome men in dinner jackets. All had been invited here for two purposes; to celebrate Kendal's successful return to the limelight and the launch of her new album *'Phoenix Rising'*.

Matt couldn't believe it had happened so fast. First the single *'Maybe It's Time.'* had been recorded and released, entering the American Billboard at number two and moving up to the number one position the following week where it had stayed for three weeks during November. As soon as the song had reached number one, Matt was set the task of putting together a collection of suitable songs for a new album. Doug had rented him an apartment overlooking Central Park, hoping that the location would prove inspirational. Matt, complete with piano, was told to lock himself away and compose. Alone with his thoughts the inspiration had flowed into eight good quality songs. As soon as they were ready, Doug pulled Kendal back into the studio to record. And now here they were, in a room full of balloons, food and celebrities, waiting for the guest of honour to arrive and celebrations to begin.

As he stood there, however, Matt wished the evening was already over. Polite small talk with strangers had never been part of his life. When he was with the Attitude the parties had been a bit of a riot, usually because Todd always devised some outrageous prank to play on the assembled guests. Here it was different. More formal. And from the body language he was observing, he got the distinct impression some of these people weren't at all at ease with each other.

'Hi there,' Marcie slid up to him in a sparkling hot pink full length evening dress and silver boots, her hair cascading around her shoulders.

'Anyone tell you, you look like Diana Ross's kid sister?' He grinned.

'I'll take that as a compliment.' she laughed, 'Are you enjoying yourself?'

'I guess so. Amazing turnout.'

'Sure is. Everyone who counts is here tonight,' she looked around the room, 'All of New York's elite. There's been a real buzz around this new album - lots of interest. Doug's delighted. And he's found a backer for Kendal's Spring Tour.'

'Yes, I wanted to talk to him about that. He'll need someone to manage that tour and I'd like to do it.'

'But you're a writer.'

'I did both with the Attitude. I enjoy the buzz, I just wondered whether he'd agree. I want a change, I've had enough of being cooped up writing. Would he go for it, do you think?'

'I guess you could ask him, I'm sure.....'

A sudden burst of applause interrupted their conversation. Doug entered the room, Kendal on his arm, his sombre evening dress a stark contrast to the shimmering red sheath she was wearing. She gave Matt and Marcie a cursory glance then turned away as champagne was offered and people came to meet and greet her, pressing cheeks with everyone, all smiles as they came to offer their congratulations.

'Typical Kendal,' Marcie rolled her eyes, 'Treats everyone at Maverick except Doug like trash. This evening belongs to you too Matt, without your talent it wouldn't be happening. Doug's really stupid at times, knows the price of everything and the value of nothing.'

'I don't mind,' Matt shrugged, 'I'm not a limelight seeker, but I see what you mean.'

Kendal was in her element now, surrounded by a crowd, talking animatedly. Watching her reminded Matt of another limelight seeker: Mel Carpenter. Straight away Abbotsbridge loomed into his mind; he saw faces and places and then unexpectedly he was back at the Mill. New Years Eve - one of his father's favourite nights. A full house - the disco volume pumped up and everyone having a good time. A strange homesickness swept over him. How he longed to be there, but, of course, such sentiment was pointless. At the moment there was still far too much pain for him to think about returning home.

'This is gonna be such a great evening,' Doug's voice interrupted Matt's thoughts as he pushed between them, an opened bottle in his hand, 'My baby's on her way back to the top. C'mon, drink up.'

'So what's next? The tour?' Matt asked innocently as he pushed the past from his mind and held out his glass.

'Yeah. In the Spring, I've got a high profile backer. Myron Barnes the Texas oil millionaire. Over there,' he waved the bottle in the direction of a fat, balding man, whose arm was currently encircling Kendal's waist, 'He's a real big fan as you can see!'

'You'll be needing a tour manager.'

'I sure will.' Doug tilted his champagne flute to his lips.

'Would you consider me?'

'You?' Doug took his glass away from his mouth and began to laugh.

'Yes, me. I was the Attitude's tour manager for two years don't forget.'

'I don't think so.' Doug gave an amused grin.

'Why not?'

'I think you should take a look at your contract.'

'What do you mean?'

'You're employed to write songs.'

'I know and I've done that. You won't need material for Kendal's next album for several months. I can start that while we're on the road. It's a good place; I get a lot of inspiration there.'

'Matt, you're not listening to me,' Doug patted his shoulder patronislingly, 'You're hired as a writer. You've done a great job with Kendal, now I want you to start doin' the business for a couple of my other acts.'

'Doug, I don't *do the business* as you put it, I write.' The irritation was evident in Matt's voice, 'and when I signed up you said I'd just be working with Kendal.'

'Slip of the tongue,' He shrugged, 'As far as I'm concerned your contract says you're a writer for Maverick Records and that means you write. For anyone I want you to.'

'In that case,' Matt said, handing his half empty glass to Marcie, 'I quit. Excuse me.'

'You can't leave, you're needed for a photo-call in ten minutes,' Doug said grabbing him by the arm.

'Stuff the photo-call!' Matt stared down angrily into the older man's face.

'Matt, be sensible, you're under contract to me for a year. Walk and I'll sue.'

'Fine,' Matt replied with a cold smile, shaking off Doug's grip, 'See you in court.'

Back in Abbotsbridge, the Mill was welcoming guests for its New Year's Eve Party, Tad and Faye in its blue carpeted foyer greeting people with a customary glass of sparkling wine.

Mick and Nina Taylor arrived, Nina in turquoise and black, her hair cut in a new shorter style.

'Well I know what his New Year's resolution ought to be.' Faye whispered watching them as they passed through to the main bar. 'Getting rid of her as soon as possible. He hasn't got a clue what's going on behind his back at the moment.'

'What's this?' Tad said nodding greeting to a large group of arrivals which included the Stewarts and the Tates, 'Up to her old tricks again is she?'

'She certainly is - with him.' Fay replied, her eye on the smiling Rich.

'But he's marrying Annabel Langley next month!'

'That's as maybe. The fact is they've been spotted together on several occasions, looking rather more than friendly.' Faye watched Rich standing there with a silly smirk on his face as the group reached their table and the men stood back to let the ladies settle themselves in. 'Not very bright our Rich,' she looked at Tad with a smile, 'Let's hope Bryan doesn't find out or he'll have him washing cars instead of selling them.'

'That'll be mild in comparison to what old man Langley will do if he gets to hear about it!' Tad said with a laugh, 'If, of course, there's anything left of him after Annabel's finished.'

Four hours later, the countdown to the New Year had begun. Tad was on stage with his microphone, the whole audience chanting with him. As *Auld Lang Syne* blared from the speakers, people hugged and kissed each other. Tad and Faye stood together on the stage toasting the crowd as they formed lines, joining crossed hands to sing.

At the far edge of the floor Faye Benedict could see Ella Macayne. Standing with Gareth, Andy and Bryony she was smiling as Gareth bent his head to shout something to her. Grudgingly Faye had to admit that pregnancy seemed to have made her even more dazzling; her skin was clear and flawless, her wild mass of shiny black hair secured on top of her head, escaping tendrils corkscrewing prettily around her face. She was dressed from head to foot in tiers of black and silver sequinned sparkle which caught the light as she moved.

Faye found her thoughts straying to Matt. How she missed him. But he was doing well with the new record company he'd signed to, that was the main thing. A successful album with one of their established artists. He still kept in touch by phone, told her he loved and missed her but she understood after all he'd been through he needed to rebuild his life somewhere away from Abbotsbridge. Once he was strong enough she knew he'd come home again.

Thoughts of Matt were pushed from her mind as she noticed a slight flurry in the crowd. People stepped back and she could now see there was an argument going on between two women and a man.

'You'd better get Max over to nip that in the bud,' She nudged Tad, wondering who was involved.

The singing came to an end and the lights went up. People turned to look in the direction of the commotion that was going on. The ever vigilant Max was already on the floor, slipping between people, heading for the area where the trouble was.

'Well well!' Tad chuckled, 'If it isn't Nina Taylor. Looks as though she's having a bit of a spat with Annabel Langley.'

'Oh dear,' Faye smiled as she looked at her husband. 'Rich's car washing days might be closer than we first thought.'

Mick Taylor was watching the crowd as his wife rushed past him pursued by Annabel Langley. He had brought her here with him to the Mill tonight to celebrate New Years' Eve alongside the usual Abbotsbridge crowd but halfway through the evening she had disappeared. Even sending Jenny off to search in places inaccessible to men did not yield any positive results - she appeared to have vanished into thin air. Irritable and angry he had contemplated his drink and watched the movement of bodies on the dance floor, wondering what was going on.

It was quarter to midnight when he decided to look for her again. After circling the dance floor to check if she was at any of the other tables, he headed for the main door where Max let him out into the crisp, cold night. The car park was full of vehicles, eerily silent, their colours distorted in the golden glow of the car park lights, a shimmer of frost on their roofs. He shivered; no one in their right mind would be out here. He was about to turn and walk back into the club, when something made him hesitate. It was barely audible at first and he paused for a moment, wondering if his hearing had deceived him. Then as quietly as he could, he took a few more steps forward. The sound became louder; muted gasps and groans and suddenly he was there, standing beside Rich Tate's Jensen Interceptor tucked into the front edge of the car park. Its windows were thick with condensation and as he stared at it he detected movement. Someone was inside, having sex. Suddenly the sounds intensified. Great moans of pleasure followed by a man's voice gasping out a familiar name, after which silence settled on the car park once more.

Mick stood there, the cold numbing his face and his fingers, trying to cope with the pain and anger he felt. He had done everything to give Nina the world she wanted; even sacrificed his most precious possession, the farmhouse. And she had repaid him with *this*. He stared at the car. The thought of Andy with her had been bad enough. But a chinless wonder like Rich was too much to cope with.

He heard Rich cough, Nina giggle and a hand inside the car rubbed at the condensation. Mick shrank into the shadows and turned back towards the club. He'd seen enough.

As he reached the club and its warm, inviting foyer he almost collided with Annabel Langley.

'Mick,' she said in her plummy accent, 'Don't suppose you've seen Rich have you? I've looked absolutely everywhere. It's nearly midnight and I need him for *Auld Lang Syne.'*

'Try his car.' Mick nodded absently towards the door.

'The car?' She rolled her eyes with irritation. 'Is he totally mad? It's freezing!'

Mick watched her go, clutching her black beaded evening jacket tightly around her as she clattered on high heels down the steps and out across the car park. He hoped when she found them she would knock the living daylights out of both of them.

In the dance hall, Big Ben was booming through the speakers on the stage and everyone was coming onto the floor, ready to link hands for *Auld Lang Syne*. He skirted the crowd, planning to slip back to his table unnoticed, but a group of boisterous strangers grabbed him as he passed and he found himself in the middle of all the noise and celebration. As the singing finished, a net full of balloons were released from above into the crowd and there was a mad scrabble for them.

Mick was in the middle of this good natured scrum when a white faced Nina pushed anxiously past him, heading back towards their table in a great hurry. Following behind her with a furious expression on her face was Annabel Langley, a flustered Rich bringing up the rear. Annabel caught up with Nina right in front of the stage only feet from where Mick was standing.

'You're a disgusting trollop Nina Taylor!' she shouted, her face flushed with anger. 'What's the matter? Isn't one man enough for you?'

'I haven't the faintest idea what you're talking about.' Nina turned brazenly to face her.

Mick watched silently as the outraged Annabel lunged at his wife and suddenly realised he didn't care about what was happening or what people thought. Somehow he felt completely detached from what was going on in front of him; it had nothing to do with him any more.

All at once the crowd parted to allow the fair suede head of Max the bouncer through. Towering above the women he parted them with a sweep of his huge arms, standing like a barrier between them. Tad appeared from the other end of the stage and walking to its edge, squatted above them.

'Ladies I'm sorry to disappoint you,' he said gently. 'But this club doesn't have a boxing licence. Now can you please break this up otherwise I'm going to have to ask you both to leave.'

Annabel pouted for a moment then pushed her thick fair hair off her face.

'I do apologise Tad,' she said giving him a gracious smile before fixing Nina with a cold, hard stare. 'The problem is when you deal with common people, you very often find yourself dragged down to their level. Rich!' She held out her hand and he approached meekly taking it in his. Without another word they both walked back to their table.

The music started up again, with Rod Stewart's *Maggie May*. Shaking his head, Tad left the stage, whilst Max gave Nina a lecherous grin before melting back into the crowds once more. Mick watched her standing there brazenly, straightening her dress and running her fingers through her hair. Then with a toss of her head and a smile for the DJ she headed for the bar.

Mick followed, catching up with her just as she was easing herself onto one of the stools.

'Ah there you are.' She gave him an easy smile. 'Fancy a drink?'

'Why not?' He watched her carefully, 'Your usual?'

'No, I fancy something completely different.' She said, spotting the barman pouring out four glasses of champagne for one of the waitresses. 'I know, let's see the New Year in properly with some bubbly.'

'Good idea.' He called the barman over.

'So, what was all that about just now?' He asked as he sat facing her moments later, glass in hand.

'All what?' She stared at him blankly.

'Your embarrassing little set-to with Annabel.'

'Oh that!' She shrugged, 'Nothing really. I went out to the car park for some fresh air. Rich was out there too, she found us together talking. Well, you know how possessive she is.'

Mick noticed the way her eyes locked onto his as she spoke, all wide-eyed innocence.

'Actually I ran into Annabel too.' He said with a smile.

'Did you?' She tipped the glass to her lips casually, uncaring.

'In fact it was me who told her where she could find you both.'

'What?' Mick noticed the uneasiness in her eyes.

'Yes,' He nodded. 'Sadly by the time she got to you both she'd missed the Oscar winning performance I'd been treated to. All that gasping and moaning - it surprised me, you know, I never had Rich down as the great lover.'

'Actually he was awful,' she stared into her glass, suddenly subdued. 'Oh Mick, I didn't mean for it to get so....involved.' She bit her lip uncomfortably. 'But I guess he caught me at a weak moment. You were on site all the time. He and Annabel were going through a rough patch. It just happened. Then when I tried to finish it, somehow I couldn't.'

'That's just your problem isn't it?' Mick said with a shake of his head, 'Being a girl who just can't say no. So, how long Nina?'

'What?'

'How long has it been going on? A month? Two?'

'Since August.'

'That long? You didn't waste much time did you? After Andy.'

'Oh Mick. I swear, it won't happen again.' She looked at him desperately, laying her hand gently on his thigh. 'Honestly.'

'You're right Nina, it won't.' He pushed her hand away.

'Mick?' She frowned, uncertain.

He drained his glass and put it back on the bar. 'No more Mr Nice Guy, Nina. It's over.'

'What are you talking about?'

'I want a divorce.'

'You can't be serious about this Mick. I told you, it was a mistake. Please, don't do this.'

'I have to Nina. There's no other way. When giving you everything's not enough there seems little point anymore. Now if you'll excuse me,' He slipped from the bar stool, 'I'm going home to pack.'

'But what about me? How will I get home?'

He considered her question for a moment and then gave a casual shrug, 'Don't know. That's no longer my problem, Nina.'

Crossing the car park moments later, Mick realised that in the first moments of the New Year he had made a decision which was going to change everything about his life. No more Kennet Close. No wife. He was about to embark on a single life once more. Of course he'd have to break the news to his parents and Jenny. As he unlocked his car, he paused for a moment, realising before he did there was something else he had to do first.

The Bridge Hotel was ablaze with light and activity. Abbotsbridge General Hospital's Consultant's New Year's Dinner was winding up. The after dinner speaker had finished to a rapturous applause, final brandies had been drunk, more coffee dispensed and now the guests were beginning to depart. People loitered outside the hotel, waiting for taxis or were caught in last minute conversations in reception as they were handed their coats.

Issy's mother Cheryl was clearing away glasses from the hotel's small lounge area. It had been a good night, sixty people in the banqueting suite, a four course dinner. All had gone remarkably well, thanks to Issy and her superb organisation.

'Hello Mick,' she looked up with a bewildered smile as Mick Taylor walked into the hotel lobby, 'What brings you here?'

'Issy,' He said, 'I need to see Issy.'

'She's clearing up in the function suite.'

'Thanks, I won't keep her long.'

'You look a bit pale love, are you OK?'

'I'm fine thanks Mrs Llewellyn.'

Cheryl watched him as he moved off down the green carpeted corridor, thinking he looked anything but and wondering whatever he could want.

In the function room, Issy was busy cleaning ashtrays and stacking them on the nearby dresser. The two waitresses with her were about to take out the last trays of dirty crockery and glasses they'd cleared from the tables.

'I'll finish up here now. You two get home to your beds.' She called after them. 'Thanks for all your hard work. It's been a great evening.'

They both smiled and nodded, wishing her a Happy New Year before they disappeared into the kitchen.

Issy sighed; her feet were killing her and she longed to kick off her shoes and join her parents upstairs for their own private toast to 1972. However, before this could happen she knew there was one last job; putting all the table cloths into bags ready for the next laundry collection.

Pulling a fresh laundry bag from one of the cupboards she was suddenly aware of someone in the room. It was then she remembered the cigarette lighter one of the waitresses had found under the table.

She looked up with a smile, about to assure Dr McKie that his lighter was safe, but to her total surprise found herself looking instead at Mick Taylor.

'Mick? What are you doing here? I thought you were at the Mill tonight.'

'I was. But.....' He hesitated. 'I had to see you,' He sounded almost desperate, 'I just couldn't leave things until the morning.'

'Have you been drinking Mick Taylor?' She eyed him suspiciously, clutching the bunched up table cloth in her hands.

'Yes....a few, but not like you think.' He swallowed hard. 'The thing is, there's something I have to say to you.' He hesitated again. 'Something that's really important.'

She put the cloth down and stared at him.

'It's about Nina.'

'Really!' Issy picked up the table cloth again and began stuffing it irritably into the laundry bag. 'As I recall, the last time her name was mentioned, you told me to mind my own business!'

'I've.....I've left her.'

As she picked up a fresh tablecloth she saw his mouth wobble and tears threaten but he shook them off and continued.

'She'd been seeing Rich Tate you see, since August. I only found out tonight. You were right all along. She did just what you said she'd do.'

Issy stood uncertainly, not knowing what to say. Although she had always predicted this, having Mick here telling her it had actually happened somehow seemed quite unreal.

'So that's why I had to come....' His words became almost a mumble as if they were heavy objects he was tired of carrying, 'I just wanted to say how sorry I am. For the way I treated you. For the dreadful things I said. I know what you must think of me.'

As his hands went to his face and he gave a great gasp, Issy abandoned the tablecloth and went over to him.

'No you don't. You haven't a clue,' she said softly, peering up at him under his hands, 'I think you're the bravest, most honourable man I've ever met.'

'You do?' He took his hands away from his face; his cheeks wet with tears, and looked down at her with surprise.

'Yes. It must have taken a lot of courage to come here tonight, to say what you've just said.'

'I feel so bad about it. I was awful to you. How could I have done that?'

'It's O.K., it doesn't matter Mick, it's in the past,' she said comfortingly. 'What does matter is where you go from here.'

'I'm moving in with Mum and Dad.' He pulled a handkerchief from his coat pocket and wiped his eyes, 'Until the divorce is through.'

'Divorce?'

'Yes.' He pushed his lips into a determined line. 'Divorce.'

'And how have your Mum and Dad reacted to all this?'

'No one knows yet. You're the first.'

'Be a bit of a shock then, won't it? You landing on them out of the blue with all this, especially on New Year's Eve.'

'I hadn't thought.' He gave a confused shake of his head. 'Yes, I suppose it will.'

'All the more reason for you to stay here, then.'

'I can't possibly do that. Whatever will your parents think?'

'They won't mind. Come on.'

She stretched her hand out to him like a mother to a small child. He took it without protest, allowing her to lead him slowly towards the door. As she reached up to turn out the lights he looked back at the room, table cloths bunched up on each of the tables, the laundry bag hanging over the back of one of the chairs where she'd left it.

'But what about the clearing up?'

With a click of the switch the room was plunged into darkness. She looked up at him with the most comforting of smiles he'd ever seen.

'The clearing up can wait. It's really not that important, Mick. Not tonight.'

1972

TWENTY TWO

Tuesday 4th January

'So what did he have to say for himself?' Doug Henderson turned away from the window and the wet New York day to look at Marcie standing in front of his desk. Swathed in a full length Afghan coat and purple platform boots, she had just returned from her visit to see Matt.

'He wasn't there,' Marcie gestured helplessly, 'I went round to his apartment just like you asked me to and the janitor told me he left on New Year's Eve. Said he'd gone to the West Coast and wouldn't be back.'

'California?' Doug frowned. 'What the hell's he gone there for?'

'Maybe to get away from you,' Marcie said with a huge sigh of irritation as she parked herself in a nearby chair. 'Ever thought of that?'

'Don't be so stupid,' Doug said dismissively, 'I gave him a damn good deal.'

'No you didn't Doug,' she said angrily, brushing her wild hair back from her face, 'You hired a remarkable talent and caged him like a bird in that apartment. You didn't give a damn about him as a person. You treated him like a machine, expecting him to write instant hits for those clapped out old has-beens you manage! You denied him his moment, to go on tour with Kendal, to actually see the fruits of his hard work. What's worse, you laughed at him! How dumb is that?'

'Be careful Marcie!' Doug's eyebrows met harshly, 'The smell of your coat I can just about cope with, your tongue I can't. The mood I'm in I just might fire you!'

'But you won't!' She shook her head defiantly. 'You need me Doug, you really do.'

'Says who?'

'Says me! And you know why? Because right now I believe I'm the only one who has a snowball in hell's chance of finding him for you and persuading him to come back!'

Saturday 8th January

A crowd had gathered at the gates of St Marks, drawn there by the wedding which was taking place. At the pavement's edge black limousines waited, white ribbons decorating their bonnets. Their uniformed chauffeurs stood clustered in a group, caps slotted under their arms, rubbing gloved hands together and stamping feet as they chatted.

The day was slate grey; a flurry of snow had dusted the pavements and the flagstones which led up to the church door. All at once heads turned expectantly as from within came the rich sound of the organ. Moments later the doors opened and bride and groom emerged, followed by a stream of guests.

Slipping from her pew into the aisle, Issy joined the slow procession out of the church. In the churchyard she watched as photographs were taken. Annabel looked absolutely amazing. Over a plain silk wedding dress she wore a full length cape of white fox fur, the hood of which she now lifted, not so much to protect her face from the cold wind but rather to give the wedding photographer the ability to capture this stunning outfit on film. She carried no flowers. Instead her hands had been encased snugly in a matching white fur muff. Her mother was now handing this to one of the ushers for safekeeping while bride and groom posed for the photographer, holding hands, showing off their matching wide platinum wedding bands.

'They've done it then.'

Issy turned at the sound of his voice.

'They certainly have.' She said with a smile as he came to stand beside her.

'I had my doubts you know, after New Year's Eve.'

'Perhaps it taught him a lesson,' Issy said, watching the way Rich was holding onto Annabel's hand and smiling down at her. She glanced at Mick again, thinking how well he looked. 'You O.K?'

'Yeah, fine,' He nodded, 'I've settled in back home. It's almost like I've never been away. Thanks for what you did, you know, letting me stop over at the hotel.'

'It's O.K,' She turned to look at him with a gentle shrug, 'Mum and Dad were more than happy to put you up.'

Issy switched her concentration from him back to the progress of the wedding photographs and their endless permutations. The photographer would step forward, move people to the left or right, fuss with the skirts of the bridesmaids, tuck tendrils of the bride's hair back into the fox fur hood. Beside her, shielding his face against the wind with the collar of his coat, Mick's voice intruded again.

'Actually, Iz, I came to ask whether you'd like a lift to the reception. You didn't look too happy when I saw you arrive with Ella and Jenny.'

'I wasn't,' She turned back with a grateful smile, 'It was an awful journey here, Andy seems to have a real strop on today. I've been finding it very difficult to bite my tongue. I think he's getting on Nick's nerves too and you know how patient Nick is with everyone. Andy is such an awful pig to Ella at times, makes me glad I'm single.'

'Not all husbands are like that, you know.'

'No,' She said quietly, 'The same as not all wives are like Nina. I expect you miss being with someone though don't you? I mean it's probably great being back home but......'

'Cooking,' He said with a smile, 'I miss her cooking. In the odd moments when she behaved like a wife she was quite a good cook. Plain stuff, of course, not like the stuff you do.'

'And what do you know about the stuff I do?' Issy gave an amused smile.

'Cordon bleu, Jen said. Went on a course didn't you?'

'Yes, I did, but I only use that sort of cooking in the business. At home I do the plain stuff as you call it. You should try my spaghetti bolognaise. Yes, why don't you come round in the week? I'll cook one for us.'

'Thank you,' He grinned, 'Invitation accepted,' and then noticing the photographer was gesturing for everyone to join the bridal party for a group shot, he said, 'Come on, looks as though we're needed.'

Sunday 9th January

Andy, propped up against the pillows was watching Ella over the top of the magazine he was reading. She was sitting in front of the dressing table running a brush through her long, dark hair, singing softly, as she watched her reflection in the mirror.

He felt irritable, not only with the way *'I'd Like to Teach the World to Sing'* was continually breaking into his concentration, but also that dinner at his father's had been thoroughly ruined by the antics of Mel Carpenter. His father's business arrangements with Liam had drawn the Carpenters into the Macayne's social circle and now that Mel was his mother-in-law, it also made them family. But exactly what was it about this dreadful woman that seemed to hold nearly every middle aged man in the town spellbound, was beyond his comprehension.

As usual she had placed herself next to his father and during the early part of the meal she appeared to be carrying on an exclusive conversation with him, leaning her head towards him in intimate fashion as he listened indulgently, or running red tipped fingers down his sleeve and giggling when she found something amusing. Then, when he had to leave the table to take an urgent business call, she homed in on Charles Fitzallyn, much to the annoyance of his wife. As the wine flowed Mel got louder, causing the other wives present to raise disapproving eyebrows across the table at each other. Andy winced and closed his eyes. It seemed lately he was angry with the whole Carpenter family. Mel for her excesses, Liam for putting up with those excesses. And Ella, for getting pregnant.

Andy watched her as she put down the brush and began gently blending night cream into her face and neck. He wished he could turn back the clock to the summer. Things were almost perfect then. In fact, after their return from Italy for a time it had been wonderful. She had matched his physical demands with a new-found healthy appetite of her own and on some days, unable to wait until the evening, he had called into her office at lunch time to whisk her back home for a little midday diversion followed by a shared shower. Life had been blissful and he had been happy. Until she told him about the baby.

The news had stopped him in his tracks. It was something he had not expected; did not want. Thoughts of the responsibility it brought, together with the ultimate changes to both their lives, frightened him. He watched her carefully for tell tale signs, but saw none. For the first few months nothing about her had changed, she positively glowed with health. The energy she put into her business doubled, the love making continued unabated. He began to think it was all a joke; that she had been playing games with him - winding him up.

Then one night in early October as they lay there together in the darkness he had turned to her with sex on his mind. Easing the straps of her night-dress from her shoulders his hands found her breasts. Tonight strangely they felt swollen and heavy. His fingers strayed slowly down over her abdomen, usually washboard flat. His hand froze and he sat bolt up right and turned on the bedside light.

'You *are* pregnant, aren't you?' He sat back, unable to disguise the horror in his voice.

'Of course I am silly,' She smiled, amused.

He stared down at her stomach. His baby was growing inside her and all he could feel was revulsion. With a puzzled frown, she pushed the straps of the oyster silk night-dress back onto her shoulders. As she did, he noticed for the first time the faint blue marbling of veins under the normally flawless skin of her breasts.

'Things are going to get a lot worse aren't they?' He looked at her, appalled.

She gave an uneasy laugh, 'Worse? It's not an illness Andy. But if you mean bigger then yes, I will get a lot bigger as the baby grows,' she ran her hand tenderly over her stomach. 'There's another five months to go yet. Remember how Jenny was? Well just like that,' she laughed. 'You men, don't you know anything?'

He stared at her, remembering how Jenny had struggled around for what seemed months with something that looked like an enormous beach ball under her clothes. The thought of Ella's body, the body he had come to depend upon daily to satisfy both his emotional and physical needs, being gradually taken over by some unseen thing living inside her, growing bigger, stretching her skin to breaking point, filled him with disgust. Suddenly he knew there was no way he would be able to touch her any more. There was nothing for it; he would just have to keep away from her until it was all over.

'Andy what's the matter?'

Her voice drew him out of his thoughts.

'What? Oh nothing,' He shook his head, 'Nothing at all.'

The bedside alarm gave him the excuse he needed, 'God is that the time?' He gave her a chaste peck on the cheek and reached over to turn out the bedside light, 'Sorry darling, think we better give it a miss tonight. I've got an early start tomorrow. Some couple coming up from Southampton. They're very keen - said they'd meet me at the show house at 8.00!'

Switching off the light he turned away, remembering the events on holiday that had caused this. Their return from a romantic restaurant they had found up in the hills, both of them suffering from Chianti overload. He'd carried her across the threshold of the bedroom like a new bride. They were both giggling like children as he kicked the door shut and staggered with her to the bed. The two of them had fallen easily into its softness, kissing and pulling off each other's clothes. Somehow through the haze of inebriation Ella had managed the presence of mind to unwrap a condom. Then afterwards, finding it had split and realising they might just as well have not bothered for all the protection it had given them. In his alcoholic haze he had been so confident there was nothing to worry about; he even remembered laughing at the panic on Ella's face.

Back in the present, her dressing table routine over, he watched her pull back the covers and slip into bed beside him. He wasn't laughing now. For him sex was a basic necessity. The baby wasn't due until the end of March. However was he going to cope until then?

Monday 10th January

Carrying an old canvas ruck sack over her shoulder, Marcie joined the queue waiting to board the early morning flight to San Francisco. As the queue moved slowly down the covered walkway to the plane, she contemplated the journey ahead. She had spent the week arguing Matt's case with Doug; trying to persuade him that a legal battle would only result in bad publicity and lawyers fees Maverick could ill afford. There was only one thing that any chance of bringing Matt back, she told him; a brand new contract that was both fair and unambiguous. In the end Doug, overwhelmed by her constant nagging, caved in and reluctantly agreed to rewrite it.

Once this was underway she returned to the apartment block to see the janitor again. After waving a handful of dollar bills under his nose, he magically produced a forwarding address for Matt. He was staying at a beach house at Hansen's Cove, just down the coast from Carmel, rented from an actor who lived on the floor above him. Luckily Marcie knew the area well; her parents lived at nearby Port Columbus. After agreeing a week's leave of absence to carry out her task, she called them to say she was flying out to escape the New York winter and she'd be with them on Monday evening.

Settling herself in her seat she smiled; so far so good. She had won her first big battle, convincing Doug of the flaws in his thinking and getting Matt's contract completely rewritten; but she knew her biggest challenge was yet to come. However she was upbeat; Matt trusted her - he was her friend and she was sure once he read the contract and the concessions she had wrung out of Doug, there would be no hesitation on his part. He'd be flying back to New York with her on the next plane.

Wednesday 12th January

Mick stood at the door nervously, holding a bottle of wine in his right hand. He paused for a moment then clearing his throat he gave the doorbell a firm press.

He heard the sound of feet in the hallway. A key turned in the door and it opened revealing a smiling Issy.

'Mick, come in.'

He crossed over the threshold, his tenseness dissolving.

'Nice place,' He said, looking around as he handed her the bottle.

'You didn't come here then? When it was Ella's.'

'No, never. Jen told me about it though.'

They looked at each other for a moment without speaking, Issy eventually breaking the silence. 'Come on; let me have your coat. What are you drinking? There's wine, or I've got some cold lager.'

'Wine will be fine.' He sniffed. 'Smells nice.'

'It's Lasagne.' She saw him frown. 'Oh dear, I promised you bolognaise didn't I? Are you O.K. with lasagne?'

He nodded his head. 'Actually, I think I'd like anything you cooked Iz.'

'Red or white?'

He looked puzzled.

'Wine. Red or white?'

'Oh, white please.'

'Go on through.' She pointed in the direction of the lounge.

He sat himself down by the warmth of the fire. The room was decorated in cream and terracotta, large abstract pictures on the wall echoing the colour theme.

'Did you do all this?' He asked moments later as she entered the room carrying two glasses of wine.

'Yes,' she handed him a glass and sat down beside him. 'Ella had pastels; I wanted something a bid bolder - a bit more me.'

'A bit more you,' He studied her for a moment as he took his first taste of the wine. 'And exactly what is a bit more you Iz? Total enigma you are. We've been at loggerheads for years and now here you are, cooking me a meal. Why the change of heart?'

'It was what you said outside the estate agents that day,' She said seriously, 'about Mr Davies. I realised you were right, it was childish, very childish. So, I thought it’s time I made my peace with you. Besides, I thought you might like some company.’’

‘It’s not because you find me totally irresistible then?’ He laughed.

‘Not yet,’ she laughed and raised her glass to her lips, ‘That’s work in progress.’

TWENTY THREE

Thursday 13th January

Marcie sat on the rocks of the breakwater at Port Columbus, watching the local ferry making its way across the sound, its bow cutting a smooth froth edged path through the dark blue water. Everything had gone wrong. She knew it served her right; she had been just a little too confident of her charm school abilities. On two occasions now, she had visited the beach house with the contract; and on two occasions he had turned her away.

The first time he did actually open the door to her, but it was obvious from the fact he didn't look surprised to see her that he had seen her arrive in her father's Dodge.

'Marcie,' He said calmly, blocking the gap in the door with his body, 'No prizes for guessing who sent you. Typical Doug, sending a woman to do his dirty work. I'm sorry, you've had a wasted journey.'

'But Matt…' Was all she managed before the door closed.

Annoyed, she pummelled the door, calling his name, trying to persuade him to open it again, but it remained firmly closed.

Forty eight hours later she was back. For some reason she thought her persistence would get her a hearing. She was wrong. This time he talked to her from the upstairs balcony which overlooked the sea. He said he was sorry she'd had yet another wasted journey, but there was absolutely nothing that would make him return to New York. As he disappeared from view she called after him, but hearing a door above close she knew he was beyond hearing or caring about anything she said.

Back in the present she sat, wondering whether to try again or pack her bags and go home. There were four days left of the seven she'd agreed with Doug. One more shot, she decided, just one. But this time I'll make sure the odds are in my favour.

Saturday 15th January

When the lunch time rush was over at the diner, Marcie went up to her room.

Pulling her wild hair into a knot, she changed into shorts, vest and canvas shoes and drove out to Culver's Cove, leaving her father's Dodge in the lay-by facing the ocean. Two hundred yards out a fine heat haze hung over the surface of the sea, obscuring the horizon. She scrambled down onto the beach, her feet sinking into the soft, loose sand of the marram covered dunes, slipping and sliding until she eventually reached the firm flatness of the smooth, pale beach. Taking a deep breath she began to run.

She was at her destination much sooner than expected and sat for a while behind a nearby dune watching the house. Eventually she saw him emerge, slinging a towel over the veranda rail before running down the steps and out onto the beach, heading for the sea. She checked her watch and smiled. Tyler, her fourteen year old cousin had done a good reconnaissance job, Matt's daily swim, confirmed by one of his neighbours, was right on time. She watched him run into the water then throw himself forward, launching into a powerful crawl. With one eye on the sea, she made her way behind the dunes to the back of the house then crept slowly down the side. Climbing quickly onto the veranda, she pulled back the screen door and slipped into the house.

Fifteen minutes later Matt returned from his swim. He stood on the veranda towelling himself down, dusted the sand from his feet and entered the house to shower. The swim had given him a chance to clear his head and free the block in his writing which had been tormenting him all morning. Shower over, he changed into a fresh pair of jeans and returned to the lounge to continue his composition, pulling on a tee shirt as he went.

'Hi Matt.'

The tee shirt was over his head, obscuring his vision and he whipped it off quickly.

'Marcie!' He stood there staring at her as it fell to the floor.

Marcie gazed at him; finely muscled arms, broad shoulders, dark hair covering his chest. She had never seen him like this before and suddenly found her pulse dancing crazily.

The sound of his voice, speaking her name had made her feel dizzy, like a seventeen year old with a crush.

'Well I have to hand it to you,' he said, 'you don't give up easily do you?'

'I thought maybe third time lucky?' Regaining some of her composure, she swung herself off the couch and began to walk casually around the room, noting the simple furnishings, polished wooden floors, durries and large piano tucked into one corner.

'You really are wasting your time, you know.' He shook his head. 'I've already told you I have no plans to return, court action or no court action.'

'Hey calm down, I'm on your side. And you're wrong if you think Doug sent me, I volunteered.'

'For Mission Impossible? That was rather a silly thing to do,' His voice was amused and mocking all at the same time, 'I had you down as a smart girl.'

'You know me Matt, never could resist a challenge,' She said leaning on the piano and trailing her fingers over the keys, 'Particularly when I can see how everything could work so well. It was going great you know, with Kendal.'

'That was before I realised what a devious bastard he was.'

'I think he just might have seen the error of his ways.'

There was a cynical edge to his smile as he retrieved his tee shirt from the floor, 'Leopards rarely change spots Marcie.'

'He's completely overhauled your contract.'

'Not interested.'

She watched him as he pulled the garment over his head and tucked it into the waistband of his jeans, amazed that such a simple action had slowed her pulse rate dramatically. Closing the piano lid she stroked the smooth mahogany, reprimanding herself; this was stupid, she had a job to do and now some silly unexplained emotion was getting in the way of the whole thing. She looked up and caught him staring at her.

'What?' She said with a grin.

'Your hair,' he seemed fascinated. 'That's the first time I've seen you wear it up like that.'

'I just tied it up for the run here, to keep it out of my face. Don't you like it?'

'Yes,' He paused, 'It's just that for a moment it reminded me of.......'

'Who?' Marcie looked at him curiously.

'It doesn't matter, it was a long time ago, best forgotten.' The words fell abruptly from his lips like the slam of a door and something in his tone told Marcie he'd touched a painful part of his past. Silently she watched him turn towards a heavy wooden dresser where an assortment of bottles stood. 'Drink?' he waved a half empty bottle of Jim Beam at her.

'Why not?' She crossed the room and settled herself back on the brown leather couch, watching as he unscrewed the cap and poured two generous measures into tumblers.

'Where are you staying?' He asked as he handed her one of the glasses.

'Port Columbus.'

He frowned. 'There aren't any hotels there.'

'I'm staying with Mom and Dad.'

'Your family's here?'

She nodded. 'Mom runs a diner on the Port - *Hash Browns* - and Dad's got a charter business, hires out boats and takes tourists deep sea fishing.'

'Fancy that!' He smiled, amused at the coincidence of it all and then taking a swallow of his Jim Beam, he studied her thoughtfully, 'So how exactly did you get from Port Columbus to New York? And why a backroom girl, when you've got such an amazing voice?'

'Oh I don't know,' she thought for a moment, 'Safer bet I guess. Dad was with one of the big bands in the late forties-early fifties. I saw what had happened to him. How the fickleness of the music business destroys peoples' hopes and aspirations,' she smiled. 'He's a great saxophonist, but that part of his life is over. The big bands are gone. Guys like him aren't in demand any more.

Still, it's not so bad,' she shrugged, 'He made enough to set himself up in business and he's happy with his boats.'

Stretching herself along the couch she relaxed, cat-like and continued.

'As a child I'd always dreamed of being famous. I loved music. Dad used to listen to Peggy Lee, Ella Fitzgerald. Amazing women. Unique voices. I knew I wanted to do something with music, but Dad warned me off singing, so, when I was sixteen I got a job here with Surf City Records as an office gofer. It was just the opportunity I was looking for. At first I did all the odd jobs, making coffee, running errands but it was great because I was learning all the time. Then after a year the boss Chuck Wiseman suggested I start helping out with tours and launches. It was fun. I loved it. I get a great buzz being with people, organising, arranging. The trouble was two years into the job the guy I worked for moved on and this woman, Gloria Defoe took his place,' she shook her head, 'She was a control freak; supervised everything I did, didn't trust me with anything on my own. A couple of things went wrong, I got the blame. I could see the writing was on the wall so I quit and flew to New York. Figured that was the happening place to be. The first newspaper I opened had Doug's advertisement in it. I applied and the rest, as they say, is history.'

'And what keeps you with Doug?' Finishing his drink he returned his glass to the dresser, turning to lean on it, staring across at her, 'He's so bloody rude to everyone.'

'Doug's a good guy really, but he's his own worst enemy,' she smiled. 'He's a committed record company boss but his weakness is he has a one dimensional view of things. For him the star is everything; he forgets that behind that one individual are a whole team of people making it happen. You took Kendal back to the top. Did he appreciate it? Hell no. All he was thinking was *who's next for the magic treatment.* I was so mad with him,' she tilted her head back and began to laugh softly, 'I told him they were old has-beens.'

'Sadly most of them are,' Matt agreed, 'and I don't think they have the potential to be resurrected. I think long term the company should invest in some new talent. Kendal can't carry the company indefinitely, even if she does have the right raw material.'

'Your songs you mean?'

'No, her voice. She's a real thoroughbred.'

See!'

'What?'

'You do care really. Please! Come back to New York and patch things up with Doug. He's offering you a wonderful new deal.'

'Marcie, I'm not interested.'

She felt a huge knot of disappointment gather in her chest.

'Look,' she saw he was watching her with his sad tawny eyes, 'It's nothing personal.'

'Well it feels like it,' she said despondently, staring into her empty glass, 'Please, don't close the door in my face. At least hear the deal before I go!'

Pushing himself away from the dresser he walked over to the window, where he stood, staring out into the fading light of the afternoon, his hands pushed deep into the pockets of his jeans. After what seemed an age he turned and with a hint of a smile said.

'I must be totally crazy. But seeing it's you and you've come all this way.........

'Oh Matt! Thank you, thank you!' She interrupted him excitedly. A lifeline, he'd thrown her a lifeline. She couldn't believe it.

'Hey, don't get too excited, I said I'd listen, that doesn't necessarily mean I'll change my mind. I'm just trying to be fair, that's all.' He joined her, perching himself on the arm of the couch. 'O.K., now exactly what is this great offer I won't be able to refuse?'

Monday 17th January

Marcie checked her seatbelt and relaxed back in her seat as the plane taxied out onto the runway ready for takeoff. Outside bright morning sunshine caught the pale stone of the airport buildings, bathing them with warmth. The engines were picking up now, the whine becoming louder. The plane shuddered slightly then was off, down the runway, gathering speed. The whole cabin angled upwards and there was that strange feeling of the air taking control, indicating they had left the ground. She looked out of the window, watching Los Angeles spread out below her as the aircraft banked and headed east. As they left the city behind she tilted her head back towards the interior of the cabin and smiled.

'O.K?'

Matt nodded, reaching across to lace his fingers with hers.

'No second thoughts?'

'I don't think so,' He shook his head, looking pleased, 'I can't believe you got so much out of Doug!'

'I told him what had to be done, that's all,' She said with an embarrassed shrug, *'And* he had to agree in the end that sending you on tour with Kendal was a great idea.'

'Ah! I wanted to talk to you about that.'

'Why?'

'Something more important has come up.'

'But what could be more important than Kendal's tour?'

'I've had an idea that could turn Maverick's fortunes around quite quickly.'

Marcie looked at him, amusement in her dark eyes, 'How you gonna do that Superman?'

'I'm going to get Doug to sign a new singer to the label. Like I said, it's time we changed direction. Broadened our appeal.'

'So who ya got in mind?'

'You.'

'Me?' She laughed. 'I'm very flattered, but....'

'No buts Marcie,' He raised a silencing finger at her, 'Listen......'

Friday 21st January

'Marcie, Matt, Morning. Have a seat.'

With a wave of his hand, a sombre faced Doug Henderson indicated the two heavy leather chairs in front of his desk. As he sat down, Matt shot a quick glance at Marcie, who lit up the room like a bird of paradise in her bright yellow leather jacket and metallic copper coloured jeans. She turned and gave him a quiet smile before settling herself beside him.

Doug leaned across his desk and handed Matt a copy of the finished contract. Matt looked at it, still unable to believe that Marcie had pulled off the coup of the century. If it were indeed true, the document he now held in his hand had completely changed his standing at Maverick. He now had a new title - Creative Director. He was no longer tied to any specific artist and he had total control over all the musical arrangements of his songs. He had an increase in salary with a review after six months. Despite this, however, he still distrusted Doug, sure that something in the small print was waiting to leap out and give him an unpleasant surprise just like last time.

'I assume you're familiar with the contents.' Doug patted his copy with the flat of his hand.

Matt nodded.

'Good!' Doug sat back, looking a little more relaxed, a smile appearing on his face as he pulled a pen from the inside pocket of his jacket. 'Now if you'll just sign where I've pencilled crosses.'

'Not so fast,' Matt replied leaning across and tossing his copy of the contract back in front of Doug. 'Before my signature goes anywhere I need you to *tell* me exactly what this contract means, so that I know exactly what I'm giving you and what you're giving me. Then I want you to swear on your Mother's grave that you'll abide by every single line of it; no blurring of the edges, no misinterpretations, I want everything to be crystal clear, understand?'

'Suspicious bastard isn't he?' Doug said, looking peevishly at Marcie.

'I guess he feels he has good cause to be.' Marcie was unsympathetic.

Doug glowered silently at both of them, feeling ganged up on, 'O.K, O.K!' he said irritably and snatching up the contract from his desk he pulled on his glasses and began to read.

Fifteen minutes later he lowered the paper to the desk, all trace of hostility gone as he looked hopefully at Matt, 'Well?'

Matt nodded silently.

'Great!' He pushed the contract back across his desk towards Matt, offering him a pen. 'Just sign then will you? The sooner this is sorted the quicker we can all get back to work.'

'Before I do,' Matt shook his head. 'There's one other thing.'

Doug's dark eyebrows knitted themselves together irritably. 'You've had the shirt off my back, there is no more.'

'It's just one simple change. I don't want to go on tour with Kendal. I want to undertake a new project, working with Marcie.'

'I don't understand,' Doug began to laugh.

'I want to turn Marcie into your next big act.'

Doug shot Marcie an angry look. 'Been cutting your own deal behind my back have you?'

'Doug,' Marcie protested. 'It's not like that! Will ya listen to what he has to say?'

'The fact is,' Matt continued, 'you need new blood. You can't keep reinventing your existing stars. Oh we can paper over the cracks with one or two good singles, but they won't go the distance like Kendal. What you need is something completely fresh! Something different. And I think Marcie is it!'

'Comedian now, are we?' Doug waved a dismissive hand at Marcie, 'Her? A star? She dresses like a road traffic accident! Gimme a break!'

'She could be big. Bigger than Kendal,' Matt's voice was full of enthusiasm. 'Her voice is better and although you might think the way she dresses is a disadvantage, believe me that's the one thing that will make people remember her. It's the youth market I aiming at, but my guess is she'll have a big appeal right across the board,' he gave her an affectionate smile, 'I guarantee, everyone will love her. And once she's established, acts will be queuing up to be managed by you.'

'Matt,' Doug shook his head with a tired sigh. 'You're way ahead of yourself here,' he pulled a Havana cigar from the silver box on his desk and lit it. 'Launching a new star isn't that simple,' he drew on the cigar thoughtfully, 'It involves time and a whole lotta money. You know the situation here. I've been lucky enough to get a backer for Kendal's tour because she's a known name and Myron knows he'll see a good return for his investment. But Marcie?' he waved a casual hand in her direction, 'We don't even know what we've got here! Who the hell's gonna risk their money on her?'

'I am.'

Doug shook his head sceptically and blew more smoke into the air. 'Then I'd say you're taking one hell of a gamble.'

'That's up to me,' Matt said quietly, 'But what is up to you is whether you still want Maverick to be here in twelve month's time.'

Monday 7th February

Nina stood on the pavement opposite the Nicholsons Estate Agents looking at the dark green paintwork and gold lettering framing a large window neatly laid out with properties. She checked her watch. Ten fifteen. Taking a deep breath she crossed the road.

A smart older woman with blue rinsed hair showed her into a large room behind the reception area and asked her to take a seat. The room was some sort of board room, with its long oval table, green and cream Regency stripe seated mahogany chairs and dark green velvet curtains tied back with gold tasselled cords. On the fine dark panelling which clad the walls hung portraits of previous generations of Nicholsons, a family who had made their money as merchants building their wealth in wool and cloth during the eighteenth and nineteenth centuries and munitions in the early part of the twentieth century. And now Alex, inheritor of all this wealth made a very lucrative living from the sale of exclusive country properties, farms and expensive town houses. Oh no, Nina thought, this was not the usual High Street estate agency, this was special.

She walked around the room, examining each portrait carefully, admiring the thick curling hair and aristocratic profiles of each one. They were all exceptionally handsome men, just like Alex Nicholson. She was disturbed from her inspection as a door opened and an immaculately dressed man with a shock of fair hair entered the room.

'Nina.' The use of her first name set the scene immediately. This interview was going to be informal, relaxed. He smiled and walked across to where she stood, his hand taking hers, shaking it firmly as his green eyes scanned her from head to foot, 'So sorry to have kept you waiting.'

She chose that moment to slip out of her coat, watching him as she carefully let the garment drop from her shoulders. As she folded it over the back of a nearby chair she could tell from his expression that he liked what he saw, his gaze lingering interestingly on her upper body.

'Please, have a seat.' He indicated a chair and joined her. 'Now then, as you know, Sylvia Ferguson, who has been with me for many years, is about to retire, which is the reason I'm interviewing today. If you don't mind, I'd like to start by finding out exactly what drew you to my advertisement.'

Nina had caught the advertisement in the paper quite by chance and realised its potential right away. Alex Nicholson was well known in town. Divorced and around ten years younger than Bob Macayne, he held as much commercial and social power within Abbotsbridge, but unlike Bob he was old money and that made him far more respectable and admired. She knew very little about him, other than he lived in a magnificent Georgian house on the outskirts of town and had divorced his French wife five years ago after she'd run off with an Argentinian polo player. Since then he had become one of the town's most eligible bachelors. She remembered seeing him at dinner dances when she had been married to Mick and knew he had a taste for young, sexy, expensive looking women.

Mick. It was strange to realise he wasn't part of her life any longer; that she was now a free spirit, in control of her own destiny. And her optimism about the divorce settlement hadn't been misplaced. Like his son, Jack Taylor was a soft touch. Letting her stay on in Kennet Close until a buyer had been found. Now contracts had been exchanged she was looking forward to moving into a comfortable first floor flat on the east side of town. So all in all it had worked out quite well, except, of course, for the maintenance she had been unsuccessful in negotiating. Instead she had been offered a single cash payment. Generous, her solicitor said, advising her to take it. Of course, there was no way it would keep her in the style she had grown accustomed to long term. To do that she would need a job to make up the shortfall and this one had really made her sit up and take notice. For, if she was successful, not only would she get to work for one of the town's most affluent men, it had the potential to take her much, much further.

With this in mind, she had taken herself into Abbotsbridge where she had spent a lot of time trying on outfits, wanting to get the look just right. Low cut tops and short skirts were out. A black suit with pencil knee length skirt and a pale green silk blouse won the day. Finishing dressing that morning, she crossed the room and gazed at herself in the mirror, then sweeping her hair back from her face she secured it at the nape of her neck with a shiny black slide and clipped pearl studs in her ears. A double string of pearls completed the look; sexy but business-like. Pleased with the result, she went to look for the new black patent high heels she had bought to go with it.

Forty five minutes later, the interview was over and Nina was walking down Bridge Street. She smiled to herself; she hadn't lost her touch, in fact it had been a piece of cake. The job was hers; she started Monday week.

Saturday 12th February

Living back at home, Mick reflected as he got ready to leave the site that evening, was almost like returning to his old bachelor days. There were some differences though. For a start, the Mill Club was gone, most of the old crowd having either married or moved on. There were atmospheres too; he found he had very little to say to Rich Tate any more whenever their paths crossed and as far as Andy was concerned, since the events of the summer of '71 he communicated with him only as a matter of necessity because of his job.

The divorce was now well underway. He had been keen to end things as quickly and cleanly as possible. Nina had been surprisingly co-operative, the only stumbling block being her insistence that she was entitled to and should have regular monthly maintenance payments. Thankfully this had now been averted by the offer and acceptance of a generous one-off payment. He missed being married though; there was a void in his life; nothing to plan, no one to share with. As he filed the latest set of site plans away, he acknowledged that six weeks into the new year had, of course, brought many positive changes in his life. The anger and pain from his break up with Nina was easing and the feeling of failure in having to resort to divorce, which he was sure would plague him relentlessly, had not materialised. Suddenly he was a new man with new attitudes and expectations and part of this he knew was down to Issy. She had come so unexpectedly into his life, giving him support and friendship when he needed it most.

He checked his watch, his thoughts turning to where he needed to be next. Liam's office for a meeting to discuss amendments to Phase Three. Pulling on his coat he locked the office and crossed to where his Stag was parked. As he opened the door he saw his father's red BMW turn into the site.

'I was hoping I'd catch you.' Jack said as he emerged from his car.

'I'm just off to see Liam. Is there a problem?'

'No, I've brought you these.' Jack dipped into his pocket and pulled out a bunch of keys.

'What are they for?'

'The farmhouse.'

'I thought you'd sold it?'

Jack shook his head, 'I was persuaded not to.'

'Who by?'

'Issy.'

'Issy?' Mick stared at his father.

'Yes. She came to me just after that first business with you and Nina. She knew I'd taken it off your hands. Pleaded with me not to sell it. Said that one day you'd need it to kick start your life again and that I'd know when. I do; it's now, so here you are.'

He reached for Mick's hand and placed the keys in his open palm.

'Thanks Dad.' Mick stared disbelievingly at the keys, then at his father who was now making his way back to the BMW.

Reaching the car, Jack turned. 'A word of fatherly advice, if you'll take it.'

'What?'

He pulled open the driver's door and leaned on it, a smile on his round face, 'When all the hard work is over. When the house is finished, ask the girl to marry you.'

Mick watched the car move off, away into the distance.

'Oh Dad,' He said with a shake of his head, 'If only it was that easy.'

Monday 28th February

'Great idea of my old man to organise this to launch his new Mercedes franchise, don't you think?'

Rich Tate lisped, casting interested eyes over the guests assembled at his father's house in North Portway.

'Yes the cars are great,' agreed Gareth Stewart, 'It's occasions like this that makes you wish you were single again doesn't it?' he watched admiringly as a pretty blonde in a pink lacy dress passed by.

Andy said nothing, but he knew he'd give anything to be single right now. He had not had sex for nearly three months and his initial feelings of revulsion were now turning to resentment. He hated the thing growing inside her. It had taken her away and not only bloated her body beyond recognition, but driven a wedge between them. For Ella no longer shared his bed. She had been uncomfortable she said, the baby pressing on a nerve. It kept her awake, so now she spent her nights in the guest room where she and the bump shared a king sized bed together. It made him feel isolated and angry.

'Sailing a bit close to the wind aren't we Rich?' Gareth gave a smirk as he looked across the room and spotted Nina standing alone with a glass of wine in her hand. 'How did she get an invite? But more interestingly how will she remain in one piece with your Annabel in such close proximity?'

'Nothing to do with me,' Rich shrugged irritably, 'She came with Alex Nicholson. 'Didn't you know? She works for him now.' He gave a disdainful smirk. 'Dad knew she was coming but there wasn't much he could do about it. Alex is pretty influential, it wouldn't do to upset him. Besides, Dad's hoping to interest him in buying a new Merc to add to his collection of cars.

'Wouldn't mind one myself,' Gareth said, taking an envious look out of the window at the selection of luxury cars parked below, 'What do you think Andy?'

'I already have one, remember?' Andy said as he consigned his glass to a passing tray.

'Who's a lucky bastard then!' Rich looked at Gareth with raised eyebrows.

'Lucky!' Andy said sharply, 'Is that what you think I am? You don't know anything!'

Gareth watched as Andy left them both, making his way back to Ella. 'Well, what's got into him, I wonder?

'A touch of PMT no doubt.' Rich replied.

They both laughed.

The doors between the huge drawing and living rooms had been folded back and a six piece band tucked among the small forest of palms in one corner were playing *'That Old Black Magic.'* Andy held Ella like a piece of treasured porcelain as they danced, aware that even if things were not all they should be, it was important to keep up appearances somewhere as public as this. When the music stopped everyone clapped and as the band struck up again, Ella rested her palm against the small of her back and smiled.

'I think I'll sit the next one out if you don't mind darling. I feel uncomfortable and just a little bit queasy.'

'What is it you want? Water!' There was barb-wire impatience in Andy's voice as he followed her to the edge of the room.

'No,' She ignored his sharpness, 'Fresh air. Can we go outside?'

They moved towards the door and she felt the coolness of the night air on her face as they stepped into the garden. Walking a little way out onto the terrace she stood for a moment, looking up at the full moon in its halo of cloud hanging over the town. She felt the baby move; new life inside her. Matt was gone now, still a painful memory, but one which she was sure would gradually fade. It was time to move on. Motherhood beckoned and she looked forward to this new role. Life was good, almost perfect; she knew she should be happy, but there was one little niggle that would not go away - Andy.

After the initial shock of her news, for a while everything was fine. But when her body started to change she sensed that Andy changed too; sex had stopped almost immediately. It appeared he was totally turned off by pregnancy. He became resentful and moody, calling the baby 'It', treating it like some sort of alien life form. Of course he always remained the caring attentive husband in public but in private he seemed to have retreated into his own world, a world from which he seemed to want to exclude her. She had spent months tip toeing round him, doing everything in her power to melt the ice wall which he had constructed around himself and to an extent she seemed to have been making some headway until a week ago when she decided to move to one of the guest rooms because of the uncomfortable nights she had been having. Although she had explained her reasons, the anger and resentment in his face was all too clear. As far as he was concerned he was being rejected. Now, alone in the garden, she felt she had to say something, she couldn't let this go on indefinitely.

'Andy,' She began, 'this situation with the baby,' she reached and covered his hand with her own, 'I want you to know I understand how you feel.'

'I wonder how Liam and Mel are enjoying the Caribbean?' He replied, gazing up at the stars as if he had not heard her, 'I wish we were there,' he shivered, 'It's a damn sight warmer than here for a start!'

'Andy please, talk to me.'

'There's nothing to say Ella,' He stared at her blankly then removed his hand from hers, 'Look, it's cold, you're beginning to shiver. Let's go back in.'

She looked at him, unable to read anything in the expressionless dark eyes which gazed into hers. Once more he'd frozen her out with his irritation and impatience. She wanted to cry but she couldn't - what was the point? She would just have to soldier on and cope with these strange moods until the baby had arrived and her body was back to normal. She was sure everything would be all right then, but the one big fear lurking at the back of her mind was that with no resolution to their problems, there was a danger he might be tempted to stray again, and that was the last thing she wanted.

As they came back in through the French doors, Annabel and Bryony were hovering anxiously.

'We saw you out there in the cold, are you O.K?' Annabel asked with a worried frown as she saw Ella's sad expression.

Ella nodded wearily. 'Just a bit uncomfortable, it's to be expected I guess.'

'Poor you,' Bryony cooed, her kohl rimmed eyes full of sympathy, 'Still not long to go now is it?'

'Perhaps we'd better go home Ella,' Andy's voice cut in abruptly, 'No point in staying if you're *ill*.'

'I am not ill Andy!' She said angrily. 'I am pregnant. There's a slight difference.'

'You come with us,' Bryony said comfortingly, giving Andy a huffy look, 'Leave Andy with the boys for a while. Mother's in the conservatory with some of her friends. She's dying to have a proper chat with you.'

Andy checked his watch, 9.00. Bryan Tate had just silenced the band to invite his assembled guests to help themselves to the buffet. A slow queue of people had progressed their way along through the pool room and out the other side, helping themselves to a wonderful array of food. Slowly he merged into the line of people, eventually finding a quiet corner to eat alone. When he had finished he went to find Ella, only to be told by Annabel that she was resting upstairs and it might be better if she was left to sleep for a while.

The music got going again, the band being replaced by a disco in the pool room. Andy amused himself for a while, partnering his friends' wives and flirting outrageously, enjoying the feel of slim bodies against his own. The evening's consumption of alcohol eventually led to high spirits with people jostling each other dangerously close to the pool's edge as *'Simple Simon Says'* blared out across the water. Suddenly there was a huge splash and a shout as Gareth Stewart went backwards into the water, fully clothed. He came to the surface shaking water from his dark curly hair and laughing.

'Come on in everybody!' He shouted encouragingly, 'The water's great!'

Andy immediately backed away, wanting to avoid a soaking, knowing despite his appetite for a laugh, he had a responsibility to get Ella home at the end of the evening. He moved away, taking up a vantage point by the DJ, sipping his wine and laughing at the antics of the people who had been pushed into the water and were now trying to drench those standing at the pool's edge. He noticed Nina Taylor on the periphery of the crowd, glass in hand, laughing and pushing with the rest. He also saw someone else watching her. Annabel was slowly edging towards her and he could see exactly what was about to happen. Darting behind her brother and father, she homed in on Nina. Nina had been trying hard to keep away from the pool's edge, but was now hemmed in by a crowd fronted by Gerald and Justin Langley. All Annabel did was to give her brother the merest of nudges and in he went, knocking Nina off balance as he fell. She screamed as they both fell backwards into the water together to a loud cheer from the assembled crowd. Andy saw the expression of triumph on Annabel's face as she looked across and gave him a huge grin.

Justin came to the surface spluttering, still holding onto Nina. Clutching her tightly like a retriever, he swam with her towards the steps and with his father's assistance hauled her out of the pool, dumping her onto the tiled floor. She sat there coughing, her hair and dress completely saturated. After giving her a few helpful pats on the back, Justin was wrapped in a bath sheet and taken away by his father to dry off. Left alone, Nina sprawled there shoeless, her tawny hair plastered to her face, the white lace dress she wore clinging to every curve. As Andy watched her lying there he thought of all the things that were wrong in his life. He was lonely and depressed, hating every minute of being an expectant father. The Ella who had returned from Italy with him had gone, replaced by a balloon full of aches, pains and constant headaches. What he needed was to put some excitement back into his life; to find someone to distract him from his misery. Good sex and a laugh, with no strings attached. Nina - he smiled to himself as he watched her. Of course, why hadn't he thought of her before.

Friday 3rd March

'Who was that on the phone?'

'Mary.'

Ella closed the lounge door and returned to her comfortable chair. She stared into the fire for a moment then retrieved her magazine from the coffee table and began to read.

'How are things?' Andy, picking up on the silence, closed the kitchen and bathroom catalogue he had been thumbing through and relaxed back into the settee, watching her intently.

'Fine.' Ella nodded, her eyes fixed on the article she was reading.

'Ella you were twenty minutes out there in the hall. Fine wouldn't have taken that long. What's wrong?'

'Mary wants me to go back to Meridan Cross for a long weekend,' she said, resting the magazine in her lap, 'She thinks it's time I cleared the air with Grandma.'

'I agree.'

'Do you?'

It was the first time in ages he'd shown any interest in her or what she was doing. Ella's expression brightened. She was rewarded with a smile.

'Yes. What's stopping you?'

'Pride I suppose,' she lied. 'We didn't exactly part on the best of terms last June. You see I didn't tell her we were having problems; as far as she was aware, I had simply gone back to the village for a visit. Then when you all arrived looking for me and my mother started throwing rather unpleasant accusations at her, she was understandably very upset. I've been phoning her regularly since we came back from Italy but it's only been small talk. I wanted to say how sorry I was, it's just that....'

She thought of Matt. It was winter in Meridan Cross, the landscape would be different; no reminders, - it would be safe.

'Oh Ella!' Andy's expression softened, he left his magazine and came and kneel at her feet, taking her hands in his. 'Darling you must go. I insist. It's important to me that you it make up with her.'

'Why?'

'Because life's too short to be at odds with each other.'

'Does that include us too?' She looked at him hopefully.

'Yes, I suppose it does. I know I've been awful to you and I'm sorry. I just find pregnancy horrible,' He made a face, 'I have great difficulty coping.'

'Oh Andy,' She leaned forward and cupped his face in her hands. 'you poor thing!' she said, kissing him tenderly on the lips.

'Now then, come on,' He said getting to his feet and pulling her up to join him. 'No time like the present. I want you to phone Mary straight away!'

'You could come too you know,' She said her eyes bright with enthusiasm, 'We could have a wonderful weekend together.'

'Darling I can't,' He shook his head, 'The next couple of months are going to be really busy, Dad wants me on site all weekend. We're having a big open day for the third phase of Bracken Down. Sales so far have been good but Dad's worried about this last phase. They're big, luxury houses; the last thing we need is to be left with stock like that on our hands tying up capital.'

'But there's a housing boom on Andy, people are asking really silly prices and getting them. When I looked over the site with you the other week I thought you said they were going well.'

'They were, but you can't guarantee anything these days. Dad's been in the business a long time, and if he's worried I know he's got good cause to be. 'Ella,' He gave her hand an affectionate squeeze, 'I insist you forget about me and any of my problems. Just take yourself off to Meridan Cross, enjoy the break and make sure you sort things out with Laura.'

'But Helen's away on holiday, there'll be no one to come in to look after you, see to your meals or get you a clean shirt.'

'I'll camp out at Dad's. Tabby will look after me.'

'Are you sure?'

'Ella I can assure you while you're away all my creature comforts will be very adequately attended to. Now come on,' He pushed her towards the door, 'Go and make that call.'

Friday 10th March

Ella stood at the front door of Little Court, her hand hovering over the bell pull. Above her the early evening sky was dark and starless and she pulled her wrap about her shoulders snugly to protect herself from the icy wind which teased her hair and tugged around her ankles. The drive down had been leisurely, the roads half empty and now here she was, standing on the threshold, about to face her grandmother. She felt odd, almost like a stranger, a trespasser, and yet there was the same warm familiarity about this place, a house she had always thought of as her second home. Of course, Mary had been keen to assure her that everything would be fine, but she had driven here full of doubt, knowing how formidable a character her grandmother was and fully expecting the worst. She knew she had been stupid, selfish even and through her actions had abused her grandmother's love and trust. She was under no illusions as to how hard she was going to have to work to get that back again.

Driving through the village, faint echoes of last summer had sprung unexpectedly from every familiar landmark. Despite this, she felt strangely calm and in control. Matt was still embedded in her heart, she couldn't change that. However, he was part of a past that would gradually fade and mellow with time. What was now important was for her to focus her energies and concentration on the present. Marriage to a man as capricious as Andy, she knew, would never be a safe, soft ride, but she hoped the baby's arrival would herald a more stable phase in their lives. She turned her attention to the task ahead. It was no use standing out here in the freezing cold. And so, cradling her hand firmly in the smooth brass of the door pull, she crossed her fingers behind her back and gave a hefty tug.

The door swung open almost immediately to reveal not Ettie, but Laura, serene and gentle, her blue eyes misty with tears.

'Ella oh Ella,' She said, stepping forward with a smile and folding her in her arms.

Ella clung to her grandmother, fighting back her own tears. She need not have worried, everything was going to be O.K., it really was.

TWENTY FOUR

Saturday 11th March

'So exactly what made you invite me to dinner?' Nina threw the question casually at Andy as they sat together in the lounge of the Highcrest Motel studying menus.

'Curiosity I suppose. About life after Mick.' He shrugged as if it was no big deal.

'About life with Alex you mean.' She corrected. 'Do I detect a hint of jealousy?'

'Certainly not. You're a free woman now; you can do as you please.'

'And I do - all the time.' Nina replied with a secret smile, turning her concentration back to the menu as the waiter arrived and hovered, ready to take their order.

They both ordered paté followed by Beef Stroganoff and skimming through the wine list, Andy ordered a bottle of Cabernet Sauvignon. As the waiter disappeared Andy studied Nina for a moment, watching the rise of her breasts beneath her blue silk blouse, running his gaze down her beige suede midi skirt, with its split just above the knee, revealing great legs. He had to hand it to Alex, he had certainly done wonders with her; not only did she look incredibly sexy, she now had something else - style.

'And where's Ella tonight?' She asked, lighting up a cigarette and relaxing into the softness of the couch.

'In Meridan Cross.'

'For how long?' She raised her eyebrows, pursing her lips and expelling smoke into the air.

'Oh, just a few days,'

'While the cat's away.....'

'The mouse is having dinner with an old friend.' His dark eyes caught hers. 'Nothing more. As I said, I was interested to see how you were getting on.'

'But why now Andy?' She asked suspiciously, leaning over and retrieving a nearby ashtray. 'You never bothered before. When you came back from Italy last year you treated me as if I didn't even exist. I hated you for that. You were as much to blame for all that trouble as I was.'

‘Yes, I probably was.’ He said with an uncaring shrug.

‘All I ever wanted was to be with you, I thought you wanted that too. I thought it was me you really wanted.’

‘That’s a pipe dream Nina. You know what my father’s like. Even if I’d wanted that, he would never have allowed it to happen.’

‘Of course, your father!’ She gave cynical laugh. ‘How naive of me to think you would ever be your own man with him around. What Daddy says goes doesn’t it? You know you and Rich Tate have a lot in common.’

‘Rich Tate,’ Andy shook his head, amused, ‘Now that was a desperate move.’

‘I wanted a little distraction because I was miserable.’ she shrugged, ‘I was lonely and married to a workaholic. You want a little distraction tonight because your wife has taken herself off for the weekend. That’s why I’m here.’

‘Hey, don’t drag my marriage into this. Ella and I are very happy.’

‘Really?’ She looked at him disbelievingly, ‘that’s not what I saw at the Tate’s party.’

‘So we had one bad evening, what’s it to you? Thought you only had eyes for Alex.’

‘As so we’re back to Alex.’ Her mouth turned up in a small satisfied smile as she stubbed out her cigarette and replaced the ash tray. ‘He happens to be a fascinating man.’

‘And a rich one.’ Andy gave a cold smile.

‘You are jealous!’

‘No I’m not. I told you I’m happy. My marriage is good.’ He responded with a smile. Nina was on good form, arguing with him outwardly but giving him all sorts of silent encouragement with her expressions and body language.

‘I think we’re just about to be called to our table.’ He nodded in the direction of the door where the waiter had just reappeared. ‘Come on, I’m absolutely famished.’

Settled into her grandmother’s comfortable sitting room, Ella peeled off her red woollen wrap and seated herself next to the warmth of the fire. After checking how long dinner would be, Laura joined her.

‘Ella,’ She said, taking her granddaughter’s hands, her face serious. ‘Before we go any farther, I need to tell you something - something very important.’

‘No, Grandma, my turn first. I owe you a huge apology.’

‘Rubbish. Please, listen to me. The way I treated you, it was a terrible thing. I should have listened to you, but when they turned up here I felt so stupid. I was so hurt that you hadn’t told me what was going on.’

‘I honestly meant to tell you, I really did,’ Ella shook her head. ‘I came back here because I knew it was where the people I loved were and the one place I thought I could get help. But I found I just couldn’t say anything to you or Mary. I was scared you both might not understand. I should have known it would all catch up with me. And it did, didn’t it? When you told me I couldn’t stay, that I had to go with Andy, I realised how stupid I'd been, and that I only had myself to blame for what was happening. I learned my lesson the hard way.'

'Never mind, it's all worked out for the best,' Laura put her arms around her and hugged her tightly. 'You've sorted yourselves out.'

'Yes, we have,' Ella ran a gentle hand over her stomach.

'You know I'm so thrilled about this baby,' Laura clasped her hands excitedly, 'It seems like only yesterday you were a small girl and now here you are grown up and about to become a mother yourself,' she leaned forward conspiratorially, 'Have you decided on any names yet?'

'No,' Ella thought for a moment, 'Not really. But I like Dominic. Andy prefers Stephen or Oliver.'

Laura frowned.

'What's the matter, don't you like them?'

'You know there is a fifty-fifty chance it will be a girl.'

'Bob says the Macaynes don't produce girls.'

Laura laughed. 'Does he now? Well we'll see about that!' she said, standing up and reaching for Ella's hand. 'Come with me.'

'What for?'

'I'm going to sort you out a girl's name.'

Obediently Ella followed her grandmother out into the main hall and climbed the stairs to the first landing where an assorted collection of oil paintings hung.

'Right, let's see what we have here.' She ran her finger along the first of the portraits, a blonde woman wearing a white muslin dress, her hair in ringlets.

'Hannah?'

Ella shook her head.

Laura walked along to the next picture, 'Jessica?' she offered hopefully.

'Mmm, not sure.'

'Ah, I think you'll like this one,' Laura raised a finger and pointed, 'Lucy.'

'Yes. Who was she?' Ella stared up at the dark haired woman in a scarlet dress looming above them.

'Lucy Palmerston-Hodges. Married your great grandfather's cousin back in 1889.'

'Lucy Macayne,' Ella repeated the name again and again, 'It has a nice ring to it and I think Bob will like it too. His wife was called Lucia.'

'Even better then, if it's going to keep your father-in-law happy,' Laura beamed. 'Ah.' She said spotting Ettie below. 'I think dinner is ready.'

They returned to the sitting room where the table was now covered with serving dishes.

'Stewed beef and dumplings, - Ettie's speciality,' Laura said as they sat down. 'Warm, nourishing and just what someone eating for two needs.'

They ate slowly, discussing Ella's business and latest events in the village. As the evening deepened, heavy needles of sleet hissed against the windows outside. Ettie came in to clear away and Laura left the table, drawing the curtains and turning on table lights, bathing the room in a warm, golden glow.

'I'm glad everything is back to normal for both of you.' She said, putting another log on the fire and returning to sit on the settee beside Ella. 'Marriage is a strange thing, it doesn't always run smoothly, even the most devoted couples have their moments!'

'What even you and Grandfather?'

'Especially me and your Grandfather!' Laura smiled. 'He could be a cantankerous old thing at times!'

'Well everything's fine now,' Ella said confidently, stretching her toes towards the warmth, 'Of course I know Andy's found my pregnancy a little difficult to cope with,' she looked at her stomach and laughed, 'but I think he'll behave himself from now on. He's grown up a lot since last summer, his womanising's all behind him now.'

'You know I like being divorced,' Nina said, pushing a forkful of rice into the stroganoff sauce, 'I've been having a great time. I've a luxury flat in East Portway, my Mini and of course, my job,' she threw back her head and gave a girlish laugh as Andy refilled her wine glass again. 'It's fascinating; I didn't realise there was so much money in land and property. I know you're convinced I've got designs on Alex, but that's not quite true. I like him as a person. He's kind and generous. He enjoys my company, says I make him laugh. Being a single man he often wants me to partner him to different functions. I've even been up to London with him. He buys all his clothes in Savile Row. He's into old stuff too; paintings and antiques for his house. It's beautiful. Hope House, just north of the town. Do you know it?'

Andy nodded.

'Then,' she continued, 'after he's done business we might take in a show or have a meal. I just love all the fancy restaurants we eat at and the hotels. It's wonderful, we get treated like royalty,' she laughed, 'and I know you won't believe this, but not once has he made a pass at me. He's a real gentleman.'

'I'm glad to hear it.' Andy said, refilling both their glasses.

Nina watched him, knowing that her words of admiration for Alex were beginning to get under his skin. Despite his protests to the contrary, she knew he was here for one thing only tonight. To persuade her to sleep with him. It was written all over his face. He was desperate for sex.

She had been very aware of the tension between him and Ella that night at the Tates and remembered Elaine telling her how Barry got all aggressive with her when she was expecting Ryan. Some men found pregnancy a big turn off, she said. Couldn't stand a woman's body getting all bloated and unattractive. Sometimes it caused them to look elsewhere.

Well if that was what Andy was after he just might have struck lucky. And what harm would it do? Just for one night, just for a bit of a laugh? With his thick, black curly hair, dark eyes, and the beauty spot which sat quite tantalisingly at the edge of his upper lip, he was still the most beautiful man she had ever seen, but she knew he was also very dangerous. When push came to shove he would always look after himself. He was arrogant and totally self absorbed. So she was going to take a leaf out of his book. Tonight, he could have her, but it would be on her terms. She wasn't hung up on him any more; she had her life sorted out. It was uncomplicated; she answered only to herself and that's how she liked it. Looking at him, she decided she would make her move over coffee.

It arrived in elegant white china cups perched daintily on a silver tray with an accompanying dish of fondants.

'Well,' She said thoughtfully, setting her cup back in its saucer, 'I think all this food and drink is a rather extravagant gesture just for old time's sake.'

'It's no big deal,' He shrugged, 'Ella's out of town and I was interested to find out what you were up to. I've had a great evening; it's a fair exchange as far as I'm concerned. '

'How can you say that?' Finishing her coffee, she leaned towards him. 'It's far too generous Andy. I insist on making some sort of contribution.'

He shook his head. 'There really is no need.'

'Oh but there is,' She pulled her bag onto her lap and opened it up. 'I want you to have this.' she pulled an object from its depths and placed it in front of him.

He frowned at the room key. 'What's this for?'

She smiled as she got to her feet and reached for his hand. 'Something that I think will round the evening off quite nicely.'

Wednesday 22rd March

'You look tired Ella,' Jenny said, as she lowered Christopher into his playpen in the corner of the living room. 'Are you OK?'

'Not really.' Ella relaxed back on the couch and closed her eyes, one hand resting on her swollen stomach. 'If you only knew how uncomfortable I've been this week. I'd give anything for a decent night's sleep. And I'm having a few problems with Andy.'

'But I thought everything was fine now.' Jenny said as she poured out two cups of coffee from a nearby percolator and brought them over. 'Since Italy you said he's changed completely.'

'He had. Thanks.' She smiled as she took the coffee.

'So what's the problem?' Jenny sat down beside her

'In a nutshell - pregnancy.' She smoothed her hand over her stomach. 'He hates it. Won't come near me.' She shook her head. 'In fact he hasn't been anywhere near me since early November when I first started to show.'

'Oh poor you,' Jenny sympathised, 'It does happen though. One of the girls at my ante-natal classes had a similar problem. Her husband's been fine since the birth though. I saw her the other day. Everything's back to normal and he just adores the baby......' she stopped in mid-sentence. 'Come on, cheer up.'

Ella managed a weak smile. 'There's another problem. Round Table. Takes him out of the house at least twice a week. He stays over with friends in Kingsford some nights,' she gave a helpless shrug. 'Says he's drunk too much and doesn't want to lose his licence.'

'And you think it might be another woman?'

'No, Jen. When he comes home from these stopovers he looks shattered, as if he hasn't slept at all; I'm worried he might be using booze to help him through this difficult time he's having.'

'Andy an alcoholic?' Jenny said, sliding her cup onto the coffee table and getting up to retrieve a selection of soft toys which Christopher had ejected rather forcefully from his playpen. 'I don't think so. Maybe he's just being sensible.'

'Maybe.'

Jenny knelt at the playpen, playing peek-a-boo through her curtain of dark hair with Christopher, who yelled with delight, reaching out with small fat fingers to touch her face through the bars.

She got to her feet and leaned in to pick him up, bouncing him on her hip. 'Look, if you're worried why don't you talk to him about it?' She said, turning back to Ella. 'Get it all out into the open, that's the best way.'

'He's not the easiest person to talk to lately,' she said as she leaned over to return her cup and saucer to the tray, 'Ooh.....ooh...'

Jenny watched as Ella sat up right and gave a small gasp, pressing her hand against her stomach. Breathing slowly and deeply she closed her eyes; then pain struck once more, making her cry out again.

'Oh Jen...' She gasped, 'I think the baby's coming!'

Nina sat behind the reception desk in Nicholson's, her fingers proficiently skimming across the keys of the black IBM golf ball typewriter, feeling pleased that at last her life had really taken off.

Alex was pleased with the new little touches she had brought to the office; fresh flowers in reception, a brighter paint scheme and coffee served to all visitors from a percolator. After only a month he had generously increased her salary. Now two months into this new job, she was always by his side. Everyone was talking about them, convinced that she was his latest conquest; the thought both amused and pleased her. She enjoyed his company, found him amusing but was more aroused by the thought of his wealth than his physical closeness. He did nothing for her, nothing at all.

Aware of the gossip which had followed her split from Mick, she had been keen to cultivate the image of the quiet, private individual trying to make a new life for herself. She was always on her best behaviour when they were together out of the workplace. And at work she did whatever was asked, staying late, coming in early, anything to get the job done - the perfect employee. She was an enigma to him too and she loved it, it put her in the driving seat. She knew he was beginning to trust her, to believe that all the stories circulating about her past were nothing but malicious gossip. He admired the energy she put into her job. He loved her quirky sense of humour, the fact she was nobody's fool. Then there were the presents; a bottle of expensive perfume, a leather coat, a beautiful evening dress from Christiana's. Everything was going well. In fact, life couldn't be better.

She let her thoughts wander for a moment to Andy and smiled as she thought of the coming afternoon at the Highcrest Motel. Good sex gave her a real buzz, recharged the batteries. Alex and Andy; a man for work and a man for play. Yes, life was really great.

Issy and Jenny sat in the waiting area of the maternity wing of Abbotsbridge General, drinking hot, tasteless vending machine coffee.

They looked up as the doors opened to see Mick arrive, his face creased with worry.

'Well?' Issy said impatiently as she got to her feet, 'Where is he?'

Mick buried his hands in the pockets of his brown leather coat and raised his shoulders in a gesture of hopelessness. 'I don't know, I can't find him anywhere.'

'Well where is he *supposed* to be?' Jenny's voice held a note of helpless frustration. 'His wife is in labour and he can't be reached. What kind of husband is he for goodness sake?'

'A totally useless one!' Issy said harshly.

'There's a diary entry for this afternoon which just says H with some sort of doodle beside it,' Mick said, frowning at Issy. 'Does it mean anything to either of you?' he looked at them both hopefully.

Issy and Jenny looked at each other and shook their heads.

'Does Bob know where he is?' Jenny asked as she threw her empty cup into the nearby waste bin.

'I haven't spoken to him yet.'

'Why ever not?' Issy looked at him, wondering how men could be so stupid sometimes not to think of the obvious.

'Because you know what Bob's like! I didn't want to stir up unnecessary trouble. All right! I'll go and phone him now.' Mick said feeling hassled. 'Is there any news I can tell him about Ella?'

'Tell him Baby Macayne is well on it's way,' Jenny said, 'and that the sooner we find its father the better.'

Mick headed off down the corridor to the nearest payphone, leaving the two girls standing in the middle of the blue cord carpeted floor looking at each other.

'Do you know what I think?' Throwing her cup into the bin Issy eyed Jenny suspiciously.

'With that expression, I don't think I want to,' Jenny replied, rubbing at a mark on her brown leather boots, 'Don't say it's another woman, not that please.'

'It is possible you know.'

'What? Lightning striking in the same place twice? I don't think so. Andy's learnt his lesson Iz, he knows Nina is trouble; he'd have to be completely stupid to resurrect all that again.'

'Oh I think he could be that stupid,' Issy replied smugly, 'But not with Nina. She's far too busy giving Alex Nicholson a run for his money at the moment.'

'Who then? Who else is there?'

Issy was about to answer that the Bracken Down development was probably full of bored middle class housewives looking for a little excitement when a young, blonde nurse appeared.

'Is there any news of Mr Macayne?' She asked, looking at both of them, 'Mrs Macayne is asking for him.'

'We're still trying to locate him,' Issy replied. 'Can we help at all? Jen here is Mrs Macayne's sister-in-law and I'm her best friend. Jen had a baby last year, so she knows the ropes.'

The nurse gave Issy an amused smile. 'It would be better if Mr Macayne was here really, but I'll just check with doctor, see what he says.'

As she disappeared through the door, Issy stood at the window looking down into the car park. 'Isn't this just typical of Andy?' She said, turning to look at Jenny.

'I'm sure we'll have news soon, now Mick's on the case,' Jenny said in her normal calming way. As she spoke her brother came back into the room, a smile on his face.

'You've found him!' Issy looked relieved.

'No,' Mick shook his head, as he stood facing the two women, his hands in his coat pockets, 'But, I think Bob knows where he is.'

'What makes you say that?' Jenny frowned.

'The way he reacted to the hieroglyphics in Andy's diary. I think he knows exactly what they mean. He'll be here soon, don't worry.'

The nurse was hovering in the doorway again, relief on her face as she saw Mick.

'Mr Macayne, thank goodness you've arrived. Would you like to come through? Your wife's been asking for you.'

'Sorry,' Mick shook his head, 'Wrong man. I'm just a family friend.'

'In that case, ladies,' She turned to Issy and Jenny, 'Would you please follow me? I really think some urgent moral support is needed.'

Bob Macayne had been lunching with a business client at *La Rotunda,* a new restaurant just opened in Bridge Street, when he had been called away to the phone. Standing in the pay booth he turned back towards his table to watch the distinguished man seated there, deciding that Peter Jeffs looked more like a solicitor than a retired farmer. The land deal was almost in the bag, the amount of money the only thing they were currently having differences on. Nevertheless, as a veteran of negotiations, Bob thought this meeting had a good feel and only needed just a little more application of wine and gentle persuasion over the sweet before the gap between what Peter expected and he was willing to pay narrowed to something they were both happy with.

The prize was a parcel of land in the nearby village of Kings Moreton next to the church. But not just land, an old cottage too, with mellowed stone walls and a honey coloured roof. Remembering what Mick had done with the farmhouse at Bracken Down, he knew this too had great potential for renovation and that by adding Liam's architectural flair some interesting designs for new houses on the rest of the site would emerge.

The fact that when he picked up the phone he found Mick there was annoying enough in the middle of such fine tuned negotiations. What matured that irritation into full blown anger was the reason for Mick's call. His initial reaction was to tell Mick he had rung at a very inopportune time and that he had no idea where his son was and cared even less. It was when Mick described what was written in Andy's diary that alarm bells started to ring loudly. It meant Highcrest. A motel twenty miles away off the A38. But why would Andy be there on a Thursday afternoon? A meeting? Certainly not with a client, as meetings were conducted either on site or in the office. No, Andy was up to something, but what? And more importantly who with?

Telling Mick he would deal with the matter personally, he returned to the table. Peter Jeffs was, of course, very understanding. A family emergency had called Bob away; they would reconvene tomorrow in his office at 11.00. After settling the bill and shaking hands Bob left, knowing all to well that any advantage had now been lost, and although he would probably not lose the deal tomorrow, the price he would have to pay would almost certainly be higher than it might have been today.

As the Jaguar ate up the miles between Abbotsbridge and the motel he wondered at the stupidity of a young man who possessed everything and yet treated it as if it was worth nothing. After all the energy he had put into getting Andy back on the straight and narrow last summer, here he was, at it again, sneaking behind Ella's back, wining and dining God knows who. He thought of Ella back in Abbotsfield General. He had been at Lucia's side when Andy was born, sharing the moment when he came into the world. He remembered the joy he felt when he heard his first cries and held him in his arms. He had had so many dreams then of what he would be when he grew up; the things he would achieve. He suddenly realised how wasted those aspirations had been.

Eventually he left the bypass, following the slip road to the motel. It widened into a large car park and he began circling around, looking to see whether Andy's red Mercedes was parked there. Eventually he found it.

Parking his car he walked, grim faced towards the motel and the glass doors which parted automatically to allow him into reception.

A male receptionist wearing a white shirt and black striped waistcoat was behind the desk sorting through a pile of letters. He looked up as Bob approached and smiled.

'Good afternoon Sir, may I help?'

'Yes, good afternoon. I am looking for a Mr Andrew Macayne who has booked in here. A lunch reservation?'

'I'll just check for you Sir.' The dark haired young man, whose name badge announced he was Simon Cavendish smiled, his eyes friendly, his tone polite as he pulled out a leather bound diary and ran his finger down the names listed, 'No, sorry Sir, he doesn't appear to be here.'

'What about room reservations?' Fearing the worst, Bob spun the leather bound register round to face him and began running his finger down the names listed there.

'I'm afraid Sir the guest register is not for public scrutiny.' Simon gently slid the register out from under Bob's hand and closed it.

'I am not the public, I am his father and I need to locate him urgently!' The tone in Bob's voice pressed his point home.

'Have you any identification Sir?'

'Will this do?' Irritably Bob pulled out his wallet, extracted his driving licence and handed it over.

'Sorry Sir, I have to follow regulations.' Simon smiled apologetically and returned the licence before placing the register carefully in front of Bob.

Bob studied it, running his finger down the list of names, checking carefully. He looked up frowning. 'I don't understand, his car's in the car park.'

'No problem Sir. Guests have to register on a card system when they arrive. Car details are included, I'll just check for you.' There was a confident smile. 'What make of car Sir, and do you happen to know the registration?'

'Red Mercedes, don't know the exact registration but it's an H plate.'

Simon Cavendish produced a small card index box and thumbed through, 'Ah, here we are,' He said as he pulled a card from the box. 'Room 311. It's registered in the name of Mr C Lyon.'

'A comedian too!' Bob said with a humourless smile.

Accompanied by Simon Cavendish with the master key, Bob Macayne took the lift to the third floor.

'Are you sure this is necessary Sir?' Simon asked as they walked along the corridor, 'If you'd only let me knock first.....'

'Believe me Mr Cavendish I know exactly what I'm doing.' Bob stopped and looked at the younger man. 'Look if you feel in any way embarrassed, I can do it just as effectively on my own.' he extended an open hand for the keys.

The young man shook his head, colouring slightly, 'I can't do that Sir. It has to be me who opens up.'

'Don't tell me, regulations?'

'Fraid so Sir.'

Bob continued along the corridor, Simon following behind. Eventually they stopped outside Room 311.

Nina lay drifting in and out of sleep. She had been in room 311 since mid afternoon and felt relaxed after a particularly energetic session with Andy. He seemed insatiable; who would have thought that fatherhood, the very thing that brought most couples together, was the very reason he was now here lying in her arms. The irony of it made her smile. Pushing herself up on one elbow, she looked at him sleeping, thinking it was criminal that any one man could have been given such perfect features. She gave a sigh of contentment, glad she had decided to change her mind about not seeing him again after the meal they'd had together. She had forgotten how good he was; how he brought her body alive; touched her in a way no one else could. At this one moment in time, she told herself, she appeared to have all of the benefits without any of the responsibilities. The thought of Andy as a sexual toy amused her. It felt great to have turned the tables on him.

Andy stirred and opened his eyes, frowning up at her as he saw her looking at him.

'What are you smiling at? Come here.' He pulled her to him, his hands reaching under the sheets for the softness of her body, arousing her slowly and deliberately. She reached under the bedclothes too; saw the expression on his face as her hands closed over what she was looking for.

'Two can play at that game,' Andy said and dived under the blankets. She moaned with pleasure and let go of him, lying back, closing her eyes, enjoying the moment. There was a sudden chill in the room, accompanied by the click of the door and soft footfalls across the carpet. She froze for a second, raised her eyes slowly above the sheets and found herself looking straight into the face of Bob Macayne.

'Oh my God!' She gasped and pulled the sheets protectively around her, realising not only was Andy's father there, but also a member of the motel staff, hovering nervously in the doorway.

'That good eh?' She heard Andy's muffled voice followed by soft laughter.

She squirmed as he moved his head lower, punching at the bed covers. 'Andy stop it! Stop it! Come out, *come out at once!*'

'What's the matter with you? I thought you were enjoying it!' Andy's resentful face appeared over the top of the sheets, his hair tousled, eyes trying to acustomize themselves to the light. He blinked for a moment then his mouth fell open. 'Christ....Dad!' He said as he sat up, the blood draining from his face.

TWENTY FIVE

Wednesday 22nd March

'Come along push Mrs Macayne!'

The small dark haired midwife standing at the end of the bed tried to sound encouraging as Ella, hair plastered damply around her face and sweat soaking the loose green gown she wore, breathed in deeply and gathered what she felt must be her last reserves of strength.

Jenny and Issy sat on either side of her, Jenny squeezing her hand, talking encouragingly to her while Issy dabbed her forehead with a cloth.

'You've almost done it Ella, you're almost there!' Jenny encouraged. 'Come on now *push!'*

Issy found the whole experience totally overwhelming. She never imagined having a baby was such a physically exhausting job. Ella seemed strung out like some sort of sacrifice with her feet slotted into stirrups, legs thrown wide apart. And then there was the pain. She had been so brave; the gas and air had helped, but she could see by the expression on her face she was exhausted. She looked towards the end of the bed where both the midwife and doctor were eyeing one another and giving little nods of approval.

The midwife straightened up and looked at Ella. 'The head is visible Mrs Macayne, one big push and it should be out. Once that happens you're nearly home and dry.'

'I'd better be, I'm all in.' Ella said as she blew a loose strand of hair from her damp face and took an enormous breath. Summoning all her strength she pushed hard and through the next wave of pain felt something within her body move.

'The head's out!' The midwife looked at her with an encouraging nod. 'Nearly there, one more push should do it.'

Ella let out a loud and exhausted groan and did as the midwife asked. Jenny jumped to her feet, her face filled with delight as she heard the baby's first cries. 'You've done it!' she patted Ella's hand, 'You've done it!'

The midwife looked at Ella and smiled. 'Congratulations Mrs Maycane, you have a lovely little girl.'

Ella lay there smiling. She felt damp and uncomfortable and her whole body felt like a punch bag but suddenly none of that mattered. She looked down at this little miracle with its perfect features and a mass of dark hair as, wrapped in a pink blanket, the baby placed in her arms. 'Welcome to the world Lucy.' She said and kissed her forehead gently.

'I'd better go and see what's happening outside.' Issy said, getting to her feet. 'Mick was trying to locate Andy. He should be here by now'

She left the delivery room and walked down the grey vinyl floored corridor with a trip of high heels, heading for the waiting area. Ahead of her she saw Mick hanging up the payphone.

'Any news yet?' He asked, slipping change back into his pocket.

'Yes, it's a girl and we're all exhausted.' She laughed, 'Who were you phoning?'

'Glamorous Gran. Bob thought we ought to let her know Ella's gone into labour.'

'Bob is here? Andy too?'

Mick nodded and leaned closer to Issy. 'Something's up though,' he whispered. 'I don't know where Andy was but Bob is as mad as hell!'

'Perhaps the good news will pacify him a little,' Issy said moving past him. She resumed her walk down the corridor until she reached the waiting room. Gently pushing open the door she saw Bob and Andy alone in the room, standing with their backs to her, facing the window. Bob was talking, his voice low and harsh. Curious, she suppressed her initial instinct to breeze in with her news, choosing instead to hover silently and listen.

'I cannot for the life of me understand what makes you tick!' Bob was saying. 'What possessed you to do such a thing? This is the second time. Are you completely bloody stupid?'

'I'm sorry Dad,' Andy responded, his voice shaky, 'she just wouldn't leave me alone.'

'Not that old chestnut! You're weak and spineless, Andy. Do you know that? And you disgust me!' Bob continued, 'But you have a wife in labour, a baby on the way. Those issues override everything else at the moment. So we'll just sit here and wait for someone to come. They shouldn't be long and when they do, I want you to go with them and take your place by your wife's side and try for a moment to behave like a normal husband. But listen and listen carefully. If I *ever* catch you anywhere near Nina Taylor again I'll wipe you out! I'll make you homeless, penniless and jobless! Do you understand that?'

Andy nodded silently.

Issy saw Bob move and knew he was about to turn from the window. Setting her face in a smile she backed out of the door then pushed in again, giving the impression she had just arrived.

Bob smiled, his expression bright, eyebrows raised in expectation. 'Isobel!' He was all good manners now. 'What's the latest?'

Issy gave him one of her sweetest smiles. 'You have a granddaughter. Ella's very tired but they are both fine. Jenny's still with them both.'

'A girl? Really?' Bob drew his eyebrows together in a disappointed frown and then looked back at Andy who still stood facing the window. 'Better go and see your wife and daughter then son,' he said softly, all hostility gone.

Andy turned to face Issy, he looked pale. 'So,' he said with a weak smile, 'I'm a father at last.'

'What kept you?' Issy eyed him frostily.

'Off site meeting, couldn't get away.'

Issy stared at him, amazed not only at the way he could lie so plausibly but also the arrogance with which he did it.

'Must have been a *very* important client, Andy.' she said as she turned towards the door, 'and somewhere quite secret. No one had *any* idea where to find you, you know. Just as well your father knew where you were.' And giving them both a amiable smile she left the room.

Thursday 6th April

You took me from the shadows

Brought sunshine to my life……

Marcie stood in the recording booth, her hands clasping the headphones tightly, singing to the music track which had been laid down the day before. For the first time since she had been with Maverick she felt she was doing what she had been born for; singing. The emotions in the lyrics held her captive, whilst the melody filled the whole cubicle, energising her. It was pure magic and it has been like this for the last week since she had begun recording her first album '*Changing Places*'. The whole thing was coming together really well and now the news of Kendal's sell out tour had made the team even more committed to launching her career as a singer. And of course where would they all have been without Matt? She watched him sitting with the technicians the other side of the glass screen; saw the enthusiasm in his face and that warm, sexy smile which more often than not was directed at her. He had spent several weeks writing solidly and produced eight commercial songs. She had run through all of them with him on the piano and surprisingly found she liked every one.

Now in the studio, putting flesh on the bones of each one, they were even better. Secretly she felt the company had a huge hit on their hands. As always, Matt had put himself into the words and music and just like Kendal, her voice had brought it all alive. It was an album full of guitar and orchestral passion and she knew it must have taken something really special to have triggered this much emotion in him. Could it be that he sensed how she felt about him? Were the lyrics his way of telling her he felt the same way too? He had sunk a large amount of money into backing her career; he wasn't the kind of man who would do that on a whim, she was sure it was because she was special to him. The exhilarating feeling she experienced in daring to believe something might be possible between them lifted her spirits.

With a smile on her face she summoned up her energies to belt out the concluding lines of the song. Of course, she told herself, being English made him different. Reserved, shy. It would be a waiting game. But why worry? Potentially she was standing on the edge of a golden career; a career which he had told her he was going to guide all the way. She had all the time in the world to help him fall in love with her; although looking at the expression on his face now as he watched her sing, she didn't think she'd have to wait that long.

Wednesday 19th April

Richard Evas was crossing the yard when he saw the blue Jaguar pull up outside the front gate. Frowning, he walked to intercept the man and woman who had emerged from it.

As he drew closer he realised it was his daughter and Bob Macayne. Wondering what they could want he took a deep breath and walked over to them.

'Mel,' He tilted his head questioningly, 'To what do I owe this honour?'

'Bob and I were at a loose end,' Mel smiled prettily as she pulled off her gloves and gestured towards her companion, 'He remembered the village from Ella's wedding. Wanted to come out to look at it properly.'

'Did he now?' Richard replied with a cursory glance at the heavy set balding man hovering by the car. He turned back to Mel, his face softening slightly. 'And talking of Ella, how is my new great-granddaughter?'

'Fine, fine.' She waved an impatient hand at him, 'Dad I didn't come for small talk about babies. Bob's a real townie. He has no idea how a farm runs. If you could spare the time we'd love to look over Willowbrook. Thought I might take him up to Fox Cottage afterwards, show him where I used to live.'

'I see,' Richard said, one eye on Bob.

'I'm sorry, I know you're busy Mr Evas.' Bob joined the conversation. 'We should have phoned....' he gazed out across the open farmland. 'A lot of land here isn't there? All those acres to maintain, must be very time consuming.'

'That's the way farming is,' Richard said with a casual shrug.

'All the same, it's an awful lot of work.'

'Farming's in the blood Mr Macayne, it's a calling not a job.' Richard replied. 'Willowbrook has been in the Evas family for five hundred years and hopefully it will continue that way for the next five hundred.'

'But there's no one to take over from you Dad,' Mel argued. 'And who knows what's round the corner. You might get to a situation where you can't manage.'

'I'll cross that bridge when I come to it Mel.' Richard said stubbornly

'But wouldn't it be better to be making plans now? Maybe scaling down a little?'

'Scaling down?' Richard looked at his daughter. 'Now that's one of Mr Macayne's terms if I ever heard one. What are you two up to?'

'Nothing.' Mel said innocently. 'Honestly. We…I'm just concerned about you, that's all.'

'Well thank you for the sentiment. Now, if you'll both excuse me, I have a herd to milk…' He raised his cap to Bob and with a shake of his head turned and walked back into the yard.

Mel went after him, seizing his arm aggressively, catching him off balance and shoving him against the breeze block wall of the dairy, 'How dare you dismiss me as if I'm some silly child!'

Leaning against the wall he angrily shook of her grip, then suddenly his face twisted in pain and his hand went to his chest, the colour draining from his face.

'Mr Evas are you all right?' Bob stood beside Mel, his face anxious.

'I'm fine thank you.' Richard replied, reaching into the pocket of his milking coat, pulling out a small tub of pills and tipping two into his open palm.

'You are ill Dad!' Mel snapped. 'And that means you should be doing something about the farm now, before it's too late.'

'Will you leave me be!' Richard shouted. 'There's nothing wrong with me, it's a touch of indigestion, that's all.' He said throwing the tablets into his mouth and swallowing them back.

Mel caught Bob's arm. 'Leave him, let's go,' she said as she watched her father slip the bottle back into his pocket, and walk away. 'If what he says is true, I'm sure my father's perfectly capable of coping with something as trivial as indigestion.'

Friday 12th May

Nina stood at the window of Nicholson's board room looking down into the street. A sudden shower had laced the windows with rain and people passing by were busy putting up umbrellas or diving for the nearest doorway. Every one of these people had a life; things to do, places to be, a husband or wife, lover or friend. All she had for company was a hangover and a wish that she could claw back time and change the situation she currently found herself in. One person had triggered all this and she held him responsible for most of her unhappiness. Bob Macayne.

'Hateful bastard!' She said miserably, her face pressed against the window.

It had all started on the day Bob bundled Andy from their room at the Highcrest Motel back in March. Turning in the doorway he had issued a warning. From now on she was to become invisible, he didn't want to see her anywhere he was likely to be. If he did then he would take the greatest pleasure in telling Alex just what had happened here today. And he was sure, he said with a look which told her he knew exactly what she was up to, that was the last thing she wanted.

Angry and outraged at being told what to do by a man she had come to hate, she made the mistake of challenging him, telling him he could do what he liked, there was no way Alex would ever take his word against hers.

Still in the doorway, Bob had simply stared at her for a moment, his face turning deathly white, his mouth setting in a hard line. Then he took a step towards her into the darkened room. The slam of the door behind him, sudden and unexpected, made her jump and she pulled the bathrobe she wore more securely around herself. He seemed to fill the room, huge and menacing and for a second she felt totally paralysed. Then gathering her wits about her, she made a dash for the bathroom, to lock herself in. But she didn't make it. Catching her easily by her hair he swung her around to face him. She clutched at the bathrobe, aware of her vulnerability. In this mood she feared he was capable of anything, even rape.

'Understand this!' He said, bringing his face very close to hers, 'Defy me and your father and brother in law might both find themselves joining the dole queue in the very near future. The choice is entirely yours.'

'You wouldn't.....' She said, trembling with fear at the black hate in his eyes.

'Wrong,' he said, pushing her onto the bed, 'I can and I will.'

She watched him leave, slamming the door behind him. The room was quiet as she lay sprawled among the bedclothes, heart beating wildly and sick with panic. Despite having alienated herself from her family, despising them and their make do and mend way of life, she realised she couldn't face being responsible for her father and brother-in-law losing their jobs.

And so, in the days that followed she began to excuse herself from Alex's company on invitations to anywhere she knew there was a chance she might run into the Macaynes. At first he was accepting about her absences - her mother was unwell, she had a school reunion, she'd had an exhausting day. She was amazed at all the excuses she could think of, but she knew she couldn't keep it up indefinitely. He would only take so much of this before he began to ask questions, then what was she going to do?

Of course, she knew she was partially to blame for the mess she was in. She had been just a little bit too smug, a little too confident, amusing herself with Andy, playing him at his own game. She was annoyed with herself for her stupidity, but even more annoyed with the way Andy appeared to have got away with it yet again. His charmed life under the benevolent eye of his father had enabled him to return to his marriage as if nothing had happened; the proud father of a beautiful dark haired baby who was to be called Lucy Gabriella Macayne. It seemed everyone she bumped into had news of this baby and its blissfully happy parents and it angered her to think she was the only one being punished, having to suffer.

She lay awake at night thinking about her problem, trying in vain to find a way round it. Lack of sleep made her irritable, she made silly mistakes at work, was abrupt on the phone and less than helpful to some of the clients who came into the office. Someone complained and before she knew where she was, Alex had called her into the office to try to find out exactly what was troubling her.

But all that did was make matters worse. Facing him across the desk, she panicked and became defensive, telling him in not so many words, to mind his own business. She could see by the look on his face she might have gone just a little too far, that she had upset him, but she hadn't realised how much until yesterday morning.

After they had gone through the day's post she returned to her desk to find Gavin Miller from Miller and Thomas, another old established agent, waiting in reception to see Alex. He had not been in the appointment book although when she buzzed through she could tell he had been expected. So she had shown him through, thinking it was no more than just a hastily arranged meeting. However, after he had gone Alex called her into his office again.

'I think I ought to let you know that I am going to be away for a while.' He said quietly, his green eyes solemn.

'Oh!' She felt just a small tug of unease at the news. She normally took charge of all his travel arrangements.

'Yes, a holiday. Greece,' He smiled pleasantly, 'I'm joining some friends. One of them has a yacht out there. We're going to cruise the islands for a while'

'How long will you be away?'

'Eight weeks or so.'

'Eight weeks? Alex why didn't you mention this before?'

'Because I've only just arranged it Nina,' He said politely. 'That's why Gavin was here. I've asked him to hold the fort while I'm away.'

'No, I mean why didn't you tell me first? Surely I had a right to know before Gavin,'

The green eyes chilled, 'Why on earth should I consult you about what I do in my private life? After all, you were quick enough tell me I had no place in yours the other day.'

The truth of his words stung her, she turned away, embarrassed.

'I'm sorry.'

'Forget it, it doesn't matter.' Getting to his feet he pulled his briefcase onto the desk and began loading it with files for his next appointment.

'No I really mean it. I am sorry,' she left her chair and walked around the desk to his side, placing an affectionate hand on his arm, eager to make peace.

'So am I Nina so am I,' He avoided her touch, his pronunciation of her name formal, creating an invisible barrier. Snapping the briefcase shut, he pushed gently past her, 'I have an appointment in Kingsford at eleven. I'll be back later this afternoon to run through everything you need to know during my absence. There's no need for you to worry, I'm sure you and Gavin are going to get on very well. He's extremely laid back when it comes to business. Enjoy the change,' he smiled. 'You'll notice the difference when I get back.'

As he moved towards the door, she watched him helplessly, feeling the room heavy with his disapproval.

'Alex, wait. Before you go.'

'What is it?' He turned in the doorway, with a frown.

'Does this mean it's all over?'

'All over?' He frowned, 'I don't understand.'

'Us, our friendship.'

He gave a tired sigh. 'To end, something needs to have a beginning Nina. With the best will in the world I hardly think what we've been doing together over the last few months constitutes friendship, do you?' He gave a light laugh, 'You're my Assistant, and I'm your employer. I thought I was doing you a favour, taking you places, introducing you to people. I hoped that in broadening your horizons it would be beneficial to you and your job and as a knock on from that, to the company.'

The matter-of-fact tone of those parting words were suddenly with her again buzzing inside her head as she stood at the window, making it ache more than ever. How foolish she had been thinking that she was different and had the power to charm him. All the effort she had made, planning and scheming her way into his favour, thinking she was making an impression. It was a bitter pill to swallow, knowing she had been wasting her time.

The shower was over now, blue sky replacing the dark clouds, the warm sun quickly drying up the pavements below. Eight weeks she murmured to herself, that should give her just about enough time. Alex was right in saying that when he came back things would be different. They would be, for by that time she would be gone.

Across town Andy Macayne, sitting in the sales office at Churchfields, noticed the first fine spots of rain as they hit the window. He watched as two workmen, stacking tiles on the felted and battened roof of Plot 7 opposite, hurried for cover just before the skies opened into a full blown downpour.

In a matter of moments the scud of rain bearing cloud was gone, the sun reappearing almost immediately with its brightness and warmth. Andy got up from his desk and walked to the open doorway, watching the activity return to the small development of twelve luxury houses. The first five plots were now occupied, curtains at the window, cars on the driveway. Plot 6 was on schedule, the second fix plumbing well underway. A couple from Taunton were making very interested noises regarding purchase. He felt positive that when they saw this emerging neat crescent of houses of red brick with their matching low walls and turfed lawns they would be completely sold on living there. The second phase was about to be released. A yellow JCB was excavating foundations on Plot 9, two men in hard hats staring into the great chasm of earth, deep in discussion.

Mick Taylor appeared around the side of Plot 5, walking slowly with Liam, who had arrived to deliver an updated set of plans for the second phase. Mick was folding a drawing as they made their way across the site towards the Sales Office.

Andy returned to his desk. Sinking into his chair he picked up the small silver photo frame by the telephone and studied it. How lucky he was to have escaped yet again from the destruction he knew his father was capable of. How easy it had been not only to slip back into the old role of devoted husband but also to pick up the new one of proud father. He looked at the photograph in the frame; Ella sitting in their comfortable lounge, smiling as she held Lucy up to the camera. Lucy. What a god send she had been, his beautiful daughter, a rainbow after the storm. How could he possibly have referred to her as It for all those months? Now he had a beautiful wife and a lovely daughter to show off to Abbotsbridge. And even better, Ella had announced she was deferring her return to her business indefinitely to spend her time with Lucy. Excellent, he smiled. It looked as if her career days were over, although he'd have to keep an eye on her to make sure things stayed that way. Perhaps another pregnancy in eighteen months time. He gave a contented sigh; everything had righted itself, come full circle. His father had been right in suggesting he marry Ella. This had been the path to follow. He was envied now; respected. He had it all and it was now up to him to make sure it stayed that way.

His thoughts strayed to Nina; he wondered where she was and what she was doing now. Of course, it had been fun, a good laugh and amazing sex; but he had no regrets. It was great while it lasted and it had run for as long as he'd wanted it to. In some ways his father's arrival had been a blessing in disguise. He had begun to worry how he was going to finish things once the baby had arrived. Now that had all been taken care of; he was back with Ella and Nina had probably gone back to her life as Alex's Assistant. The world would turn peacefully again as if nothing had happened.

'Morning Andy, how are things?' Liam appeared suddenly in the doorway, Mick close behind him.

'Things are fine Liam,' Andy smiled broadly as he replaced the photo frame next to the telephone. 'In fact they couldn't be better!'

Wednesday 21st June

'You're looking pleased with yourself,' Faye looked up from her accounts as Tad came into the office.

'I certainly am.' Tad smiled confidently, pulling up a chair and seating himself beside his wife. 'I've just come from seeing Liam. He's prepared to do the refurbishment plans for me and make all the submissions to the Council's Planning Committee. We had a long chat. I'm well impressed. He's got some first class ideas.'

'Are you sure we're doing the right thing Tad?' Faye closed the heavy journal and pushed the top back on her pen, 'It's not going to be the same without the Mill you know; it's been part of Abbotsbridge for so long.'

'Not any more Faye, you more than anyone should know that,' he nodded towards the leather bound ledger. 'The weekly takings have been down for some time. We have to face facts, the sixties are over; seventies kids have different tastes. If we want to stay alive we have to change direction, find a different market. Of course, I'll always remember the Mill with affection. However my new plans for the building will be as ground breaking as they were in 1965,' he smiled. 'Once the work has been completed I'm going to have a grand opening night with free drinks and a big donation to charity. It'll be just great!' He stopped for a moment, aware his enthusiasm was getting the better of him, 'But you don't want to hear this do you? You'll be more interested in my other news!'

'Other news?'

Tad nodded. 'About Matt.'

She brightened immediately. 'How is he?'

'He's fine,' Tad said reassuringly, 'Doing well too. I spoke to Sonny earlier this morning. You know that small independent he was working for in New York? Well he's only gone and got himself a number one album with one of their new artists. Sonny thinks it will do well over here too.'

'No mention of when he'll be home I suppose?' Faye looked at him hopefully.

'As a matter of fact, yes,' Tad laid a gentle hand on her shoulder, 'He'll be back in June, for the launch night of the new club.'

'What makes you think he'll come back for that?' Faye looked at Tad sceptically.

'Because, I'm going to ask him to open it.'

Friday 14th July

'Will you come into the office for a moment please Nina?'

Nina looked up to see Gavin Miller hovering in the doorway, a smile creasing his face.

It was her last day at Nicholson's and after eight weeks of unsuccessful job hunting she was timing her departure to coincide with Alex's return, determined that when he walked in on Monday morning she would be gone.

She knew Gavin had been in touch with Alex so he was aware of exactly what was happening, and she had expected the news to have brought some reaction from the eastern end of the Mediterranean. She was bitterly disappointed when there was none. He hadn't even wished her well. It reinforced her opinion of him; he was just like the rest - an uncaring bastard.

'Nina,' Gavin had settled himself comfortably in Alex's heavy leather chair. 'I have a job for you.'

'What sort of job?'

'Have you heard of the Ragbourne Grove Hotel?'

Nina nodded again. It was the old manor house five miles out on the Taunton Road. Five star. Very expensive.

'Well, I know it's your last day, but I need you to go there for me this afternoon to meet a client.'

'Me? Meet a client?'

Gavin nodded, flicking through the pages of his diary, 'I've a clash of appointments. I can't be in two places at once, so I'm delegating the new one to you. It only came in this morning, but it's too good a deal to miss out on. An overseas client who has substantial funds and wishes to purchase something rather special. Here....,' he handed her a folder, 'I did find the time to put these together, I think you will be fairly familiar with the details, after all you did type up the specifications for them. All you have to do is take Mr Dalgetty to lunch and go through the portfolio with him, and then leave him to make a decision. Nicholson's will pick up the bill. Feel free to order anything you want.'

'Thank you,' Nina smiled, determined to put as big a dent as possible in the company's hospitality budget by the time the afternoon was through. On her last working day it would be an excellent way to finish.

The Ragbourne Grove in all its Victorian ivy clad glory stood at the end of a winding gravel driveway. Its lawns green and lush, its borders colourful; every inch a luxury country hotel.

Nina, wanting to look the part, had gone home to change into a cream sleeveless linen dress, coffee jacket and black patent sling backs. Parking her car in the visitors' car park she walked into its cool foyer, carrying the precious portfolio in the black leather briefcase she had borrowed from Gavin.

The clerk at the desk smiled appreciatively at her as she explained the purpose of her visit and after confirming her lunch reservation directed her to a lounge full of antique furniture and comfortable settees to wait for her guest. Moments later a waiter arrived and offered her a complimentary glass of champagne. She smiled as took the glass of pale effervescent liquid, watched curiously by one or two elderly gentlemen guests over the top of their newspapers. Raising her glass to them in toast, she tipped it to her lips, enjoying her moment of indulgence.

The same waiter returned ten minutes later to tell her that her table was ready and Mr Dalgetty, who was staying at the hotel, would be with her shortly. Nina smiled; the moment had arrived to appraise the menu and make her expensive choices before her visitor joined her. Picking up her brief case, she walked into the dining room, with its high ceilings, heavy brocaded chairs and white starched table cloths.

Another white shirted waiter appeared, fussing over her, leading her across the room, indicating a window table with a magnificent view of the gardens. Seating her, he spread the starched napkin across her lap and handed her the menu. She relaxed, running her fingers down the menu. So much to choose from, what should she have? The fish or the beef? And what of Mr Dalgetty? Just what form did he take she wondered? She looked forward to the coming lunch and their meeting; slivers of conversation already forming in her mind. It was a shame she was leaving, she really enjoyed the job, but at least her last day was seeing her go out on a high.

She flipped the menu over to the wine list. The initial glass in the lounge had activated her taste buds. Something sparkling. Something expensive. She looked at the price of the champagnes. Tattinger or Bollinger? Or Moet? She was undecided. Perhaps it would be better to leave the choice to Mr Dalgetty.

Continuing to study the wine list, she was aware of someone arriving at the table, sliding into the seat opposite her. She lowered it with a smile. 'Good afternoon Mr. Dal.....' The words trailed away as she sat there in shocked surprise. 'What are you doing here?'

Alex, bronzed and healthy from his two months away sat facing her, his gaze steady, a smile hovering on his lips.

'Hello Nina,' He said, taking the menu from her hands, 'Now what's all this nonsense about you leaving?'

Later Nina smiled at Alex as they left their table and moved into the lounge to take coffee. How strange, she thought; this morning I hated him. I was leaving, no idea where my next job would be and now everything's back to normal.

They had just eaten a delicious lunch, Sole Meunière with a light salad and new potatoes, washed down with crisp Sauternes. The sweet had been simple, fresh strawberries and cream, but they could have been eating at a Wimpy Bar for all she cared. The way he looked at her, spoke to her, reached for her hand across the table to apologise had taken her completely by surprise and turned everything completely on its head.

There had been guilt in his green eyes, 'I was so harsh with you, it was unforgivable! I've spent the past eight weeks hating myself for being such a pig. And then when Gavin phoned to say you were leaving, well, I had to do something, that's why I tricked you into coming here today.'

'I'm glad you did,' she smiled happily at him, 'I felt bad too. I was rude to you; I had no right to push you away when you were trying to help me. I was as much to blame for what happened.'

'And is everything O.K. now? Have you sorted out all the things that were troubling you, the ones you didn't want to talk about? Are you happy?'

'Yes,' She lied, desperate to cling tightly to the wonderful return of her meal ticket, 'Yes everything's fine now.'

'So you will be back in the office on Monday?' He sounded anxious.

'Dear Alex, yes, of course I will.' She laughed, amused, as they got up from the table. She felt the familiar touch of his hand in the small of her back as they crossed the foyer into the lounge with its comfortable couches.

'Alex,' She said as they sat down together, feeling the need to respond, to flatter him, 'I'd just like to say thank you.'

'Whatever for?'

She dropped her gaze as if embarrassed, then looked up at him warmly. 'For teaching me so much and giving me a taste of the kind of life I used to read about in magazines. I've really enjoyed it and I'd just like to say given the chance, if there was anything I could do for you then I would.'

'But you have,' His eyes never left hers as he took her hands in his, 'In so many ways; I don't think you realise how much you've changed me. You're so different from all the others I've known. Bright, funny, you make me laugh. I feel so at ease with you. It's almost as if I've known you all my life. I like what goes on in here,' he touched her forehead with his finger tip, 'You know when I thought I might come back here and find you gone, I couldn't bear it.'

'Oh Alex.' She could see tears glinting in his eyes. He really did care about her. The thought made her feel not only secure but strangely powerful.

'Nina,' He hesitated for a moment and then she felt the pressure of his hands tighten around hers, 'There is something. Something I've been giving really careful thought to while I've been away.'

'Yes?'

'I know you'll think this is totally crazy, but - will you marry me?'

Thursday 27th July

'I have pleasure in declaring Anderson Gate open.'

With a flourish of scissors a florid faced Maurice Webster, Chairman of the Council, cut the blue ribbon tied across the elegant bricked arch which formed the entrance to Abbotsbridge's new shopping precinct. Enthusiastic clapping followed and then a huge crowd swarmed down the steps and into the building to begin their exploration of the new shops, most heading for the new Gateway where free frozen chicken were on offer to the first fifty customers through the door.

Watching them go Maurice turned with a satisfied smile.

'It's a great day for Abbotsbridge Liam; this development will put us well and truly on the map. It's quite unique you know.'

Mel stifled a yawn, wishing Maurice Webster would stop twittering on and get them all across the road to the Town Hall where lunch and an inviting glass of champagne was waiting.

'Ah but it's not just down to me Maurice,' Liam replied, 'I've an excellent team. Mac Wilson has to take a lot of the credit too.'

'Ah but you had the original vision Liam. Just like the Civic Centre, now that's another masterpiece,' Maurice enthused, and then catching sight of Mel at Liam's elbow turned his attention to her.

'Mrs Carpenter. Your husband's a genius. Simply a genius!'

Mel nodded in agreement, painting on a smile, playing the part of the silent adoring wife. Beneath the surface, however, irritation bubbled. Why did Liam always have to be so self-effacing, so humble, when his true worth was recognised? She'd spent years suffering scenarios like this one. Where through his modesty others got to shine and take credit they often weren't due. Of course things would be different with Bob. He wasn't afraid to stand in the spotlight. Soon, very soon, she'd be by his side smiling demurely as praise and accolades were heaped on him for the mark he was planning to leave on Abbotsbridge. And all this frustration with Liam wouldn't matter, because he would be out of her life, a thing of the past.

TWENTY SIX

Friday 27th July

The applause was deafening as Marcie Macguire took a bow and flung out an outstretched arm of appreciation for her band and backing singers. Around her the audience shouted and whistled loudly, demanding more, but she merely waved and smiled, blowing them a kiss before finally disappearing from the stage.

Backstage, Doug and Matt stood together, watching her as she came towards them in a shimmer of blue and magenta, breathless and smiling.

'Another great evening, Marcie,' Doug threw a fatherly arm around her and hugged her tightly, 'I take back everything I said.' He looked from her to Matt, 'This is the most wonderful moment of my life. For the first time in six years, Maverick has a new star. Destined for big things! Matt you're a genius!'

'Congratulations Marcie,' Matt leaned forward and kissed her cheek, 'Doug's right, we could do this all over again tomorrow, sell every ticket and still have them queuing in the street.'

As they moved down the corridor back to the dressing rooms, Marcie shot a sideways glance at Matt and smiled. She had never doubted him. First the single, then the album followed by a sixteen venue tour, finishing up tonight back home in Asbury Park, New Jersey. It had been so wonderful out on the road with him, supporting her all the way. In that time she felt they had grown even closer. She remembered how every night just before she had gone on stage he had put his arms around her and given her a big hug and a kiss for good luck and in return, in love with him as she was, she had given every last ounce of her energy.

'Excuse me a moment.' Doug said, giving her hand a final squeeze before moving off towards a small crowd of reporters who had gathered at the end of the corridor.

'You'd better come in; we'll have a long wait,' Marcie gave a grin as she opened the dressing room door, 'Once Doug starts talking he loses all sense of time and tonight he's got a hell of a lot to say to them.'

Matt followed her in, settling himself on the green velour couch while she disappeared behind the screen to change. She emerged moments later wrapped in a pale blue silk robe. Scooping her hair back off her face, she secured it at the nape of her neck before seating herself in front of the dressing table.

'Matt,' She watched his reflection in the mirror as she dipped her fingers into the small pot of cream on the dressing table, 'One thing that's constantly nagged at me -where do you get the inspiration for your songs?'

'All around I guess,' He gave a casual shrug, 'Events, places, people.'

'There's one special person too isn't there?' She smiled as she removed the lid from the small glass jar on the dressing table and retrieved a cotton wool ball. 'I can feel it in your love songs.'

'Can you?' He looked at her curiously. 'Well if you must know, the inspiration for my love songs usually comes from seeing a pretty girl or a couple on the sidewalk, or in the park. My imagination automatically kicks in and I weave a song around them.'

'Oh c'mon Matt,' Marcie applied the cotton wool in smooth strokes across her forehead. 'No one writes with the kind of emotion you do after seeing a complete stranger. I sing it; it's powerful stuff. It's gotta be written for someone you know.' When he didn't answer she hesitated, cotton wool in hand. 'Ah,' she gave a teasing laugh as she turned and leaned over the back of the chair. 'I know! You're embarrassed because it's me isn't it? Admit it, I'm your muse; your inspiring goddess.'

'Yes, you're very special to me, Marcie.' He nodded, his smile pensive. 'In fact, right now, I'd say you're the centre of my world. Everything I do revolves around you. And yes, I do love you....'

'Oh Matt!' She interrupted him, her hand going to her mouth as he said the words she had dreamed of for so long.

'Please, 'He took her by the hand, 'let me finish. I was about to say, I do love you, but I'm not in love with you. There is a difference. When I think of you, I think of a best buddy. You're always there for me, you keep me sane, make me laugh. With you I've learned not to take life or myself too seriously. ' He kissed her hand gently. 'You're a great girl Marcie!'

But I don't want to be a great girl something inside her screamed as bitter disappointment tightened like an iron band around her heart. All the months they'd been together, the way he looked at her, his smile, the lyrics he'd penned. It had all gone to convince her that all this reserved Englishman needed was time. Time to find the courage to declare his real feelings for her. The ones he hid; the ones he was too shy to reveal. Only they had never existed - it was all a crazy dream. Now all she wanted to do was to cry, but knew she couldn't. Not here, now like this, on a night of great celebration.

'I'm sorry, I didn't mean to upset you,' He let go of her hand, concern in his face.

'You do write for someone though, don't you?' She was insistent, holding back the tears, trying to keep her voice steady.

He nodded and she saw a shadow cross his face and his expression cloud as if her words had triggered a painful memory. Tossing the cotton wool into the waste paper basket, she leaned on the back of her seat, watching him. 'Is it the same someone you didn't want to talk about the day we were at the beach house?'

'Yes.' On this occasion the utterance of this word didn't feel a door slamming; Marcie knew there was more to come. 'She was very special to me,' He began quietly, leaning forward, hands clasped loosely, 'So special that I find it impossible let go of her memory. Writing songs is the only thing that helps me cope. Call it bereavement therapy if you like.'

'She's dead?' Marcie whispered, her own self-pity swept away by this tragic revelation. 'Oh Matt!'

Matt stared at her stunned expression, felt the soft, comforting caress of her hand as she reached out and touched his cheek and realised she had taken his words literally, 'Yes,' he nodded automatically. 'She's dead.'

'Oh Matt, I'm so sorry,' He heard her say, her brown eyes brimming with tears. 'So very, very sorry.'

Matt looked at her compassionate face. He couldn't love her in the way she wanted him to. And now, even worse, he was lying to her. And yet it wasn't really a lie. For Ella might as well be dead, and if Marcie believed she was, it meant she was less likely to ask questions. Questions which at this moment in time he simply couldn't answer, because it was far too early and the pain still too raw.

Saturday 28th July

'About next Saturday - the bash at the Civic Hall,' Jenny said as she sat with Issy in the emptiness of the banqueting suite. 'I just wondered if you were, you know, going with anyone.'

Issy spread the clean cutlery across the wooden surface of the built in cupboard and began checking it into place settings before returning it to the green baize of a large open drawer.

'Like who?' She turned and looked at Jenny suspiciously before resuming her counting.

'Oh, I don't know,' Jenny gave a faint shrug. 'Someone.'

'What are you plotting Jenny Kendrick?' Issy said as she continued counting.

'Oh don't be like that, I just thought, you know, as you've been seeing quite a lot of Mick lately......'

'That I might be interested in going him. Is that it?' Fork and spoon in hand Issy turned to look at Jenny who was nodding enthusiastically.

'Well, it's very kind of you to take an interest in my welfare, but I'm afraid you're too late,' She gave Jenny a self-satisfied smile. 'I'm spoken for.'

'Oh!' Jenny's expression arranged itself into something half way between curiosity and disappointment, 'Now that's a shame, I thought you two would make an ideal couple.'

'That's just what he said.'

'Who?'

'Mick, when he asked me.' Issy said casually as she continued to replace the cutlery carefully in the drawer.

'He's already asked you? And you've turned him down ! Oh poor Mick!' She put her hand to her face, 'He'll be so upset that you've decided to go with someone else.'

Issy grinned at Jenny, 'Just as well he's the someone else then isn't it?'

'What?'

'He's my partner.'

Jenny shot her an exasperated look. 'Well why didn't you tell me that in the first place?'

'Are you two arguing again?' Ella stood in the doorway smiling at both of them.

'Oh it's just our usual banter.' Issy laughed. 'Where's Lucy? Oh my God! You haven't left her with your mother I hope?'

'Certainly not. Helen's looking after her this morning. What's happening? I thought we were all supposed to be hitting the shops to look for something to wear for next Saturday night?'

'We are; I've nearly finished here.' Issy placed the last piece of cutlery and closed the drawer. 'Give me two minutes, I'll just get my bag.'

Later, after a successful morning, their purchases made, the three sat relaxing in Ella's sun lounge. Helen had stayed on and prepared them a wonderful lunch. The plates had now been cleared away and coffee had arrived.

'I hear the Mill will be closing at the end of the year.' Issy said, reaching over to help herself to sugar.

'I'm not surprised,' Ella replied. 'I can't imagine who goes out there now. Sad though, it was great in its day.'

'Ah but Tad has plans.' Jenny smiled secretly.

'Has he?' Issy looked astonished. 'First I've heard of this.'

'It's at a very early stage.' Jenny said resting her cup in its saucer, 'I only know what I know because he had a chat with Dad the other day. Apparently he's planning to turn it into a supper club with entertainment.

'Really?'

'Yes,' Jenny continued, 'I think Liam is going to be asked to do the plans which will mean Taylor Macayne are bound to be in line for the refurbishing contract. Everything should be finished by early next summer. And guess who Tad is going to ask to open the new club?'

Ella thought for a moment. 'A celebrity no doubt.'

Jenny nodded.

'And it's bound to be someone involved in the entertainment business.' Ella added.

''It is, and they are well established.'

Issy thought for a moment. 'I bet it's Des O'Connor. Doesn't Tad know him?'

'I think he does, but no, it isn't. Think transatlantic.'

'Not Frank Sinatra!' Issy was all wide-eyed awe.

'How would Tad know Frank Sinatra, Issy?' Jenny began to laugh.

'I don't know - you said transatlantic, meaning American. He's an American entertainer, isn't he?'

'Be realistic please! Think English transatlantic.' Jenny prompted.

Issy thought for a moment. 'Got it! Tom Jones - he lives in America doesn't he? My God! If it's him we'll be expected to throw our knickers!'

'He's Welsh, you idiot! Jenny was shaking with laughter at Issy's attempts to guess.

'Oh! I give in - please, just put me out of my misery.' Issy pleaded.

It's Matt.' Jenny said reaching for a tissue.

'Matt?' Issy wrinkled her nose disappointedly, 'Oh!'

'Well,' Jenny shrugged, 'Matt's a celebrity and he lives in America doesn't he?'

'Who's Matt?' Helen was standing in the doorway, holding the coffee pot, 'Sorry, I couldn't help overhearing.'

'Matt Benedict,' Issy looked up at Helen. 'Local boy made good. He left several years ago. You must have heard of The Attitude.

'Yes I have.' Helen nodded. 'Not my kind of music, I have to say, but they're very famous aren't they? Well, well,' her face lit up. 'so you all grew up with a rock star. How fascinating.'

'We did indeed!' Issy continued, 'But Ella knew him better than any of us; they were very friendly once.' she turned to Ella. 'When was it you last saw him?'

'Oh, I don't know, I can't remember.' Ella said with a shake of her head, looking at them all and feeling like a rabbit caught in the headlights. The events of last year were a deep, dark secret hidden from everyone. The only person who knew she had been with Matt in Meridan Cross was Rachel and as far as she was concerned they were merely two old friends catching up with each other. However, the way Issy and Jenny were looking at her now, it appeared they knew something. Stop it, she told herself. You're getting paranoid. They can't possibly know anything.

'I remember!' Jenny exclaimed. 'You were with him in Meridan Cross weren't you?'

'I don't think so Jen.' Ella could feel the heat creeping into her face and her pulse beginning to pick up speed.

'Yes, you were. Grandma Laura mentioned it to Nick.'

'Did she?' Ella began to feel uneasy. She couldn't imagine what had caused

Laura to say anything at all to Nick about it. But if Jenny knew then there would now be questions and she didn't know whether she was up to bluffing her way out of it. Because bluffing was the only option open to her; she had deliberately buried the truth, determined to forget Matt Benedict forever and she was not about to dig it up, even for her two best friends.

'Yes.' Jenny thought for a moment. 'Oh but what am I saying? It was ages ago. You must remember - after you came back you found out he was getting married and he hadn't mentioned a word to you about it. You were very upset - when was that now?

'The summer of '69,' Ella, painting on a smile, gave an inward sigh of relief and tried to sound as casual as she could. 'It was just before we started the business.'

'That's right.' Issy agreed. 'We all went for a week in Cornwall didn't we? And Andy turned up out of the blue and proposed.'

'And you obviously accepted.' Helen smiled at Ella then looked at the coffee pot she was still holding. 'Sorry, I actually came to see if anyone wanted a top up.'

'Not for me thank you.' Issy said looking at her watch. 'I must be going. I'm meeting Mick for a drink this evening.'

'I'd better go too.' Jenny got to her feet. 'Mum's baby sitting. I expect Christopher will have worn her out by now.'

They said their goodbyes and Ella watched Jenny's Escort disappear down the driveway. Closing the door she went to find Helen, who was clearing away the coffee things.

'Let me give you a hand,' she said, picking up the tray.

'Thanks.' Helen smiled.

'I must pay you for the lunch,' Ella said as they both walked into the kitchen, 'it was wonderful and really kind of you to stay on and organise it for us.'

'It's not a problem, I love cooking and I always think of this kitchen as mine anyway. I quite miss it in some ways, you know.'

Ella nodded, 'Yes, I find it strange being at home all the time now. Still, it won't be for ever, so please don't take your talents anywhere else.'

'Don't worry, I won't.'

They both laughed.

As soon as the kitchen was cleared and the dishwasher filled and running, Ella retrieved a bottle of white wine from the fridge. Pouring out two glasses, she handed one to Helen, 'I think you deserve this.' she said. 'In fact,' she picked up her glass and took a mouthful, 'I know I do.'

'Ella, 'Helen looked at her, her expression serious. 'If it makes you feel any easier, I don't think they noticed.'

'Noticed what?'

'The fact that you're obviously still in love with Matt Benedict.'

'We were friends, that was all,' Ella replied matter-of-factly, 'Besides it was a long time ago.'

'Ella,' Helen shook her head. 'You're going to have to do better than that.'

Ella turned away towards the window and stared out across the garden.

'I'm sorry,' Helen gave an embarrassed shake of her head, 'the last thing I wanted to do was to intrude into your personal life.'

'It's O.K., you haven't,' Ella responded, giving Helen a haunting smile as she turned and leaned against the kitchen unit. 'You want to know the truth? Matt Benedict is probably the only man I've ever really loved. He was so special. But he hurt me - very badly. I can't forgive him, but worse than that, I can't forget him. And now he's coming back Helen, and I don't know what I'm going to do. A memory I can cope with - the real thing, I'm not so sure about.'

In New York it had just turned one thirty in the afternoon. Sitting at the piano in his Manhatten apartment, Matt Benedict's fingers ran over the keys, bringing the melody he had just written to life. When he had finished he gave a satisfied smile and took the sheet of composed music, laying it flat on top of the Steinway. The room was still in shade, the blind pulled down to keep out the intruding brightness of the early afternoon sun. He put the palms of his hands against the sides of his face, sitting for a moment in deep concentration. As inspiration filtered slowly into his consciousness, he took them away and picked up his pen. He began to write slowly above the lines of music; carefully weaving the lyrics of the song - about love, lies and promises, wondering as he wrote, if he would ever be able to free himself from the ghost of Ella Macayne.

Breinigsville, PA USA
29 March 2010

235133BV00001B/3/P

9 780755 204953